THE BEST SHORT STORIES: 1936

THE
BEST SHORT STORIES
1936

AND THE

YEARBOOK OF THE AMERICAN
SHORT STORY

Edited by

EDWARD J. O'BRIEN

BOSTON AND NEW YORK
HOUGHTON MIFFLIN COMPANY
The Riverside Press Cambridge
1936

The Riverside Press
CAMBRIDGE · MASSACHUSETTS
PRINTED IN THE U.S.A.

TO
ROBERT WHITEHAND

BY WAY OF ACKNOWLEDGMENT AND REQUEST

GRATEFUL acknowledgment for permission to include the stories in this volume is made to the following authors, editors, and publishers:

To the Editors of *The Red Book Magazine, Harper's Bazaar, Story, Harper's Magazine, The American Mercury, Pictorial Review, Scribner's Magazine, Esquire, The Frontier and Midland, The New Masses, The Virginia Quarterly Review, Vanity Fair, The Atlantic Monthly, Literary America, The New Yorker,* and *American Prefaces;* and to Mr. Roger Burlingame, Mr. Morley Callaghan, Mrs. Dorothy Canfield Fisher, Mr. A. H. Z. Carr, Mr. Charles Cooke, Miss Evan Coombes, Mr. William Faulkner, Mr. Michael Fessier, Mr. S. S. Field, Mr. Roy Flannagan, Miss Martha Foley, Mr. Walter Gilkyson, Miss Elizabeth Hall, Mr. Frank K. Kelly, Mr. Karlton Kelm, Mr. Manuel Komroff, Mr. Erling Larsen, Miss Meridel Le Sueur, Miss Dorothy McCleary, Mr. Albert Maltz, Miss Katherine Anne Porter, Mr. Roaldus Richmond, Mr. Allan Seager, Miss Tess Slesinger, Miss Elisabeth Wilkins Thomas, Mr. Howell Vines, Mr. Robert Whitehand, Mr. Calvin Williams, Mr. William E. Wilson, Mr. Thomas Wolfe, and the Scholastic Corporation, publishers of *Scholastic, The American High School Weekly.*

I shall be grateful to my readers for corrections, and particularly for suggestions leading to the wider usefulness of these annual volumes. In particular, I shall welcome the receipt from authors, editors, and publishers of stories printed during 1936, which have qualities of distinction and yet are not printed in periodicals which are brought regularly to my attention. Editors of new periodicals are invited to assist me by calling attention to their undertakings.

Communications may be addressed to me at 118 Banbury Road, Oxford, England.

E. J. O.

For those who are studying the technique of the short story and of short story writing, Mr. O'Brien has prepared a thirty-two page pamphlet which analyzes each story in this volume. These pamphlets will be supplied by the publishers at ten cents each.

CONTENTS

CONTENTS

INTRODUCTION

I

I THINK the time has come to speak frankly and clearly, so far as I am concerned, about a number of things. During the past year or two I find that a number of assumptions are being made publicly about my work. Some of these assumptions are disinterested and some of them are very far from being disinterested. Let us see what these assumptions are.

Various people profess to be interested in the supposed fact that my interest as a judge of short stories is political. Some writers who have jumped to hasty conclusions consider that my judgment is warped because I have strong fascist tendencies. Other writers consider that my judgment is warped because I have strong communist tendencies. As a fascist I am supposed to flee from reality and to exhibit a preference for stories of romantic escape in which events are seen through the eyes of a child. As a communist, it is supposed that my interest in the short story is limited by my strong preference for rude brutal slices of life. I shall make no attempt to defend myself against either of these charges. Obviously they cancel each other out. To the fascists and to the communists, however, I say frankly: 'A plague on both your houses!' I am interested in good short stories, and wherever I find them I shall call attention to them, whether they are fascist, communist, or merely human.

Another common assumption is that I am a tiresome old gentleman with a long beard and snuffy clothes who has grown hoary with age in the service of old-fashioned newspapers. This legend is useful, no doubt, but surely it is a little childish. Those who have taken pains to spread such a rumor begin to realize that it is childish, and during the past year they have created a variant of this legend. I am an old man of the sea whose overwhelming influence on the American short story is undoubted but tragic. Years ago I served a useful function, but my mind is now covered with barnacles, and I serve now chiefly to retard the path of progress. The unspoken implication is that the path of progress should lead the promising short story writer to the standardized short story of the commercial magazines, and that in some unexplained way I am deterring most young writers from writing as the commercial magazines wish them to write.

It is furthermore assumed that I am extremely pompous, that I strut like a turkey cock, and, worst of all, that I totally lack a sense of humor. Well, I may be pompous and I may strut. Please allow me these weaknesses, but do not blame me for lacking a sense of humor. You may be wrong, you know. Is it not possible that the American short story lacks a sense of humor? How many good humorous short stories have you read during the past year in American magazines? Did you find any? If you do not find them in American magazines, how do you expect to find them in my books? Is it not possible that the American short story is a little too self-conscious? Is that not perhaps the reason for the present dearth of humorous short stories in this country? What do you expect me to do about it?

More base insinuations about my critical integrity are beginning to appear. They are always carefully worded so as to avoid the libel laws. The principal insinuation of this sort is that I am financially interested in two magazines, one in America and one in England, and that I show undue favoritism in reprinting stories from these magazines at the expense of other magazines. The two magazines to which indirect reference is thus made are, of course, *Story* and *New Stories*. A little more knowledge and a little less conjecture would have prevented my critics, had they been so disposed, from pressing this particular insinuation. I have no financial interest, direct or indirect, in *Story*. During the past five years it has paid me twenty-five dollars for a posthumous story by my wife Romer Wilson and twenty-five dollars for an article which I contributed to *Story* myself. My interest in the magazine and my friendship for its editors is entirely based on the magazine's achievement, which is acknowledged by disinterested critics on both sides of the Atlantic to be exceptional.

As to *New Stories*, I founded the magazine two years ago in conjunction with five English writers as an open forum for new English short story writers. Neither I nor my associates have drawn a penny from the magazine up to now, its profits and losses have been entirely the concern of its English publisher, and its running editorial expenses have been borne cheerfully by the six of us. May I suggest to such critics that it is just possible that both the editors of *Story* and the editors of *New Stories* have a more disinterested attitude toward the short story writer than these critics choose to assume?

At this point, I shall state frankly that I have enemies against whom I fight and against whom I propose to continue to fight. These enemies may be defined succinctly as the base editor and the teacher of short story writing. The base editor has never bothered to fight me, even indirectly. The burden of the battle against me nowadays is usually fought by the teachers of short story writing. By their works ye shall know them. If you are a hopeful short story writer, you will receive circulars from them explaining how they can make your unsaleable manuscripts saleable either by their critical advice or by rewriting your story for you. In either case, you are invited to pay through the nose for their services. If you do not receive their circulars, you will find their advertisements in certain magazines which claim to be published for the benefit of the writer. Some magazines for writers are valuable, others are not. A perusal of their advertising pages will assist any reader of average common-sense to decide between them. Some teachers of short story writing have taken a cue from me. They profess to love the little magazines and to wish to assist contributors to them by offering them at a generous fee the advantages of their loving nurture. 'Grandmother, what big eyes you have!' The story of Little Red Ridinghood still has its point in these matters. Do not misunderstand me. The advice of a competent critic is often valuable to any mature short story writer, but the value is never a commercial one, and it is usually unwise to reward it with money. I always tell any short story writer who offers me money to criticize his manuscripts to put the money back in his pocket. If I have time, which is not often, I then try to help him as best I can.

Another general assumption in recent years is that I favor stories without a plot. Those who make this assumption also believe as a general rule that I love gloom. Well, to be frank, I may say at once that a story without a plot is apt to be handicapped on this account, but that the lack of a plot does not necessarily handicap it. It all depends on what you expect from a short story. What I do object to is the short story that exists for the sake of the plot. The plot, after all, is merely a skeleton which the story clothes. The story which exists for the sake of the plot is merely a grinning and repulsive skeleton without flesh and blood. As to the accusation that I love gloom, I reply frankly that I do not. Has it possibly occurred, however, to my critics, that a short story is by its very nature something which deals with relatively heightened moments, that by reason of its brevity it is likely to be tolerably tight in its compactness, and that in its resemblance to the one-act play it is very likely to have a compressed dramatic situation? In other words, if it is dealing at all honestly with life, it will probably be serious. There is no need whatever to confuse seriousness with gloom. On the other hand, a writer is entitled to be gloomy if he likes, and if he writes a sufficiently good gloomy story, I shall certainly print it without giving him bad marks for his crime.

Finally, I am regarded as illogical because for some years I preached the gospel of the little magazines and because last year I said that it was time to establish a moratorium on most new little magazines for a while because they were beginning to take in each other's washing. However, time has justified my statement, I think. Most of the silly little magazines died off like flies last year. So did a few sensible little magazines. Most of the better little magazines appear to be still flourishing, and I have not the slightest wish to shorten their lives. Shall I name them?

If the American public would subscribe to the following magazines and read them, they would be familiar with most of the best short stories published in this country. Here is the list: *American Prefaces, The American Spectator, The Anvil and Partisan Review, Direction, Fantasy, The Frontier and Midland, The Husk, Literary America, Manuscript, The Prairie Schooner, The Southern Review, Story,* and *Vernier.* One or two of them have outgrown their humble beginnings. Among the valuable little magazines which appear to have ceased publication during the past year, I should like to mention particularly *Avenue, The Magazine, The Plowshare, Space,* and *The Windsor Quarterly.* Probably neither of these lists is complete, but the magazines which I have mentioned will give you a fairly accurate picture of the kind of little magazine on which, it seems to me, no moratorium need be declared.

The most promising new magazine of the year is *American Prefaces.* An attentive reading of the first few issues of this magazine leads me to believe that it has a good chance of focusing all the best literary talent of the Middle West in its pages. Next to *Story* and *The American Mercury*, it is the American magazine the stories in which interest me most.

II

To repeat what I have said in these pages in previous years, for the benefit of the reader as yet unacquainted with my standards and principles of selection, I shall point out that I have set myself the task of disengaging the essential human qualities in our contemporary fiction, which, when chronicled conscientiously by our literary artists, may fairly be called a criticism of life. I am not at all interested in formulae, and organized criticism at its best would be nothing more than dead criticism, as all dogmatic interpretation of life is always dead. What has interested me, to the exclusion of other things, is the fresh, living current which flows through the best American work, and the psychological and imaginative quality which American writers have conferred upon it.

No substance is of importance in fiction unless it is organic substance, that is to say, substance in which the pulse of life is beating. Inorganic fiction has been our curse in the past, and bids fair to remain so, unless we exercise much greater artistic discrimination than we display at present.

The present record covers the period from January 1 to December 31, 1935, inclusive. During this period I have sought to select from the magazine stories published by American authors those which have rendered life imaginatively in organic substances and artistic form. Substance is something achieved by the artist in every act of creation, rather than something already present, and accordingly a fact or group of facts in a story only attains substantial embodiment when the artist's power of compelling imaginative persuasion transforms them into a living truth. The first test of a short story, therefore, in any qualitative analysis, is to report upon how vitally compelling the writer makes his selected facts or incidents. This may conveniently be called the test of substance.

But a second test is necessary if the story is to take rank above other stories. The true artist will seek to shape this living substance into the most beautiful and satisfying form by skilful selection and arrangement of his materials, and by the most direct and appealing presentation of it in portrayal and characterization.

The short stories which I have examined in this study, as in previous years, have fallen naturally into four groups. The first consists of those stories which fail, in my opinion, to survive either the test of substance or the test of form. These stories are not listed in the yearbook.

The second group consists of those stories which may fairly claim that they survive either the test of substance or the test of form. Each of these stories may claim to possess either distinction of technique alone, or more frequently, I am glad to say, a persuasive sense of life in them to which the reader responds with some part of his own experience. Stories included in this group are indicated in the yearbook index by a single asterisk prefixed to the title.

The third group, which is composed of stories of still greater distinction, includes such narratives as may lay convincing claim to a second reading, because each of them has survived both tests, the test of substance and the test of form. Stories included in this group are indicated in the yearbook index by two asterisks prefixed to the title.

Finally, I have recorded the names of a small group of stories which possess, I believe, the even finer distinction of uniting genuine substance and artistic form in a closely woven pattern with such sincerity that these stories may fairly claim a position in American literature. If all these stories by American authors were republished, they would not occupy more space than a few novels of average length. My selection of them does not imply the critical belief that they are great stories. A year which produced one great story would be an exceptional one. It is simply to be taken as meaning that I have found the equivalent of a few volumes worthy of republication among all the stories published during the period under consideration. These stories are indicated in the yearbook by three asterisks prefixed to the title, and are listed in the special 'Roll of Honor.' In compiling these lists, I have permitted no personal preference or prejudice to influence my judgment consciously. Several stories which I dislike personally are to be found on the 'Roll of Honor.' The general and particular results of my study will be found explained and carefully detailed in the supplementary part of this volume.

III

I shall now comment briefly on the thirty stories which I am reprinting this year. I make no attempt to analyze the stories. I merely wish to suggest why these stories seem to me more memorable than the others which I have read during the past year.

In the Cage by Roger Burlingame.   This seems to me an admirably compressed but very full character study.   It is worth comparing with that well-known story by Manuel Komroff, *How Does It Feel to be Free?*   Mr. Burlingame has not been content merely to record a series of events.   His wise use of symbols lifts the story to a level in which it is an excellent allegory of American life.   The cage encloses every man and woman in America nowadays, and we all grow comfortable in our cages.   The mechanization of man has not proceeded as far in any other country.

The Blue Kimono by Morley Callaghan.   I specially admire in this story, apart from its perfect sense of form, the unstressed reticence of its telling.   It is customary to regard Mr. Callaghan as the best of Ernest Hemingway's disciples.   On the contrary, he is entirely free of any literary influence and has been free for years. The texture of his work is very close and fine, his eye is exact and keenly selective, and the story is full of quiet implications subtly conveyed to the reader.   Mr. Callaghan's gentleness is deceptive. There is deep feeling behind it.

The Murder on Jefferson Street by Dorothy Canfield.   While this story would perhaps have gained by greater economy of treatment, it is a searching and successful study of a not uncommon psychological situation.   It is realized vividly, and the values of the story are carefully balanced.   The self-consciousness of the shabby genteel in a social position which is precariously maintained offers the writer an opportunity for a study in what Henry James called 'the finer grain.'   The struggle between evil based on fear and the inability to return evil for evil, also based on fear, has offered a rich dramatic opportunity.   The irony of the story is implicit, but none the less real.

The Hunch by A. H. Z. Carr.   The easy circumstantial directness of this intimate study of a gangster shows close visual imagination and unusual humorous sympathy.   While the story is told quite unpretentiously, it is actually unfolded rather subtly and shows a fine sense of form. The suspended ending is worthy of special study. Technically the manner in which the author takes the reader into his confidence is noteworthy.

Catafalque by Charles Cooke. This study of vanity and greedy clutching at power and money is told with considerable sobriety. As an essay in musical psychology it is more than adequate. The pictorial treatment shows sharp selection of detail and unusually good composition of background and foreground. The story might easily have been crude, but the author's detached treatment, like that of Chekhov, only adds to our sense of pity and sympathy, not only for the little musician but for her stupid uncle. We do not even resent the uncle's self-pity.

The North Wind Doth Blow by Evan Coombes. This is a study in atmosphere and mood full of implicit poetry and should be compared with a recent story by H. E. Bates, *Beauty's Daughters*. There is very little action in the story, but great intensity and sharp focusing on a series of pictures. Success in this kind of story is uncommon in America. This reticence of adolescence on the threshold of manhood, fascinated and irresolute before the element of strangeness and romance which it confers on an apprehended experience, is full of smouldering fire. It is worth contrasting with the story by Erling Larsen in this volume.

That Will Be Fine by William Faulkner. This story should be compared with the author's masterpiece, *That Evening Sun Go Down*. Both stories are told from the point of view of a child remembering what it does not completely understand. The child sees events in pieces and adds them up one by one into a picture which is imperfect from the child's point of view, but from which the mature reader can make all the inferences necessary to grasp the situation completely. Technically this is a difficult achievement. The method usually fails, but in this case it serves to increase effectively, not only the dramatic values of the story, but its deep ironic implications. The merciless candor of the child gives us an exact picture of the characters which conceals nothing.

That's What Happened to Me by Michael Fessier. The best 'tall stories' are written in America, and this humorous variant of the type is quite deftly worked out. Notice particularly how the characterization is achieved entirely through monologue. Compare the story with *Fame Takes a J Car* by George Albee in *The*

Best Short Stories: 1933. The story has a surprise ending, but it does not depend principally for surprise for its effect. In fact, the ending is quite unstressed. Apart from being a 'tall story,' it is an excellent psychological study of wish fulfilment.

Torrent of Darkness by S. S. Field. This sombre tragic story is built up in sharply etched pictures with great care and an exact feeling for dramatic values. Although it appears to show the influence of William Faulkner, it is in no sense derivative, and technically it is much more direct. Faulkner gets his dramatic effects by implication, while the author of this story focuses our attention directly on the scene. He has imparted a legendary quality to the story which gives it an effect of reality poised in distance. The irony and inevitability of the ending are Greek in feeling.

The Doorstop by Roy Flannagan. This story of Negro devotion is worth contrasting with the previous story, not only in the manner of telling, but also in the author's attitude towards his characters and his general angle of vision. The irony is subtler, the situation more fresh, and the moral intention a little more obvious. Why has Mr. Field written the better story?

Her Own Sweet Simplicity by Martha Foley. I have selected this story for publication because of the clear vigor of its telling, its sharp perception and exact portraiture, and its closeness of texture. Like Mr. Fessier's story it illustrates the most characteristic qualities of contemporary American humor. Humor is a rare quality in contemporary American short stories, and should be valued accordingly when found. Miss Foley preserves exactly the right distance from her subject and there is no overemphasis. Overemphasis is the usual fault of American humorous stories.

Enemy Country by Walter Gilkyson. Although this story is a little diffuse, the characterization is good, and the use of atmosphere in the service of an intellectual idea is unusually good. The allegory is nowhere unduly stressed, and the bitter irony obtained from contrast between dream and reality is unforced and natural. The story serves to illustrate very well how the best moral effects are achieved without direct propaganda, a fact which is apparently realized by very few proletarian writers. We are shown in this story two kinds of new world, and both kinds are experienced by the same blood.

Two Words Are a Story by Elizabeth Hall. This story won the first prize in the recent undergraduate contest sponsored by *Story*. It seems to me important as the voice of a new generation coming to terms with reality successfully in its own way. The psychological analysis is close and exact, but never tortuous. The story has a sense of space and a quiet interior glow. It records fugitive moods with exact faithfulness and relates them to the fundamental human emotions which engender them. The story is worthy of the closest study.

With Some Gaiety and Laughter by Frank K. Kelly. This story is an improvisation on the theme suggested by the title. Good allegorical stories based on fantasy have been rare in American writing since Hawthorne, but, allowing for the changes in life and mood in America since Hawthorne's time, the story would have won his interested approval. Notice particularly how the allegory fits the conditions of American life in our own time. It is rooted in contemporary reality.

Tinkle and Family Take a Ride by Karlton Kelm. I reprint this story as a model for proletarian writers. Most proletarian stories, as I have said before, fail because they are obviously preaching in a tiresome way to the converted. In this story a moral is implicit, and all the more bitterly effective on that account. Compare it with the story by Mr. Maltz in this volume. You may call the story a study in wish fulfilment if you like and dismiss it as a fairy tale, but there is a great deal more in it than that. Notice particularly the implications in the sentence: 'That car's freedom, it is a way out.' The ending of the story is faultlessly achieved. The contrast between the children watching the butterfly and the others drives the point home exactly.

That Blowzy Goddess Fame by Manuel Komroff. I have had occasion more than once in the past to point out the importance of Mr. Komroff in American story-telling as a tale-teller rather than as a story-writer. Like A. E. Coppard in England, he believes that the short story should return to something like oral tale-telling in the bazaar. Notice the conversational quality of this story. It is best read aloud. You can hear every modulation in the teller's voice, and his personality is an important part of the tale, though it is never obtrusive. This story is another good example of the best humorous writing in the short story form today.

A Kind of a Sunset by Erling Larsen. Compare this story with

The North Wind Doth Blow. It has a fine sense of space and distance and a legendary poetic atmosphere which does not prevent the pictures it presents from being realistic and exactly focused in a clearly realized foreground. Like the story by Miss Coombes, it is a vividly realized study in adolescence. Does the tragic ending seem to you inevitable? If not, has the author induced in you the necessary temporary suspension of disbelief?

Annunciation by Meridel Le Sueur. For the second time in twenty-two years I have broken a rule and reprinted a story which I have not previously seen in a magazine. The other story was by Ernest Hemingway. While this story is entirely without plot and is, in fact, nearly static in outward event, it actually implies a great deal in the past and future and is by no means without interior event. It is an excellent example of the story without plot which is fully justified. It unites intense realization with quiet writing. The sense of radiance in a hopeless situation which it contains points the way to the best kind of constructive revolutionary attitude for the making of a new world. Instead of preaching, the story drenches us with beauty and yet never overflows into unreal sentiment. It is taut and dynamic throughout.

The Shroud by Dorothy McCleary. I commend this story for its rich warm human characterization, its lifelike dialogue, and quasi-Shakespearean humor. The picture of these two dressmakers is unforgettable, and yet we see them almost entirely through what they say. There is a slight excess of sensibility on the part of the author, but the purity of the characterization largely offsets this.

Man on a Road by Albert Maltz. This is another proletarian story which successfully avoids direct preaching. It is a model of its kind in its emphasis of understatement, full realization of all social implications, admirable characterization, and simple dignity. The story designed to awake social consciousness will always achieve its end most successfully by making the reader feel the exact vibrations of life itself. It is always better not to have a professional guide when looking at pictures.

The Grave by Katherine Anne Porter. This simple clear objective story of the discovery by a child of the mysteries of life and death is noteworthy for a cool precision of narrative in which the value of each detail is exactly calculated. Notice particularly the economy of statement and the quiet of the prose writing. The writer is as detached from the subject matter and as free from being involved in it emotionally as Mérimée. This serves to make the emotional impact of the story all the more direct and vital.

Thanks for Nothing by Roaldus Richmond. This seems to me the best story of the year in the Hemingway tradition, a tradition which is not, of course, to be overvalued. The characters and situations are fully realized, the dramatic episodes are in no way forced, and the treatment is quite detached. In all these respects the story is in marked contrast to the usual story in the Hemingway tradition. The method depends entirely on the human valuation of the characters for its success. There must be no effort to romanticize them and no sham brutality masking as naturalism.

Fugue for Harmonica by Allan Seager. Allan Seager, who was the most important new American short story writer to appear in 1934, seems to me to take rank in his best work with Sherwood Anderson, Ernest Hemingway, Ring Lardner, Whit Burnett, and Morley Callaghan. These six short story writers are probably the best who have emerged in America since the Great War. Compare this story with *This Town and Salamanca* which I reprinted last year. Mr. Seager's realism has much implicit poetry behind it. You should listen for the overtones of his stories. He has fine selective ability and his special gift is to make us see his characters simultaneously from without and from within.

A Life in the Day of a Writer by Tess Slesinger. Miss Slesinger's notable gift is her ability to use the stream of consciousness technique to reflect poignantly that curious insulation of modern metropolitan man and woman divided between inward aspiration and chromium-plated outward event. She can register for us better than any other writer I know the continuous bombardment of petty and irrelevant experience upon the soul of modern man. Her characters all dance in Heartbreak House with fixed smiles on their faces concealing the tragedy within.

Traveling Salesman by Elisabeth Wilkins Thomas. I am not sure that this story is not a little sentimentalized, but the author's manner of telling it, as if it were an objective experience put into the mouth of the chief character, serves to conceal such sentimentality as there may be. The narrator's emotional interest in the other principal character determines the rhythm of the story and quietly enlists the sympathy of the reader. This story has moved me deeply, and technically it is a most interesting achievement.

The Mustydines Was Ripe by Howell Vines. I should like you to study this story with two points specially in mind. First of all, it is a tale that is told rather than a story that is written, and it should be compared with Mr. Komroff's story in the present volume. Secondly, it is an admirable prose idyll which is quite simple and clear, and, as such, should be compared with Mr. White-hand's story. It is one of the best stories of a regionalist nature which the year has produced.

American Nocturne by Robert Whitehand. Mr. Whitehand has interested me more than any other writer who has published short stories for the first time this year. Innocence is a rare thing in American life, and this story is perfectly innocent and as beautiful in its reticent stillness as Meredith's account of the meeting of Lucy and Richard Feverel. Mr. Whitehand knows very well the hairline which must not be crossed without offending good taste, and he has not crossed it. I specially admire the background of the story, its sense of space and freedom, and the significant quiet which it succeeds in imparting to an arrested moment in the lives of this boy and girl.

On the Sidewalk by Calvin Williams. Compare this story with that by Mr. Richmond in the present collection. It is a *genre* picture etched with vigor and economy of line. The influence of Ernest Hemingway is strong, but the story is a remarkable achievement for a high-school student. Its defect is that the writer carries economy so far that it obscures his story.

The Lone Pioneer by William E. Wilson. The rich variety of American short story material to be found in regional happenings is only beginning to be tapped, and this story is an interesting and unusual piece of Americana. The characterization of the narrator through monologue is superb, and, though the story itself is a little sentimentalized and may be criticized unfavorably on that account, the author has the right to retort that the sentimentality is only part of his characterization of the narrator. There is a freshness in the point of view which is unusual and the implicit irony of the story is never unduly stressed.

Only the Dead Know Brooklyn by Thomas Wolfe. This is another interesting piece of Americana and should be compared with the previous story. The writer's photographic ability to register detail is as unusual as his gift for mimicry. He is much more objective in this story than in his novels, and no pathetic fallacy weakens its effect. Notice once more here, as well as in the previous story, the technical means by which characterization has been successfully achieved through monologue.

And now, after you have read all these stories, I should like you to consider the book as a whole in retrospect. American life has many facets of interest, and I have sought to make this book a representative cross-section of contemporary American life as it is being interpreted by our best short story writers. Will you not ask yourselves whether this collection has not contributed a good deal to your knowledge of America in your own time? I like to think of these annual collections as records of the changing moods and emotions of the American people. No one of the writers in this collection takes America for granted. A continual process of re-discovery is going on. Our short story writers are explorers, and these books record from year to year the most interesting things about American life which they have found.

EDWARD J. O'BRIEN

OXFORD, *January* 15, 1936

THE BEST SHORT STORIES: 1936

IN THE CAGE[1]

By ROGER BURLINGAME

(From *The Red Book Magazine*)

I

WHEN Timson first came to the bank more than thirty years ago, it was a small bank: The Vigilant National, housed in a modest brick building in East Thirteenth Street. Timson was young then, a boy almost; he came in as a bookkeeper, having been trained elsewhere to the first stages of banking. Old Mr. Hardwick, the president, hired him as he hired everyone, himself, even the runners, even the man who opened the doors of the carriages.

Old Mr. Hardwick used to embarrass men in their first interviews asking them, 'What are you reading, young man?' and frightened boys used to pretend, saying Dickens or Thackeray or the Bible, but Timson answered frankly, 'I don't get much time for reading, Mr. Hardwick,' and smiled so pleasantly that the president liked him for his open honesty.

But Timson had large ambitions. So when old Mr. Hardwick leaned back in his squeaking swivel chair and said, 'You can't tell, Timson, some day you may be sitting here,' Timson's eyes grew big. The president patted him, then, on the shoulder. 'Slowly, slowly, my boy,' he said. So Timson looked round at the lesser desks where the assistant cashiers sat and beyond, at the cages thinking of himself in those places; but when he went home after his first day, he thought of himself in old Mr. Hardwick's squeaky swivel chair behind a rolltop desk with a labyrinth of pigeonholes. That was thirty years ago and boys, entering a bank in those days, often thought such things.

Banks in those days were simple mechanisms. Bookkeeping was done by hand and letters were wetted and pressed to record them between the thin pages of books. There were shelves of books everywhere; enormous books. The bank was divided in two by the counter structure which the public rarely passed. Beyond the

---

cages, assistant cashiers and the vice-president (of which a bank like the Vigilant had only one) sat at a variety of desks, and even the president had no partition to protect him. Along the back wall, on high stools, sat the bookkeepers in a row.

Soon Timson saved his wages and married, and he and his bride went to live in Brooklyn because it was cheap.

'It won't be long, though,' Timson told her, 'before we can have a fine apartment in New York.'

'How long?' said Mary Timson.

'Well, in just a few years I'll be in a cage...'

'Years...' said Mary Timson, who did not understand banks, but had ambitions as high as her husband's.

'Yes,' Timson went on, 'but once I'm in a cage, I'll go up quickly. Why, Mr. Hardwick said... But you have to be in a cage where you can talk to the customers... Yes, once I get in a cage, I'll be out of it in no time. You can't keep a good man down, Mary. You'll see. Why, Mr. Hardwick himself said...'

Timson told all his friends what the president had said and they looked at him with admiration. But when it got back to the bank that he was quoting Mr. Hardwick in this way, some of the boys tried to take him down off his high horse.

'Hardwick tells everybody that,' they said. 'Even the doorman.'

This did not disturb Timson. Look at these men, he thought, loafing along at their jobs, taking out their watches an hour before closing time, and always thinking of something outside their work — where would they get? Timson was always the first to come in the morning and often the last to leave. He was gracious and friendly to everyone. He was good-looking, too, and as neat as the figures in his books. When there was extra work to be done to keep men late, Timson was the first to volunteer. And he was so gay and pleasant about it that no one hesitated to ask him, so there were many nights when he was late to supper.

'Well, that's the way, Mary,' he told his wife when she protested. 'That's the way to get on. It won't be long now.'

And, sure enough, by the time his son was three years old, Riker, the receiving teller, made a serious mistake and had to go, so Timson was promoted to a cage. It was a quick promotion, the bookkeepers said; almost a record for the Vigilant National and some of them thought Timson must have outside pull.

II

'But isn't it dreadful,' Mary Timson asked one night, 'to be always in a cage? All day long in a cage?'

'Well, I can go in and out,' Timson said. 'I have half an hour for lunch, too, and a chance to get out in the air. And, anyway, Mary, before you know it, I'll be out and have a desk to myself. Remember I've gone this far in record time. And just look at the other tellers! Look at red-head Rawlins, he's almost a freak with those freckles. Quick-tempered, too. And Biglieri, that cross-eyed Dago. And Billings, the assistant cashier, he'll be out first thing you know. One more mistake on an overdraft and there'll be a vacancy. You just watch me now!'

And Timson, in the cage, was surprised, watching himself. He began to develop all sorts of new abilities. He worked up a great memory for faces so that he recognized the depositors as soon as they came in the door, and he had a pleasant word ready by the time they got to his window. 'Well, Mr. Grover,' he would say, 'been away South? You're looking so well!' or, 'Well, Mr. Hoops, how's that strapping young son of yours? At St. Paul's, isn't he? Thought I recognized that school pin he had on.' And he always followed these remarks with his winning smile so that the customers began to think he was the most personable young man in the bank.

Yet several years more went by before there seemed to be any chance of Timson getting out of the cages. When he was moved up to paying teller, he became more restless.

'I don't understand it,' he told his wife. 'Why, I know more about banking now than any assistant cashier in the place.'

'You ought to,' Mary Timson said, 'working all night over your correspondence schools, using up the money for Junior's education.'

But at last Billings left, and it was whispered about the bank that Timson was slated for assistant cashier and Mary Timson bought the boy a new outfit on credit. After that, for several weeks, Timson could think of nothing else so that he made two mistakes from thinking about it and looking out of his cage at the empty chair by Billing's desk. Then, suddenly, the whole bank was rocked to its foundations by an announcement issued by the president.

The Vigilant National, it appeared, was about to lose its identity. It had been bought, entire, by the Peter Stuyvesant Loan and Trust Company and everyone might lose his job. Rumor and fear ran through the cages and among the desks. Every time the president sent for anyone, a wave of excitement swept the bank and the men would look over their shoulders at the unhappy victim. Several serious mistakes occurred in those days.

Then, at last, Timson had his triumph. By the time the news came, he had forgotten about promotion and the only thing for which he and his little family prayed was that he might be allowed to stay in his job.

Mr. Hardwick would retire on his profits. The vice-president had 'resigned.' The Peter Stuyvesant Loan and Trust Company brought its own assistant cashiers and three tellers. The freckled Rawlins and the Dago Biglieri went out. Timson and a handful of the old bookkeepers stayed on.

III

When the Peter Stuyvesant Bank took over, there were many changes. The whole place was rearranged and redecorated. The old desks were taken out and the executives had new, big, flat-topped mahogany desks, all alike. Dark green filing cabinets replaced the shelves of books. It was all quite different and strange; colder and less genial, Timson thought, than the old Vigilant National. He complained to his wife about this.

'And there are so many people,' he told her. 'It will be hard to get to know them all — and they are so busy! They've got a new efficiency system with calculating machines and a dozen typewriters and there is a telephone on almost every desk. No,' he said, 'it isn't like the old Vigilant.'

Mrs. Timson was unsympathetic.

'You ought to be grateful you've got your job,' she said, 'with all those changes.'

Yes, Timson thought, he had nothing, really, to complain of and he settled down, then, in his new cage. It was a larger cage; everything in it was made of steel and there was a tricky lock on the sliding door so that it was difficult, till he got the hang of it, to get out. Soon he had struck up a friendship with Heimburger, the young blond receiving teller, and they went out to lunch together. Timson was older now and he felt years ahead of Heimburger in experience.

'I'd have been assistant cashier,' he told Heimburger, 'if it hadn't been for the merger.'

'Um,' said Heimburger. 'In a bank as big as this, there isn't much chance.'

'Yet vacancies must occur,' said Timson, who still hoped to be a vice-president some day. There were so many vice-presidents in the Peter Stuyvesant! And once you got to be a vice-president . . .

But Heimburger said: 'Yup, when there's a vacancy, they fill it from outside.'

'Not if there's a man on the inside that can't be kept down.'

Heimburger looked at him queerly at that and changed the subject.

Yet for all the efficiency and busy aspect of the people, Timson made friends. Once Mr. Talbot, the cashier, said to him:

'By God, Timson, you never make a mistake, do you? Have you ever made a mistake?'

Timson, who was blushing at this praise, said:

'Yes, I made two in the old bank. Mr. Hardwick was very decent about it. It was rather unusual — I mean the circumstances. H'm, yes, in the old bank. I was slated for assistant cashier — when the merger came.'

Once Talbot, who always introduced his remarks by a profane ejaculation, said:

'By God, Timson, you know a surprising lot about banking.'

'Yes,' said Timson, 'I study in my spare time. I've even got a book or two here.'

They were in Timson's cage then and Timson pointed proudly to a couple of books on one of the steel shelves. So Timson went home that night and told his wife he was in line for promotion.

It was true, too, for not long after that the president, Mr. Teale, sent for him and they had a talk. 'Because I want to know, personally, all of my employees,' said Mr. Teale.

Then Talbot said: 'I'm leaving soon to take a job with the Guaranty. That will put McGregor in my place and I've recommended you for assistant cashier.'

So Timson was excited about this, and after Talbot left he kept watching his desk for the time when McGregor would sit there. But he watched for a month and there was no change. McGregor, curly-haired, growing gray and with a round bald spot at the back of his head, stayed at the assistant cashier's desk.

Then, out of the blue, a panic broke in Wall Street. For a few black days, the people at the bank were too busy and worried even to talk to each other. At the end of the first terror, Timson stopped Heimburger one morning on his way to his cage. There was something about Heimburger's face that made him know he must speak to him.

'Well,' said Timson, 'of course all of us who have followed the market knew it would come sooner or later.'

'Yes,' said Heimburger, 'but now I've been fired,' and he could not keep the tears out of his pale blue eyes.

'Fired?' said Timson, feeling the chill along his back. 'What for?'

'They're cutting,' said Heimburger. 'Cutting right and left. They'll let twenty per cent of us go. Yes, you'll be lucky, Timson, if you stay where you are, let alone being assistant cashier.'

Timson stayed where he was. The Peter Stuyvesant Loan and Trust Company cut off some twenty per cent of its employees in the bad times after the panic. McGregor moved up, but his old desk stayed empty. After a while they took McGregor's desk away, so the bank had one less assistant cashier. And Timson stayed in his cage and felt as if he had had a promotion.

'No,' he told his ten-year-old son, 'you can't keep a good man down.'

The years rolled on then, and they came and went so fast that Timson did not realize that he was growing older, but after a time he knew that he was less restless. He was quite comfortable, now, in his cage.

IV

With the years the bank grew prosperous. New people came; new young men, and Timson found, after a time, that he had been there longer than any of them. The business grew so, at last, that the bank had to move into larger quarters. The new building was very impressive, done in the 'chaste' style of the period with everything square-edged and solid and smooth. It was near Forty-Second Street, whither business had moved — a crowded and rather alarming part of town with its hurried swarms of people and tremendous traffic.

For years, now, Timson had been taking the subway home to Brooklyn. The subway ran under the river, and it was exciting to

Timson to go down underground and never see daylight again until he was almost home. But the new building was especially remarkable because it had a stairway leading directly into the subway, so when Timson, at night, turned out the light in his cage he could go to Brooklyn without ever going outdoors.

Soon after the bank moved, Timson found a flat to rent immediately behind the Brooklyn subway exit from which he was accustomed to walk some five blocks home.

'But the walk is good for you,' said his wife. 'It freshens you up after being all day in that cage.'

'Um,' said Timson, 'but think on rainy days being able to pop right from the subway into your own home!'

They argued it back and forth for a time; they would be moving, Mrs. Timson said, from a fine open place on a square into one of the most crowded sections of the city.

'All the same,' Timson said, 'it's a *much* bigger apartment.'

Mrs. Timson finally said, 'Look, Jim, are you growing old that you're afraid of a little walk?'

That frightened Timson so that for a few weeks he did not mention the new flat. Morning and night he would walk briskly to and from the subway, taking long breaths and puffing out his chest, but, arriving at the bank, the idea of walking up the stairs directly into the bank was always pleasing to him. Of course, he thought, when I get to be a vice-president, I can go back and forth in a taxi or, if I was president, I might go in my own limousine. But it ended by his moving into the new apartment house, the entrance of which was only four steps from the entrance of the subway.

v

In the meantime the young Timson had grown up. He had finished high school and was in a job of his own in a high-class stationery store. He would not, now, be called Junior, but insisted on James to distinguish him from Jim, his father.

He was in a good, dignified business and Timson was pleased.

'Remember, James,' he said, 'don't be afraid to work overtime. If you're the first to come in the morning and the last to leave at night, you'll — some day — well, you need never be afraid of losing your job.'

For years, now, it had been customary on Sunday for the Timsons to go on some sort of excursion. In summer they would go to Coney Island or Brighton Beach and swim, or, in winter, they would go up to Queens, take one of the new buses across the bridge and go up Riverside Drive. But after the Peter Stuyvesant Bank had gone into its new Forty-Second Street building and the Timsons were in their new flat, Timson would say on Sundays,

'Look, Mary, you and the boy run along and enjoy yourselves, I've got reading to do.'

Less and less often, he would go with them. When they had gone, he would shut himself up in his 'den,' which was the smallest room in the flat, and read all the banking magazines from cover to cover. Later, when the boy got to going off on his own, Mary Timson would sit at home in the living-room until, at last, her husband came out for dinner and complaining of the draughts.

'I can't think what's come over you,' Mary would say, 'to stick in that room all day reading your eyes out. Honestly, Jim Timson, anybody'd think you were an old man.'

But Timson would answer:

'Just you wait, Mary, just you wait. They're coming, now, in the bank to ask my advice about very important problems. Why, only yesterday, Mr. Teale himself ——'

'Yes,' said Mary, 'but it's been a long time. And you never go out and see people or take any exercise. You say, yes, you're going to be the head of the bank, but you've been saying that, Jim Timson, for over twenty years now.'

'Well,' said Timson, 'it's a slow business. And what's the use of going out and walking in parks and on beaches and all that when we've got this fine cozy apartment. Anyway, if I'm going to get anywhere, I've got to work.'

Timson was now fifty. Yet he had not changed very much. He had less hair on the top of his head, but it grew thick over his temples and there it was quite gray. But his face had few lines. His mouth was still young. People at the bank said he was quite distinguished-looking as they saw him through the window. But the old doorman, who was the only person (except the watchmen) who was still in the bank when Timson left at night, said Timson had a queer look as he went across the big space down the center of the bank. 'He always seems in a hurry, leaving,' the doorman said to

Buster the big uniformed attendant; 'he looks around over his shoulder like he was scared of something.'

'Well,' said the attendant who always carried a pistol in his pocket, 'it's no wonder folks'd be scared these days with all the stick-ups.'

'No,' said the doorman, 'I don't believe it's that. I don't know.'

Timson was not afraid of holdups. When his wife worried about such things, he said, 'Pooh, pooh! The cages are protected with every kind of fancy device.'

VI

About this time, prices began to go up and the Timsons were put to it to make ends meet. So one day, Timson suggested that it would be a great economy if his wife would put him up a little lunch to take to the bank so he would not have to go out and buy lunch.

'But,' she said, 'you wouldn't eat your lunch in the cage!'

'Why not?' said Timson.

'Eat your lunch there in the cage! Why, Jim, that would be terribly undignified — as if you couldn't afford — and besides it does you good to get out! To get away from the old bank for an hour!'

'All the same,' said Timson, 'a lunch, these days, costs thirty cents at least.'

But Mary put down her foot on this.

'You'll never get anywhere in the bank if you do that kind of thing,' she said. 'Do the assistant cashiers eat their lunches at their desks?'

Young James laughed at this, and there was a quality in his laugh that echoed in Timson's mind for weeks.

'I'll show him,' Timson would say to himself. 'I'll show that fresh, ungrateful boy.'

And, a month later, Timson showed him.

In the meantime, Timson found a cozy little cafeteria in the long narrow corridor that led, under the building, to the subway, where he could get a substantial lunch for not more than thirty-five cents. It was a crowded place, but it was a lot better than going out.

VII

A month after young James had laughed in that queer way, Mr. Auchincloss, assistant treasurer, sent for Timson after hours. He was very gracious and friendly.

'Sit down, Mr. Timson,' he said. 'I want to have a talk with you.'

Timson was trembling with excitement. Mr. Auchincloss's desk was out in the enormous open space with the rail round it where all the executives sat at their big desks: the place Timson had looked at with awe and envy all his life. Yet now, sitting there after hours with all the desks empty, he felt uncomfortable in a queer way. Of course, during hours, he often had to go to one of these desks on business, but he had hurried away briskly as soon as the business was done.

But then Auchincloss began to talk and Timson forgot everything.

'We've been looking over your record, Timson,' he said. 'You've been here twenty-four years.'

'Twenty-nine,' said Timson, trying to keep the excitement out of his voice, 'that is, counting the old Vigilant National.'

'Is that so?' said Mr. Auchincloss. 'Well, Well!'

'Yes,' said Timson.

'As far as we can make out, you've never made a mistake in your work.'

'Yes, two,' said Timson. 'But Mr. Hardwick was very kind about it. You see the circumstances were unusual ——'

'No,' Mr. Auchincloss interrupted, 'I'm not talking about that old bank. Furthermore, you seem to know as much, if not more, about some of our problems than most of our assistant cashiers.'

'Well, yes. I've kept pretty careful track...'

'In short' — Mr. Auchincloss went on quickly — 'we feel that you deserve a better position in the bank. Mr. Teale was saying yesterday that you belong out here. Now we have a vacancy — Mr. Archer, our assistant cashier, is leaving us... we've hoped for some time... you are eminently fitted... now in the matter of salary...'

But Timson did not hear the rest distinctly. He had begun to tremble and he wanted to get away before Mr. Auchincloss noticed. Thinking it over afterward, it seemed to him that he wanted to get away anyway — get back to his cage to think.

That night Timson took a bottle of champagne home to his family. He had trouble getting it, and he was quite tired, what with the new excitement and going about to find the champagne. It was a hot spring night.

'Well,' he said, after dinner when he was quite warm and mellow from the wine, 'you follow your father's example, my boy, and never make a mistake. You young men think you can get on in the world by pushing yourself forward and being clever and bold, but I tell you you can get ahead too by just sticking to your desk and not making mistakes. Of course I look on this position as just a step ...'

'Let's go out,' said Mary. 'Let's go out and celebrate.'

'Where?' said Timson, looking up at her sharply.

'Well, we might go up to the Bossert Roof. It'll be fine up there this fine warm night.'

'Roof!' said Timson. 'What an idea!'

'Yeah, sure,' said James. 'I'll call up Sadie. That'll be swell, we can dance there.'

But Timson felt that he would rather stay at home.

'It's so cozy here,' he said. 'You're always wanting to go out somewhere, Mary.'

'It's hot and stuffy,' said Mary. 'I can't stand it.'

'Well,' said Timson, 'we could go to the movies. Why don't we try that nice new little Prospect Theatre? There's a good picture ...'

VIII

After Timson had moved from his cage to the new big mahogany desk, his habits of life changed a little. He surprised his family by coming home early, evenings.

'Why, it isn't six yet, Jim,' Mary would say.

'Well,' said Timson, 'everybody leaves at five.'

For the first few days, he kept saying to himself, over and over, 'This is the ambition of my life, realized at last! Still, I must remember, it's only a step.' The president, he thought, had a private office to himself.

In his new position, Timson often had occasion to ring his bell for a page boy to take some paper or other somewhere or bring him something. It seemed to him that whenever he rang, the page boy would come from behind. The boys would come up behind him and

stand at his shoulder, and say, 'Yes, sir.' This always startled him
a little and after a while, he liked better to take the papers himself.
'If you want a thing done right,' he would say, 'do it yourself.'

One day, when he was absorbed in his work, a voice spoke close
at his back and he jumped right out of his chair. Someone, he
thought, before he remembered, had got through the sliding door.
But then he blushed hot with embarrassment, for he was facing
Mr. Teale, the president.

Mr. Teale looked at him queerly.

'Did I startle you, Timson?' he said. 'I'm sorry.'

'It's nothing,' said Timson. 'I've been drinking too much coffee
lately.'

Mr. Teale sat down then by Timson's desk and talked to him
quite warmly.

'Yes,' said Timson when Mr. Teale had finished, 'the work is
quite easy for me. I've read and studied a good deal. But I find
that if I have a job to be done — even quite a small job — the only
way to be sure is to do it myself.'

Mr. Teale frowned unexpectedly at this.

'No, Timson,' he said, 'that's the wrong idea. We've got a large
staff of competent people to handle the mechanical details. You
must use them and save yourself for the work they cannot do.'

Much of Timson's new work was with Bright, the paying teller,
who occupied Timson's old cage. Bright would come to ask about
overdrafts and other questions which were beyond him . . . Timson
had, for years, been making these decisions himself without bothering any assistant cashier, but Bright was young and less experienced
and could not be expected to do this.

But the queer thing was that, now, when Bright came with a
question, Timson could not be sure.

'Well,' he would say, 'yes, Miss Bigg's account has always been
good. And yet, I don't know. I've always honored her checks.
Let's go back and look.'

Bright would say he *had* looked, there was an overdraft last
week. So Timson would get up and walk back to the cage with
Bright. When he got there, in the familiar cage, he would often
say 'Yes' or 'No' quite definitely, and once he said to Bright in the
cage: 'Why, of course, you needn't have bothered me about that.'

Nowadays, Timson took a full hour off for lunch. He made

friends with young Bright and they would go to lunch in the cafeteria. But after a while this young man, Bright, complained that he wanted to get outside for lunch.

'Yes,' said Timson, 'I used to feel that way when I began. Well, now, of course, I'm out most of the time — out there.'

He was at Bright's cage as he spoke with the sliding door between them, and Timson, looking over at the space where his desk was, had a feeling that he would like to prolong the conversation with Bright. But Bright was in a hurry to get out, so Timson went to lunch alone.

A few days after that, Timson said to Mr. Auchincloss:

'I'd be glad to help out at lunch time by taking over Mr. Bright's cage for an hour. I'm thinking of giving up lunch, myself. My digestion needs a rest.'

He patted his stomach at this, but Mr. Auchincloss did not understand.

'Oh, no,' he said, 'an assistant cashier can hardly work in a cage ... No, no, Mr. Timson.'

But Timson thought his suggestion was reasonable and could not see why Mr. Auchincloss looked at him so queerly.

IX

In the next few months, people in the bank began to talk about Timson. He must be having domestic troubles, they said. He had grown quite pale and there were lines in his face. He was thinner, too, and he had that funny scared look always in his eyes.

'He's jumpy as the devil,' said Bill Schulz, the page boy. 'Every time I come to his desk, he turns round at me as though I'd hit him or something.'

But the change in Timson was still more noticed at home.

'I can't understand it,' Mary said to their son. 'He goes later in the morning and he comes home earlier. He isn't working near so hard as he used to. And last Thursday when he had to stay after hours he had the regular jitters over it. But I can't get a word out of him what's the matter.'

About the fourth month, there were complaints against Timson in the bank. Young Bright said he was always bothering him at the cage, distracting him from his work. One day Bright turned on him.

'I can't work,' he said, 'with you coming up all the time to talk to me.'

'Hum,' said Timson, 'you've got a door behind you with a lock on it.'

To everyone's surprise, then, Timson began making mistakes. Mr. Auchincloss was quite gentle with him.

'I hate to have to bring this up,' said Mr. Auchincloss, 'especially as you've been so long in the bank and had such a fine record of service.'

'I don't know what's the matter,' said Timson. 'I don't, really.'

'Perhaps you're tired. Perhaps you need a rest. Now a week or two at the seashore would put you on your feet.'

'No, no,' said Timson. 'Oh, no, Mr. Auchincloss!'

Then, one day, Mr. Teale sent for him. Timson was afraid, but when he was in the president's office with the door closed, he felt more comfortable. Mr. Teale was very kind.

'I can hardly criticize your work,' he said, smiling, 'after all your years of loyal, excellent service. But these complaints...'

'Yes,' said Timson, 'it's queer. Now in my old job, I never made mistakes. And yet, I knew the assistant cashier's work thoroughly.'

'You do know it,' said Mr. Teale. 'But you seem to have trouble making decisions. That sometimes happens when a man is tired. Now what I suggest is a vacation.'

'Oh, no, sir,' said Timson. 'Vacations are not good for me, really! No, I'm sure I'll do better when I get used to — when I get accustomed — to the change...'

But Timson did not get used to the change. He did better for a few days and then the old, queer feeling came back. He could not go, now, to Bright to talk. He could not, in fact, talk to any of his old friends in the cages. They seemed, almost, to dislike him. Then, slowly, his mind came to a solution.

When he had decided, he was more cheerful. At home, they began to notice a change in his spirits. I won't tell them, he thought, but I'll just go ahead... There's no need for them to know. I can just say that with the hard times and so on... no, they won't know.

So, one day, with quite a firm voice, he asked the president's secretary for an appointment. She smiled up at him, glad to see the trouble gone from his face.

But Mr. Teale, when Timson told him, was puzzled.

'But I don't understand,' he said. 'We have no other position we can offer you.'

'No,' said Timson, 'but Mr. Bright, I'm sure, will do quite well as assistant cashier. He's the kind of boy you can't keep down, you know. And maybe it isn't good to keep that kind of a lad too long — too long — in such a place . . .'

'But, Timson, surely you don't mean you want to leave us?'

'No, no!' said Timson, feeling the sweat prick out on his forehead. 'No, no, not that, sir!'

'Well, then, what do you mean?

Mr. Teale was beginning to get impatient.

'Why, just this, sir, that perhaps it would be better for Bright to come out of the cage and let me . . . I mean, give me back my old job. I'll be fine at it now and I can help Bright, too, to work in!'

Mr. Teale stared at him.

'You mean you want to go back?' he said.

'Why, yes, sir. It's a queer favor to ask. But after all these years, you know. Mr. Teale . . . I don't know . . .'

Mr. Teale looked at him a long time and drummed with his fingers on the desk. Then a strange, sad look came in his face and Timson felt sorry at disappointing this man who had been so kind to him. After a while, Mr. Teale said:

'It's very unusual, Timson. Very unusual, indeed. But you've been with us so long it's hard to refuse you. I suppose we can arrange it. But ——' and suddenly, the president's eyes were incredulous again. 'But can you be sure?' he said. 'Can you honestly mean, Timson, that you want to go back? Back there — in the cage?'

Timson's arms suddenly flung out across the president's desk as if they moved in a kind of reflex and a lot of words came to his lips, but all he said was:

'Yes, Mr. Teale, yes, sir, that's what I mean. In the cage . . .'

THE BLUE KIMONO[1]

By MORLEY CALLAGHAN

(From *Harper's Bazaar*, New York.)

IT WAS hardly more than dawn when George woke up so suddenly.
He lay wide awake listening to a heavy truck moving slowly on
the street below; he heard one truck-driver shout angrily to another;
he heard a hundred small street sounds multiplying and rolling
with the motion of the city awakening.

For many mornings in the last six months George had lain awake
waiting to hear all the noises of people preparing to go to work,
the noises of doors slamming, of women taking in the milk, of cars
starting, and sometimes, later on in the morning, he had wondered
where all these people went when they hurried out briskly with so
much assurance.

Each morning he awakened a little earlier and was wide awake
at once. But this time he was more restless than ever and he thought
with despair: 'We're unlucky, that's it. We've never had any luck
since we've come here. There's something you can't put your
hands on working to destroy us. Everything goes steadily against
us from bad to worse. We'll never have any luck. I can feel it.
We'll starve before I get a job.'

Then he realized that his wife, Marthe, was no longer in the bed
beside him. He looked around the room that seemed so much
larger and so much emptier in that light, and he thought: 'What's
the matter with Marthe? Is it getting that she can't sleep?' Sitting
up, he peered uneasily into the room's dark corners. There was a
light coming from the kitchenette. As he got out of bed slowly, with
his thick hair standing up straight all over his head, and reached for
his slippers and dressing-gown, the notion that something mysterious and inexorable was working to destroy them was so strong in
him that he suddenly wanted to stand in front of his wife and shout
in anger: 'What can I do? You tell me something to do. What's
the use of me going out to the streets today? I'm going to sit down
here and wait, day after day.' That time when they had first got

[1] Copyright, 1935, by Harper's Bazaar, Inc.

married and were secure now seemed such a little faraway forgotten time.

In his eagerness to make his wife feel the bad luck he felt within him, he went striding across the room, his old, shapeless slippers flapping on the floor, his dressing-gown only half pulled on, looking in that dim light like someone huge, reckless, and full of sudden savage impulse, who wanted to pound a table and shout. 'Marthe, Marthe,' he called, 'what's the matter with you? Why are you up at this time?'

She came into the room carrying their two-year-old boy.

'There's nothing the matter with me,' she said. 'I got up when I heard Walter crying.'

She was a small, slim, dark woman with black hair hanging on her shoulders, a thin, eager face, and large soft eyes, and as she walked over to the window with the boy, she swayed her body as though she were humming to him. The light from the window was now a little stronger. She sat there in her old blue kimono holding the boy tight and feeling his head with her hand.

'What's the matter with him?' George said.

'I don't know. I heard him whimpering, so I got up. His head felt so hot.'

'Is there anything I can do?' he said.

'I don't think so.'

She seemed so puzzled, so worried and aloof from even the deepest bitterness within him, that George felt impatient, as if it were her fault that the child was sick. For a while he watched her rocking back and forth, making always the same faint humming sound, with the stronger light showing the deep frown on her face, and he couldn't seem to think of the child at all. He wanted to speak with sympathy, but he burst out: 'I had to get up because I couldn't go on with my own thoughts. We're unlucky, Marthe. We haven't had a day's luck since we've come to this city. How much longer can this go on before they throw us out on the street? I tell you we never should have come here.'

She looked up at him indignantly, but he couldn't see the fierceness in her face because her head was against the window light. Twice he walked the length of the room, then he stood beside her, looking down at the street. There was now traffic and an increasing steady hum of motion. He felt chilled and his fingers grasped at the collar of his dressing-gown, pulling it across his chest. 'It's cold here, and you can imagine what it'll be like in the winter,' he said.

And when Marthe again did not answer, he said sullenly: 'You wanted us to come here. You wanted us to give up what we had and come to a bigger city where there were bigger things ahead. Where we might amount to something because of my fine education and your charming manner. You thought we didn't have enough ambition, didn't you?'

'Why talk about it now, George?'

'I want you to see what's happened to us.'

'Say I'm responsible. Say anything you wish.'

'All right. I'll tell you what I feel in my bones. Luck is against us. Something far stronger than our two lives is working against us. I was thinking about it when I woke up. I must have been thinking about it all through my sleep.'

'We've been unlucky, but we've often had a good time, haven't we?' she said.

'Tell me honestly, have we had a day's luck since we got married?' he said brutally.

'I don't know,' she said with her head down. Then she looked up suddenly, almost pleading, but afraid to speak.

The little boy started to whimper and then sat up straight, pushing away the blanket his mother tried to keep around him. When she insisted on covering him, he began to fight, and she had a hard time holding him till suddenly he was limp in her arms, looking around the darkened room with the bright wonder that comes in a child's fevered eyes.

George watched Marthe trying to soothe the child. The morning light began to fall on her face, making it seem a little leaner, a little narrower and so dreadfully worried. A few years ago everybody used to speak about her extraordinary smile, about the way the lines around her mouth were shaped for laughter, and they used to say, too, that she had a mysterious, tapering, Florentine face. Once a man had said to George: 'I remember clearly the first time I met your wife. I said to myself, "Who is the lady with that marvelous smile?"'

George was now looking at this face as though it belonged to a stranger. He could think of nothing but the shape of it. There were so many angles in that light; it seemed so narrow. 'I used to think it was beautiful. It doesn't look beautiful. Would anybody say it was beautiful?' he thought, and yet these thoughts had nothing to do with his love for her.

In some intuitive way she knew that he was no longer thinking of his bad luck, but was thinking of her, so she said patiently, 'Walter seems to have quite a fever, George.' Then he stopped walking and touched Walter's head, which was very hot.

'Here, let me hold him awhile and you get something,' he said. 'Get him some aspirin.'

'I'll put it in orange juice, if he'll take it,' she said.

'For God's sake, turn on the light, Marthe,' he called. 'This ghastly light is getting on my nerves.'

He tried talking to his son while Marthe was away. 'Hello, Walter, old boy, what's the matter with you? Look at me, big boy, say something bright to your old man.'

But the little boy shook his head violently, stared vacantly at the wall a moment, and then tried to bury his face in his father's shoulder. So George, looking disconsolately around the cold room, felt that it was more barren than ever.

Marthe returned with the orange juice and the aspirin. They both began to coax Walter to take it. They pretended to be drinking it themselves, made ecstatic noises with their tongues as though it were delicious and kept it up till the boy cried, 'Orange, orange, me too,' with an unnatural animation. His eyes were brilliant. Then he swayed as if his spine were made of putty and fell back in his mother's arms.

'We'd better get a doctor in a hurry, George,' Marthe said.

'Do you think it's that bad?'

'Look at him,' she said, laying him on the bed. 'I'm sure he's very sick. You don't want to lose him, do you?' and she stared at Walter, who had closed his eyes and was sleeping.

As Marthe in her fear kept looking up at George, she was fingering her old blue kimono, drawing it tighter around her to keep her warm. The kimono had been of a Japanese pattern adorned with clusters of brilliant flowers sewn in silk. George had given it to her at the time of their marriage; now he stared at it, torn as it was at the arms, with pieces of old padding hanging out at the hem, with the lighter-colored lining showing through in many places, and he remembered how, when the kimono was new, Marthe used to make the dark hair across her forehead into bangs, fold her arms across her breasts, with her wrists and hands concealed in the sleeve folds, and go around the room in the bright kimono, taking short, prancing steps, pretending she was a Japanese girl.

The kimono now was ragged and gone; it was gone, he thought, like so many bright dreams and aspirations they had once had in the beginning, like so many fine resolutions he had sworn to accomplish, like so many plans they had made and hopes they had cherished.

'Marthe, in God's name,' he said suddenly, 'the very first money we get, even if we just have enough to put a little down, you'll have to get a decent dressing-gown. Do you hear?'

She was startled. Looking up at him in bewilderment, she swallowed hard, then turned her eyes down again.

'It's terrible to have to look at you in that thing,' he muttered.

After he had spoken in this way he was ashamed, and he was able to see for the first time the wild, terrified look on her face as she bent over Walter.

'Why do you look like that?' he asked. 'Hasn't he just got a little fever?'

'Did you see the way he held the glass when he took the orange juice?'

'No, I didn't notice.'

'His hand trembled. Earlier, when I first went to him, and gave him a drink I noticed the strange trembling in his hand.'

'What does it mean?' he said, awed by the fearful way she was whispering.

'His body seemed limp and he could not sit up either. Last night I was reading about such symptoms in the medical column in the paper. Symptoms like that with a fever are symptoms of infantile paralysis.'

'Where's the paper?'

'Over there on the table.'

George sat down and began to read the bit of newspaper medical advice very calmly; over and over he read it, very calmly. Marthe had described the symptoms accurately; but in a stupid way he could not get used to the notion that his son might have such a dreadful disease. So he remained there calmly for a long time.

And then he suddenly realized how they had been dogged by

bad luck; he realized how surely everything they loved was being destroyed day by day and he jumped up and cried out, 'We'll have to get a doctor.' And as if he realized to the full what was inevitably impending, he cried out: 'You're right, Marthe, he'll die. That child will die. It's the luck that's following us. Then it's over. Everything's over. I tell you I'll curse the day I ever saw the light of the world. I'll curse the day we ever met and ever married. I'll smash everything I can put my hands on in this world.'

'George, don't go on like that. You'll bring something dreadful down on us,' she whispered in terror.

'What else can happen? What else can happen to us worse than this?'

'Nothing, nothing, but please don't go on saying it, George.'

Then they both bent down over Walter and they took turns putting their hands on his head.

'What doctor will come to us at this hour when we have no money?' he kept muttering. 'We'll have to take him to a hospital.'

They remained kneeling together, silent for a long time, almost afraid to speak.

Marthe said suddenly, 'Feel, feel his head. Isn't it a little cooler?'

'What could that be?'

'It might be the aspirin working on him.'

So they watched, breathing steadily together while the child's head gradually got cooler. Their breathing and their silence seemed to waken the child, for he opened his eyes and stared at them vaguely.

'He must be feeling better,' George said. 'See the way he's looking at us.'

'His head does feel a lot cooler.'

'What could have been the matter with him, Marthe?'

'It might have been a chill. Oh, I hope it was only a chill.'

'Look at him, if you please. Watch me make the rascal laugh.'

With desperate eagerness George rushed over to the table, tore off a sheet of newspaper, folded it into a thin strip about eight inches long and twisted it like a cord. Then he knelt down in front of Walter and cried, 'See, see,' and thrust the twisted paper under his own nose and held it with his upper lip while he wiggled it up and down. He screwed up his eyes diabolically. He pressed his face close against the boy's.

Laughing, Walter put out his hand. 'Let me,' he said. So George tried to hold the paper mustache against Walter's lip. But that was no good. Walter pushed the paper away and said, 'You, you.'

'I think his head is cool now,' Marthe said. 'Maybe he'll be all right.'

She got up and walked away from the bed, over to the window with her head down. Standing up, George went to follow her, but his son shouted tyrannically so he had to kneel down and hold the paper mustache under his nose and say, 'Look here, look, Walter.'

Marthe was trying to smile as she watched them. She took one deep breath after another, as though she would never succeed in filling her lungs with air. But even while she stood there, she grew troubled. She hesitated, she lowered her head and wanted to say, 'One of us will find work of some kind, George,' but she was afraid.

'I'll get dressed now,' she said quietly, and she started to take off her kimono.

As she took off the kimono and was holding it on her arm, her face grew full of deep concern. She held the kimono up so the light shone on the gay silken flowers. Sitting down in the chair, she spread the faded silk on her knee and looked across the room at her sewing basket which was on the dresser by the mirror. She fumbled patiently with the lining, patting the places that were worn; and suddenly she was sure she could draw the torn parts tight together and make it look bright and new.

'I think I can fix it all up so it'll look fine, George,' she said.

'Eh?' he said. 'What are you bothering with that for?' Then he ducked down to the floor again and wriggled his paper mustache fiercely at the child.

THE MURDER ON JEFFERSON STREET[1]

By DOROTHY CANFIELD

(From *Story*)

I

WITH its low, bungalow-style, stucco cottages, and its few high old-fashioned clapboarded houses, Jefferson Street looked like any side street in the less expensive part of any American large town, small city. And it was like any one of them. Like all collections of human habitations everywhere, its roofs sheltered complex and unstable beings, perilously feeling their way, step by step, along the knife-edge narrow path of equilibrium that winds across the morasses and clings to the precipitous cliffs of life.

Mrs. Benson, the slender, middle-aged, well-bred widow who had moved to Jefferson Street because it was cheap, was the only one of them — as yet — whose foot had slipped too far from that path for recovery. With her every breath since her husband's death, she had slid down toward that gray limbo of indifference in which all things look alike. She was lost and she knew it; but as she fell, she grasped at anything that could hold her for a little longer; till her daughter grew up. At fourteen, Helen, plain, virtuous, intelligent, charmless, needed all the help she could get, if she were to have even a small share of the world's satisfaction.

Although Mrs. Benson went through the normal maneuvers of life, speaking, smiling, asking and answering questions, her secret aloofness from what other people prized was, of course, obscurely felt by the people around her. It was both felt and feared by the Warders, who were her nextdoor neighbors. It was one of the many things that made them feel insecure in Jefferson Street life. They felt everything, feared everything, started back at the snapping of a twig, all their senses strained like those of nervous explorers cautiously advancing, hand on cocked trigger, into an unknown jungle. For they were undertaking a hazardous feat compared to which hunting big game or living among hostile savages is sport for children. They were moving from one social class to the one above it.

Their family (as far as Jefferson Street knew it) was made up of Bert Warder, his wife, their daughter Imogene and a brother Don, employed in a bank in Huntsville. But this presentable floe, visible above the white-collar surface, was the smallest part of the tribe. Below it was a great substructure, sunk deep in the ocean of manual work — overalled uncles who were factory hands, drab, stringy-necked aunts who 'worked out,' brothers who were garage mechanics, sisters who sold over the counters of ten-cent stores. Only Bert and his bank-clerk brother Don sat at desks with pens in their hands. Bert, like most of the men who lived on Jefferson Street, was an employee of the great Stott McDevitt Electric Company. His desk there felt to him like a pedestal. His bungalow home was another. To the occasional Packard car which, trying to locate a dressmaker or a trained nurse, sometimes purred into it and rolled noiselessly out, Jefferson Street looked plebeian and small-employee-ish enough. For Bert Warder and his wife, brought up in tenement houses in a black brutally industrial city, Jefferson Street was patrician with its small lawns, its shade trees, its occasional flower-beds, above all, its leisure-class tennis courts on the two vacant lots at the end. They could hardly believe that Bert's night-school-educated brains had lifted them to such a height. The watchful tips of their antennae soon told them that in the class into which they were transferring themselves it was considered no notable feat to live in a home with a yard, so they took care to speak of the street as other people did, with amused condescension for its humbleness; but in reality they all three worshiped it, admired, feared, and tried to imitate its inhabitants, lived in dread that something from their past might cast them out from it, and did what we all do, passionately collected their neighbors' weak points as potential ammunition with which to resist attacks on their own. They would have fought to the death against a threat to their social standing on the street — as indeed they did, quite literally, when they felt themselves so threatened.

Tautly on the lookout as they were, they naturally felt that Mrs. Benson's preoccupied good manners might be intended as a reflection on their own, and suspected that the Tuttles (neighbors on the other side) looked down on them and on Jefferson Street. There was nothing definite in Francis and Mary Tuttle around which this suspicion could crystallize. It was everything. In their every contact with the Tuttles, the Warders uneasily felt the need to make an effort toward more ease, pleasantness, reticence, and quietness than was natural to them. It was fatiguing. And they were never sure they had quite caught the new tune.

Yet, as a matter of fact, the Tuttles did not look down on Jefferson Street, but were as glad to live there as the Warders. And, exactly like the Warders, had escaped to it from a life they shuddered to look back on. It was true, as Bert Warder's quiveringly suspicious nose for class differences told him, that both Francis and Mary his wife had been brought up in a house grander than any Bert had ever set foot in, and that Francis' youth (which he mentioned as little as Bert mentioned his) had been spent, not with hired girls and factory hands, but with senators and bank presidents. But his past had something else in it — misery and failure, and a period of total black eclipse such as the vigorous Bert had never dreamed of. Francis thought of his past as seldom as possible. Till Mary had dragged him up out of the morass of self-contempt in which he lay, already half drowned, and set his feet beside hers on the knife-edge narrow path of equilibrium, he had taken for granted that his failure in life was inevitable, was because he was an all-around misfit. Living with her he had begun to hope that perhaps it was only his family he did not fit. He said — he thought — 'family.' What he meant was 'brother.' Away from Roger there might be a place for him in the world, after all, he began to hope.

When Mary thought of that past, as wretched for her as for Francis, it was to Francis' mother, not his brothers, she cried, 'Shame on you! Shame!' His mother had long been dead, but no tombstone could hide her from Mary's wrath. In the old bad days when both sons were little boys, and the mother's favoritism was at its maddest worst, people used to say, if they noticed Francis at all, 'It's hard on an ordinary boy, and rather a weakling at that, to have such a successful older brother. Doesn't give him a chance, really.' But Mary knew that Roger was not the one to blame for the tragedy of their relation. She had thought him stub-fingered and tiresome, the sort of successful person who bores sensitive and intelligent ones; but living as she did — mouselike invisible poor relative — close to both of them, she had always known that Roger felt wistful and clumsy beside Francis' accurate rightness of taste, and that he had even a dim divination of Francis' exquisite undeveloped gift. No, part of Roger's exasperating rightness was that he had never accepted his mother's overvaluation. The older brother had steadily tried to be friendly; but Francis' mother had early conditioned the younger to see in any friendliness from anyone only a contemptuous pity for his own ineptitude.

'You, *you!*' cried Mary ragingly to the woman in her grave. 'Before your little poet-son could walk alone, you had shut him into the black vault with your stupid admiration of Roger's commonplace successes, your stupid notion that Francis' fineness was weakness. And every year you added another padlock to the door. What strange hateful mania possessed you, you wicked woman with your mean perverted bullying...' Whenever another bitter adjective came into her mind, she said all this and more to Francis' dead mother, ending triumphantly: 'But *I* know what he is and I've always known — a poet, a spirit so fine and true that just to breathe the air with him lifts an ordinary human being to nobility! I, the little poor young cousin-drudge you never noticed, I married a broken man, and he's a whole man now — or will be soon. I've given him children who adore him, *who depend on him!* And I depend on him. He earns their living and mine. He's escaped from the rôle of defeated weakling you bullied him into. He creates happiness and knows it! He's coming to life! And every day I bury *you* a little deeper, thank God!'

Never a word of this did she say to Francis. He did not recognize personal resentment as one of the permissible elements in life. Not in his life. It belonged in a lower, meaner world than his. Mary had climbed through the keyhole of his vault, had triumphantly thrown open the door and led him out to happiness, without letting him hear a single reproach to his mother or brother at which his magnanimity could take fright. She knew magnanimity to be the air he must breathe or die. It was part of what she adored in him, part of what she loved in the world he shared with her. But she did not practice it in her own thoughts. Francis, she knew, would have cut his hand off before he would have admitted even to himself that the smallest part of his passionate delight in the twins came from the knowledge that Roger's brilliant marriage was childless, and that he had — at last — something that Roger envied. She felt no such scruples. Hugging her babies to her, she often reveled, unabashed, in happy savagery, 'You dumb conspicuous go-getter, you haven't anything like *this* in your expensive empty house!' Sometimes in reaction from the loftiness of Francis' ideals she thought: 'Why can't he *be* unfair like anybody, and hate Roger, even if Roger's not to blame? It's nature. Who but Francis could feel guilty — not over *being* unfair, but over the mere temptation to be not angelically just. It'd do him good to let himself go.'

But she did not believe this. 'He couldn't let himself go into unfairness like just anybody,' she thought, 'for he's not just anybody. He's a poet with a poet's fineness of fiber. And about the only civilized being on the globe.'

So there was Jefferson Street; its low bungalows, its awkward high older houses with their jigsaw ornamentation filled with people who, day by day, set one foot before the other along the knife-edge narrow path that ran — for the Warders across a treacherous black bog, for the Tuttles along the face of a cliff with crashing breakers below, for the others here and there, high and low, as Fate decreed. Nothing happened. Mrs. Benson was the only one who had lost the path. And she sank but slowly toward her final fall. Three years went by. Her daughter was a senior, getting high marks; unnoticed by the boys. Bert Warder had held his job, not yet realizing that he would never do more than hold it, would never get any higher; only beginning to feel aggrieved because other men were stepped up over his head. He had also, with what sweating pains and secret study nobody would know, learned to play tennis without betraying that he had never before held a racket in his hand. Imogene Warder had passed her examinations — well, nearly all — and was, with some conditions, a senior in the high school, intensively noticed by a certain kind of boy. Francis Tuttle had not only held his job and had had two raises in salary, but had learned to grow roses. His June garden now made him catch his breath. And he had written a little shy and beautiful poetry. Poetry not verse.

'Give me three years more,' cried Mary his wife to Fate. 'Give me only *two* more, and he'll be safe.' The exquisite happiness Francis gave her and gave their children even softened her heart toward his mother. Once she thought — just once! — 'Why, perhaps she was a victim too. Someone may have hurt her in childhood as she hurt Francis, hurt her desperately, so that her will to live was all warped into the impulse to hurt back.'

Yes, just once, Mary had a moment of divination and guessed that the will to hurt comes by subterranean ways from pain and fear, not from malignancy.

It was but a flash. A partial guess, so weak and newborn a beginning of understanding, that it had no more than an instant's universal life before Mary, frightened by a glimpse at the vicious circle of the human generations, seized it and made it personal, 'Oh, yes — horrors! — of course, if Francis were still sick with that self-hating Roger-obsession, he couldn't help making the children wretched with it, one way or another. And when they grew up, they would pass it on to *their* children . . .'

She looked across the room at Francis and the twins, wrestling together on the couch, wildly, happily, breathlessly laughing, and thought contentedly, 'Well, there's *one* misery that won't be handed on. His hurt is all but healed.'

Leaning on her sword she stood, negligently smiling, at the gate of the garden where Francis grew poetry and roses, from which she had walled his demon out.

II

And then, one day four years after the Warders had moved to Jefferson Street, Fate, unheeding Mary's appeal for only a little longer respite, rode in on the bicycle of the evening newspaper boy, flinging up on each front porch the usual hard-twisted roll of trivial and ugly news. But this time, among the ugly items was a headlined statement about the arrest of one Donald Warder in Huntsville. He had been stealing from the bank he worked for, it seemed; had been playing the races; spending money on fancy women; he would probably get a long term in the penitentiary.

When Bert Warder walked across his front porch on his way home from the office that April afternoon, he was wondering resentfully why dumb-bells like Frankie Tuttle got one raise after another, while he with three times Frankie's pep just barely held his own, with frequent callings-down. 'But I can beat hell out of him at tennis, anyhow.' He applied his tried-and-true old remedy to his soreness and felt the pain abating. The evening paper was still lying in front of the screen door. He stooped, picked it up, glanced at the headlines.

Although the news took him so by surprise as to leave him stunned, his body acted as bodies do when left to themselves, in obedience to the nature of the soul dwelling in them. He rushed into the house, shut the front door, locked it and jerked down the shades of the front windows. His wife and daughter stared at him surprised. 'Look here! Look here!' he said in a strangled voice, and beckoned them to read the headlines.

They read the news together, dropped the paper, looked at each other in despair. The same thought was in them all — if only they need never open that door, if only they could leave town that night, never again be seen by anybody on Jefferson Street. For they knew that as they stood there, all their neighbors up and down the street were opening screen doors, taking in the paper. And, knowing what their own exclamations would have been, had those headlines referred to someone's else brother, they cowered before the gloating, zestful comments they could almost literally hear, 'Say, that must be Bert Warder's brother, Don. What-do-you-know-about-that? Well, *well* — maybe we'll have a little less kidding from Bert about our Harvey's being suspended from high school.' 'Why, look here, I see in the paper where Bert Warder's brother is jailed for stealing. What kind of low-down folks are they anyhow? And Bert so high and mighty about your mother's being divorced.'

Imogene drowned out the twanging of these poisoned arrows by a sudden outcry: 'I can't *ever* go back to school. Those mean kids'll just razz me to death. Helen Benson's so jealous of me about the boys, she'll be tickled pink to have something terrible like this on me. Oh, I think Uncle Don ought to be *shot!*'

Her father and mother, too, had been thinking that Don deserved to be shot for wrecking their lives. For of course they could not run away from this disgrace. Of course they must, and the very next morning, appear before their neighbors with a break in their armor far worse than anybody's. Harvey Starr's suspension from high school, Joe Crosby's not getting his raise, Mary Seabury's divorced mother, Frankie Tuttle's weak tennis, Helen Benson's unattractiveness to boys — they had been held up by the Warders as shields against possible criticism of slips in their manners. But against the positive disgrace of a brother in the penitentiary! And, of course, now everybody would find out about their folks — the aunt who was somebody's hired girl, the old grandmother who couldn't write her name. All that would be in the newspapers, now. 'If I had Don Warder here, I'd...' thought his sister-in-law vindictively. But Don, of course, was in jail. 'Safe in jail!' thought his brother bitterly. '*He* won't have to walk into an office tomorrow morning, and all the mornings, and face a bunch of guys that'll...' Like his wife, his mind was full of foreseen descriptions by newspaper reporters of his illiterate tenement-house relatives. He held the newspaper up to go on reading it. It rattled in his shaking hands. Imogene flung herself on her mother's shoulder, sobbing, 'Mamma, you *got* to send me to boarding-school. Every kid in school will be picking on me.'

Behind the newspaper her father gave a choked roar of rage. Lowering the sheet, he showed a congested face. His jaws were set. 'Boarding-school! More likely you'll have to get out of high school and go to work.' They looked at him, too stunned to ask what he meant. Still speaking between clenched teeth he told them, 'Our savings were in Don's bank and I see in the paper here where it says the bank's on the rocks because of the money he stole.'

With a wringing motion of his hands as if they had a neck between them, he crushed the paper, flung it to the floor, and turned on his weeping wife and daughter as if he would like to wring their necks too.

'What's the good of standing there hollering?' he shouted at them. 'Haven't you got any guts? Don't take it lying down like that! Stand up to them! Get back at them before they begin!'

He tramped into the next room and they heard him locking doors and windows.

It was true, just as the Warders thought, that the neighbors began to talk about them as soon as the headlines were read. Helen Benson had taken her mother over to the Tuttles' garden to look at the newly opened tulips. Mrs. Tuttle, newspaper in hand, came out of their shabby tall old house, read out the news to them and they all said how hard it was on the Warders.

'Oh, I bet there's some mistake,' said Francis Tuttle. 'The paper just says he's accused of it. There's no proof he's done it, you notice. I remember Don Warder very well, the time he came to visit Bert, last summer. He's not that kind at all. I bet when they get to the bottom of it that they'll find somebody's double-crossed him. Maybe one of the other men in the bank. I'm going to tell Bert Warder I bet that's what happened, the first time I see him.'

Thinking intently of the accused man's probable innocence, he was absent-mindedly fingering his sandy hair which, he had noticed for the first time that morning, had begun to thin a little.

Mrs. Benson said: 'It'll be a terrible blow to the Warders. We must be sure to show our sympathy for them. Helen, it'd be nice if you could think of something specially nice to do for Imogene.' She had by now slipped so far from the narrow path trod by those who still cared what happened, that this like all news was no more than a murmur in her ears. But, that Helen might learn what is correct, she brought out the right formula in the right voice.

'Yes, indeed,' said Mary Tuttle, in her warm eager way. 'People's friends ought to stand close around them when trouble comes.'

Mrs. Murray across the street, seeing the four of them standing close together, not looking at the flowers, knew what they were talking about and came over to say compassionately, 'I could cry when I think of poor Emma Warder! She'll take this hard.'

Helen Benson was awed by her first contact with drama. 'My! Imogene must be feeling simply terrible,' she said. 'I wonder if she wouldn't like to be vice-president of our class. I'd just as soon resign. Mother, how would it be if I went right up now to the Warders and told Imogene...'

But Helen's mother said, her sorrow salt in her heart, 'No, when people have had a blow it's better to leave them to themselves a little, at first. Don't you think so, Mrs. Tuttle?'

Mary, annoyed to see Francis once more passed over as if he were not present, said resolutely in a formula she often used, 'Yes, that is what my husband always advises in such cases, and I have great confidence in his judgment.'

But Francis had turned away. How like Mary it was to try even in little things to make it up to him for being a nonentity! But sometimes he thought she but pointed out the fact that he was. A little nettled, as any man might be (no, considerably more than a man who had had in his past no nightmare nervous collapse), he walked along in the twilight toward the house. On the other side of Mary's wall his exiled demon kept pace with him, trying hard to reach him with old dark associations of ideas, thinking longingly how easy it would be to tear open that nearly healed wound if only these passing relapses could be prolonged. He succeeded in starting a familiar train of thought in Francis' mind, like a brackish taste in his mouth.

'And now to grow bald!' he meditated moodily. 'What Bert Warder calls my "moth-eaten" look will be complete.' His fingers strayed up to his head again to explore the thinning hair. Deep under the healthy scar-tissue forming over his inner wound, an old pulse of pain began to throb. Roger was getting bald, too, he remembered, but of course baldness gave Roger dignity and authority, would actually add to his prestige. Francis, bald, would drop to a lower insignificance. 'To him that hath, and from him that hath not — the motto of my life,' thought Francis. His demon's eyes glittered redly in hope.

But Mary had built her wall high and strong. And inside its safe protection Francis' roses had struck down deep roots. The gardener came to himself with a smile at his absurdity that sent his demon scurrying away into outer darkness.

'Good gosh, only a thin place in my hair, and seeing myself bald a'ready!' he thought, amused. It had been through that mental habit as through a secret back door, he reflected, that many a dose of poison had been smuggled into his life. He stooped to straighten a drooping tulip. As he stood up, the evening star shone brightly pale in the eastern sky. The inner eye of his intelligence focused itself to a finer accuracy: the world stood before him in its true, reassuring proportions. 'Suppose I do get bald — bald as an egg — what of it!' he thought; and, loose, at ease, forgot himself to admire a young pear tree, its myriad swelling buds proclaiming with pride that, mere humble living cellulose that it was, its roots had found the universal source of growth. 'And all amid them stood The Tree of Life,' thought Francis, his eyes deeply on the miracle.

'Da-d-d-dy,' came cautiously from the sleeping porch. The bars of the railing there were high and set close together because of the dangerous three-story drop to the cement-floored basement entrance below, but Francis could make out the twins in their pajamas like little bears in a cage. 'How about a sto-o-ory?' they called down.

'With you in a sec,' called Francis, running into the house.

The twins rushed out on the landing to meet him, hopping, twittering, and as he snatched them up, planting loud kisses on his cheeks, his ears, his nose. 'Praise be to God who gave me life!' sang Francis' heart as he had never dreamed it could. On the swelling tide of this joy, this thankfulness, he rode up with a surge to the highest point — but one — of his long struggle with himself. Quite effortlessly, quite naturally, he thought, 'Too bad that Roger's wife can never give him children,' and went warm with delight that he had wished his brother well.

III

Francis had meant to tell Bert Warder when he next saw him that he was sure Don had never stolen a cent, that somebody had double-crossed him. But the next time he saw Warder, he did not tell him that or anything else.

The morning after the newspapers had announced the arrest of Bert's brother, Francis stepped out to the border along his front-yard path to get some tulips for Mary to take to Emma Warder, Bert's wife. But there was something so beautiful on the first one he cut that he stood still to look at it, marveling, forgetting the errand his sympathy had sent him on. Dew-drops clung to the flower, every tiny globe a magic mirror reflecting all the visible universe. Francis smiled dreamily down on the extravagance of this beauty. At first he remembered with amusement that he was the man who only last night had thought life hard to bear because his hair was getting thin. Then he forgot himself in contemplation of the divine playfulness that shrinks the great far blueness of the sky, the nearby intricacy of trees, immeasurable space itself, to ornament the white perfection of a flower. The doors of his heart swung softly open, as they do when a poem knocks and asks to be written.

Another door opened, the door of the next house. Through it — because he must — Bert Warder came resolutely out from the safety of his home to face the arena full of enemies waiting to spring upon him. The odds were against him now. He knew that. But he was no coward. He was no man to take things lying down. He was worn with sleeplessness, and half sick with dread of this first impact with a world echoing to his disgrace. But he did not lose his head. He remembered the plan for defense he had worked out in the long dark; he tried to keep clearly in mind the old rule of warfare that the way to head off attack is to attack first. But would he be able to carry out this plan? Cornered by Fate as he was, how could he reach anyone with a first thrust? He had no hope that he could, no hope at all; but he bared his teeth savagely with the desperation of the trapped, and would not give up. The instinct of self-preservation, feeling him appeal as if for his very life, responded with a wild rush of its inordinate stimulants to action. His eyes fell on Frankie Tuttle in the garden next door. He was mooning over a flower he held in one hand, while the other hand in a mechanical gesture drew up the sandy hair over a spot at the top of his head. When a man's hand does that without his realizing it, he fears baldness. The instinct of self-preservation, as it can when driven hard by fear, rose to genius, and showed the endangered man how to strike, in all safety, a first blow to ward off the attack he could not parry. He took off his hat, put his hand up to his head and walked rapidly along the sidewalk toward the Avenue, keeping his eyes on Frankie.

When Francis, his heart still unguardedly opened to its very depths by ecstasy, looked up from his tulip, he saw Bert Warder passing by on his way to the trolley, holding his hat in one hand. With the other he was ostentatiously patting and ruffling his abundant dark hair in uncouth caricature of Francis' unconscious fumble. As their eyes met, Bert let fly his arrow with all his might. His words were but trivial and a little common, but his panic tipped them well with the poison of the wish to hurt, and he put his back into the bending of his bow, his broad beefy back. Long before the meaning of the vapid pleasantry had penetrated to Francis' mind, the malignity of its intention was quivering deep in his opened, softened heart. 'That's the way to do it, Frankie!' called Bert in a loud, coarse tone, his fingers leaping about grotesquely in his hair. 'You've *got* a clearing up there. Scratch 'em up into it where you can get at 'em. Scratch 'em up into the clearing.'

For a nightmare second, Francis, like a man who dreams he sees a friend run on him sword in hand, felt not pain so much as a wild incredulity. His eyes widened, his dumbfounded face was blank, his upraised arm and fumbling fingers froze foolishly where they were. From his confusion a gleam of light shone into the other's darkness. The constriction around Bert's heart loosened. It might really work, then, the system of attacking first. He'd sure knocked old Frankie cold, his first try. No man who looked like that could collect his wits for taunts about jail-bird brothers. After the hours of helpless dread that lay back of Bert, his relief was exquisite. And the hope it gave! Hope! He might, after all, be able to defend himself. Drinking in greedily Francis' stunned expression and grotesque attitude, he burst into a yelling haw! haw! of triumph and clutching hope to his breast, ran on courageously to where a fellow worker stood waiting for the trolley.

By that time the meaning of his words reached Francis' mind. He snatched his hand down from his thinning hair with a betraying jerk. Through the quiet morning air Bert's voice came, loudly repeating his joke to Joe Crosby, who remarked, turning back to look at Francis, 'Why, I never noticed he has a bald spot.' The trolley roared along the tracks and carried the two men away to the office where Francis was at once to follow them.

By the end of that day everybody over in the Stott McDevitt Works and out on Jefferson Street knew that the Warders didn't want to have anything said to them about this trouble. 'Some folks take trouble that way,' said their neighbors with sympathy.

So, since that was the way the Warders took it, nobody did say anything about it to them. And since it was never mentioned, nobody knew exactly what was happening. People naturally took for granted that Bert's first thought had been of his brother's innocence, and that, like Joe Crosby at the time of his sister's divorce, he was spending his last cent to pay defending lawyers. Since his face grew steadily more haggardly anxious, they supposed that his efforts were all in vain. They sympathized silently, and read without comment day after day the abbreviated accounts of his brother's trial in the local newspapers.

For they were both brief and colorless. Huntsville was far away in another State; one more revelation of the doings of a dishonest bank employee was hardly news; the reporters apparently found Don too obscure a thief to be interesting. No revelations about a grubby working-class family were ever printed. But the Warders saw in every newspaper mention of Don's trial plenty of other material for malicious satisfaction on the part of their neighbors. When finally Don was found guilty and sentenced to fifteen years in prison, Bert Warder said wildly to his wife, 'Nobody need tell *me* what they're saying to each other. By God! I'd like to knock the words down their dirty throats.'

Drunk first with shame and then with anger — for two weeks after Don's conviction, the bank did fail and the Warders did lose their savings — he had a drunken man's glowering readiness to take offense at nothing. He snarled and hit out in response to harmless greetings; he started every conversation with an unprovoked verbal aggression; he protested every decision made against him at the North Side Tennis Club — as Jefferson Street people called the two vacant-lot courts; he took every happening in the office as flagrant and unfair discrimination against him. His neighbors, his fellow workers knew that his snarls were cries of pain, and for a time — a short time — said to each other tolerantly, 'Poor old Bert, no wonder he's got a grouch.' But they had tempers of their own, grievances of their own, their tolerance soon wore thin, his unprovoked attacks began to strike sparks. Two could play as well as one, they reminded him forcibly, at being offensively personal. He was not the only one who knew how to give a nasty dig. Nobody, of course, dreamed of sinking so low as to throw his brother up to him, Don now in stripes behind prison bars. In fact that story soon passed out of their minds. They had seen Don only once or twice. They were full of their own affairs, their own secret troubles and hidden disgraces. They did not mention the convicted thief, or remember him. But the convict's brother had not forgotten. He imagined in the turn of every exasperated retort a reminder that they had something on him, a threat that he would hear a thing or two about jail-birds if he went too far. So he did not go too far — with them. Every rough rejoinder to a brutal sally from him frightened him into choking down his ill-nature. A sort of approximate balance was found. After a week or so, a Jefferson Street maxim ran, 'Anybody can get along with Bert Warder — all you got to do is to tell him to go to hell once in so often.'

But there was one among them foolishly unable to return evil for evil. Or to defend himself from boorishness by being boorish. And Bert's first handful of mud had told him where he could fling more without having it flung back on him. Mary, annoyed to have Bert's ragging increasingly center on Francis, used to think, 'If Francis only had more vanity! He'd get mad then at teasing instead of feeling ashamed that he's bothered by it; and he'd defend himself.' But she was wrong. Against the blackguardism of the wish to cause pain, Francis now as in his youth could devise no defense that he was willing to use. The others on Jefferson Street and in the office snatched up whatever weapon came to hand, dirty or not. If a hit below the belt was what reached Bert's sensibilities most sharply, all right — sure — they'd hit below the belt — why not? But to Francis a choice between committing an ignoble act or suffering from one was no choice at all. For him only one of those two alternatives was conceivable.

When in an idiotic pleasantry that became threadbare that summer, Bert came suddenly behind him, blew hard on the thinning spot in Francis' hair, rattling off with a noisy laugh, 'Let-the-air-*blow*-on-the-head-the-hair-will-*grow*-on-the-head,' Francis only jerked away in a gesture of nervous annoyance, and then grinned apologetically for feeling sore. He was incapable of hitting back as the others did, with a gibe about Bert's pendulous paunch any mention of which, it was an open secret, made him wince, or about his big flat feet, or his bulging eyes, or his occasional bad grammar. He could not understand the idea the men around him had that hurting Bert Warder's feelings eased their own. Rather the contrary, it seemed to him. To find a festering wound in Bert's life and to press on it hard with a word well chosen for its power to cause him pain — how could that do anything but make a bad matter worse? A good deal worse. For Bert's uncouth tormenting caused him only discomfort and annoyance. But it would be shame, as at a real disgrace, which he would feel, to spy upon another's unhealed sores and dash his fist into the one that looked as though it would hurt the most. From his shadowed childhood on, Francis Tuttle had never understood why, with all the unavoidable pain in the world, anyone could wish to add to it.

So he could do no more than try to hide under an apologetic grin the annoyance he could not help feeling when week after week Bert rang the changes about his looking moth-eaten, twitted him with his poor tennis, his mistakes in gardening, his inability to carry a tune. He even managed a grin, though a faint and weary one over a new stunt of Bert's which emerged in June, a strenuous imitation of Francis' tennis serve, winding up with grotesquely strenuous contortions to deliver at the end a ball of a lamentable young-ladyish feebleness.

But it was his watchful demon not he who grinned, when Bert, in a chance remark, stumbled on one of the two secrets in Francis' life he was ashamed of. This was the lesser secret, the one he had thought he had quite outgrown. One Saturday afternoon in June, at the end of some doubles, as they were pulling on their sweaters, Bert Warder chanced to comment on the election of his daughter Imogene to be vice-president of her class in the high school —'... right over the head of Helen Benson, I understand. She's all right, Helen is, but kind o' slow. No S. A. as the boys say.' The other men all knew that Helen had resigned to make place for the Warder girl and had insisted on her election. A self-conscious silence fell on the group. Sensitive to silences as a sick man to draughts, Bert went hot and cold with his usual reflex of panic — were they thinking that because Imogene was a convict's niece — he backed into his corner and bared his teeth.

But Joe Crosby thought of something to turn the conversation. 'I never heard that sex appeal is what swings elections,' he said.

The casual quality of the remark blew away Bert's suspicion. But his nerves had been shaken. They needed an outlet. A safe one. His eyes fell on Francis Tuttle. 'Sure, S. A. is what settles elections!' he cried at random, giving Francis a great dig in the ribs. 'That's why our own Valentino gets elected to all the fat offices in town.'

Francis was astonished to feel a sharp twinge from old bitterness. He had not then, not even yet, left behind the boyish chagrin over all those elections in school, in college, when Roger again and again had been chosen to any office he would accept, and Roger's dead loss of a brother had never been so much as thought of. It was absurd that he still cared anything about that. But an involuntary quiver had passed over his face, just one. It was enough for his tormentor. 'Why, for fair! Frankie, there's more truth than poetry in what I say. You never do get elected to anything, do you? Were you *ever?*'

This was the time, of course, for Francis to tell him to mind his own damn business. But he could never tell anybody that, and now could think of nothing but a sorry shame that he felt even a last throb of that trivial adolescent hurt. He kept his eyes on the racket he was putting into its case; he fumbled with its fastenings; he was silent. He felt diminished and looked it.

As half-asphyxiated lungs strain joyfully to draw in a life-giving gush of fresh air, Bert felt his own painfully diminished self expanding in the other's discomfort. What suffocating man would hold his hand from the one window he can open?

'Poor old Frankie!' he cried gloatingly. 'Never had no luck with 'lections. Let's 'lect him to something right now. I nominate him to be Honorary Fly-Swatter to the Ladies' Aid Society. Haw! Haw!'

As they walked down the street together, he composed variations on this new theme. Mary, coming out to meet Francis, heard his horse-laugh, heard him as he turned in at his front walk bawl out, 'I nominate Mr. Francis Tuttle to be scorekeeper in the One-Legged Men's Athletic Meet. Who will second my motion?'

'What's he talking about?' she asked.

Francis answered, 'Oh, nothing.'

Sitting that evening over her accounts, Mary chanced to glance up at Francis, reading, and was startled to see an old shadow on his face. He wore the shrunken look that had always frightened her. She had not seen it for a long time now. His relapses in the last years had come seldom and were short; but they still made her almost as miserable as he. Adding up a total and transferring it to the next page she thought: 'It is like an old tubercular lesion. Doctors tell you that even when they are healed — or almost — they feel strains that are nothing to normal tissue.' Looking down fixedly at her column of figures but not seeing it, she fell for the hundredth time into a puzzled wonder at the inexplicable difference between what people feel about bodily and mental sickness. 'If it had been a temporary breakdown in a normal lung, acquired in childhood by direct infection from the outside, now almost but not quite healed — why, we'd have told everybody about it, sure of their sympathy. We'd have given it as the natural explanation for the things Francis isn't quite well enough to do yet. There'd have been nothing to hide. Everybody would be interested, and sort of proud and encouraged when Francis recovered. But because it's a temporary breakdown of a normal personality he's recovering from — and yet that was forced on a sensitive mind by a direct infection from the outside as much as any disease germ! — we have to hide it as though it were a disgrace. We can't even talk it over together, and plan what's best to do.'

More than by anything else, she was worn by the need to appear unconscious of what was the center of her thoughts. Now, for instance, to be forced to cast about in the dark for a possible explanation of the recurrence on Francis' face of that old look of sickness. Not even to be sure she was not imagining it. What strain could have come into their safe Jefferson Street refuge that was just the same now as ever? Nothing had happened there to change anything. She did give one fleeting thought to Bert Warder's joshing. But he had always been a boor. And anyhow, he was only teasing. Teasing! The word brought up recollections of child play. And child play was always unimportant. The thought reassured her. She began to emerge from her concentration, set her pen down to the paper again, added 23 to 44, and thought in the phrase she had heard her elders let drop so often, 'Oh, teasing's nothing.' She shot a sidelong look at Francis again. He was reading. His face looked quiet. Yes, she must have been mistaken. It could be no recurrence of his old trouble, vague and dimmed as that was now. Perhaps his tennis had tired him. Presently the idea occurred to her that he might have a real worry, a present one, something at the office, perhaps. No matter how bad that was, it would be less dangerous.

IV

She was right. It was a present worry. About a real danger. But not in the office. In his past, close to the foolish weakness uncovered by Bert's random thrust lay his other secret — the base and bad one. The two were woven together by a thousand connecting nerves. Bert's hammering on one had set the other a-quiver. Suppose — he thought, horrified, that some day, with a reflex reaction like this, some involuntary quiver of his face should betray his feeling about Roger. That he had such a secret to hide was his shame. That Mary might learn it was his terror. Great-hearted as she was, she would never go on sharing life with him if she knew of his mean jealousy of Roger — fiercely suppressed, always festering in the dark hollow of his heart. He thought, as he had a thousand times in his boyhood, that there could be no depravity so low as this vicious ill-will toward his unconscious, blameless brother. He told himself once again that he was cheating Mary — he knew why she overlooked his personal insignificance, his poverty — it was because she had the illusion that he was true-hearted, above baseness. If she should learn that he was capable of this obscene resentment of the kind and generous Roger's superiority — she would turn away from him forever. Was there any real difference — no, there was not — between such a feeling toward a brother and the upraised arm of Cain?

But Mary was looking at him! She had lifted her eyes from her account book! He had not seen when. How long had she been watching him? A man with a guilty secret is always terrified to be watched. Had she guessed? Had she read this thought in his face? He froze. And waited.

But Mary smiled. The room shone. The golden light around him brought Francis with a start out of his nightmare.

'Why, you've been asleep,' said Mary.

'Yes, I must have dropped off for a moment.' He thought he had been having a bad dream. What a relief to be waked up!

Before he lay down to sleep that night, he stepped over to the twins' little cribs. Through the high railing of the sleeping-porch the barred moonlight shone on their round faces, bland in sleep. How safe they looked! And it was he who made them safe, their father. His heart grew great with love.

But after he was in bed Mary heard him draw the long sighing breath of disheartenment. 'What is it, dear?' she murmured. He did not answer. Probably he was already asleep, she thought.

He was awake. His sigh had been of disheartenment. He had perceived that his love for his little boys was tarnished and sullied by satisfaction in his brother's childlessness.

The tide that had been sweeping in so strongly had begun to ebb.

The two vacant-lot courts had never been so busy as that summer. Bert Warder made them the center of Jefferson Street life as much as he could. For there he knew success. By concentrating fiercely on his game, he had made himself one of the best players, and looked forward all through his uneasy days to the hour with his racket at the end, which was almost his only respite from misery. His big unused workingman's body grunted with satisfaction in the hard physical effort and the copious sweat: the strain of his fixed idea relaxed in a momentary forgetfulness of Don in jail: and his perpetual doubt of his equality with those about him fell with the ravening zest of starvation on the chance to inflict defeat.

He steered clear cunningly of the two or three men who could beat him. And naturally played a good deal with Frankie Tuttle. They did not work in the same department of Stott McDevitt, but he scarcely let a day go by without hunting up Francis, inviting him to play, and saying facetiously that he did hope *this* time he might get by Francis' cannon-ball serve and maybe score a few points against him: promising, if he did, to campaign for Frankie's election to be town dog-catcher, or chief reader-aloud at the Sewing Society. Day by day he scored more points.

Mary went up to watch the play once, and afterwards said, 'See here, Francis, why don't you give up tennis for the rest of the summer? You're wearing yourself out.' But the turn of her phrase, the quality of her voice showed Francis how pitiful he looked on the courts, going to pieces under Bert's ragging, trotting about, broken-kneed, like a futile old woman, unstrung, unable to command even his usual modestly competent strokes. If he stopped playing now after such exhibitions of feebleness, there would be no limit to the joshing he would get at Bert's hands.

And by this time Bert's joshing did not so much annoy as frighten him. He was terrified at the thought that another chance lunge in the dark might lay open to Bert's rough handling the secret shame he was trying to leave behind. Bert had, so far, never twitted him with Roger, but at any moment he might try that line; certainly would if he guessed that to be a sore point. Francis' nerves tautened in vigilance if he even caught sight of Bert from afar. He seemed to feel Roger in the air, whenever Bert was present.

He was right in feeling that Roger's name was often in Bert's mind. The contrast between Francis' brother, distinguished, wealthy, well-known, and his disgraced convict brother was one of the sorest of Bert's stripes, the worst of all his envies. Glaring across the net at Francis, going forlornly and hopelessly through the complicated wind-up for his serve, he often thought (as he called out in his witty way, 'Play ball, bald head!'), 'There's one sure thing, 'bo... you'll never know from *me* I ever heard of that big stiff!'

Mary was rather troubled by the way Francis seemed to feel the heat that summer. But the hot weather would soon be gone. And wasn't he growing thinner? She'd have to start the evening hot chocolate and crackers again. He didn't seem to have the interest in his garden of other summers. Perhaps only that he hadn't much time left over from tennis. He hadn't written a line of poetry for weeks. But of course the wind of poetry blew fitfully. Was he enjoying the twins as much as he did? Or was that only a fancy of hers?

It was no fancy of hers. Coming in to his children after his daily defeat in tennis, worn out with standing guard over his threatened secret, it was soon borne in on him that he had been in a fool's paradise. Now, while his little sons were babies, yes, of course, they were his, as other men's children were theirs. But they grew so fast. Over and over he lived helplessly through in imagination, as if it had already happened, how they would turn from him. They would soon naturally be asked to visit their Uncle Roger. They could not but be struck by the difference between the two homes. They would begin to compare their father with his brother. And then they would see how their father always took a back seat, never was consulted, never elected to any office, had no influence. As they grew, they would note people's surprise that a senator — Roger would probably be a senator by that time — had such a queer singed-cat of a brother... 'And now,' Francis often thought, his fingers fumbling with his thinning hair, 'now a mangy singed-cat.'

Twenty times a day, it seemed to him, he was startled to find that without his knowing it, he was nervously drawing his hair up over the crown of his head.

He was even more startled to discover that he was not the only one to notice this involuntary reflex. 'Have you hurt the top of your head lately, Mr. Tuttle?' Mrs. Benson once asked him. He was shocked and turned on her such a darkening face that she hurriedly excused herself, 'I just noticed that you often put your hand up to it.'

He snatched down his hand — to his amazement it was once more lifted to his head — and told her shortly, 'No, I'm all right.' As he moved away a strong thought came to him, one that soon became familiar by repetition. 'It would be better if all the hair on my head would come out. And have it over with!' Sometimes he imagined for an instant between sleep and waking that this had happened. And it was a relief. He was sickened to find that he could not control himself even in such a little matter as fumbling with that thin place. How could he hope to hide his secret vice?

Every time he found his fingers in his hair he thought anew, disheartened at his own weakness, that he would never be quick enough to hide what would come leaping up to his eyes at a mention of Roger.

V

But until now he had had Mary. As long as Mary was there. . .

Then early in August a tragic telegram took Mary away for a time. Her delicate sister, now a young wife, was lying at the point of death, her baby prematurely born. 'Come at once. Florence calling for you,' the telegram read. She telephoned the news to Francis, who looked up the hour of the next train for her and hurried to draw the money from the savings bank to cover her expenses. Mary, wild with sorrow and alarm, began to pack, interrupted herself to run over to ask Mrs. Benson to keep a neighborly eye on Francis while she was away, tried to think what clothes the twins would need, stopped to telephone the cleaning-woman about getting Francis' meals, stood still in the middle of the floor and wrung her hands.

When Francis came with the money, he was startled to see her so distraught. 'If it were only time for my vacation, so I could go along to take care of the twins,' he said.

'Oh, if you only could be there to take care of *me!*' cried poor Mary, weeping on his shoulder. 'I'm scared to death to go by myself. I don't know how to face *anything* without you now!'

The memory of this cry of Mary's, the thought of her need for him, Mary's real and actual need for *him* hung like incense around Francis as he stood on the station platform that evening looking after the train from which the twins' handkerchiefs still fluttered. It was a sweetness in the night air as he let himself into the empty house. He was breathing it in as he fell asleep, his arm on the pillow sacred to Mary's dear head. Mary had not yet wholly gone.

The next day, the first day since his marriage that he had wakened alone, he arrived early at the office. To his surprise Bert Warder was at a desk farther down the same room, among the apprentices. Francis wondered if this meant that Bert had been definitely put out of the drafting-room. There had been some gossip about his mistakes there. Bert's eyes were roving about unhappily. He saw the surprise in Francis' glance. 'You, damn you, with your rich brother and your pull! Of course you get on!' he thought, savage over the injustice of the world. To say something he called out foolishly, 'Hey, there, Francis, I got special orders to report here to keep the air blowing through your clearing.' As Francis took out the papers from his drawer he heard Bert's loud, unmodulated voice explaining the joke about 'the clearing.' 'Have I got to go all through that again?' thought Francis shrugging his shoulders wearily. But the men near Bert thought the joke a flat one, found Bert's noise about it tiresome, and took no pains to conceal their impression. Smarting, humiliated, apprehensive, resentful, Bert drew glumly back into himself, waiting bodefully for a chance to pay Francis out for his rebuff.

At lunch he went out of his way in the cafeteria to sit at the same table with Francis, ostentatiously familiar with him, and after work he let trolley after trolley go by the corner where he waited till Francis arrived. Knowing that he had been punished for being too fresh, he was impelled, by the fatality that hangs over people who have struck a false note, to strike it yet more loudly.

Francis had never found him harder to endure. As they walked up Jefferson Street together, he said peremptorily: 'Run on in and get your tennis things on, Frankie. We'll have a set before supper. Maybe if I try *hard*, I can score a point or two on you.'

'It's gosh-awful hot for tennis,' protested Francis.

Bert's heavy eyebrows lifted ironically over his bulging eyes, he began a certain menacing one-sided smile which was the introduction to his worst joshing. It was uglier than usual, ominous and threatening.

There was but one threat that Francis feared. It came instantly into his mind. He lost his head, 'This is the time he is going to bring Roger up — and I have not yet thought what to say or how to look!' and said in a hurried panic: 'All right, all right. Yes, let's play. It may do us good.'

A couple of hours later he came in. He had lost one love set after another to Bert. Too tired to bathe and change, he sank down in a chair. The cold supper that was to be left for him every evening by Mary's cleaning-woman, faced him on the table. After a time he ate a little of it, and went stiffly to bed. But for a long time not to sleep. Out of the darkness white balls hurtled toward him. Every time he began to doze, he saw one, like a bullet, driving straight toward his eyes, and starting to one side to avoid it woke up to find himself sweating, his heart beating fast, all his muscles taut.

The cleaning-woman, come in early by Mary's instructions to get Mr. Tuttle's breakfast, told him, 'You don't look so good, Mr. Tuttle.'

'It was hot last night,' he told her, pushing his uneaten breakfast away.

It was hot all that day too. But in spite of it he lingered in the furnace-like office till the five-twenty trolley. To no avail. As soon as he stepped off the trolley, Bert and a couple of others shouted at him to come and make a fourth at doubles. They played set after set, shifting partners in all the possible combinations. But defeat always came to the side that Francis was on. He could have told them that beforehand, he thought, playing more and more feebly.

When he went home he found two letters waiting for him in the hot shut-up living-room. One from Mary. One from Roger. What could Roger be writing for? Looking at that letter with apprehension, he opened Mary's. The twins were well, she wrote, her sister had recognized her, but was not expected to live. The rest was love. ' . . . take care of yourself, darling, *darling!* I miss you so! I need you, dearest. I love you. I love you.' A murmur as from Mary's voice rose faintly from the paper. But died away in the silence coldly breathed out from the letter he had not read. He sat a long time looking at it, forgetting his dinner. But it had to be read. He tore it open.

Roger wrote to give Francis the news everybody was to see in the newspaper the next day, that through a new business combine he was now one of the vice-presidents of the Stott McDevitt Company, as well as of his own. 'We'll see to it that this means some well-deserved advancement for you too, Francis, old man,' wrote Roger pleasantly. His letters were always kind. 'It'll be fine to see more of you and Mary. We may even decide to become neighbors of yours. Nothing holds us here. And I certainly would enjoy getting acquainted with my splendid little nephews.'

The darkness fell slowly around Francis holding the letter in a clutch he could not relax. He had not eaten since noon. His old inner wound opened slowly, gaping here and there, and began to bleed. No, no, he told himself, shamed to the heart, it was nothing so clean and wholesome as bleeding; it was the drip of pus from a foul old ulcer. Well, a man was a leper who could feel nothing but mortal sickness over his own brother's success.

The blackness deepened. Out of it, one after another, there hurtled toward him bullet-like revelations of his own pitiful abjectness. He had always known he was a dub at business, a dub at tennis, a dub at life — everybody's inferior in everything! But till now he had hoped he might at least grow into a harmless dub. But he was not even that. He was incurably vicious, with the mean vice of feebleness. The beast in his heart would not die, starve it though he might. It snarled and gnashed its teeth over every new triumph of Roger's and sprang up from its lair, rattling its chain in sordid hope every time a faint shadow came over Roger's life. He would rather die, oh, infinitely rather die, than have Mary learn that her husband could not kill that hope tighten his hold as he might around its filthy throat.

Through the darkness a voice in a loud snarl came to Francis' ears, 'He'll never have any children. And I have two sons.' Francis leaped to his feet. Who was there in the dark with him? He had thought he was alone. He snapped on a light and looked wildly around the empty room. He was alone.

Had *he* said that? Or had he only thought it so fiercely that it rang in his ears like a cry? His knees shook. Suppose Mary had been there? Suppose Bert Warder had heard him? Why, he was likely to betray himself wholly at any moment, even without the dreaded mention of Roger's name. How it would be mentioned tomorrow at the office, after everyone had seen the announcement in the morning paper! And he who could control his voice no more than his fingers — he found them again fumbling involuntarily at the crown of his head!

He turned off the light, undressed, and sat down on the edge of his bed to think, to plan, to prepare himself for tomorrow's ordeal. Everyone would speak of Roger to him, not Bert only, everybody. And he had only this one night in which to find the right look, the right intonations, the right answers.

Yet when it happened he was somehow equal to it. Tense and careful as a man handling a bomb, he thought he had come through safely. Everybody had said the proper thing about what good luck it was to have his brother one of the company's vice-presidents, and he had made the proper answers. At least they had sounded all right when he said them. Why did he still have this terrified uneasiness? Then he realized that his apprehension came from the fact that Bert Warder alone had not said a word to him. He, alone of all the men, had only nodded with a sardonic smile, and sat down silently to work. Francis' heart gave a frightened leap. Bert knew something. Somehow he had found out. Perhaps spying on him from a distance as he had doggedly answered the congratulations of the other men, Bert had seen through the mask he had tried to keep closely clamped over his face.

All that morning Bert stuck closely to his desk. But Francis knew that he was not thinking of his work. As the hot morning went on, and Bert said nothing, did not so much as look at him, Francis was surer and surer that somehow he knew. But how could he have found out?

A few moments before lunch time, Bert took his hat and without a word went out by himself. He was not at the cafeteria at all. In the alarm over this inexplicable variation from routine, Francis suddenly knew how Bert had found out. He had been standing outside the open windows last night listening in the dark, and had heard that cry of evil joy in Roger's childlessness. Yes, of course, that was what had happened.

All that afternoon Francis covertly watched Bert. It was strange how easy it was to watch him without seeming to. Even when his back was squarely turned, he could see Bert continually leaving his desk to go from one man to another, whispering in their ears. And then not knowing that Francis could see them even though his back was turned, the listener would stare at him, nodding, nodding his head with pursed-up lips, as Bert went on whispering, whispering, telling about the shameful secret he had heard as he stood listening in the dark.

Through the breach in Mary's wall the demon had stepped softly in, bringing blackness with him.

VI

Bert said nothing about tennis that day and went home early. Francis got off the trolley at Jefferson Street alone. Forgetting to look in the mailbox he let himself into the unaired, empty house. He did not go about to open windows. He sat down heavily, alarmed to feel his legs shaking under him. He could not afford to be agitated. He must collect himself. His only hope lay in not losing his head. The situation was grave. Bert might even now be coming up the walk to . . . He looked out to reassure himself, and saw not Bert, but a shining limousine drawing up in front of the house.

Before he knew that he had recognized it was Roger's, his trembling legs had carried him in a wild rush of panic to the back of the house. The locked kitchen door halted him. If he went out there he would be seen. Where could he hide? Glaring around, he saw the closet where the mops and cleaning-cloths were kept. He flung himself into it. He was just in time. He had no more than drawn the door shut when the front doorbell rang, and it came to him sickeningly that he could not remember whether he had locked the front door when he came in. He had not breathed till now, when, his lungs almost collapsing, he gasped deeply and drew into his last capillary the stench from the dirt on the damp mops, decomposing in the heat. The bell rang again. The noise found out his hiding-place so accurately that for an instant he felt he was discovered, and gave up hope. He tightened his clutch on the doorknob. Even if they found him out, he would hold the door shut, no matter how they pulled on it. He braced himself. A long silence. Had they stepped into the house? He tried to listen. The drumming of his pulse was the only sound. He stood rigid, clutching the doorknob to him, breathing the fetid air deeply in and out of his lungs. Presently from the street the sound of a starting motor came dimly through the closed door.

He waited a long time before he ventured to come out. This might be a trap to make him think they had gone. If he opened the door, he might see someone's cold, contemptuous eyes fixed on the door, waiting for him. But when he finally did cautiously turn the knob and look out, the kitchen was empty. He tiptoed to the front door, found he had locked it, that he had been safe all the time.

And then, coming to himself for a moment's respite, he turned so faint in a revulsion of feeling that he could not stand. What in God's name had he been doing? But was it *possible!* It was so remote from anything he wished that he thought for an instant he must have dreamed it. He, Francis, had had no intention of hiding from Roger! Why should he? There was no reason. Suppose Mary had been there? What possible reason could he have given her?

The respite was over ... *suppose someone had seen him!* A cold sweat drenched him. Someone had seen him, of course. Everyone! They all must have known what he had done. Everyone on the street must have seen him leave the trolley and go into the house. They all knew Roger by sight. They must all have been looking from their windows, saying to each other, 'But he's there. I saw him go in just now.' Perhaps they had gone out to the street to tell Roger that. Tomorrow they would say to him, suspicious eyes boring into his, 'Why in the world didn't you let your brother in yesterday?' What could he say?

He wrung his hands. 'What can I say? What can I say?' Then he thought of a way out. It was simple. He could say he had gone at once to sleep, that he had not heard the bell. He would hurry up to the sleeping-porch now and lie down so that if anyone came in he would be found there, his eyes closed. He raced up the stairs and flung himself down on the bed, clenching his eyelids shut. It was essential that he should seem to be asleep. Then he remembered that nobody could come in because the doors were locked. He opened his eyes. He tried to get up.

But he was by now exhausted. He fell back, his wide-open eyes facing a new danger. He imagined Bert Warder asking him the next morning, 'What were you up to yesterday that you didn't want your brother to catch you at?' He must think of an answer to that question. Perhaps if he went over it all now in anticipation, question and answer, he might be able to... Suppose Bert said suddenly, 'What did you get into the mop-closet for yesterday, when your brother...'

Oh horror! He had forgotten to keep his eyes shut to prove to people who came in to spy on him that he really had been asleep when Roger rang the bell. He shut them hard. Then slowly remembered, no, no, that was not necessary. The front door was locked. No one could come in. He opened them again and stared out through the high railing of the sleeping-porch.

He had been trying to think what he could answer Bert Warder tomorrow. But how could he hope to control his face to hide his secret when he had no control over his fingers — he snatched his fumbling hand down from his head — over his body — he felt himself cowering again in front of the foul-smelling mop. His desperate thoughts of how to ward off tomorrow's danger were cut short by a sudden cold divination of the present peril. Danger was stealthily closing in on him now, this instant. He felt it creeping up on him from behind. He had known what that danger was. He tried wildly to remember. Oh, yes. He was to keep his eyes closed so that people would think him asleep. He had forgotten that. He shut them tightly, and weak with relief, felt that he had been just in time.

He opened them in the morning, rose and under the cleaning-woman's eyes went through the motions of eating breakfast. He and Bert happened to walk into the office together. He was incapable of speech, all his vitality concentrated on being on his guard. Bert looked pale and out of sorts and said he hadn't been feeling very well yesterday. But he was all right today, he said, goggling his eyes, 'And how about some tennis?'

Francis saw through this trick instantly. He knew Bert was lying, and why he was lying . . . to throw Francis off his guard. His plan was to wait till Francis was exhausted at the end of the tennis that afternoon and then suddenly to shoot his question like one of his cannon-ball serves . . . '*Why didn't you let your brother in yester-day?*' Yes, it would come to him like one of those fiercely driven balls he could not return.

All day he tried to invent a way out of the trap laid for him. But it was not till he was on the trolley with Bert that his inspiration came to him. The ride home was triumphal. He told Bert with a happy smile that he was going to change his clothes for tennis, and ran into the empty house. He stepped lightly, exultantly, into the kitchen and putting all his weight against it, tipped the heavy refrigerator to one side. As it toppled he stooped, still smiling, and held his right hand under it.

VII

But of course the bandaged hand that could not hold a racket could not hold a pen or run a typewriter either. When he went to the office, he was sent home on sick-leave. This pleased him. It meant he could lie on the bed all day, his eyes tightly shut to prevent the discovery that threatened him, that threatened Mary through him. The moment he opened them — as he must if he went down-stairs to eat — Mary was in danger again, might at any moment be dragged in the filth of knowing what kind of man her husband was. But he had grown very clever in thinking of ways to protect Mary from that discovery. 'I seem to be very sleepy,' he said cunningly to the cleaning-woman. 'The doctor who took care of my hand told me the accident might have that effect and wanted me to sleep as much as I could. Just keep some food on a tray for me, will you, outside the door. When I wake up I will eat it.'

After this he need not open his eyes. He could lie, hour after hour, reveling in the pain of his mangled hand, glorious anguish with which he was buying security for Mary. He could, waiting till black night, grope his way into the bathroom, find scissors and razor blades by feel, and use them without looking. Without opening those tightly shut eyelids he could find the food left for him on the tray, and empty it out in the corner of his closet so that the cleaning-woman would think he ate it. Mostly he lay rigidly still, as still as if he were in his coffin. Now that there was no reason to raise his hand to his head, his arms lay quiet at his side. What a heavenly rest! He was resting almost as well as if he were dead. And Mary was as safe as if he were dead. He was very tired, but infinitely proud of knowing how to protect Mary.

Sometimes his tense eyelids relaxed and he really slept. That was the best. Oh, that was the best...

VIII

Since he no longer knew whether it were night or day he could not judge of time. How long had he lain there keeping Mary safe? A day... a week... a year? The silence of the empty house seemed to be broken by voices. The cleaning-woman's. And — could it be — it sounded like Mary's! It *couldn't* be Mary's, could it, come back into danger when he was so sure he had made her safe? Not *Mary!* This must be a ruse of his enemies to frighten him into opening his eyes.

He sat up in bed, staring into the red blackness of his closed lids. Horrified, he strained his ears and recognized the children's voices. And that was Mary's step in the hall downstairs. His heart beat in time with it as with no other. Mary had come back, walking straight into mortal peril.

Once more he had failed. He had not saved her after all. For a moment he was undone with defeat, and trembling from head to foot sat dumb with stupid panic.

He heard the dear remembered step start up the stairs. With an effort greater than any in all his life, he summoned his soul to rise on the wings of love and be strong. And saw how even now it was not too late. Even now, though Mary's dear step was mounting the stairs, unsuspecting... Now, now was the time to play the man, once for all.

He flung himself on his love for Mary, and with one beat of its mighty wings it bore him beyond Destiny that thought to have him vanquished. Weak he might be — his love, immortal and divine, made him, at the last, mightier than Fate.

IX

Only after the excitement of the clearing of Don's name was all over, when the Warders were on the train going home from their exhausting week in Huntsville, did they begin to understand all that the proving of Don's innocence meant to them. Their days in Huntsville, after the melodramatic discovery of the real thief, were so crammed with raw emotion they had been bewildered. They had passed without a pause from their first incredulous excitement to incredulous joy and then indignant sympathy for their brother with all those months of undeserved wretchedness back of him. What a nightmare they had all lived through, they said over and over to each other. They had wept together, and the tears had washed the poison out of their wounds so that now, in the train on their way home, they were faint in the sweet weakness of convalescence. Bert's heart, that had been crushed shut by shame and fear, softened, opened, and let him out from the bitter desolation of self-pity. His imagination that had been smothered under the consciousness of disgrace drew breath again. He forgot what he had suffered; his thoughts were for his brother. 'Poor Don!' he said over and over. 'Poor *Don!*' After what he had lived through, it was like dying and going to heaven, to feel love and compassion. He was proud with a noble and new pride that the loss of all his savings weighed as nothing with him compared to his brother's vindication.

The news had been in the newspapers. With headlines. Everybody must have read it. The Warders almost expected a congratulating delegation of neighbors to meet them at the station. But when they climbed heavily down from the dusty train and saw that the platform was empty, they thought at once that it was only uneducated working-class people who made a fuss in public, and laid the lesson humbly to heart.

There was no one to be seen on Jefferson Street when they stepped from the trolley at the home corner. They set their suitcases down with a long breath, to look. There was their street! It was theirs, with its genteel lawns, its ornamental useless flower-gardens, its dignified parklike shade trees. There it stood brooding dreamily in the blue summer twilight, and welcomed them back.

'I'll carry the bags, both of them,' said Bert to his wife, chivalrously.

They trudged along toward their home, their own home, redeemed, shining, safe. They belonged here, they thought, with deep content. They were accepted by these refined people who took lawns and trees and flowers for granted. Their purged hearts swelled with thankfulness, with friendliness, with good resolutions. They must be worthy of their good fortune.

As they approached the Benson house, they saw that Helen was standing on the front porch, looking at the newspaper. What a nice girl Helen was, they thought fondly. Imogene called, '*Ooh*-hoo, Nellie!' and skipped up the front walk. Stricken by Helen's face she fell back, shocked. 'Oh . . . why . . . what's the *matter?*'

Two or three short sentences were all Helen had to say. Her news, whining ominously like a loaded shell, flew over her listeners' blanched faces, not exploding till long after it had passed.

They stood like stocks, stupidly listening to the sound of the words they could not understand. Then Bert said in a flat voice, 'Not Frankie Tuttle! You didn't say it was *Frankie Tuttle!*' He took the newspaper from Helen's hand. Through the brooding summer twilight the headlines shrieked.

JEFFERSON STREET MAN
GOES SUDDENLY INSANE
LEAPS FROM THIRD STORY
TO DEATH.

The paper fell from his hand.

'This very morning,' said Helen.

'That deep cement-covered entrance to the basement,' began

Mrs. Benson. 'Right over the high railing around the sleeping-porch. Mary had come home — you knew she'd been away with a sick sister — and she had just started up the stairs.'

The Warders, stunned, sank down on their suitcases. Bert's mouth hung slackly open.

Joe Crosby came over from across the street. His lips twitched. His eyes were red. He shook Bert's hand without a word. The Warders had been but bludgeoned into stupefaction by the head-lines. They had not believed them. But this silence told them what had happened. Mrs. Warder and Imogene began to cry. A film came over Bert's bulging eyes. He got out his handkerchief, blew his nose, and took his hat off, holding it on his knee and looking fixedly down at it.

After a time, when they could, they asked the usual questions. And had the usual answers. No imaginable explanation. His accounts in perfect order. His health all right — he'd hurt his hand, of course, but that was not serious; the doctor said it was healing without any sign of infection. And everything going extra well with him, seems though — his brother just made vice-president of the company, the luckiest kind of a break, his brother thinking the world and all of him — came right over the minute he heard of this and took Mary and the children back. To make their home with him. Always. Said he'd always wanted children in his home. No, everything in the business end of his life was fine, couldn't be better. His brother kept saying there wasn't *anything* he wouldn't have done for him. And no trouble at home, Lord, *no*! He and Mary were the happiest couple on the street. Suspicious of their good faith, Bert said it seemed as if there *must* have been some warning. 'No, there wasn't. He was just exactly the same as ever, the last time anybody saw him. He'd hurt his hand, you know — was that before you went to Huntsville? No, I guess it was afterwards — and that kept him away from the office for a while. It must have been while he was at home with that, that he . . .'

Bert Warder was shocked at a glimpsed possibility of unneigh-borly neglect. 'For the Lord's sake, hadn't anybody gone in to see that he was all right?' he asked sternly.

Mrs. Benson defended herself hastily. 'Oh, yes, yes. Before she left, Mary had asked me to look after him, and I went over there every day. Sometimes twice. But the cleaning-woman always said he was asleep. She told me the doctor had given him something to deaden the pain in his hand and make him drowsy.'

Joe Crosby confirmed this. 'Yes, every time I went in, too, he was asleep. I went clear up to his room, several times. The shades were pulled down and it was dark. But I could see he was asleep all right.' He answered the stubborn question in the other's face. 'Yes, I know, Bert, I felt just the way you do, as if we might have done *some*thing, if we'd been any good. But you know there isn't anything *any*body can do when it's a case of ' — he drew in a long breath before he could pronounce the word — 'it was just plain insanity, Bert.'

'Frankie wasn't insane!' rapped out Bert, indignant. 'He was a *swell* fellow!'

Joe lowered his voice and, with a dark, shamed intonation and yet with a certain relish of the enormity he was reporting, said: 'Bert, when they picked up his body they found he'd shaved his head. All over. Every spear of hair shaved off. Down to the skin. The way you shave your face.'

This did stagger the questioner. He said feebly: 'You don't *say*...! Good gosh, his *head!* Why, what in the...whatever would make anybody do *that?*' and fell back into his stockish, uncomprehending blankness.

Mrs. Benson murmured an explanation. 'The doctors told his brother that's one of the signs of religious mania—the tonsure, you know. They told his brother that sometimes insane...'

'Oh, they make me tired!' cried Joe Crosby in angry sorrow. 'They don't know anything about it. Why don't they keep still!'

Bert Warder agreed sadly. 'I guess nobody knows anything about what causes insanity.'

It came over him that this was no waking nightmare, was fact. But he could not admit it as fact. 'It just don't seem *possible* to me!' he told them, his voice breaking grotesquely in his pain. 'Why, Frankie and me... why, I never *had* a better pal than Frankie Tuttle!'

THE HUNCH[1]

By A. H. Z. CARR

(From *Harper's Magazine*)

NO ONE has ever called me superstitious or even tender-minded. In the past when people have told me at second hand about mysterious phenomena and occult forces ('I didn't see the spirit myself, exactly, but I know the fellow who did'), I have generally been a little bored. But since my experience with the man called Leg-'n'-half I have sometimes — well, wondered.

These are the facts. I was driving through suburban Westchester one warm Sunday afternoon with a girl. She was — is — a very pretty girl. Possibly I was less concerned with the car and the road than with her profile; we were not married then. At any rate, while we were going through Ryeneck, one of Westchester's wealthy towns — you know the type: wide streets, stone and stucco mansions for the upper middle class, Tudor-style apartment houses for the middle middle class, dingy wooden cottages for the lower middle class, neat, red-brick, glass-fronted stores downtown — while we were in the commercial district I passed a traffic light — a red light.

I advanced in excuse that the light was badly situated and partly obscured by some construction work, although the crosswise stream of traffic should have warned me. However, seeing no signal, I inferred that here was one of those every-man-for-himself lightless intersections that used to make motoring exciting. The prospect of waiting indefinitely while New York-on-wheels returned home did not attract me; and at a propitious moment I charged across the road.

Blasts from horns, remarks reflecting on my parentage and intelligence, and requests for data on my eyesight and my destination rose all about us. The girl said, 'Oh. I see the light now. You passed it.' Simultaneously a large policeman advanced from nowhere and yelled, 'Pull over to the curb, you!' I did.

This policeman was elderly, and life, no doubt, had thwarted him; he was bitter and vengeful. I have always believed that when dealing with Nemesis in a blue coat a candid admission of one's iniquities goes farther than a claim to know the chief of police, unless one happens actually to know him. But what I intended to be a disarming apology evoked in this instance only the little pad of summonses and a sarcastic, 'Smart guy, hey?'

Stimulated by a deep-rooted aversion to the payment of fines, I pointed out that although I had been at fault, the violation had been (a) unimportant, (b) unintentional, and (c) due in part to the inconspicuous position of the traffic light. To this the policeman replied, while examining my licenses, 'Trying to lie your way out of it, hey?' and his tone was more than usually offensive.

Had I been alone it would never have occurred to me to resent what a policeman said, lest worse befall. I suppose the girl's presence made my ego unduly sensitive. At any rate, I replied something to the effect that I did not like his manner.

He said, 'Oh, is 'at so? Tough guy, hey?'

Having committed myself thus far, I became reckless. I said, no, I was not tough. I said that I merely wanted him to be civil.

He said, 'Shut up.'

Up to this point I had been astonished and delighted at my own temerity; the summons seemed cheap at the price. But now, like so many inexperienced orators, I was carried away by my own eloquence. I pointed out that he was a public servant (a statement that does not ring cheerfully in the ears of an American policeman) paid by the community's taxes to exercise a little intelligence, although, I implied, the community should have known better. I proclaimed my determination to make an issue of this case. I told him that he would regret his insolence, his arrogance, his discourtesy, and so forth. These were, of course, empty mouthings.

The speech was very soothing to me, but not to him. His complexion was red to begin with; it became apoplectic now; and breathing hard, he made some notes in his notebook, which, he said, would do me no good in court.

While this was going on, I was dimly aware that several men were watching us from a sleek black touring car parked at the curb some fifty feet away. I doubt whether they overheard the dialogue, but the pantomime was sufficiently clear. They grinned broadly; and one of them winked sympathetically at the amused girl next to me.

The policeman finally handed me the summons, and with an

attempt at dignity, I drove away. When we came abreast of the other car, a man who had been standing at its side detached himself and called, 'Hey!'

I stopped. He was a heavy-set, powerful man, round-faced, small-featured, swarthy, with a greasy skin — a South-Italian, I should guess. His costume consisted of a pair of shapeless gray trousers, a dirty yellow 'wind-breaker,' and an old cap. When he moved out into the street limping, I instinctively glanced at his feet. One leg was perhaps three inches shorter than the other; and he wore on its foot a shoe with a grotesquely high heel to make up the difference.

He said casually, 'Get a ticket?'

I said, 'Yes.'

He said, 'Aw, 'at's only ol' Scanlon. Let's have it, 'n' I'll fix it fuh yuh.'

My first idea was that I had stumbled onto a new racket, in which a policeman gave out tickets which his associate down the street then 'fixed' for a consideration. But there was an air about this man, a kind of placid confidence, that did not fit into this view. He was not sly or furtive. He stared at me steadily and waited for my answer.

I said, 'What do you mean, you'll fix it? Why should you?'

He said, 'Whut duh hell's 'uh difference s'long 's it's fixed?'

I said, 'How do I know you can fix it?'

He looked surprised. 'Sure I'll fix it. Jeez, I fix a dozen of 'em ev'y week.'

'How?' I asked.

'How yuh think?' he retorted with a trace of irritation. 'I know all 'uh right guys. Christ, fella, I'm tryin' 'uh do yuh a favuh.'

'Yes,' I said doubtfully, 'but suppose you didn't fix it. That'd leave me in a fine spot, wouldn't it?'

'But I'm gonna fix it,' he repeated impatiently. 'Hell, ev'ybody here knows me. Henry Milano, 'ey call me Leg-'n'-half. I run all 'uh rackets roun' here. Ask anybody.' He did not say this boastfully, but with a quiet authority, as a statement of fact.

I believed him. But I could not understand why he should go to any trouble on my behalf. While I was hesitating, he said, 'You f'm Brooklyn, aintcha?'

I said, 'No, I'm from Manhattan.'

'Oh,' he said, 'I thought yuh was f'm Brooklyn, f'm yuh license plates.'

I shook my head.

He continued, 'I thought maybe you was one of Augie' — I think he said Geronimo — 'Augie Geronimo's boys. Yuh know Augie?'

I had never heard of Augie. But while Leg-'n'-half — to give him the name by which I always think of him — was talking, I became aware of several things. Scanlon, the policeman, had watched the scene for a moment and then moved away with a discomfited air too authentic to be simulated. The young men in the car were gesturing at the girl alongside as if to say, 'Go ahead. Do it.'

I no longer seriously doubted Leg-'n'-half's good intentions; but his motive remained incomprehensible. Then a theory occurred to me. I was wearing a new hat, an excessively jaunty affair into the purchase of which an unscrupulous salesman had intimidated me. It gave me, I felt, a rather sinister appearance. Could this fact, together with a sunburned skin, an unfortunate assemblage of features, an unpleasant attitude toward the police, and a presumptive Brooklyn license number have suggested that one of Augie's boys was taking his moll out for a drive? Was Leg-'n'-half extending the courtesies of the town to a fellow racketeer? I could think of no less implausible explanation.

Obviously, I saw, a connection with this Augie should not be too quickly disowned if I wanted to avoid the trouble which had visited me. Accordingly I said with what I hoped was the proper inflection, 'Well, I don't know Augie personally, but one of my pals knows him very well.'

I heard the girl in the car choke, but Leg-'n'-half seemed relieved. He said, as if everything was settled, 'Deh y'are. Let's have it.'

I handed him the ticket. Perhaps there was a trace of doubt still in my manner, because he said, 'I'll give yuh my 'phone numbeh. Four-three-six. If yuh worried, just gimme a call so I won't f'get.' With that, he crumpled the ticket, stuffed it into his pocket, and began to limp away.

A few flakes of gratitude were crystallizing out of my bewilderment. I said weakly, 'Thanks very much.' He looked round and said, 'Okay.' I got the impression that he was waiting for something, and an uncensored impulse made me ask, 'Do I owe you anything?' He answered curtly, 'Nah. What the hell.' And this time with finality he turned his back.

We drove off while the men in the other car laughed. For a while the girl and I were amused and excited; but after a few hours the incident dropped out of our consciousness. I forgot to telephone Leg-'n'-half; a week elapsed, and I had not heard from the Ryeneck police, and the episode began to slip into the mists of the faintly unreal.

About ten days later I went to the public library to consult recent copies of the metropolitan newspapers for the purposes of an article on which I was engaged. Glancing down a page, my eye caught a brief item which read:

> Ryeneck, July 8th. Late last night Henry Milano, reputed Westchester racketeer, was shot outside the Helicon Restaurant by two unknown men who effected their escape by automobile. Milano was wounded in the abdomen and chest and was taken to the Ryeneck hospital. His assailants, with whom he exchanged several shots, escaped unrecognized, but the police believe that they are members of a Brooklyn gang who have lately been attempting to 'muscle in' on Milano's 'territory.' Milano's condition is grave.

My encounter with Leg-'n'-half had taken place on the sixth. He had been shot the next night. I was vaguely sorry; and I dismissed a faint uneasiness about my summons, with the reflection that time would tell.

But a new worry arose to plague me. Suppose this Brooklyn gang was that with which I claimed connection. My name and address were on the summons. Might not Leg-'n'-half's friends regard me with suspicion?

I remained unmolested, however, by gangsters or police, and my fears gradually wore thin, until a day about six months later, when while riding in the subway I became aware of another strap-hanger who was watching me intently. I turned and saw Leg-'n'-half.

As soon as our eyes met, he forced his way through the crowd and took the strap next to mine.

'Yeah,' he said without any preliminaries. 'I thought it was you.'

His manner struck me as being alarmingly enigmatic. 'How are you?' I stammered.

'Okay,' he said.

An embarrassing pause ensued. 'I read in the newspapers that you got shot,' I said, frantically wishing I could think of something else to talk about.

'Yeah,' he said. 'Right after you came along.'

My imagination began to conjure up discouraging possibilities. If in Leg-'n'-half's mind I was in some way associated with the attack on him the immediate future was not inviting. I wanted to protest my innocence, but I felt that anything I said might be interpreted as a consciousness of guilt. With desperate caution I began, 'The papers said some fellows from Brooklyn did it.'

He answered significantly, 'Yeah. 'Ey got theirs las' month.'

I was not troubled about the fate of the fellows from Brooklyn, but I recall being a bit confused about the proper etiquette for the occasion. Did one offer congratulations? I mumbled something vague and hurried on. I said, 'I've never thanked you enough for fixing that ticket.'

He shrugged. ''At's okay.'

I decided to clear the matter up once and for all. 'You know,' I said jocularly, 'you asked me whether I was from Brooklyn — whether I knew some fellow — Augie something?'

His eyes flickered, and I plunged into awkward explanation. 'I was kidding when I said I knew a friend of his. I really never heard of him, but I thought maybe you wouldn't fix the ticket if I said I didn't know him.'

He smiled slightly, for the first time. 'Sure, I knew yuh was lyin',' he said. 'I jus' ast yuh tuh make sure yuh wasn't one o' Augie's guys. If you'd 'a' bin, you'd 'a' said yuh neveh hoid of him. Deh was a couple of 'em around just 'uh day b'fo', and I wasn't takin' no chances. I wasn't fixin' no tickets fuh none o' his guys.'

This revelation of subtlety startled me, and all my former curiosity returned. 'Look here,' I said, 'if you didn't fix the ticket for me on account of — well, why did you fix it anyway?'

His face became somber and he was silent for a moment. Then he said: 'Well, I'll tell yuh. I play hunches, see? I was in kind of a spot wit' Augie, see, 'n' I was lookin' fuh a hunch. When I see you and yuh dame ahguin' wit' Scanlon, right away I get a hunch. I say to the boys, "Dat guy's gonna gimme luck. I'll fix it fuh him, 'n' I'll tell Augie tuh"' — he repeated what he had told the boys he would tell Augie to do. Then he added, rather bitterly, 'Well, I fixed 'uh ticket okay, but a hell of a lot o' luck you was. A jinx.'

'I hope not,' I said, trying to smile.

'Not any mo',' he answered promptly, with an air of having considered the question. ''S soon as I see yuh just now I had a hunch it was okay. 'At's why I come over tuh talk tuh yuh. I got a deal on t'night, 'n' I need some luck. Well, I'm countin' on yuh to give it tuh me dis time.'

There was a challenge in his voice.

'I'll do my best,' I said idiotically.

'Okay,' he said, as if satisfied. There was a long and difficult pause. Then he added, 'Well, here's wheh I get off,' turned abruptly as the train pulled into a station, and limped onto the platform, where he stopped and looked at me with an expressionless face.

Without quite knowing why, I was perturbed, but my wife, to whom I related the incident, laughed, possibly at the thought of my bringing good luck to anybody. In an effort to create a little concern on my account, I pointed out that he was an avowed murderer, whose annoyance might easily carry a fatal connotation. But the detective stories and gangster movies to which my wife is addicted have made murderers too familiar to be very terrible.

'The least you can do,' she said, 'is give the poor man what he wants. Try concentrating.'

The next morning at breakfast I turned a page of my newspaper to find a small headline staring at me: 'Gangster Killed, Slayer Wounded in Gambling House.' The story read:

> Last night, a little after nine o'clock, Henry Milano, whom the police describe as a racketeer living in Ryeneck, New York, shot and killed Pasquale Vincenti, of 1258 West End Avenue, who was discharged from Sing Sing only last month. The shooting occurred at Jack Maguire's Club at 10th Avenue and 57th Street, raided by the police as a gambling dive on several occasions. Milano was seriously wounded in the right shoulder, but whether by Vincenti or another is not known. At City Hospital he refused to give any information to the police.

The report went on at some length.

It was quite clear to me that Leg-'n'-half's superstition, derived from heaven knew what obscure Mediterranean origins, would hold me responsible for his casualty. And, actually, an absurd feeling of responsibility for what had happened to him did bother me. I could not get him out of my thoughts. A childish but none-theless oppressive notion that I had been singled out to play a mysterious rôle in the life of this man defied every reference to common-sense and seemed to adumbrate some impending calamity. Although my wife continued to dismiss my fears with regrettable lightness, I could not help hoping that Leg-'n'-half would go to jail for a long sentence. I watched the newspapers closely. In a month or so I read that he had proved to the district attorney's satisfaction that the killing had been in self-defense, and had pleaded guilty to a technical charge of manslaughter. Sentence had been deferred. After that I saw no reference to the case.

Under the pressure of my own affairs, the matter slowly slipped out of my mind. Then, one evening about eight months after the previous encounter, my wife and I stopped for dinner in a West-chester roadhouse. My first intimation of Leg-'n'-half's presence was a shuffle of feet behind me and a gasp from my wife. I turned and saw him standing back of my chair.

He was thinner and paler than the last time I had seen him. I looked for a clue to his feelings in his face, but it was as impassive as ever. When he spoke, however, his voice had an ominous under-tone. For the first time I sensed the genuinely dangerous nature of the man.

'Listen,' he said to me, 'I wanna talk tuh yuh. Come on oveh to duh bah.'

Before I could reply, my wife said, smiling pleasantly, 'Why not talk here? I'm not in the way, am I?'

He looked at her for perhaps ten seconds, then said, 'Naw, I guess not,' and dropped into a chair at our table.

'Listen,' he resumed. 'You jinxed me.'

My wife said to me reproachfully, 'I do think you might introduce me.'

I mumbled an introduction, which Leg-'n'-half acknowledged with a nod.

'I remember your kindness very well, Mr. Milano,' said my wife.

He cleared his throat, and turned to me again. 'Listen,' he said, 'I jus' got sprung on parole yestiddy. Duh las' six mont's I bin thinkin' about you.'

'I was mighty sorry,' I said, 'to hear about that business — you know, the time we met on the subway?'

He paid no attention to my words. 'Funny,' he said thoughtfully, 'my hunches a'ways clicked up t' I met you. Twice yuh jinxed me. I thought for a while you was doin' it on poipus, but when I look atcha, I dunno. I keep gettin' 'uh same hunch I had b'fo'.'

He broke off, and there was a little silence. Then he looked at me from under his heavy lids and said, 'Yuh know, if I thought you was jinxin' me'... and stopped again, with a glance at my wife. She was no longer smiling, and I did not like the situation in the least.

I said, 'You know I'm not jinxing you. How could I?'

He merely looked at me, and I hastened to drop the rational argument.

'Well, then,' I said, 'why should I? You were decent to me up in Ryeneck. I wouldn't want to see you in trouble, would I? It's just a coincidence.'

He passed his fingers slowly across his lips. 'Yeah,' he said. 'Only how do I know?'

My wife started to speak, and he interrupted.

'Listen,' he said. 'Yuh needn't be scared. If I was gonna do anything, I'd 'a' done it. It's like I say, when I look atcha, I dunno. I keep gettin' 'at hunch. When I saw yuh t'night, I says t' myself, "Deh's duh jinx. I can't rub him out here, so I better beat it b'fo' he sees me." Den I'm not so sure. I keep thinkin' maybe duh jinx is oveh. I keep feelin' you're luck if I can make it come.'

I shook my head and then hastily reversed the motion to a nod.

He said: 'Listen, guy. I don't have nothin' against yuh. But I don't stand for no more jinxes. Twice is enough. Three times is out. T'night I'm goin' back to Ryeneck to split wit' duh guys that's been lookin' after things while I bin away. Maybe dey'll split easy, and it'll be okay. Maybe it won't. It's up to you. Get it?'

I nodded again, vaguely.

'If you put the jinx on me again,' he said simply, 'it'll be duh last time. Yuh gotta be lucky. Get it? Lucky!'

With that he rose, in his usual abrupt fashion, and left us.

For the first time I saw my wife frankly alarmed. She wanted me to go to the police. I objected, however, that to do so would be a direct invitation to disaster; whereas if events were left to chance,

Leg-'n'-half's luck might turn. Certainly the law of probabilities owed him — and me — something. Besides, what could I tell the police that would not sound like the timidities of a neurotic; and what could they do?

But Leg-'n'-half had said, 'Three times is out.' I did not like the sound of that. The next morning my wife and I scanned every column of our newspaper. We found nothing. I was plunged into a state of unresolved suspense. Had I been confirmed as Leg-'n'-half's jinx? Or had the boys 'split easy'? The incredible fact grew upon me that some night, any night, as I walked along the street, I might quite casually, quite abruptly, be shot to death.

This was not a pleasant thought to live with. And although for a while nothing happened, there can be a kind of terror in nothing happening. At first my wife and I buoyed up our spirits with wishful thinking. We told each other that Leg-'n'-half's affairs had probably prospered, failing reports of a shooting in Ryeneck; and that even if something had gone wrong the man could not be fool enough to hold me responsible. But neither of us had any faith in this theory. We had seen and heard Leg-'n'-half.

The truth is that the obvious insistence of circumstance on turning what should have been a joke into a tragedy had an air of predestination. My wife denies that she expected my murder hourly; but I know that I began to entertain a sort of resigned conviction that I was doomed. I found excuses for not leaving our apartment building; and I astounded a strange insurance solicitor, who called on me in a spirit of hopeless routine, by taking out a policy.

It was after three days of morbid tension that Leg-'n'-half reappeared. He came while my wife and I were at the dinner table. We had been trying to talk of inconsequentialities, when she rebelled, saying, 'This Suicide Club atmosphere is getting on my nerves. Let's go away for a while. Let's go to the country.'

I had been secretly toying with the same notion, but naturally, I did not want to admit it. I said that I would not be forced out of my home by a gangster's threat; a man owed something to his self-respect; what were we coming to; and so on.

My wife is not easily deceived by heroics, especially mine. She said: 'Nonsense. We can't go on like this, looking up and down the street every time we go out-of-doors, jumping at every noise. And we're so helpless.'

With the nonchalance expected of me, I said, 'Oh, if he intended to kill me he'd have done it by now.'

At this point the doorbell rang. I answered; we had previously agreed that Leg-'n'-half would not dare to call at our apartment, under the eyes of doormen and elevator boys. I had imagined several versions of an encounter with him, in all of which I came off with credit and alive; but as I opened the door and saw him standing there with another man, I could not speak or move or slam the door; I was paralyzed.

He said, 'Hello, guy.'

I muttered something that I did not understand myself.

He said, 'I come to tell you it was okay.'

'Okay?' I gasped, and he nodded. I remember that my knees literally trembled with relief as I caught the implications of his words. 'That's great,' I managed to say. The thought crossed my mind that it was extremely decent of him to have taken the trouble to call.

'Yeah,' he said. 'Duh boys come through okay.'

My wife, with a look of panic, had joined me at the door, and I said hurriedly, 'Mr. Milano just stopped by to say that everything went off all right the other night.'

'Oh,' she cried, beaming at him, 'I'm so glad. How nice of you, Mr. Milano, to let us know.'

He cleared his throat, and said, ''At's okay.' And then, with sudden bravado, 'My hunches a'ways bin good. 'At's how I got wheh I am.'

'I'm sure of it,' my wife smiled.

He turned to the man with him, a big, tough bruiser, and said, 'Beat it a minute, Pete. I wanna talk tuh dis guy alone'; and the man strolled down the corridor.

'Listen,' Leg-'n'-half said to me, lowering his voice. 'I knew my hunch couldn't be wrong if you was pullin' fuh me.'

'No,' I said, cheerfully making conversation. 'Of course not. I'm no jinx.'

He paused for a moment before replying, as if considering my remark, and I began to feel vaguely uneasy. Then he said: 'Listen. I'm f'gettin' about 'ose uddeh times. My hunch is, you're duh guy I been waitin' fuh.'

'Waiting for?' I repeated stupidly.

He said: 'I bin lookin' fuh a good-luck guy. I used tuh have a lucky kid, but he died on me. Now I know yuh okay, I'm all set tuh make a couple o' deals I bin thinkin' about fuh a long time, see?'

I merely stared at him, and he went on.

'I'm makin' a deal wit' a couple o' big shots downtown next Satiddy night, an' I ain't takin' no chances. I'll need plenny luck. So I'll be comin' in tuh see yuh on my way down. About eight o'clock, you be here.'

This was not a question; it was an order, given by a leader to his henchman.

I said, bewildered, 'But look here...'

He broke in impatiently. 'I ain't got time now. If yuh know whut's good fuh yuh, guy, yuh won't try no funny stuff. You'll pull fuh me. You be here.'

There was no mistaking his seriousness. He waited for an instant, but as I did not renew my objection, he nodded, and said, ''At's right. You pull fuh me, guy, an' I'll take care o' yuh.' With this he turned and started to limp away. But after a few steps, as if not wishing to fail in politeness, he glanced back, made a short jerky motion with his hand, and said, 'G'night.' I saw him join his man Pete at the elevator.

My wife closed the door, and we looked at each other. The bitter unfairness of it all was what I resented most, I think. I felt rather like Job. Why should I, among millions, have been chosen by Leg-'n'-half to bear the responsibility of his dangerous fortunes? And I wondered again, was there in truth some unfathomable human relations between us that he could sense, and I could not? Was I mascot, if not jinx? Could there be unrecognized forces of nature that might bind together two lives in an apparently magical pattern of luck or adversity?

My wife, however, is a realist. She wasted no time in idle reproaches to Destiny, or in philosophical excursions. While I was dismally contemplating the agonies of uncertainty that would fill my brief future before its inevitable, violent end, she went to the telephone, where I heard her calling a real-estate dealer of our acquaintance.

The result was that after a few days of unbelievable effort, on the morning of the very Saturday when Leg-'n'-half was to call, we moved into a small house in the country, about a hundred miles from

New York. The place is not entirely satisfactory; but one cannot expect too much when one rents on such short notice.

I do not know what has happened to Leg-'n'-half. We left no forwarding address, and I think I am safe from him. In my more optimistic moments, I hope that he is dead. But every now and then I get the quite ridiculous feeling that if he is dead, I may somehow — I don't know how — be to blame.

CATAFALQUE[1]

By CHARLES COOKE

(From *Story*)

THE earth's majestic rotation gradually edged the Atlantic coast into the eternal radiance of the sun. In the pale blue sky of a crystal winter dawn, the glowing disc hung just above the pastel canyons of New York, flooding its rays through the icy air to paint a wash of delicate rose over the snow-hushed city, filling with early light a room high in one of the great windowed cliffs that line Central Park West.

The room was a milling pandemonium at this strange hour. Newspaper photographers jostled and cursed each other as they crowded around a sofa, flashing their bulbs, barking 'Right into *this* camera, girlie!' 'Give us the old smile, both of you!' A score of reporters, notebooks in hand, waited impatiently.

Two figures sat on the sofa, smiling through the flickering roar: a slight, bald man, thin-lipped and sharp-nosed, wearing big tortoise-shell spectacles; a sturdy child in a scarlet frock, chubby little hands folded complacently in her lap. Her name — Milda Buksnaitytė — was on the front pages of all the morning papers, under by-lines of the music critics who had gone to Town Hall the evening before in weary expectation of hearing another commonplace child performer and had left two and a half hours later in a glow of ex- hilaration and awe, titillated by the knowledge that they had been present at the unveiling of one of Nature's miracles. When the night editors had read their critics' copy they had whistled and placed it in the unaccustomed glare of the first-page spotlight —

NINE–YEAR–OLD LITHUANIAN GIRL HAILED
AS GREATEST PRODIGY SINCE MOZART

CHILD PIANIST STUNS TOWN HALL AUDIENCE...

The photographers, in an uncouth wedge, rushed off to develop their plates, and the reporters closed in around the pair, grudgingly

[1] Copyright, 1935, by Story Magazine Inc.

making way for the two trays of breakfast which were brought in by white-jacketed waiters. The little man's smile had faded as soon as the pictures had been taken: though he plainly basked in the sudden notoriety, there was a peculiar, unremitting truculence in his manner, as though he were at bay, fighting hated enemies with his back against a wall.

The child still smiled amiably. The winter sunshine glazed her scarlet dress and extraordinary little face, its wide mouth that, smiling, bunched her cheeks into chubby mounds, its strong nose under strongly arched eyebrows, its fine forehead, its dancing russet eyes, its thick blond child hair. She was so small that, when playing, she could not sit on the piano bench: had to lean against it and stick her legs out straight, in order to touch the pedals. But her head was large in proportion to the rest of her body, and many who had watched and listened the night before had wondered, under their amazement and emotion, whether the key to her genius might not be a physiological one, a simple matter of larger, longer brain corridors. As she sat munching her breakfast toast in the buzzing, morning-drenched room, the intensity and poise of her face and manner created a startling impression that she was actually an adult — an adult reduced to doll size but retaining all the personal force of maturity, a brilliant adult looked at through the wrong end of opera glasses.

The reporters, pencils poised, were an intent arc, sitting on chairs, squatting on the floor, leaning against the black grand piano: 'Where was she born?' 'How long has she played the piano?' 'Who taught her?' 'Plans for future?' 'Who is her favorite movie star?' The bald man gulped his coffee greedily, his nervous eyes, behind the big tortoise-shell circles, alertly sweeping back and forth. He put his cup down on his tray, sat up straight, holding up a hand.

'If you will pleece be silent for moment, gentlemen, I will tell you whole story in nutshell. You will pardon my English. This little girl was born right here in New York.' Each word was curt, as though spoken in argument rather than simple narrative. 'Her mother and father were old-country Lithuanians, like me. They died before she was two years old and I — her mother's brother — have brought her up. I am her legal guardian. I have taught her how to play, all what she can do is because the way I teach her. Her name you could never say it right — nobody but real Lithuanian could — but this is close enough: Book-shnye-*tee*-teh.' The child giggled. 'See,' said the man, 'she knows that is not right even though she hardly speak any Lithuanian — she is real American girl.' He blinked solemnly as the pencil points rustled. 'Now my name is fine old Lithuanian name like hers; you spell it like this: Kastytis Dobilas. But you *say* it: Kus-*tee*-tis *Daw*-bi-lus. Got that?'

'Were her parents musical?' a reporter asked.

'No,' said the little man, 'and that is why, though sad she lose her mother and father so young, it is really fortunate thing. I am concert pianist, you see; studied in Kovno and played in Berlin, Paris, New York, all over. Right away, before she is yet four years old, I see she is musical genius and I begin to teach her piano. I am only teacher she ever had ——'

A tabloid reporter was looking at him sharply. 'I heard that you never had a complete musical education and that you never did any concert work. I heard you played the piano in a little East Side movie house until the talkies came and you lost the job. There isn't any truth in that, is there?'

The bald man's entire head had turned scarlet. 'Where you hear that?' he croaked. 'Where? It is low-down lie!' The lenses of his glasses glittered like mica spangles on a red globe. 'You put down I am *concert pianist*, don't put down no lies.'

The same reporter spoke again. 'All right, all right,' he said. 'We're only trying to get the facts straight. But you know all the critics say that she is a real genius but that her teaching has been very bad. They say she should be taken off the concert stage for years while she studies with the best piano teachers in the world ——'

'Milda!' snapped her uncle. 'Run get me my cigarette case; it is on my bed. Quick now!' Wriggling down from the sofa, trotting out of the room, she was a scarlet streak of vitality and good humor.

He lowered his voice as she disappeared, his thin jowls trembled. 'Gentlemen, gentlemen,' he said: 'do not say such things in my niece's hearing. That is *very* bad. It is important she keep confidence in me and her mind is so quick you have no idea; everything what she hear she remember forever. Now you have put idea in her head she may never forget ——'

'Good thing, perhaps,' a sourceless voice said, deep in the crowd of reporters.

The little man put his head in his hand and groaned. 'Why you all against me? Is because she make such big success? I have taught her all she know, I am best possible teacher in whole world for her because I know good how to teach, and she will mind me. And I am only trying to give you good story for your papers, and you —'

She stood beaming chubbily in the doorway. 'It isn't on the bed,' she shrilled.

'All right, Milda, never mind, come back,' said her uncle.

She trotted to the sofa and wriggled up on it, folding her hands in her lap again.

A reporter turned toward her radiant little smile. 'What is the hardest piece you play, Milda?' he asked. All the others were alert for the reply.

'Why, the Campanella —' she began, but her uncle cut in sharply.

'That is foolish question, why should she answer it? *Nothing* is hard for her. I have taught her to play any music in the world. Just put down that through my teaching she can play *any* music. And she can learn any piece in two days, some in two hours. Now, gentlemen, pleece, we cannot give you more time. Milda must get to work and I allow no one to hear her practice. You have plenty there for stories. But you can add that she will play entirely new program in Carnegie Hall in three weeks, then twenty-five recitals from here to California, then London, Paris, Berlin, Stockholm, Copenhagen —' he paused for breath.

The reporters, scribbling, were moving toward the door. One said: 'What, all those concerts, and she is only nine years old!'

This time the little man exploded. 'There you go again,' he blurted, the veins standing out in his crimson forehead. 'I asked you not to talk like that when she can hear. What business of yours if she play a lot of concerts? She makes two thousand dollars every one — she should throw that away because what some damn-fool critic or damn-fool reporter say?' He was angrily herding them toward the door.

He opened it; hand on the knob, he faced them and spoke with triumph under his rage:

'And you can put in that tonight I am taking Milda to call on Volkonsky. He was at concert last night and called me up here before I went to bed. Put that in. And you can put in that day after tomorrow I am taking her to call on Mrs. Payne Augmont to arrange big recital before we sail for Europe in spring — what is it, Milk Fund Benefit? Yes. Put that in, too. Good-bye.'

He slammed the door after them and turned back toward the child, who submissively awaited his command. His anger had ebbed and his weasel face was lighted by the tonic thrill of publicity and the bewildering, delicious intoxication of soaring transversely upward through artistic and social strata to the exotic air of the highest levels. The tiny figure on the sofa was, momentarily yellow with a rich crust of gold pieces, like a magnet furred with filings. His brain marinated in glory.

Then his face hardened. 'Get to the piano,' he barked. 'We have lose an hour's work with those newspaper fools. And mind, if last movement of *Appassionata* is not finished and perfect by two o'clock, you'll get box on ears what you won't forget.'

She ran to the piano, leaned against the bench, stuck out her chubby legs until they touched the pedals, placed her miraculous little fingers on the keyboard. The room was filled with the flaxen light of winter morning.

The butler ushered them into the music-room. Sergei Volkonsky had arisen from an armchair; tall and aristocratic, he came toward them. His gait was slow, almost a shuffle, and this, together with the slight droop of his shoulders, underlined the weary sadness of his craggy, old-ivory face — weariness of unflagging, titan labor to attain year after year a cruelly high standard, sadness of exile. The Russian virtuoso, one of the greatest pianists of all time, inclined his famous close-shaven head in a courtly bow as he gently patted the little girl's hand with his steel-strong fingers; a smile transfigured his fine-fibred melancholy. He waved Kastytis Dobilas to a chair and sat opposite him, drawing the child against his knee. She wore a blue dress with white ruffles; her bright eyes sparkled as she nestled against him, glancing up, unafraid, at his paternal and sympathetic expression.

'I am so glad you have come,' he said, speaking slowly and carefully, a hint of Slavic thickness in his words. 'This little girl's playing interested me greatly last night. I seldom attend recitals, but Mr. Lhevinne spoke to me about her, and I am interested in young talent. I believe she played part of her program for Mr. Lhevinne at your apartment last week?'

Dobilas had taken off his tortoise-shell spectacles and was polishing them vigorously with his handkerchief; his bald pate gleamed. 'Yes,' he answered, replacing them with jerky fingers, 'but I tell you. I was very disappointed. He make crazy suggestions, try to put new ideas in her head after I have taught her so careful just how to play. I was sorry he come, honest.'

Volkonsky was not smiling now. 'I heard something of all that from Mr. Lhevinne,' he said politely. 'It is one of the reasons I attended the concert. It is only because your niece has such remarkable possibilities that ——'

The little man leaned forward belligerently. 'What you mean "possibilities"? She is great artist right this minute, because I have taught her how. Didn't she fill Town Hall packed full, with hundreds on the stage too, and they cheer and cry and make her play ten, twelve encores? "Possibilities," you say?'

The two phenomenal pianists, one venerable and gray, the other tiny and dew-fresh, gravely watched the bald man's excitement.

Volkonsky continued:

'I didn't mean to offend you, Mr. Dobilas. I was only going on to say that Mr. Lhevinne is quite right. Your niece has genuine virtuoso temperament; her handling of the big bass octaves in Chopin's A minor Etude in the Opus 25 shows this very clearly. But that is not enough; it can never serve, alone, for the whole complexity of rounded artistic playing. I am sorry to have to say this, Mr. Dobilas, but her purely musical side, which is potentially as rich as her astonishing gifts of technique and memory, has been crim — has been quite neglected.' Dobilas, flushing, began to sputter, but Volkonsky went on: 'She plays many wrong notes, and — please do not be angry — she has no conception whatsoever of the difficult and subtle art of phrasing.'

Dobilas leaped out of his chair. 'How can you say such thing?' he cried.

'Milda,' said the great musician, looking down into her eager face with deep affection, 'I wonder if you would go over for me the first few bars of the *adagio* from the *Pathétique* sonata which you played last night.'

'Oh, yes,' she answered, leaving his knee to run to her beloved keyboard. She leaned against the bench of the big concert grand piano, began. The resonance of a fine instrument in perfect tune throbbed in the room.

After a moment, Volkonsky said: 'That's all, my dear. Thank you very much.'

She ran back to his knee and this time rested her head on his sleeve.

'It is a perfect illustration, Mr. Dobilas,' said Volkonsky. 'I have no doubt you teach her conscientiously and to the best of your ability. But if you do not realize that her phrasing of that short passage is atrocious, if you do not realize that that phrasing is an insult to a trained musical ear, then clearly you should not presume to continue teaching her. The child's gifts are of an unearthly quality which gives her the *right* to be turned over, immediately, to one of the best living piano teachers. It should have been done long ago ——'

Dobilas stood beside the pair, glaring at them. He gave a short laugh. 'I suppose *you* want to teach her, to take her away from me and try to give her ideas she is too young to understand — then she would be Volkonsky pupil in all write-ups. You would like that, eh?' His thin lips were ugly in a sneer.

'My dear Mr. Dobilas,' said Volkonsky, 'nothing was further from my mind. I do not teach and do not wish to teach. But perhaps Mr. Lhevinne, if properly approached, would undertake to instruct her, or even Mr. Hofmann, if he heard her play. That is the kind of teaching she deserves: a master who, like Toscanini, can hear in his mind the sublime songs of ideal, perfect interpretations and who is able to lead others to create a close approximation of them. Every lesson this girl takes is crucial; obviously, she leaps in an hour's study as far as the average talented child goes in two months.'

Milda Buksnaityté, still leaning against the Russian's knee, looked from one face to the other, then dropped her eyes, which turned self-absorbed as she mentally ran over one of the pieces in her huge repertoire. Volkonsky leaned forward in his chair, looking earnestly up at Dobilas.

'Please forgive me, Mr. Dobilas, for speaking so frankly about what is, in the last analysis, not my province. But, if nothing else, it is grossly unfair to the world of music and music-lovers to allow this marvellous instrument to fall short of its superb possibilities and through no fault of its own. And there is the future to be thought of. Today Milda is able to entrance audiences by the — what shall I say? — the melodramatic fact of her age and size. When she gets older, she will have to be supported by music alone, not melodrama. And will she be able to meet the sterner test? Ruth Slenczynski, for instance, is, to my mind, being pushed far too fast for her own good; she is approximately Milda's age, you know. But Yehudi Menuhin is eighteen now, no longer a boy wonder, and he must stand on his own; it is deeply satisfying to me to realize that, through the perfect behavior of his parents, he has come through splendidly into artistic maturity. I heard him play the Bruch Concerto like a young god the other night; on my word of honor, there was not a cough or a rustled program through its entire length. Sheer selfishness on the part of the audience; it didn't want to miss a single golden note from his bow. Will Milda be able to command such rapt attention when she is eighteen? Will the stick be everlasting, feeding the flame richly, growing larger with the years? Mr. Dobilas, unless her training is changed immediately, the flame will burn the stick to ash and the ash will float away on the wind. She plays wrong notes, she does not know how to phrase, the conceptions she has been taught of her pieces are immature and sometimes actually vulgar. Yet she receives rapturous applause. This is a frightful danger; it will give her habits which she simply cannot overcome. She will always play inaccurately and immaturely and her career will be ruined by the time she is ——'

Something like fear came into Dobilas's face under the impact of the slow, earnest words spoken with such profound sincerity by the master musician; his posture of outraged rectitude wavered.

'Well,' he said, still watching Volkonsky narrowly; 'what you suggest? You say when you call up that you want to discuss Milda's future and that is why I come, why I bring her ——'

Volkonsky's mood brightened as the other's opposition relaxed. 'Why, the first thing, of course, would be to remove her from public playing for, say, six years. During this time she would be under the constant guidance of her new teacher and she would be tutored so that her general education would keep pace with her musical development. And all the rush and strain and excitement of concert life would be avoided.' He warmed to his plan, too absorbed in it now to notice that Dobilas's face was reddening with anger again. 'At the end of six years, she would be fifteen. Then a limited number of recitals would, I think, be wise. Then another three years of training, the final polish, and at eighteen or nineteen she could begin as a mature artist, and might, I feel, develop into the greatest woman pianist the world has known.'

In the silence which followed, Dobilas took Milda abruptly by the hand and pulled her to him. She stood obediently as he poised to release the torrent of emotion which had built up in his brain.

'I have listened to you all this time,' he said, sobs of self-pity trembling on the brink of audibility, 'because you are great musician and I think maybe you give me good ideas for Milda. But you talk like Mr. Lhevinne and the little girl she hear it all and that is terrible for her and for me. Even she hear the newspaper men say same thing. Why is whole world against me? Everybody want to take Milda away from me after I have taught her so careful——'

Volkonsky's face was grave again, hopelessness was in his voice now. 'It is not a question of taking her away from you, Mr. Dobilas. You would remain her guardian and be with her always. These years of study ——'

'These years of study! And what about the bookings we have made? Carnegie Hall in three weeks, then a tour all way to California, then Europe. And two thousand dollars every time she play! She should give that up because these damn ideas? No! You will not take her away from me and nobody else will. She love to play, I can't never make her stop encores. This is the life she love and she will keep right on. And I will teach her myself. She has had big, enormous success already and only I have taught her.' Volkonsky had risen and was looking down at them with horror in his eyes; his silence spurred Dobilas to continue. 'Ruin her career?' he shouted. 'How can career be ruined that is already booked solid even now when she only nine? And she learn so quick and I teach her so good — so *god damn good*, you hear me?'

'Do I understand she is to play in Carnegie Hall in only three weeks? A new program?'

'Yes, new program. And she can do it easy, practicing only six hours a day. She loves to practice ——'

'I have nothing further to say, Mr. Dobilas,' said Sergei Volkonsky, tall and sad in the amber light.

Outside, cold night winds swept newly fallen snow up and down Riverside Drive; the Hudson was an ebony sheen. Kastytis Dobilas and Milda Buksnaitytė stood at the curb, their breath making little clouds. A taxi pulled up, they entered. As they settled back, he put his arm around her with a sigh of infinite relief. The taxi started. He darted a backward glance at the granite, snow-tufted structure from which he was fleeing as though it were a plague-stricken house of death.

She lay motionless in the profound slumber of exhaustion, tiny in the big bed. He switched off the light and groped to the window, opened it and stood looking out as icy air rushed in. The ghostly purple-black expanse of Central Park was spangled with points of yellow light under the star-studded night sky. The earth was muted in its own vast shadow.

THE NORTH WIND DOTH BLOW

By EVAN COOMBES

(From *The London Mercury*)

THE boy had stayed home alone that he might watch the house across the fields, himself unwatched. Only when his mother and father had gone to town could he stare as he liked up the sloping ground to the small dark house that so aroused his wonder and defied it.

No matter where he looked, his eyes were drawn there, and no matter what he might be doing: working on the farm now that he had finished school, or standing idle on the back steps as he was standing this afternoon. He might look away over the November fields and pastures, strewn with rocks and bounded with them, as though the rocks had been swept into walls by some mysterious tide. He might follow with his eyes these low walls as they straggled down the hillside, past the orchard and down to the clustered roofs of the village, but he must come back as if magnetized. All these curving, undulating lines led to one place, were drawn together and brought up sharply in the small dark angles of the house.

There were no trees or bushes near it; nothing grew there to soften its stark ugliness. Isolated, exposed, the house stood on bare ground, and neither man nor Nature had tried to deal with the unsightly structure in the usual way. Only the weather had given a suitable coloring to the unpainted boards, the color of the fields themselves, especially rich and dark after the recent rain. The wind also had assisted in making it native; the strong gales from the north actually giving a slant to the walls of the house and to the stakes that served as a crude trellis for a vine that bore no grapes.

The house held its interior secret. The small windows revealed nothing and the boy had never been inside. Since he had moved to this farm so many months ago, he had never even set foot across the wall that divided the two properties. He had only gazed from a distance, fascinated in some obscure way by the very bleakness of the place. Its exposure to the winds, to the greater heat in summer, to the snows of winter, aroused a longing in him to be up there on that high ground. Standing there, one could look far, and the whole countryside would roll away with its scattering of little homes, all like his own, painted white, vined over, nestled down comfortably under trees. None was so bare and ugly, none so exposed as this. Perhaps that was why he could not keep his eyes from the place; why he kept watching it, and watching for the woman who lived there.

She seldom came outside, but when she did, she was as conspicuous as her house. Her hair was an unnatural red, having no part in Nature's reds; her dress, a faded washed-out blue, strained over her rather large body as though she wore nothing under it. Sometimes she only came out to sit on the steps; sometimes to walk down to the village for food, usually early in the morning when other women were busy in their kitchens. That was one of the things that made her so different from the women he knew: she was never busy. When she sat on the doorstep, it was wonderful how long she could sit there. She made him think of Old Man River in the song; she didn't plant 'taters, she didn't do nothin'. She didn't even roll along, but just sat as if she were waiting; like the sea, waiting for rivers to come to her. Busy people couldn't understand doing nothing, but the boy could. There was much of that in himself. He liked to stand still in the rows of bean-hills, leaning on his hoe, or lie on his back in the orchard watching the apples redden in the sun. If he could watch the woman sitting on her steps, so much the better. But how sharply his father would call him to his task, and in what a curious tone his mother would ask what he was staring at.

How reluctant his mother had been to leave him home alone that afternoon. She had stood there smoothing down the fingers of the brown kid gloves she always wore to town, but such was the reserve existing between the practical woman and the dreaming boy, she could only say:

'Cousin Mamie will think it mighty queer, your stayin' home like this. What'll I tell her?'

'Tell her I'm going to supper at Lucy's. Anyway, she asked me.'

'Why didn't you say so before? Are you sure you're going? Will you promise me, Jerry?'

'Sure. Why not?'

And yet she still stood there, smoothing down the fingers of her gloves, not looking at him, not saying the thing that was on her mind.

'Take a bunch of dahlias when you go. There's some of those big red ones left.'

'I don't want to take them to Lucy. That would be silly.'

'Well, take them to her mother, then, and don't forget.'

Even then she seemed dissatisfied, and as she climbed in the car, appealed to his father: didn't he think Jerry should come with them? But his father was indifferent as long as work was not being neglected. Let the boy stay home. Let him go to Lucy's. The hired man was coming up to milk the cows, anyway. The boy staying home waited at the open door until the little car had scuttled out of sight down the road, until all sound of it had gone and there was nothing to be heard but the wind. He stood as if he were still being watched, hands thrust in pockets, head bent, while he kicked at the blistered paint on the doorsill. Funny thing about mothers, he thought, how much they know. She knew he was more likely to stay home than he was to go to see Lucy.

Why was she so keen about Lucy, anyway? Always having her to supper and then he had to walk home with her. The girl would hold tightly to his arm as they went stumbling down the black road at night, sometimes shy and silent, sometimes chattering. He didn't know how it happened, but the last time they said good night, she reached up and kissed him. It was a queer little oblique meeting of lips, the touch of her mouth soft and quick like nothing he had ever known. He had pondered long over this first kiss of woman. It meant that she liked him, he supposed.

He stood now listening to the wind in the trees, hearing it creak and sway the great branches, watching it delicately ruffle the white feathers of a hen pecking the ground beneath. He stood in the doorway between the warm kitchen and the sombre November scene. Dark enough the house looked now, set out pitilessly on the stony fields. One could imagine the stones had been thrown there, the house for a target. The place was so stripped that the wind found nothing to take with it, nothing even to tug at but the dry network of grapevine and a tendril of smoke at the chimney corner. Inside those dark walls, the woman was sitting as idle as he was, no doubt, and waiting; between them, only a field and a tumbling line of rocks. The thought of going to see her came to him as an extraordinary thought. And yet, he suddenly realized, that was what his mother feared he might do, and this startled him. As though her fear of his going there made it possible for him to do so, he considered it. If he had some gift to take her, but he had nothing she wanted. He did not even have anything to say to her. The thought of summoning her to the door while he stood tongue-tied, unable to open his mouth, confused him so that he was about to shut himself in the kitchen, when he was held motionless.

Something bright caught his eyes. The woman had come out of the dark house, and what was bright was her hair, the unnatural blaze of her hair. It was seized upon by the wind, tossed and whipped back like flame. The sweater she wore tightly buttoned across her full breast was also red, but a soft dull red, like that of old barns, tempered by the sun and rain into a lovelier tone than man could produce. She stayed at the door of her house like a figure on the prow of a ship, and the blowing clouds gave an illusion of motion so that the house seemed to be riding high on the slopes of the earth as on a sea. Then she detached herself, striding down over the fields, her thin blue skirt torn at by the wind; and the boy watched her go through the orchard, watched her colors through the trees, until the last flickering of red had gone and there was nothing more of her to be seen. Sombreness reasserted itself; the dark clouds pressed lower; the fruit had been gathered. Earth grew cold, awaiting the frost, under a sky without memory or hope of sun.

Shivering, he went in and shut the door. He tried to warm himself at the stove, but the fire was low. Restlessly, he moved about the little room, going to the window to stare down the empty road, turning back to the kitchen with its comfortable, familiar things trying to reassure him. He cut a wedge of apple pie, and eating it hungrily, looked at the clock. If he were going to see Lucy, he must go soon. He would have to take the road the woman had taken. Perhaps he would meet her on her way home, and meeting her so casually, he might be able to speak. At least, he could say good evening. He wished she knew that he did not share the prejudice of the village. It meant nothing to him, what they said about her.

And yet, it was not what they said, it was what they did not say. There was a knowing conspiracy of silence, and the boy, too, not to appear unknowing, was silent. It seemed to him that her coming from town and not going back there was the chief cause of their resentment. Morgan, the man who had built the house up on the hillside for all to see, who had made it ugly and left it ugly, used to interrupt his solitary life with trips to the nearest town. After several days of drunkenness, he would return to sobriety and toil, but on his last trip he had brought back the woman with him, and had died a month later, leaving her his property. She had only been there through the summer, but even that was too long for the village. Why doesn't that woman of Morgan's go back where she came from? This was the only question he ever heard asked about her. He heard it asked of his father down in the store and he heard his father ask it of the hired man; and Charlie, oddly enough, for the boy had never seen him talking to the woman, seemed to know her plans. Charlie knew that she was trying to sell the property and was going back to town now the cold weather was coming. We'll have to buy it ourselves, his mother said, if that's the only way to get rid of her.

His mother was not home to watch him now, but everything in the kitchen watched him for her. It was useless to stare out of the window, his face close to the glass; he could feel the room at his back. He must get away from it, out to shoulder the wind. Let it be cold and bitter, but no more of this shut-in place. He must get out in the strong wind which would be like a rude embrace, encompassing his body, a thing to struggle with, to throw himself against. He hurried to get away, pulling his sweater down from a hook, and as he did so, an apron of his mother's fell with it across his arm. For a moment, he stood looking at it curiously. The apron was so light he could not feel it on his arm, and yet it held him there. But why? He was only going to see Lucy and he had not forgotten about the flowers. It is time to go, he said aloud, looking at the clock and carefully hanging the apron up; it is time.

As he opened the back door, the wind engulfed him, plunged past him into the room. Slamming the door shut behind him, he ran down to the dahlia patch by the barn, putting on his sweater as he ran. He picked all that were left, five heavy red ones, drooping on their stems. Then he took to the wagon road that followed the wall down the hill. It was deeply rutted and pooled with rain, but the cold would soon be binding it over. He continued to run because he must, because it seemed to him nothing was still. The air was filled with leaves blowing and birds in difficult flight. He watched a small bird beating its wings, trying to make headway, only able to maintain its position in mid-air. The dark plummet of its body, the levity of its wings. The north wind doth blow, he remembered the child's verse, and we shall have snow, and what will poor robin do then? But the robins had gone south long ago. Perhaps the verse meant the winds in March, snow coming then to send the robin to the barn to hide his head under his wing, poor thing; the robin who had flown north too early thinking spring had come.

The road was still empty; there was no one on the road as far as he could see down it. He stopped running and began to walk, and then to walk more and more slowly. After all, there was no hurry. He would be coming out on the main road too soon. But he could not walk slowly enough, and in order not to get where he was going, he had to sit down. On the top of the stone wall, he sat under an old apple tree strayed from the orchard. Its little useless apples littered the grass; he had crushed them underfoot and the odor was rather sweet. Holding the dahlias, he sat there, the heavy blossoms drooping with their weight of redness. Mother sent these, he would be careful to say, handing them to Lucy's mother.

The stone wall climbed away from him up the hill; it tumbled away from him down the hill. Looking up, he could see both houses from where he sat: the little white farmhouse and the dark house on barren ground. They were neighbors, set far apart, but only a badly kept wall between. What made it seem like a barricade? Idly, he swung one leg over, sitting astride the wall. His foot touched the alien soil and he felt as though he had trespassed, more than that, he had come nearer the woman herself. In touching the earth of her field, he seemed to have touched the hem of her dress. He caught his breath, and then, he could not breathe at all.

For she was coming toward him up the road. Her head was lowered, her eyes looking where she walked. She had not seen him, he knew, and for one tumultuous moment, he stayed there, watching her come nearer. He tried to think of what he should say, he gave one desperate look round, and in complete panic, dropped down on the other side of the wall. Face down, lengthwise, he lay close to the wall, as still as the stones themselves, as compact and as cold. His eyes shut, deep in the grass, he could only listen. But all he could hear was the roar of the wind above him and the pounding of his own heart within. He could not hear her step on the road, but he knew when she was near; he sensed her nearness as she walked by. Closer and closer, he pressed his body to the hard earth and the harder stones, and even after she had gone by, he stayed there, prone, exhausted. He became aware of the odors of the wet earth, the crushed apples, and the dahlias he still held. He felt as if he had been there hours, when slowly, cautiously, he drew himself up.

Something had happened to the world. The clouds low in the west had parted and the sun shone, a violent, incredible sun. He had never seen so red a sun as the one burning between those heavy purple clouds. It brought him to his feet and he looked from the sun to the woman. She was far up the road now, starting to climb over the wall to reach her house. He knew that she might look back, but he could not move; and when she did look back, still he could not move. They were standing far apart, but the wall no longer separated them. The ancient stones were running from where he stood to where she stood; both were touching the wall and it was like a communication between them. After a moment, she climbed over and walked up to her house, the wind beating her garments against the strong curves of her body until she was like a woman stripped, walking among the stones that looked as if they had been thrown there.

The wet earth of the field gave under his feet; he stumbled awkwardly, his feet becoming heavy with earth. He kept his eyes on the woman as she waited in the doorway and then went inside, leaving the door open. At that moment, the sun caught on the windows and they blazed as if the rooms within were alight. He was mounting strange land, leaving his known world behind him. When he glanced down toward his own home, he scarcely recognized it. He was a long way from there, going at last into the house and its mystery. Dark enough it looked now, the nearer he came. The sun had left the windows, and he hesitated, almost repelled by the cold dark look of it. But he had the dahlias in his hand to give her, the door was open for him to enter, and he went in.

THAT WILL BE FINE[1]

By WILLIAM FAULKNER

(From *The American Mercury*)

I

WE COULD hear the water running into the tub. We looked at the presents scattered over the bed where Mamma had wrapped them in the colored paper, with our names on them so Grandpa could tell who they belonged to easy when he would take them off the tree. There was a present for everybody except Grandpa because Mamma said that Grandpa is too old to get presents any more.

'This one is yours,' I said.

'Sho now,' Rosie said. 'You come on and get in that tub like your mamma tell you.'

'I know what's in it,' I said. 'I could tell you if I wanted to.'

Rosie looked at her present. 'I reckon I kin wait twell hit be handed to me at the right time,' she said.

'I'll tell you what's in it for a nickel,' I said.

Rosie looked at her present. 'I ain't got no nickel,' she said. 'But I will have Christmas morning when Mr. Rodney give me that dime.'

'You'll know what's in it, anyway, then and you won't pay me,' I said. 'Go and ask Mamma to lend you a nickel.'

Then Rosie grabbed me by the arm. 'You come on and get in that tub,' she said. 'You and money! If you ain't rich time you twenty-one, hit will be because the law done abolished money or done abolished you.'

So I went and bathed and came back, with the presents all scattered out across Mamma's and Papa's bed and you could almost smell it and tomorrow night they would begin to shoot the fireworks and then you could hear it too. It would be just tonight, and then tomorrow we would get on the train, except Papa, because he would have to stay at the livery stable until after Christmas Eve, and go to Grandpa's, and then tomorrow night and then it would be Christmas and Grandpa would take the presents off the tree and call out our names, and the one from me to Uncle Rodney that I bought with my own dime and so after a while Uncle Rodney would prize open Grandpa's desk and take a dose of Grandpa's tonic and maybe he would give me another quarter for helping him, like he did last Christmas, instead of just a nickel, like he would do last summer while he was visiting Mamma and us and we were doing business with Mrs. Tucker before Uncle Rodney went home and began to work for the Compress Association, and it would be fine. Or maybe even a half a dollar and it seemed to me like I just couldn't wait.

'Jesus, I can't hardly wait,' I said.

'You which?' Rosie hollered. 'Jesus?' she hollered. 'Jesus? You let your mamma hear you cussing and I bound you'll wait. You talk to me about a nickel! For a nickel I'd tell her just what you said.'

'If you'll pay me a nickel I'll tell her myself,' I said.

'Get into that bed!' Rosie hollered. 'A seven-year-old boy, cussing!'

'If you will promise not to tell her, I'll tell you what's in your present and you can pay me the nickel Christmas morning,' I said.

'Get in that bed!' Rosie hollered. 'You and your nickel! I bound if I thought any of you all was fixing to buy even a dime present for your grandpa, I'd put in a nickel of hit myself.'

'Grandpa don't want presents,' I said. 'He's too old.'

'Hah,' Rosie said. 'Too old, is he? Suppose everybody decided you was too young to have nickels: what would you think about that? Hah?'

So Rosie turned out the light and went out. But I could still see the presents by the firelight: the ones for Uncle Rodney and Grandma and Aunt Louisa and Aunt Louisa's husband Uncle Fred, and Cousin Louisa and Cousin Fred and the baby and Grandpa's cook and our cook, that was Rosie, and maybe somebody ought to give Grandpa a present only maybe it ought to be Aunt Louisa because she and Uncle Fred lived with Grandpa, or maybe Uncle Rodney ought to because he lived with Grandpa too. Uncle Rodney always gave Mamma and Papa a present, but maybe it would be just a waste of his time and Grandpa's time both for Uncle Rodney to give Grandpa a present, because one time I asked Mamma why Grandpa always looked at the present Uncle Rodney gave her and Papa and got so mad, and Papa began to laugh and Mamma said Papa ought to be ashamed, that it wasn't Uncle Rodney's fault if his generosity was longer than his pocketbook, and Papa said Yes, it certainly wasn't Uncle Rodney's fault, he never knew a man to try harder to get money than Uncle Rodney did, that Uncle Rodney had tried every known plan to get it except work, and that if Mamma would just think back about two years she would remember one time when Uncle Rodney could have thanked his stars that there was one man in the connection whose generosity, or whatever Mamma wanted to call it, was at least five hundred dollars shorter than his pocketbook, and Mamma said she defied Papa to say that Uncle Rodney stole the money, that it had been malicious persecution and Papa knew it, and that Papa and most other men were prejudiced against Uncle Rodney, why she didn't know, and that if Papa begrudged having lent Uncle Rodney the five hundred dollars when the family's good name was at stake to say so and Grandpa would raise it somehow and pay Papa back, and then she began to cry and Papa said 'All right, all right,' and Mamma cried and said how Uncle Rodney was the baby and that must be why Papa hated him and Papa said 'All right, all right; for God's sake, all right.'

Because Mamma and Papa didn't know that Uncle Rodney had been handling his business all the time he was visiting us last summer, any more than the people in Mottstown knew that he was doing business last Christmas when I worked for him the first time and he paid me the quarter. Because he said that if he preferred to do business with ladies instead of men it wasn't anybody's business except his, not even Mr. Tucker's. He said how I never went around telling people about Papa's business and I said how everybody knew Papa was in the livery-stable business and so I didn't have to tell them, and Uncle Rodney said Well, that was what half of the nickel was for and did I want to keep on making the nickels or did I want him to hire somebody else? So I would go on ahead and watch through Mr. Tucker's fence until he came out to go to town and I would go along behind the fence to the corner and watch until Mr. Tucker was out of sight and then I would put my hat on top of the fence post and leave it there until I saw Mr. Tucker coming back. Only he never came back while I was there because

Uncle Rodney would always be through before then, and he would come up and we would walk back home and he would tell Mamma how far we had walked that day and Mamma would say how good that was for Uncle Rodney's health. So he just paid me a nickel at home. It wasn't as much as the quarter when he was in business with the other lady in Mottstown Christmas, but that was just one time and he visited us all summer and so by that time I had a lot more than a quarter. And besides the other time was Christmas and he took a dose of Grandpa's tonic before he paid me the quarter and so maybe this time it might be even a half a dollar. I couldn't hardly wait.

II

But it got to be daylight at last and I put on my Sunday suit, and I would go to the front door and watch for the hack and then I would go to the kitchen and ask Rosie if it wasn't almost time and she would tell me the train wasn't even due for two hours yet. Only while she was telling me we heard the hack, and so I thought it was time for us to go and get on the train and it would be fine, and then we would go to Grandpa's and then it would be tonight and then tomorrow and maybe it would be a half a dollar this time and Jesus it would be fine. Then Mamma came running out without even her hat on and she said how it was two hours yet and she wasn't even dressed and John Paul said, 'Yessum,' but Papa sent him and Papa said for John Paul to tell Mamma that Aunt Louisa was here and for Mamma to hurry. So we put the basket of presents into the hack and I rode on the box with John Paul and Mamma hollering from inside the hack about Aunt Louisa, and John Paul said that Aunt Louisa had come in a hired buggy and Papa took her to the hotel to eat breakfast because she left Mottstown before daylight even. And so maybe Aunt Louisa had come to Jefferson to help Mamma and Papa get a present for Grandpa.

'Because we have one for everybody else,' I said, 'I bought one for Uncle Rodney with my own money.'

Then John Paul began to laugh and I said, 'Why?' and he said it was at the notion of me giving Uncle Rodney anything that he would want to use, and I said, 'Why?' and John Paul said because I was shaped like a man, and I said, 'Why?' and John Paul said he bet Papa would like to give Uncle Rodney a present without even waiting for Christmas, and I said, 'What?' and John Paul said, 'A job of work.' And I told John Paul how Uncle Rodney had been working all the time he was visiting us last summer, and John Paul quit laughing and said 'Sho,' he reckoned anything a man kept at all the time, night and day both, he would call it work no matter how much fun it started out to be, and I said, 'Anyway, Uncle Rodney works now, he works in the office of the Compress Association,' and John Paul laughed good then and said it would sholy take a whole association to compress Uncle Rodney. And then Mamma began to holler to go straight to the hotel, and John Paul said 'Nome, Papa said to come straight to the livery stable and wait for him.' And so we went to the hotel and Aunt Louisa and Papa came out and Papa helped Aunt Louisa into the hack and Aunt Louisa began to cry and Mamma hollering, 'Louisa! Louisa! What is it? What has happened?' and Papa saying, 'Wait now. Wait. Remember the nigger,' and that meant John Paul, and so it must have been a present for Grandpa and it didn't come.

And then we didn't go on the train after all. We went to the stable and they already had the light road hack hitched up and waiting, and Mamma was crying now and saying how Papa never even had his Sunday clothes and Papa cussing now and saying, 'Damn the clothes.' If we didn't get to Uncle Rodney before the others caught him, Papa would just wear the clothes Uncle Rodney had on now. So we got into the road hack fast and Papa closed the curtains and then Mamma and Aunt Louisa could cry all right and Papa hollered to John Paul to go home and tell Rosie to pack his Sunday suit and take her to the train; anyway that would be fine for Rosie. So we didn't go on the train but we went fast, with Papa driving and saying Didn't anybody know where he was? and Aunt Louisa quit crying awhile and said how Uncle Rodney didn't come to supper last night, but right after supper he came in and how Aunt Louisa had a terrible feeling as soon as she heard his step in the hall and how Uncle Rodney wouldn't tell her until they were in his room and the door closed and then he said he must have two thousand dollars and Aunt Louisa said where in the world could she get two thousand dollars? and Uncle Rodney said, 'Ask Fred' — that was Aunt Louisa's husband — 'and George' — that was Papa; 'tell them they would have to dig it up,' and Aunt Louisa said she had that terrible feeling and she said, 'Rodney! Rodney! What' — and

Uncle Rodney begun to cuss and say, 'Dammit, don't start snivel-
ing and crying now,' and Aunt Louisa said, 'Rodney, what have
you done now?' and then they both heard the knocking at the door
and how Aunt Louisa looked at Uncle Rodney and she knew the
truth before she even laid eyes on Mr. Pruitt and the sheriff, and
how she said, 'Don't tell Pa! Keep it from Pa! It will kill him ...'
    'Who?' Papa said. 'Mister who?'
    'Mr. Pruitt,' Aunt Louisa said, crying again. 'The president of
the Compress Association. They moved to Mottstown last spring.
You don't know him.'
    So she went down to the door and it was Mr. Pruitt and the
sheriff. And how Aunt Louisa begged Mr. Pruitt for Grandpa's
sake and how she gave Mr. Pruitt her oath that Uncle Rodney would
stay right there in the house until Papa could get there, and Mr.
Pruitt said how he hated it to happen at Christmas too and so for
Grandpa's and Aunt Louisa's sake he would give them until the day
after Christmas if Aunt Louisa would promise him that Uncle
Rodney would not try to leave Mottstown. And how Mr. Pruitt
showed her with her own eyes the check with Grandpa's name
signed to it and how even Aunt Louisa could see that Grandpa's
name had been — and then Mamma said, 'Louisa! Louisa! Remember Georgie!' and that was me, and Papa cussed too, hollering,
'How in damnation do you expect to keep it from him? By hiding
the newspapers?' and Aunt Louisa cried again and said how everybody was bound to know it, that she didn't expect or hope that any
of us could ever hold our heads up again, that all she hoped for was
to keep it from Grandpa because it would kill him. She cried hard
then and Papa had to stop at a branch and get down and soak his
handkerchief for Mamma to wipe Aunt Louisa's face with it and
then Papa took the bottle of tonic out of the dash pocket and put
a few drops on the handkerchief, and Aunt Louisa smelled it and
then Papa took a dose of the tonic out of the bottle and Mamma
said, 'George!' and Papa drank some more of the tonic and then
made like he was handing the bottle back for Mamma and Aunt
Louisa to take a dose too and said, 'I don't blame you. If I was
a woman in this family I'd take to drink too. Now let me get this
bond business straight.'
    'It was those road bonds of Ma's,' Aunt Louisa said.
    We were going fast again now because the horses had rested while

Papa was wetting the handkerchief and taking the dose of tonic, and Papa was saying, 'All right, what about the bonds?' when all of a sudden he jerked around in the seat and said, 'Road bonds? Do you mean he took that damn screw driver and prized open your mother's desk too?'

Then Mamma said, 'George! how can you?' only Aunt Louisa was talking now, quick now, not crying now, not yet, and Papa with his head turned over his shoulder and saying, did Aunt Louisa mean that that five hundred Papa had to pay out two years ago wasn't all of it? And Aunt Louisa said it was twenty-five hundred, only they didn't want Grandpa to find it out, and so Grandma put up her road bonds for security on the note, and how they said now that Uncle Rodney had redeemed Grandma's note and the road bonds from the bank with some of the Compress Association's bonds out of the safe in the Compress Association office, because when Mr. Pruitt found the Compress Association's bonds were missing he looked for them and found them in the bank and when he looked in the Compress Association's safe all he found was the check for two thousand dollars with Grandpa's name signed to it, and how Mr. Pruitt hadn't lived in Mottstown but a year but even he knew that Grandpa never signed that check and besides he looked in the bank again and Grandpa never had two thousand dollars in it, and how Mr. Pruitt said how he would wait until the day after Christmas if Aunt Louisa would give him her sworn oath that Uncle Rodney would not go away, and Aunt Louisa did it and then she went back upstairs to plead with Uncle Rodney to give Mr. Pruitt the bonds and she went into Uncle Rodney's room where she had left him, and the window was open and Uncle Rodney was gone.

'Damn Rodney!' Papa said. 'The bonds! You mean, nobody knows where the bonds are?'

Now we were going fast because we were coming down the last hill and into the valley where Mottstown was. Soon we would begin to smell it again; it would be just today and then tonight and it would be Christmas, and Aunt Louisa sitting there with her face white like a whitewashed fence that has been rained on and Papa said, 'Who in hell ever gave him such a job anyway?' and Aunt Louisa said, 'Mr. Pruitt,' and Papa said how even if Mr. Pruitt had only lived in Mottstown a few months, and then Aunt Louisa began to cry without even putting her handkerchief to her face this time and Mamma looked at Aunt Louisa and she began to cry too and Papa took out the whip and hit the team a belt with it even if they were going fast and he cussed. 'Damnation to hell,' Papa said. 'I see. Pruitt's married.'

Then we could see it too. There were holly wreaths in the windows like at home in Jefferson, and I said, 'They shoot fireworks in Mottstown too like they do in Jefferson.'

Aunt Louisa and Mamma were crying good now, and now it was Papa saying, 'Here, here; remember Georgie,' and that was me, and Aunt Louisa said, 'Yes, yes! Painted common thing, traipsing up and down the streets all afternoon alone in a buggy, and the one and only time Mrs. Church called on her, and that was because of Mr. Pruitt's position alone, Mrs. Church found her without corsets on and Mrs. Church told me she smelled liquor on her breath.'

And Papa saying 'Here, here,' and Aunt Louisa crying good and saying how it was Mrs. Pruitt that did it because Uncle Rodney was young and easy led because he never had had opportunities to meet a nice girl and marry her, and Papa was driving fast toward Grandpa's house and he said, 'Marry? Rodney marry? What in hell pleasure would he get out of slipping out of his own house and waiting until after dark and slipping around to the back and climbing up the gutter and into a room where there wasn't anybody in it but his own wife?'

And so Mamma and Aunt Louisa were crying good when we got to Grandpa's.

III

And Uncle Rodney wasn't there. We came in, and Grandma said how Mandy, that was Grandpa's cook, hadn't come to cook breakfast and when Grandma sent Emmeline, that was Aunt Louisa's baby's nurse, down to Mandy's cabin in the back yard, the door was locked on the inside, but Mandy wouldn't answer and then Grandma went down there herself and Mandy wouldn't answer and so Cousin Fred climbed in the window and Mandy was gone and Uncle Fred had just got back from town then and he and Papa both hollered, 'Locked? on the inside? and nobody in it?'

And then Uncle Fred told Papa to go in and keep Grandpa entertained and he would go and then Aunt Louisa grabbed Papa and Uncle Fred both and said she would keep Grandpa quiet and for both of them to go and find him, find him, and Papa said, 'If only the fool hasn't tried to sell them to somebody,' and Uncle Fred said, 'Good God, man, don't you know that check was dated ten days ago?' And so we went in where Grandpa was reared back in his chair and saying how he hadn't expected Papa until tomorrow but, by God, he was glad to see somebody at last because he waked up this morning and his cook had quit and Louisa had chased off somewhere before daylight and now he couldn't even find Uncle Rodney to go down and bring his mail and a cigar or two back, and so, thank God, Christmas never came but once a year and so be damned if he wouldn't be glad when it was over, only he was laughing now because when he said that about Christmas before Christmas he always laughed, it wasn't until after Christmas that he didn't laugh when he said that about Christmas. Then Aunt Louisa got Grandpa's keys out of his pocket herself and opened the desk where Uncle Rodney would prize it open with a screw driver, and took out Grandpa's tonic and then Mamma said for me to go and find Cousin Fred and Cousin Louisa.

So Uncle Rodney wasn't there. Only at first I thought maybe it wouldn't be a quarter even, it wouldn't be nothing this time, so at first all I had to think about was that anyway it would be Christmas and that would be something anyway. Because I went on around the house, and so after a while Papa and Uncle Fred came out, and I could see them through the bushes knocking at Mandy's door and calling, 'Rodney, Rodney,' like that. Then I had to get back in the bushes because Uncle Fred had to pass right by me to go to the woodshed to get the axe to open Mandy's door. But they couldn't fool Uncle Rodney. If Mr. Tucker couldn't fool Uncle Rodney in Mr. Tucker's own house, Uncle Fred and Papa ought to have known they couldn't fool him right in his own papa's back yard. So I didn't even need to hear them. I just waited until after a while Uncle Fred came back out the broken door and came to the woodshed and took the axe and pulled the lock and hasp and steeple off the woodhouse door and went back and then Papa came out of Mandy's house and they nailed the woodhouse lock onto Mandy's door and locked it and they went around behind Mandy's house, and I could hear Uncle Fred nailing the windows up. Then they went back to the house. But it didn't matter if Mandy was in the house too and couldn't get out, because the train came from Jefferson with Rosie and Papa's Sunday clothes on it and so Rosie was there to cook for Grandpa and us and so that was all right too.

But they couldn't fool Uncle Rodney. I could have told them that. I could have told them that sometimes Uncle Rodney even wanted to wait until after dark to even begin to do business. And so it was all right even if it was late in the afternoon before I could get away from Cousin Fred and Cousin Louisa. It was late; soon they would begin to shoot the fireworks downtown, and then we would be hearing it too, so I could just see his face a little between the slats where Papa and Uncle Fred had nailed up the back window; I could see his face where he hadn't shaved, and he was asking me why in hell it took me so long because he had heard the Jefferson train come before dinner, before eleven o'clock, and laughing about how Papa and Uncle Fred had nailed him up in the house to keep him when that was exactly what he wanted, and that I would have to slip out right after supper somehow and did I reckon I could manage it? And I said how last Christmas it had been a quarter, but I didn't have to slip out of the house that time, and he laughed, saying, 'Quarter? Quarter?' did I ever see ten quarters all at once? and I never did, and he said for me to be there with the screw driver right after supper and I would see ten quarters, and to remember that even God didn't know where he is and so for me to get the hell away and stay away until I came back after dark with the screw driver.

And they couldn't fool me either. Because I had been watching the man all afternoon, even when he thought I was just playing and maybe because I was from Jefferson instead of Mottstown and so I wouldn't know who he was. But I did, because once when he was walking past the back fence and he stopped and lit his cigar again and I saw the badge under his coat when he struck the match and so I knew he was like Mr. Watts at Jefferson that catches the niggers. So I was playing by the fence and I could hear him stopping and looking at me and I played and he said, 'Howdy, son. Santy Claus coming to see you tomorrow?'

'Yes, sir,' I said.

'You're Miss Sarah's boy, from up at Jefferson, ain't you?' he said.

'Yes, sir,' I said.

'Come to spend Christmas with your Grandpa, eh?' he said. 'I wonder if your Uncle Rodney's at home this afternoon.'

'No, sir,' I said.

'Well, well, that's too bad,' he said. 'I wanted to see him a minute. He's downtown, I reckon?'

'No, sir,' I said.

'Well, well,' he said. 'You mean he's gone away on a visit, maybe?'

'Yes, sir,' I said.

'Well, well,' he said. 'That's too bad. I wanted to see him on a little business. But I reckon it can wait.' Then he looked at me and then he said, 'You're sure he's out of town, then?'

'Yes, sir,' I said.

'Well, that was all I wanted to know,' he said. 'If you happen to mention this to your Aunt Louisa or your Uncle Fred you can tell them that was all I wanted to know.'

'Yes, sir,' I said. So he went away. And he didn't pass the house any more. I watched for him, but he didn't come back. So he couldn't fool me either.

IV

Then it began to get dark and they started to shoot the fireworks downtown. I could hear them, and soon we would be seeing the Roman candles and skyrockets and I would have the ten quarters then and I thought about the basket full of presents and I thought how maybe I could go on downtown when I got through working for Uncle Rodney and buy a present for Grandpa with a dime out of the ten quarters and give it to him tomorrow and maybe, because nobody else had given him a present, Grandpa might give me a quarter too instead of the dime tomorrow, and that would be twenty-one quarters, except for the dime, and that would be fine sure enough. But I didn't have time to do that. We ate supper, and Rosie had to cook that too, and Mamma and Aunt Louisa with powder on their faces where they had been crying, and Grandpa; it was Papa helping him take a dose of tonic every now and then all afternoon while Uncle Fred was downtown, and Uncle Fred came back and Papa came out in the hall and Uncle Fred said he had looked everywhere, in the bank and in the Compress, and how Mr. Pruitt helped him but they couldn't find a sign either of them or of the money, because Uncle Fred was afraid because one night last week Uncle Rodney hired a rig and went somewhere and Uncle Fred found out Uncle Rodney drove over to the main line at Kingston and caught the fast train to Memphis, and Papa said, 'Damnation,' and Uncle Fred said, 'By God, we will go down there after supper and sweat it out of him, because at least we have got him. I told Pruitt that and he said that if we hold to him, he will hold off and give us a chance.'

So Uncle Fred and Papa and Grandpa came in to supper together, with Grandpa between them saying, 'Christmas don't come but once a year, thank God, so hooray for it,' and Papa and Uncle Fred saying, 'Now you are all right, Pa; straight ahead now, Pa,' and Grandpa would go straight ahead awhile and then begin to holler, 'Where in hell is that damn boy?' and that meant Uncle Rodney, and that Grandpa was a good mind to go downtown himself and haul Uncle Rodney out of that damn poolhall and make him come home and see his kinfolks. And so we ate supper and Mamma said she would take the children upstairs and Aunt Louisa said, 'No,' Emmeline could put us to bed, and so we went up the back stairs, and Emmeline said how she had done already had to cook breakfast extra today and if folks thought she was going to waste all her Christmas doing extra work they never had the sense she give them credit for and that this looked like to her it was a good house to be away from nohow, and so we went into the room and then after a while I went back down the back stairs and I remembered where to find the screw driver too. Then I could hear the firecrackers plain from downtown, and the moon was shining now but I could still see the Roman candles and the skyrockets running up the sky. Then Uncle Rodney's hand came out of the crack in the shutter and took the screw driver. I couldn't see his face now and it wasn't laughing exactly, it didn't sound exactly like laughing, it was just the way he breathed behind the shutter. Because they couldn't fool him.

'All right,' he said. 'Now that's ten quarters. But wait. Are you sure nobody knows where I am?'

'Yes, sir,' I said. 'I waited by the fence until he come and asked me.'

'Which one?' Uncle Rodney said.

'The one that wears the badge,' I said.

Then Uncle Rodney cussed. But it wasn't mad cussing. It sounded just like it sounded when he was laughing except the words.

'He said if you were out of town on a visit, and I said, Yes, sir,' I said.

'Good,' Uncle Rodney said. 'By God, some day you will be as good a business man as I am. And I won't make you a liar much longer, either. So now you have got ten quarters, haven't you?'

'No,' I said. 'I haven't got them yet.'

Then he cussed again, and I said, 'I will hold my cap up and you can drop them in it and they won't spill then.'

Then he cussed hard, only it wasn't loud. 'Only I'm not going to give you ten quarters,' he said, and I begun to say, 'You said —' and Uncle Rodney said, 'Because I am going to give you twenty.'

And I said, 'Yes, sir,' and he told me how to find the right house, and what to do when I found it. Only there wasn't any paper to carry this time because Uncle Rodney said how this was a twenty-quarter job, and so it was too important to put on paper and besides I wouldn't need a paper because I would not know them anyhow, and his voice coming hissing down from behind the shutter where I couldn't see him and still sounding like when he cussed while he was saying how Papa and Uncle Fred had done him a favor by nailing up the door and window and they didn't even have sense enough to know it.

'Start at the corner of the house and count three windows. Then throw the handful of gravel against the window. Then when the window opens — never mind who it will be, you won't know anyway — just say who you are and then say, "He will be at the corner with the buggy in ten minutes. Bring the jewelry." Now you say it,' Uncle Rodney said.

'He will be at the corner with the buggy in ten minutes. Bring the jewelry,' I said.

'Say "Bring all the jewelry,"' Uncle Rodney said.

'Bring all the jewelry,' I said.

'Good,' Uncle Rodney said. Then he said, 'Well? What are you waiting on?'

'For the twenty quarters,' I said.

Uncle Rodney cussed again. 'Do you expect me to pay you before you have done the work?' he said.

'You said about a buggy,' I said. 'Maybe you will forget to pay me before you go and you might not get back until after we go back home. And besides, that day last summer when we couldn't do any business with Mrs. Tucker because she was sick and you wouldn't pay me the nickel because you said it wasn't your fault Mrs. Tucker was sick.'

Then Uncle Rodney cussed hard and quiet behind the crack and then he said, 'Listen. I haven't got the twenty quarters now. I haven't even got one quarter now. And the only way I can get any is to get out of here and finish this business. And I can't finish this business tonight unless you do your work. See? I'll be right behind you. I'll be waiting right there at the corner in the buggy when you come back. Now, go on. Hurry.'

V

So I went on across the yard, only the moon was bright now and I walked behind the fence until I got to the street. And I could hear the firecrackers and I could see the Roman candles and skyrockets sliding up the sky, but the fireworks were all downtown, and so all I could see along the street was the candles and wreaths in the windows. So I came to the lane, went up the lane to the stable, and I could hear the horse in the stable, but I didn't know whether it was the right stable or not; but pretty soon Uncle Rodney kind of jumped around the corner of the stable and said, 'Here you are,' and he showed me where to stand and listen toward the house and he went back into the stable. But I couldn't hear anything but Uncle Rodney harnessing the horse, and then he whistled and I went back and he had the horse already hitched to the buggy and I said, 'Whose horse and buggy is this; it's a lot skinnier than Grandpa's horse?' And Uncle Rodney said, 'It's my horse now, only damn this moonlight to hell.' Then I went back down the lane to the street and there wasn't anybody coming so I waved my arm in the moonlight, and the buggy came up and I got in and we went fast. The side curtains were up and so I couldn't see the skyrockets and Roman candles from town, but I could hear the firecrackers and I thought maybe we were going through town and maybe Uncle Rodney would stop and give me some of the twenty quarters and I could buy Grandpa a present for tomorrow, but we didn't; Uncle Rodney just raised the side curtain without stopping and then I could see the house, the two magnolia trees, but we didn't stop until we came to the corner.

'Now,' Uncle Rodney said, 'when the window opens, say, "He will be at the corner in ten minutes. Bring *all* the jewelry." Never mind who it will be. You don't want to know who it is. You want to even forget what house it is. See?'

'Yes, sir,' I said. 'And then you will pay me the ——'

'Yes!' he said, cussing. 'Yes! Get out of here quick!'

So I got out and the buggy went on and I went back up the street. And the house was dark all right except for one light, so it was the right one, besides the two trees. So I went across the yard and counted the three windows and I was just about to throw the gravel when a lady ran out from behind a bush and grabbed me. She kept on trying to say something, only I couldn't tell what it was, and besides she never had time to say very much anyhow because a man ran out from behind another bush and grabbed us both. Only he grabbed her by the mouth, because I could tell that from the kind of slobbering noise she made while she was fighting to get loose.

'Well, boy?' he said. 'What is it? Are you the one?'

'I work for Uncle Rodney,' I said.

'Then you're the one,' he said. Now the lady was fighting and slobbering sure enough, but he held her by the mouth. 'All right. What is it?'

Only I didn't know Uncle Rodney ever did business with men. But maybe after he began to work in the Compress Association he had to. And then he had told me I would not know them anyway, so maybe that was what he meant.

'He says to be at the corner in ten minutes,' I said. 'And to bring all the jewelry. He said for me to say that twice. Bring all the jewelry.'

The lady was slobbering and fighting worse than ever now, so maybe he had to turn me loose so he could hold her with both hands.

'Bring all the jewelry,' he said, holding the lady with both hands now. 'That's a good idea. That's fine. I don't blame him for telling you to say that twice. All right. Now you go back to the corner and wait and when he comes, tell him this: "She says to come and help carry it." Say that to him twice, too. Understand?'

'Then I'll get my twenty quarters,' I said.

'Twenty quarters, hah?' the man said, holding the lady. 'That's what you are to get, is it? That's not enough. You tell him this, too: "She says to give you a piece of the jewelry." Understand?'

'I just want my twenty quarters,' I said.

Then he and the lady went back behind the bushes again and I went on, too, back toward the corner, and I could see the Roman

candles and skyrockets again from toward town and I could hear
the firecrackers, and then the buggy came back and Uncle Rodney
was hissing again behind the curtain like when he was behind the
slats on Mandy's window.

'Well?' he said.

'She said for you to come and help carry it,' I said.

'What?' Uncle Rodney said. 'She said he's not there?'

'No, sir. She said for you to come and help carry it. For me to
say that twice.' Then I said, 'Where's my twenty quarters?' because he had already jumped out of the buggy and jumped across
the walk into the shadow of some bushes. So I went into the bushes
too and said, 'You said you would give ——'

'All right; all right!' Uncle Rodney said. He was kind of squatting along the bushes; I could hear him breathing. 'I'll give them to
you tomorrow. I'll give you thirty quarters tomorrow. Now you
get to hell on home. And if they have been down to Mandy's house,
you don't know anything. Run, now. Hurry.'

'I'd rather have the twenty quarters tonight,' I said.

He was squatting fast along in the shadow of the bushes, and
I was right behind him, because when he whirled around he almost
touched me, but I jumped back out of the bushes in time and he
stood there cussing at me and then he stooped down and I saw it
was a stick in his hand and I turned and ran. Then he went on,
squatting along in the shadow, and then I went back to the buggy,
because the day after Christmas we would go back to Jefferson, and
so if Uncle Rodney didn't get back before then I would not see him
again until next summer and then maybe he would be in business
with another lady and my twenty quarters would be like my nickel
that time when Mrs. Tucker was sick. So I waited by the buggy
and I could watch the skyrockets and the Roman candles and I could
hear the firecrackers from town, only it was late now and so maybe
all the stores would be closed and so I couldn't buy Grandpa a present, even when Uncle Rodney came back and gave me my twenty
quarters. So I was listening to the firecrackers and thinking about
how maybe I could tell Grandpa that I had wanted to buy him
a present and so maybe he might give me fifteen cents instead of
a dime anyway, when all of a sudden they started shooting firecrackers back at the house where Uncle Rodney had gone. Only
they just shot five of them fast, and when they didn't shoot any

more I thought that maybe in a minute they would shoot the sky-rockets and Roman candles too. But they didn't. They just shot the five firecrackers right quick and then stopped, and I stood by the buggy and then folks began to come out of the houses and holler at one another and then I began to see men running toward the house where Uncle Rodney had gone, and then a man came out of the yard fast and went up the street toward Grandpa's and I thought at first it was Uncle Rodney and that he had forgotten the buggy, until I saw that it wasn't.

But Uncle Rodney never came back and so I went on toward the yard to where the men were, because I could still watch the buggy too and see Uncle Rodney if he came back out of the bushes, and I came to the yard and I saw six men carrying something long and then two other men ran up and stopped me and one of them said, 'Hell-fire, it's one of those kids, the one from Jefferson.' And I could see then that what the men were carrying was a window blind with something wrapped in a quilt on it and so I thought at first that they had come to help Uncle Rodney carry the jewelry, only I didn't see Uncle Rodney anywhere, and then one of the men said, 'Who? One of the kids? Hell-fire, somebody take him on home.'

So the man picked me up, but I said I had to wait on Uncle Rodney, and the man said that Uncle Rodney would be all right, and I said, 'But I want to wait for him here,' and then one of the men behind us said, 'Damn it, get him on out of here,' and we went on. I was riding on the man's back and then I could look back and see the six men in the moonlight carrying the blind with the bundle on it, and I said did it belong to Uncle Rodney? and the man said, 'No, if it belonged to anybody now it belonged to Grandpa.' And so then I knew what it was.

'It's a side of beef,' I said. 'You are going to take it to Grandpa.' Then the other man made a funny sound and the one I was riding on said, 'Yes, you might call it a side of beef,' and I said, 'It's a Christmas present for Grandpa. Who is it going to be from? Is it from Uncle Rodney?'

'No,' the man said. 'Not from him. Call it from the men of Mottstown. From all the husbands in Mottstown.'

VI

Then we came in sight of Grandpa's house. And now the lights were all on, even on the porch, and I could see folks in the hall, I could see ladies with shawls over their heads, and some more of them going up the walk toward the porch, and then I could hear somebody in the house that sounded like singing and then Papa came out of the house and came down the walk to the gate and we came up and the man put me down and I saw Rosie waiting at the gate too. Only it didn't sound like singing now because there wasn't any music with it, and so maybe it was Aunt Louisa again and so maybe she didn't like Christmas now any better than Grandpa said he didn't like it.

'It's a present for Grandpa,' I said.

'Yes,' Papa said. 'You go on with Rosie and go to bed. Mamma will be there soon. But you be a good boy until she comes. You mind Rosie. All right, Rosie. Take him on. Hurry.'

'Yo don't need to tell me that,' Rosie said. She took my hand. 'Come on.'

Only we didn't go back into the yard, because Rosie came out the gate and we went up the street. And then I thought maybe we were going around the back to dodge the people and we didn't do that, either. We just went on up the street, and I said, 'Where are we going?'

And Rosie said, 'We gonter sleep at a lady's house name Mrs. Jordon.'

So we went on. I didn't say anything. Because Papa had forgotten to say anything about my slipping out of the house yet and so maybe if I went on to bed and stayed quiet he would forget about it until tomorrow too. And besides, the main thing was to get a holt of Uncle Rodney and get my twenty quarters before we went back home, and so maybe that would be all right tomorrow too. So we went on and Rosie said, 'Yonder's the house,' and we went in the yard and then all of a sudden Rosie saw the possum. It was in a persimmon tree in Mrs. Jordon's yard and I could see it against the moonlight too, and I hollered, 'Run! Run and get Mrs. Jordon's ladder!'

And Rosie said, 'Ladder my foot! You going to bed!'

But I didn't wait. I began to run toward the house, with Rosie running behind me and hollering, 'You, Georgie! You come back here!' But I didn't stop. We could get the ladder and get the possum and give it to Grandpa along with the side of meat and it wouldn't cost even a dime and then maybe Grandpa might even give me a quarter too, and then when I got the twenty quarters from Uncle Rodney I would have twenty-one quarters and that will be fine.

THAT'S WHAT HAPPENED TO ME[1]

By MICHAEL FESSIER

(From *Story*)

I HAVE done things and had things happen to me and nobody knows about it. So I am writing about it so that people will know. Although there are a lot of things I could tell about, I will just tell about the jumping because that is the most important. It gave me the biggest thrill. I mean high jumping, standing and running. You probably never heard of a standing high jumper, but that's what I was. I was the greatest jumper ever was.

I was going to high school and I wasn't on any team. I couldn't be because I had to work for a drugstore and wash bottles and deliver medicine and sweep the floor. So I couldn't go out for any of the teams because the job started soon's school was over. I used to crab to the fellows about how old man Patch made me wash so many bottles and so they got to calling me Bottles Barton and I didn't like it. They'd call me Bottles in front of the girls and the girls'd giggle.

Once I poked one of the fellows for calling me Bottles. He was a big fellow and he played on the football team and I wouldn't have hit him because I was little and couldn't fight very well. But he called me Bottles before Anna Louise Daniels and she laughed and I was so mad I didn't know whether I wanted to hit her or the football player, but finally I hit him. He caught my arm and threw me down and sat on me and pulled my nose.

'Look, Anna Louise,' he said, 'it stretches.'

He pulled my nose again and Anna Louise put her arms around herself and jumped up and down and laughed, and then I knew that it was her I should have taken the first poke at. I was more mad at her than the football player, although it was him pulling my nose and sitting on me.

The next day I met Anna Louise in the hall going to the ancient history class and she was with a couple of other girls and I tried to go past without them noticing me. I don't know why, but I had a funny feeling like as if somebody was going to throw a rock at me or something. Anna Louise looked at me and giggled.

'Hello, old rubbernose,' she said.

The girls giggled and I hurried down the hall and felt sick and mad and kind of like I was running away from a fight, although nobody'd expect me to fight a girl. And so they called me Bottles sometimes and Rubbernose other times and always whoever was near would laugh. They didn't think it was funny because Jimmy Wilkins was called Scrubby or Jack Harris was called Doodles. But they thought it was funny I was called Rubbernose and Bottles and they never got tired of laughing. It was a new joke every time.

Scrubby pitched for the baseball team and Doodles was quarterback of the football team.

I could have pitched for the baseball team or played quarterback on the football team. I could have pitched no hit games and I could have made touchdowns from my own ten yard line. I know I could. I had it all figured out. I went over how I'd throw the ball and how the batter'd miss and it was easy. I figured out how to run and dodge and straight-arm and that was easy too. But I didn't get the chance because I had to go right to Patch's Drug Store after school was out.

Old man Patch was a pretty good guy but his wife she was nothing but a crab. I'd wash bottles and old man Patch he would look at them and not say anything. But Mrs. Patch, old lady Patch, she would look at the bottles and wrinkle her nose and make me wash half of them over again. When I swept up at night she'd always find some corner I'd missed and she'd bawl me out. She was fat and her hair was all straggly and I wondered why in the deuce old man Patch ever married her, although I guess maybe she didn't look so awful when she was a girl. She couldn't have been very pretty though.

They lived in back of the drug store and when people came in at noon or at six o'clock either old man or old lady Patch'd come out still chewing their food and look at the customer and swallow and then ask him what he wanted.

I studied salesmanship at high school and I figured this wasn't very good for business and I wanted to tell them but I never did.

One of the fellows at school was in waiting for a prescription and he saw me working at some of the things I did at the drug store. So when another fellow asked me what I did this fellow he laughed and said, 'Old Bottles! Why, he rates at that store. Yes he does! He rates like an Armenian's helper.'

That's about the way I did rate but I was planning on how I'd someday own a real, modern drug store and run the Patches out of business so I didn't mind so much.

What I did mind was Anna Louise at school. She was the daughter of a doctor and she thought she was big people and maybe she was but she wasn't any better'n me. Maybe my clothes weren't so good but that was only temporary. I planned on having twenty suits some day.

I wanted to go up to her and say, 'Look here, Anna Louise, you're not so much. Your father isn't a millionaire and some day I'm going to be one. I'm going to have a million dollars and twenty suits of clothes.' But I never did.

After she laughed at me and started calling me Rubbernose, I began planning on doing things to make her realize I wasn't what she thought I was. That's how the jumping came about.

It was the day before the track meet and everybody was talking about whether or not our school could win. They figured we'd have to win the high jump and pole vault to do it.

'Lord, if we only had old Heck Hansen back,' said Goobers MacMartin. 'He'd outjump those Fairfield birds two inches in the high and a foot in the pole vault.'

'Yeah,' somebody else said, 'but we haven't got Heck Hansen. What we got is pretty good but not good enough. Wish we had a jumper.'

'We sure need one,' I said.

There was a group of them all talking, boys and girls, and I was sort of on the outside listening.

'Who let you in?' Goobers asked me.

Frank Shay grabbed me by the arm and dragged me into the center of the circle.

'The very man we've been looking for,' he said. 'Yessir. Old Bottles Rubbernose Barton. He can win the jumping events for us.'

'Come on, Bottles,' they said. 'Save the day for us. Be a good old Rubbernose.'

Anna Louise was one who laughed the most and it was the third time I'd wanted to pop her on the nose.

I went away from there and didn't turn back when they laughed and called and whistled at me.

'She'd be surprised if I did,' I said.

I kept thinking this over and pretty soon I said, 'Well, maybe you could.'

Then when I was sweeping the drug store floor I all of a sudden said, 'I can.'

'You can what?' Mrs. Patch asked me.

'Nothing,' I said.

'You can hurry about sweeping the floor, that's what you can do,' she said.

There was a big crowd out for the track meet and we were tied when I went up to our coach. It was just time for the jumping to start.

'What the hell you doing in a track suit?' he asked me.

'I'm going to save the day for Brinkley,' I said. 'I'm going to jump.'

'No, you aren't,' he said. 'You run along and start a marble game with some other kid.'

I looked him in the eye and I spoke in a cold, level tone of voice.

'Mr. Smith,' I said, 'the track meet depends on the high jump and the pole vault and unless I am entered we will lose those two events and the meet. I can win and I am willing to do it for Brinkley. Do you want to win the meet?'

He looked amazed.

'Where have you been all the time?' he asked. 'You talk like you've got something on the ball.'

I didn't say anything, I just smiled.

The crowd all rushed over to the jumping pits and I took my time going over. When everybody had jumped but me the coach turned and said, 'Come on now, Barton, let's see what you can do.'

'Not yet,' I said.

'What do you mean?' he asked.

'I'll wait until the last man has been eliminated,' I said. 'Then I'll jump.'

The crowd laughed but I just stared coldly at them. The coach tried to persuade me to jump but I wouldn't change my mind.

'I stake everything on one jump,' I said. 'Have faith in me.'

He looked at me and shook his head and said, 'Have it your own way.'

They started the bar a little over four feet and pretty soon it was creeping up toward five feet and a half. That's always been a pretty good distance for high school jumpers. When the bar reached five feet seven inches all our men except one was eliminated. Two from Fairfield were still in the event. They put the bar at five feet nine inches and one man from Fairfield made it. Our man tried hard but he scraped the bar and knocked it off.

The crowd started yelling, thinking Fairfield had won the event.

'Wait a minute,' I yelled. 'I haven't jumped yet.'

The judges looked at their lists and saw it was so. Maybe you think it was against the rules for them to allow me to skip my turn but anyway that's the way it was.

'You can't make that mark,' one of the judges said. 'Why try? You're not warmed up.'

'Never mind,' I said.

I walked up close to the jumping standard and stood there.

'Go ahead and jump,' one of the judges said.

'I will,' I said.

'Well, don't stand there,' he said. 'Come on back here so's you can get a run at it.'

'I don't want any run at the bar,' I said. 'I'll jump from here.'

The judge yelled at the coach and told him to take me out on account of I was crazy.

I swung my arms in back of me and sprung up and down a second and then I jumped over the bar with inches to spare. When I came down it was so silent I could hear my footsteps as I walked across the sawdust pit. The judge that'd crabbed at me just stood and looked. His eyes were bugged out and his mouth hung open.

'Good Lord!' he said. 'Almighty most loving Lord!'

Our coach came up and he stood besides the judge and they both looked the same, bug-eyed.

'Did you see that?' the coach asked. 'Tell me you didn't. Please do. I'd rather lose this track meet than my mind.'

The judge turned slowly and looked at him.

'Good Lord!' he said, 'there's two of us.'

All of a sudden everybody started yelling and the fellows near me pounded me on the back and tried to shake my hand. I smiled and brushed them aside and walked over to the judge.

'What's the high school record for this state?' I asked.

'Five feet, eleven inches,' he said.

'Put her at six,' I said.

They put the bar at six and I gathered myself together and gave a heave and went over the bar like I was floating. It was easy. Well, that just knocked the wind out of everybody. They'd thought I couldn't do anything and there I'd broken the state record for the high jump without a running start.

The crowd surrounded me and tried to shake my hand and the coach and judge got off to one side and reached out and pinched each other's cheek and looked at the bar and shook their heads. Frank Shay grabbed my hand and wrung it and said, 'Gosh, Bottles, I was just kidding the other day. I didn't know you were such a ring-tailed wonder. Say, Bottles, we're having a frat dance tonight. Will you come?'

'You know what you can do with your frat,' I said. 'I don't approve of them. They're undemocratic.'

A lot of the fellows that'd made fun of me before crowded around and acted as if I'd been their friend all along.

When Anna Louise crowded through the gang and said, 'Oh, you're marvelous,' I just smiled at her and said, 'Do you think so?' and walked away. She tagged around after me but I talked mostly with two other girls.

They didn't usually have a public address system at our track meets but they started using one then.

'Ladies and gentlemen,' the announcer said, 'you have just witnessed a record-breaking performance by Bottles Barton ——'

He went on like that telling them what an astonishing thing I'd done and it came to me I didn't mind being called Bottles any more. In fact, I kind of liked it.

Mr. and Mrs. Patch came up and Mrs. Patch tried to kiss me but I wouldn't let her. Old man Patch shook my hand.

'You've made our drug store famous,' he said. 'From now on you're a clerk. No more bottle washing.'

'We'll make him a partner,' old lady Patch said.

'No, you won't,' I said. 'I think I'll go over to the McManus Pharmacy.'

Then they called the pole vault and I did like I'd done before. I wouldn't jump until our men'd been eliminated. The bar was at eleven feet.

'It's your turn,' our coach told me. 'Ever use a pole before?'

'Oh, sure,' I told him.

He gave me a pole and the crowd cleared away and grew silent. Everyone was watching me.

I threw the pole down and smiled at the crowd. The coach yelled for me to pick up the pole and jump. I picked it up and threw it ten feet away from me. Everybody gasped. Then I took a short run and went over the bar at eleven feet. It was simple.

This time the coach and the judge took pins and poked them in one another's cheeks. The coach grabbed me and said, 'When I wake up I'm going to be so mad at you I'm going to give you the beating of your life.'

Anna Louise came up and held my arm and said, 'Oh, Bottles, you're so wonderful. I've always thought so. Please forgive me for calling you Rubbernose. I want you to come to our party tonight.'

'All right,' I said. 'I'll forgive you but don't you call me Rubbernose again.'

They moved the bar up again and the fellow from Fairfield couldn't make it. I took a short run and went over. I did it so easy it came to me I could fly if I wanted to but I decided not to try it on account of people wouldn't think it so wonderful if a fellow that could fly jumped eleven feet without a pole. I'd won the track meet for Brinkley High and the students all came down out of the stand and put me on their shoulders and paraded me around and around the track. A lot of fellows were waving papers at me asking me to sign them and get a thousand dollars a week as a professional jumper. I signed one which threw in an automobile.

That's what I did once and nobody knows about it, so I am writing about it so that people will know.

TORRENT OF DARKNESS [1]

By S. S. FIELD

(From *The American Mercury*)

I

SHE was part way up the next hill where the sun hadn't yet come — walking in the middle of the red clay road and pulling behind her the little painted wagon in which sat the child all bundled up because it was still early and the ground was still cold down in the hollows. The child was waving his arms up and down with that morning excitement they get on fall days, like jack-rabbit's ears. It was about five miles south of Waterbridge that I saw her.

I had shot right on through Waterbridge this last trip without even slowing down, there being two good reasons for doing so: one that I had nothing to stop for and the other that, running good like my machine was in the morning air, I could pull right on up that log-sluice hill by Rust's and keep going, providing the good God hadn't whispered to those pigs of Rust's that I was coming and to get out in the middle of the road and lie down. (Damn if I don't believe that's how come I stop by Rust's when I do: his pigs. Maybe he trains them.) So it wasn't until later that I learned how they had lynched that nigger the night before, and about five miles south of Waterbridge I saw her and the kid pulling up the next hill.

First I thought that can't be her because she's back at Rust's place, but it was that wagon and there isn't another child's wagon like that in fifty miles, so I thought 'Why, damn if it don't look like someone has stolen that wagon of hers,' and then I saw the kid was sitting in it, hopping up and down with health, and so I said, 'No, that must be her. Now what is she doing a way out here?' and I figured something was wrong.

I reckon she didn't remember me at once. It's the first time I had realized how small she was, standing there on the top of that hill in the morning sun with no hat on and some of that mist from the hollow still in her hair.

'Ma'am,' I said, 'I'd be honored to take you where you're going. It's a right smart piece wherever it is on this road.' The little fellow was waving his arms up and down like he was glad to see me. 'Ain't he fine,' I said.

First I thought she was sick, and then I said to myself, No, it's that trouble of hers, and then I said, No, that's not it either. This is something bad. Because I could tell by her eyes; because her eyes were still seeing it. So I helped her in and put the little wagon in back and the little fellow on the seat between us, and damn if it wasn't as if he recognized me from the last time I was at Rust's because he commenced bouncing up and down and saying, 'Dubba chabbe yeps?' like me and him was picking up matters where we left off before. So I said, 'Ma'am, I'd be honored to take you wherever it is you're going.'

She just sat there for a while, looking straight ahead with her arm around the little one as if they might be holding one pose for a long time while a man took their picture.   When she spoke I knew she recognized me all right but it kind of gave me a start when she called me by my given name — me being old enough to be her father.

'Home,' she said. 'To New Orleans.'

'Ma'am?' I said.

'Home,' she said.

She wasn't looking at me or at anything. That was when she called me by my given name. 'Home,' she says, 'Robert.' It has been a long time since anyone called me Robert; my wife's family used to before we were married, but for the past twenty-five years it has been Bob or B. D. from one end of the county to the other.

And the next thing I knew she was crying. With her mouth open like a child's, making no sound at all — as if at eight o'clock of a fine morning on the top of a hill she might be seeing something that she'd never dared to look at before.

I've an idea it's the first time she ever cried in her life, the first time she ever looked back, having spent all her time, maybe, seeing tomorrow different from other people. Maybe whatever it was she was seeing all the time had just run out the night before; snapped off.

I guess it was the first time she had ever really seen.

II

It was close to a year and a half ago that she got off the through train at Waterbridge with that baby that couldn't have been more than a month or two old at the time. I first saw her at Rust's a year ago September when I stopped by there on my way over to Lauder in my brother-in-law's county. She had been at Rust's about three months when I first saw her, and Brody told me how she had got off the evening north-bound carrying that little month-old critter the way a little girl will carry one of those big dolls. Brody is the station master there; has been for years.

'That's what I thought she was at first,' Brody said. 'Just a over-grown kid, maybe, with one of them dolls, that had got herself left behind when Simon released his pressure and give his throttle a notch. It was the way she carried it,' Brody said. 'With one arm around its middle and part of it hanging down as if it was stuffed, and it not making any more fuss than a doll. But I reckon she just didn't know much about carrying one.'

Brody said that the reason he thought she was left behind was because people didn't get off the through north-bound unless they were left behind. Waterbridge is about midpoint in the division and the only reason they stop there going north is to take on water. They've got a three per cent grade all the way to Asheville after that. When the south-bound comes through you have to hold your hat.

'It was almost dark and I didn't see her at first,' Brody said. 'I had been up to the cab with a dispatch for Simon and he had opened the throttle and was already rolling when I came back and found her standing there like a kid with a doll, watching the last car roll by all lit up like a Christmas Tree.

'"Why that train has done gone on off and left you, and you standing right there looking at it," I says to her. Then I saw that she wasn't a kid at all and that that wasn't no doll and she had a traveling bag. "Yes," she says. "Wasn't it a beautiful train?"'

Brody told me how she stood there watching the lights of the north-bound bend out of sight and how she then said she wanted a taxicab to go up to Rust's. 'You could tell she hadn't ever set foot outside a city before,' Brody said.

'A taxicab?' Brody said. 'Why young lady, this here's Water-bridge, North Carolina. It ain't but a quarter of a mile to Rust's place, straight up this hill, but I reckon it's a right smart piece to any taxicab that could carry you there. Close to ninety-five miles.'

It's easy to see why people began to talk about her. She was just about everything those people had never been able to talk about before and with that taxicab thrown in. Because Waterbridge is nothing but a railroad water-tank town between two mountains. They changed the name to Waterbridge about ten years ago. It used to be called Ninety-Seven, maybe because it was back in ninety-seven that the saw mill slipped down into that valley one rainy day and couldn't climb back out, and then the railroad came running in and out of the hills like a trickle of water chasing down grade and the line built a trestle over Rocky Run, so they changed the name to Waterbridge. They could have dropped the name altogether without doing the world out of much future. It is fine country, though, and in those hills in the fall you can smell the chestnuts and the deep shade of the valleys, and the hunting is fine.

It was Brody who figured out how she happened to land in Waterbridge with that child and the suitcase and the destination — Rust's.

'I reckon she would have got off the train at Cuba if he'd said so,' Brody said. 'This Duke, I mean. This fellow that must have told her she was married and then put the bee on her. Maybe he ran his finger down a timetable,' Brody said, 'and it stopped at Waterbridge. And then maybe the brakeman or somebody gave him Rust's name, being that a man named Rust trains more pigs than anybody else in the state to get out in the middle of the road and lie down. That's about the size of it,' Brody said.

Because Brody said that she hadn't gotten any further than from the station to Rust's before it was plain that she wasn't married at all. 'Maybe she thought she was,' Brody said.

He carried her suitcase up the hill that night, the two of them trudging along with the lantern, and her with that month-old doll in one arm and talking fast about why she was there in that singing voice, he said, that put you in mind of water chasing along over rocks. 'So that by the time we reached Rust's I reckon I knew more about why than she did,' Brody said. 'What with her carrying that little fellow and wearing no rings on her left hand. But that wasn't what told me,' he said. 'I reckon it was like the daddy of that kid had took a piece of chalk and wrote Good-bye all over her back. It was all of them lies about himself that he had told her,' Brody said. 'About how she could wait for him at this nice quiet old place (meaning Rust's damned old place) until he was ready to come down for the hunting season, and about who he was supposed to be and all.'

Brody said that it wasn't until she began writing letters to herself — in that big careful handwriting of a child — that they got straightened out on what it was his name was supposed to be; what he had told her it was. This was when she gave off being fooled by him and commenced trying to fool herself.

'It got to be a kind of a joke,' Brody said, 'with them railroad mail clerks. She would come down here once or twice a week with the baby and watch old Seventeen come in and say to me, like that first night, what a beautiful train it was. "Why you'll go a long way before you find a more beautiful train than that one," she would say. "Europe, perhaps." And then she would hurry up ahead to the mail car with this letter she had wrote to herself and drop it in the slot. So it got to be a kind of a joke with the boys and one night I was up talking with Simon while the fireman was watering, when one of them leans out and says, "I got something for the Duchess," he says, and gives me this letter. One she had mailed just two minutes before. And there it was,' Brody said. 'Addressed to herself, and up in the left-hand corner, big as all outdoors as if she wanted people to see it: "From the Duke of Rayon, New York." Yes,' Brody said, 'because maybe he traveled for one of them nearly-silk underwear companies, and maybe the boys called him "Duke." And maybe he put them two together when he sold this convent or wherever it was he found her (asylum, maybe) and called himself the Duke of Rayon,' Brody said.

III

So when I made Waterbridge a year ago September, what with some government business I had over at the mill (I'm the county assessor), I stopped off at Rust's. It was a Saturday and that night it rained hard and the next day that road was like a log-sluice, so I had to stay over an extra day. That was when I first set eyes on her.

They were at supper when I got out and dragged back the gate and drove my machine in. It was already dark and the wind had come up cold, driving one of those black September storm clouds across that valley like sliding a lid over a pot, so I ran my machine under the wagon shed and then I saw Henderson — that's Rust — holding a lamp in the doorway. He had his coat on.

I believe that was when I first remembered that I had heard them talking about her back at Boonton. Maybe it was the sight of Rust wearing a coat who you knew had all his life been satisfied to decorate his table with his undershirt or shirt and suspenders, Sundays excepted.

There's not much to Rust. A hard-shelled, bony sort of man who has been smart enough to get hold of a bad piece of property and put a good house on it, neither farm nor home, with a porch and a lot of gingerbread work on the gables, where once in a while a feed drummer will stop or an occasional hunter in season (together with any wet-weather up-hill trade forced in by those pigs lying in the road) and where Bidwell, the mill foreman, boards. Rust held the gulping lamp against the wind and I could see his face. He had on the coat but no collar and tie.

'Come in,' he says. 'We'll make a place for you.'

Rust does no work. He used to do some farming but after he built that house and found out that pigs will grow themselves, he took to tinkering about with his carpenter tools in that way some men have of seeming always to be busy and doing nothing. About five years ago he built the wheel chair and that was the last piece of work he's done.

The wheel chair was for old Grandma Rust. She lives in the room next to the dining room where at supper time she will bring to the table that sickening sweet odor of the very old that is like a pall from the tomb, while she will chew her food idiotically, secretly watching and hearing everything. She puts me in mind of some old horror, her pale dead eyes watching beneath the hood of her coal-scuttle bonnet, and that hairy gray jaw hanging loose like an old stove-in-mare's. And late at night she can be heard rolling around downstairs in that wheel chair Rust made for her out of a pair of surrey wheels and a rocking chair, sounding like soft thunder or a horse and wagon on a bridge, and whispering her Bible. They say she keeps her tombstone under her bed.

Besides her there is Rust's wife and her maiden sister, tall, gnarled, hard-faced, the two of them living without conversation; sullen and with few words, not like other women, more like Indians.

And Ruffon. Ruffon is that twelve-year-old oaf of Rust's that the devil let live.

So Rust says: 'Come in, we'll make a place for you.'

I didn't see her at first, small the way she was in that ring of hard-faced women of Rust's. They put me in mind of white Indians, the way they sit around the supper table (it's got oilcloth on it), the lamp throwing shadows on those high jaws of theirs. She was only a little shadow beyond the lamplight that somehow glistened as if wet or jeweled in the region of the face. But when she came up from where she was, half down behind the table feeding that little fellow some warm milk with a spoon, it was like one of our late autumn evenings had moved right into the house. She had some of that fine mountain laurel twisted in her hair, and some red berries, all tangled and wild.

She was perhaps five feet, four inches tall, slight, and with that child's-hair gathered at the back as if she had just been washed. She wore or supported about her a kind of oversized and makeshift garment that put me in mind of attics and old satin and sewing she had done herself, all bunched around her and tied up in back. She was fine, all right. But it was the way she seemed to flash up from the shadow, her face toward the doorway, and the little cry she gave. Because it was already open season on doves, and quail and rabbit were coming in soon, and her looking for this Duke to come riding in in a red coat, maybe, and blowing a horn; except it was only me.

'Come in,' Mrs. Rust says. 'We've done made a place for you.' But I saw her watching Rust.

IV

It was Bidwell who told me about Ruffon, that hellion of Rust's: how he would plague the girl and (later) how he figured in the lynching. Bidwell is the foreman of the mill, a soft-spoken man, a bachelor but a man you knew was one because he didn't have all that torment chasing through his veins.

'Like all the hatefulness that goes on behind that old grandma's face has done come to life in Ruffon,' Bidwell said. 'And he ain't ascared of nothing,' he said. 'You see that there little gray squirrel?'

We were sitting in the sun outside the planing shed up at the mill.

This was Sunday morning. It had rained hard the night before — one of those regular September mountain storms — but the morning had turned up bright and clean and crisp, so that you knew summer was gone, had moved out the night before like a lot of hot fat relations and their children leaving after a visit.

'That's a little fox squirrel,' I said. 'She's setting in stores for the winter. Why?'

'Because,' Bidwell said, 'what Ruffon would like to do better than anything in the world is to get a axe in his hand and run around wild like a Injun and chop that little squirrel into pieces. Sometimes I think of him at night. Not like a child sleeping; like some kind of devilish hell laying in wait for a signal. That Ruffon.' Then he told me how the apple tree got ruined.

I had noticed it after breakfast — split right down the middle, and it the only tree in the yard: a fine old one, loaded down with good eating apples. ('Why look what that storm has done to your tree,' I had said. I noticed that Rust's women didn't answer.)

'Storm?' Bidwell said. 'That's good. Storm. I reckon Henderson would have give a right smart for a storm that night.' Then he told me. Squatting there in the sun, listening to Bidwell, I commenced to see the whole thing....

'It's Henderson,' Bidwell said. 'You know how it is. A man that ain't never had much but God and that wife of his. And then she come along with her little baby.

'I first noticed it when he commenced putting on his coat at the table, but you know how it is. I reckon them women of his knew even before that. I could tell by the way they would set the food on the table and Miz Rust would watch him until you could hear her thinking: "Go ahead. Just put on your collar and tie. Just you dare put on your collar and tie," and her setting there with that fine little croodlin' baby that don't never cry, and talking fast the way she does, and Rust afraid to even look at her.

'It was one night about a week and a half ago that I heard the noise. I had done already gone to bed and I was laying there in the dark when I heard it, like a horse stumbling. It was a lot of apples falling. And the next thing I heard was the crash. That was when I pieced the whole thing together and seen how it must have all commenced with this here little X-ray thing that Rust ——'

'X-ray?' I said. 'Hold on a minute. You were telling me about that apple tree and now you start to tell me something about a X-ray. What's any X-ray got to do with all this?' I said.

'That's just it,' Bidwell said. 'It was this here X-ray. It's how it all started.'

'What kind of X-ray?' I said. I thought maybe he had lost his mind.

'Not no real X-ray,' Bidwell said. 'It was one of them little child's toys that the mailing houses advertise along with how to be a ventriloquist and jujitsu in one lesson. One of them little old ten-cent tubes that you hold up to your eye and don't see nothing through. It come in the mail one day addressed to Rust and Miz Rust says, "What's this here parcel addressed to you?"

'I reckon Rust must have figured he was caught. Maybe he had aimed to get the mail first. "It's a X-ray," Rust says.

'"A X-ray?" Miz Rust says. "What do you mean, a X-ray?"

'"It ain't nothing but a little one," Rust says. "I got it for the boy. It didn't cost nothing."

'"So that's how you spend my egg money," Miz Rust says.

'"It didn't cost but a dime," Rust says. "It'll be handy to have around."

'It wasn't until that night that I figured it out. Figured out how he had been settin' downstairs by the lamp night after night in his sock feet, reading them farm magazines from cover to cover: slow studying out the words with his finger, until he come to this advertisement about a X-ray. You know how they read: "Boys! Look! A gen-u-ine X-ray for only ten cents. See the bones in your hand, see the inside of your body." And then how they say: "Important! This gen-u-ine X-ray is sold for the scientific study of anatomy; not for looking through doors and walls into no lady's room." How they go on to say, "And now remember, you boys who are interested in science. You boys be good sports and don't use this gen-u-ine X-ray to watch the lady next door undress." You know how it is. And the bright ones figure it out. So Rust sent off.

'And so that night after supper the little lady had done took the baby on up to bed and I had gone on up and was fixing to read for a while when I seen my lamp was nigh out of oil, so I took the lamp and opened the door and that was when I saw him. He was at her door. Leaning over like an idiot, holding that damn little ten-cent nothing to his eye up against the door of her room. He thought

I didn't see him at first. He tried to make it look like he was just standing there in that dark empty hall, looking through his hand.

'"It's got to have daylight," he says. "You can't see nairy a bone in the dark. It ain't a very good one."

'"No," I says. "I reckon not, since it ain't nothing in it but a little old feather."

'And so three nights later I heard the noise, the crash when that apple tree split in two. That was when I pieced the whole thing together. "So the X-ray didn't work," I said to myself. "But he figured the apple tree would." Only the apple tree didn't work much better than the X-ray because the apple tree was made to bear apples, just as that X-ray was made to do nothing, and both of them fooled him.

'Because that there apple tree looks right into her window. Right into where she has to stand to bathe herself, poor little kid, outen that old cracked basin. And her believing there wasn't nothing but God and the apple tree could see, and them eyes hid back in the leaves like a bobcat's.

'So I reckon there was a serpent in that apple tree, too. And then half the tree come crashing down and it seemed like I could hear a right smart of scuffling around on the ground, but it wasn't until the next morning that I knew it was the two of them. They must have been perched up there like two buzzards, young and old. Scratched up like they had done been in a cat fight. That old fool Rust and that young devil Ruffon.

'Sure,' Bidwell said. 'I guess Rust would have give a right smart for a storm, all right.'

V

Now that it's all over and she has gone (the last of it happened one night just five weeks ago), now that it's all over I like to look back on the whole thing. On how it all started that night when she got off the big train with her baby and stood there watching the lights disappear, thinking it was all kind of important and she would get a taxi and go up to this nice quiet old hunting lodge and later this Duke would come down, maybe in a red coat with a lot of horses and dogs and blowing a horn so she'd know. And then I think of how she must have kept on believing in this something — a person can stand so much with something to believe in — alone in that ring of rock-jawed Rusts, having to write letters to herself to keep on believing it, and how they commenced to say she was possessed. And then I think of how it all ended: of the violence and horror that was those people's vindication of a simple darkness they couldn't fathom. Because nature will work on them just the way it will work on a snake that gathers its bafflement and rage into a coil and strikes at the simplest little rabbit. And that snake isn't after killing that rabbit; he's after destroying the blind spot in his brain that the rabbit put there.

And then I think of her on that crisp October morning just five weeks ago, on the top of that hill with the sun and the dew in her hair and crying, her little mouth shaped in horror and her eyes sightless with seeing backward into the dark remembering of that valley of the world . . . And I say this: They drove her into seeing.

It was dinner time when Bidwell and I got back to Rust's. We had sat up there talking about her and watching the squirrel the whole morning. Down below we could see a wagonload of niggers idling back from church on the brown scar of road, and across the valley, high up on the slope in a clover patch, we could see this solitary figure and beside it a flash of red. 'That's that there little red wagon,' Bidwell said. Then he told me how she had got the storekeeper to send off and get it for her and how she would wander up and down the hills on bright days, with the little fellow all propped up in the wagon and throwing his bottle out every now and then. 'Like it wasn't nothing but just a old bottle,' Bidwell said.

They were ready to sit down when we reached the house and found the Reverend Howard there. I didn't know the Reverend. I reckon she didn't know him either and sometimes I look back and wonder if the good Lord knew him. You know how it is. When you see a man who has worked himself thin in the single-track rigor of his own conviction; who has toiled all his life getting himself narrowed to the point where he has only one thing to do and then he does it wrong.

And so when I look back on it all I think I see where the turning point was, where the power was that could lead to Rust's final vindication of his own lust by violence and bloodshed. It was that they had God on their side and against God was the devil, and in between was Rust shaken like a reed in a tempest, and it was all like some stage play, only little and hard and violent, down in that valley.

'So this is Sister Rayon,' the Reverend Howard said. 'My, my.' His voice was a long soft breath, like a sigh of inner comfort. Then he led in prayer.

It was like she was in a cauldron, in that dim circle of faces all looking as if they had been hammered into a hard formality like iron statues and their Sunday clothes as if cast out of metal, and no sunlight in the room. They were all at the table. That old Grandma Rust in between her wheels like some old stove-in horse and wagon driven up to the table and with her lip hanging loose from her big lower teeth that were false and old and even like a horse's, and spilling food out while she watched and listened. Rust and the preacher sat at opposite ends of the table, their heads matted in identical poultice plasters of hair like harsh, cheap wigs. And those high-cheeked women of Rust's, and Ruffon. Ruffon looked like one of them ventriloquist's dummies, all polished up and dirty underneath.

'So this is Sister Rayon?' Howard says. 'Well, well.'

'I'd thankee for the salt meat,' Rust says.

'I reckon it's high time the voice of the Lord sat down at this table,' Mrs. Rust says. I saw her watching Rust.

It was pitiful and it was mean. I remember how the girl sat there hemmed in at the table with the baby in her lap and some of that mountain laurel in her hair and trying to look busy and glad, like a frightened child: kind of half hiding beneath the table and bending over the little fellow with sudden concern when Howard would fix her with that greasy sword of a voice and the others would watch her.

'And where was Sister Rayon at the church meeting this morning?' Howard purrs, looking from one to the other of them brightly like he had pulled a fast one. 'And whe-r-r-r-e was Sister Rayon?'

She gave a little laugh, suddenly down around the child where he was bouncing up and down with a spoon, saying, 'Da da ya ya.'

'He wants to play,' she said quickly. 'Now here.'

It was like she was embarrassed, like the only answer she could give in any common language was the child, with her eyes darting back and forth with the modesty of a bird.

'I reckon it's high time,' Mrs. Rust says, watching Rust, her

jaws throbbing. I could see the old grandma watching and listening down in between her wagon wheels, food stringing out of her mouth.

'I'd thankee for the beans, Brother Howard,' Rust says.

And then I commenced to see which way *he* was leveling: Brother Howard. Because it didn't take him long to get around to the part about the marriage license, and her sitting there with her scared eyes darting down to the little baby and bending over quick to straighten his dress or wipe his chin. 'Now here,' she said. Howard had commenced to spread-eagle.

'She'll want to be counted in the flock,' Howard told them. 'She'll want to be numbered in the fo-o-o-o-ld,' his long hands spread-eagling over that room for attention. And then he commenced to level.

It was shrewd, it was smooth, with those questions not direct like 'Whe-r-r-r-e was Sister Rayon?' and those answers he made up himself in his sure, oily voice, and old Rust sitting there with his soul stark naked, mute in his bafflement and rage at the lust within him which he didn't understand. Damn if there wasn't something pitiful about Rust; about the shape of his bony head while that preacher's voice went on putting a web around those darting eyes of hers. It was like a snake charming a bird.

He had worked right up to the marriage license before Mrs. Rust spoke again, not smooth but flat and final, her voice.

'S'posing you go on upstairs and git it,' she said, looking half at old grandma surrey wheels. 'If Reverend Howard wants to see yer license, just s'posing you go on upstairs and git it,' and old grandma surrey wheels watching like a hawk.

It was right then that the train blew for Waterbridge: the fast south-bound, filling that valley with a long low wail and I saw her eyes rush up to follow the dying echo, holding that roomful of Sunday Rusts like statues turned to iron in some long-forgotten afternoon of the past.

'All right,' she said, her wild bright eyes gone from the room. But I believe she was answering that train, and in the next instant she too was gone.

She didn't return to the table. They just sat there for a minute and then I noticed old grandma surrey wheels' narrow eye sockets burning the spot where she had been. It was the first time the old woman had spoken.

'She's crazy,' the old woman said, looking across the room at nothing.

VI

It was spring before I made Waterbridge again after that Sunday in September when I first saw her. I was on my way over to Boonton when I passed through last spring and so I stopped off at the mill to see Bidwell, and I asked him about her and that was when he told me that she had moved.

'Moved?' I said. 'What do you mean she has moved? Why what street is she living on now?' I said. (Because nobody ever moved in Waterbridge. There's no place to move but out and out isn't moved, it's gone.)

'Yes,' Bidwell said. 'Over on the other side of the hill. They drove her out. I figured you would have heard.' Then he told me.

Bidwell said they must have gone through her room searching for the marriage license. It was just after I left, he said, that they commenced to whisper outright that she was bad. And when the Reverend Howard gave her up (Bidwell said that he came to dinner for five straight Sundays before he gave her up) they were sure of it. And when they found out that she was writing the letters to herself, he said they began to believe she was possessed. 'Being that possessed was about the only thing left to believe,' he said. 'Since they had already decided she was crazy and bad. And then I guess of all the things to do next in the world, the next thing she did was the worst. Hemstitching.'

Because it wasn't only just plain sewing; it was *what* she was sewing on that made it bad, and that was how they came to find out that it was New Orleans she was from and all about her maiden aunt down there who ran some kind of little Mardi Gras costume shop, she called it, and how she had learned to make these here red devil suits that they would sell to all those niggers down there because it was this big white devil or something called the Mardi Gras that would clean out all those niggers every year if they didn't put on these suits, or something.

'And so she aimed to sell them,' Bidwell said. 'To niggers. Maybe it keeps the Ku Klux offen them — or something. She figured on selling them to pay for her board.'

Because along about February she ran out of money, Bidwell said, and then one day she received the anonymous letter with a one-dollar bill in it, this too postmarked Waterbridge like the ones she would write to herself. She bought a lot of that cheap red cotton material with the dollar, at Fry's general store.

Bidwell said it was like one of those hard ones you would find on page two of the first-grade arithmetic, figuring out where that dollar came from. 'John has eleven dollars and Robert has nine,' Bidwell said. 'If John give Robert one of his dollars, how much has each?'

Because she paid Mrs. Rust ten dollars a month — two and a half a week besides the thirty or forty cents she paid a little family of niggers to come for and deliver each week (they would all come for and all deliver like a solemn parade) her washing — and when the first of February turned up she had only nine dollars left to her name. And when two days later the letter came and Mrs. Rust watched her open it and find a dollar bill and then went straight to the kitchen cabinet where she hides her egg money, Bidwell said it was like looking in the back of the book for the answer.

'Rust had it bad,' Bidwell said.

Mrs. Rust wouldn't take the dollar. Bidwell said she stood there at dinner looking down at the girl, her hard jaws throbbing like granite with a pulse, and you could hear Rust outside with a hammer and saw trying to sound as if he was building a four-story annex, and that afternoon he hitched up and loaded some half-grown shoats in the wagon and drove off for Boonton and he was gone for three days. So the girl bought the red cotton cloth.

Nobody knew what she was making with it. She spent a whole week making the suits up in her room, coming down only for her meals and to take the baby for a walk. And then one dark day the Devil himself came galloping down the stairs and whooping through the house like something fresh out of hell. It nearly killed the old grandma. He had horns and a tail and he was red all over and he went whooping past that old woman, shrieking and screaming with joy.

'Yes,' Bidwell said. 'Ruffon had done got hold of one of them suits.'

They thought the old woman was dead, at first. She can't see any too well anyway and they saw her head snapped back and her eyes stuck out like glass, and she pitched headlong onto the floor and

lay there wall-eyed and they had to throw water on her. Then they
got her onto the bed and Rust took Ruffon out to the barn and beat
him with a stick of stove wood until he didn't cry any more. That
night, when she could speak again, the old woman said it was a sign
from heaven that her time had come and she summoned them all
to her bedside.

So they drove the girl out. It must have been pretty terrible for
her. Not even Bidwell was there, having gone back into the hills
with one of the logging crews, so she was without a friend in that
house. I can imagine the deathbed scene: one of those black, windy
nights with the branches of the dead apple tree rattling like skeleton
fingers and that old woman propped up in bed, with them kneeling
in the cold lamplight, in the cold odor of death, while she adminis-
tered her last words on each of them.

And I can imagine how they went to that little girl's room and
forced her to come down and kneel among them on the cold boards,
with the tombstone and the chamber pot and Rust's miserable head
a carved image of bafflement, and those high-jawed women all
kneeling in the lamp-light, their shadows black upon the wall, and
that old woman croaking above the sobbing and praying that was
working up to a yelling and a singing like a hog-wild revival meeting,
saying: 'Dip your robes in the blood of the lamb for I've washed
my hands in the fou'tain; let us sing.' Saying: 'Cleanse your feet
in the waters of Jordan; and you, Henderson Rust, drug into the
way of sin, chain down that imp of torment a-ranting in the devil's
image! Chain him to the hind wheels of the Lord; sing all!' And
how that old woman's dying eye must have fixed itself upon that
little girl when she pointed her bony finger at her, saying: 'Drive
her out! Drive out the Jezebel!'

'Leave her remain,' Rust said, shaking like a reed. 'The Lord
says leave her remain.'

'I say to you drive her outen this house for she's a witch and
a harlot,' the old woman said. 'Drive out the Jezebel and leave me
my deathbed in peace!'

So that night they drove her out. They must have risen up from
their bended knees, those women, singing and praying and pointing
their fingers, and told her to pack up and go and they called her baby
a name. This was the middle of last March, the night that grandma
was dying. But the old woman was still helling around on them

wagon wheels the thirty-first of October, the night the nigger Sylvester was lynched.

'Yes,' Bidwell said. 'A average of twice a year for the past six or seven years. It's the only act she knows, dying; the only way she can get attention, and then she kind of keeps in training, too. Like a athlete.'

VII

There lived in the vicinity of Waterbridge, until that night five weeks ago, a ragged, hard-working nigger named Sylvester who raised a lean crop each year on the side of a stump-pocked hill a mile south of Rust's. He had a mule and a wife and half a dozen little ragged children. I have seen them: standing in a row on the sagging porch, their big eyes uplooking.

It was the family of this nigger Sylvester that used to come for and deliver each week, like a solemn parade, the girl's washing, and it was Sylvester who, astride his mule with a sack of feed and a lantern late that night in March, came upon this little figure struggling in the black road with a suitcase and a little red wagon and the child. 'Whoa!' Sylvester said. I reckon he signed his death warrant with that speech to his mule. Because she went with him.

And this is the last of it, the ugly part, the violent and the terrible part:

For a long time no one knew where she was. Bidwell said that it was breaking down Rust's health; that he took to reading his Bible at night and praying aloud, and then he commenced to stalk. 'Like a sick Indian,' Bidwell said. 'Maybe it was them leaves she used to wear in her hair.'

It was a family named Aaron that first learned where she was. Old man Aaron lives with his two hairy-faced grown sons in a dilapidated shanty on a piece of fallow land also about a mile south of Rust's, where they will sit or lie for endless days on a weather gray porch in the sun as if proud of their dilapidation; as if dilapidation and the endless doing of nothing were in themselves both the vainglory and the labor of life, like farming. And one day old man Aaron and one of his sons were tilted back on their porch, hats slanted against the afternoon sun, when they saw a strange phenomenon at the western end of their land: a pair of red devil's horns and a red tail peeking from behind a boulder — then another and a third and then three small red devils shimmering over the hill.

The younger Aaron sat upright with a clump. 'Git me my gun,' he said, his jaws snapped tight.

'Git me the Book,' old Aaron said without moving. 'I'm an old man, Jesus, but just tell me what You want.'

So they learned where she was. It was those devil suits — Sylvester's children had them on.

They learned how an old ragged nigger and his family had been providing for her who they thought had gone: learned how she had been living alone in a one-room cabin, windowless and with a mud fireplace, long abandoned even by niggers, that Sylvester's father or grandfather before him had built down in a hollow a quarter of a mile from the road. And they learned that it was niggers who had furnished her a bed and who provided her food and wood for the fireplace and brought warm milk to her each morning and night.

Then Rust commenced to stalk.

It happened on a Saturday night. Ruffon had got hold of an old bony horse somewhere — one that a nigger had given Rust in payment of some trifling debt — and they say that each day Ruffon would set out to kill the horse again, riding the lean beast in a daily succession of shampoo lathers over the hills and through the woods like some harpy out of hell crouched on its shuddering back. And Bidwell said that then the two of them would go stalking through the hills, not together, the one on foot, the other on the foam-flecked nag circling him, watching him, following him probably, seeming probably (to a ragged nigger plodding in the early darkness with a pail of fresh warm milk) to converge like a mounted tribe from several trails at once upon the desolate little hollow where there lurked near the warped lamplight of the doorway the figure of a man.

Maybe the nigger stopped still in the sloping path, watching. He must have seen the figure approach the single board step of her door, and heard the cry from within. He must have run then, down the gully of path, his head high, his nostrils and eyes wide. He must have said, 'What you doing here? White man, you got no business down in thishyere holler!' and with Rust wheeling suddenly in passion and rage, caught in shame between the terrified sobs within the cabin and the figure of the nigger in the door. Maybe he struck the nigger or cursed him. Sylvester was a big man; humble, they say, but without fear.

And so that Saturday night Fry and the two hard Aaron boys and four or five of the mill hands were lounging on the porch of Fry's store in kerosene lamplight, drinking now and then from a jug, playing a harmonica, cursing, boasting, when over the blue edge of the hill came Ruffon, riding that spectre of a horse down the night road to another sweat-covered death. He laid the old sack of bones back on its quivering haunches and plowed a furrow to a halt in front of the store.

'The nigger!' he shrieked. 'He's a-killin' my pa! The nigger Sylvester's a-killin' my pa and a-shaming that gal!' His voice was a high shrieking sob like a tantrum of rage.

'Gimme that horse,' one of the Aaron boys said. He was up on his feet and moving with the swiftness of a prize fighter. He jerked the horrified head of the horse, the bridle, from Ruffon's hands.

'We'll git our shotguns!' he shouted. 'You boys git a rope and meet us up at the forks! Come on!'

With a single lanky vault, like a circus act, the two Aaron boys were astride the horse, back-shouting to the figures that were running in the dark, yelling, waving lanterns, scattering and converging, all terrific on the hillslope, while Ruffon streaked up the dark road shrieking, 'He's a-killin' um! Wait for me! I'll git my gun too! That black bastard's a-killin' um,' his voice falling into breathless whimpering to the pounding of feet as he rushed into the house and out again down the path to where old Grandma Rust sat in her wagon wheels (one end of the porch is level with the ground; she had heard the shouting; she had wheeled herself into the yard) tugging at her wheels and cawing. She blocked the path.

'What is it!' she yelled. 'Who's a-killin' who! Here, you imp of hell, tell me what it is!'

Ruffon crashed into the back of the chair in the dark with a lunge that snapped the old woman's false teeth shut and spun her wheels into motion headed downhill. He gave a single fierce cry of pain and rage, shrieking, 'He's a-killin' um, I tell you!' and waving the shotgun he dashed down the embankment and up the dark hill as the old woman vanished downward.

They all met back on a slope of the road at the juncture of a wagon trail, weed-grown from disuse — the five or six of them, intense in the wasted motion of violence, with the lantern light swinging gustily across their faces and hats and gun barrels, with the devastated horse and the rope and the straining dust-colored faces.

'Come on,' one of the Aaron boys said. He took the lead. Stumbling, crowding each other like cattle, they came suddenly upon the dark outline of the nigger's house and stopped dead.

'Come out!' the Aaron boy shouted. He stood in front, tall, lean, hard, his legs apart, his jaws showing in the lantern light. 'Come outen there, you nigger.'

Inside the house there were sounds. A thin brown mask of horror appeared in a ribbon of light in the partially opened door. 'Who that?' the voice said. It was the nigger woman. 'Aw Lawdy, who that?'

'Send him outen the house or we'll set far to it,' the Aaron boy shouted.

'Set far to it!' someone shouted. 'Set far to it!'

Someone hurled a lantern. It burst in the bare yard short of the house and extinguished.

'Aw Lawdy,' came the woman's voice, 'Aw Lawdy,' rising to a smothered wail within the cabin as the door grated shut. 'Aw Jesus, aw Lawd —' when suddenly out of the darkness of the path stumbled the figure of Rust, his face blood-covered and terrible.

'Back that-a-way,' he said.

He flung a limp arm backward down the path toward the hollow. He stood dangling and spent as a scarecrow while the men wheeled the lanterns and guns and faces and swept down the crooked slope of path, leaving Rust and the nearly dead horse alone and heaving in the night.

Halfway down they saw the nigger. He stood motionless in the path, once more stark and apparition-like in the funnel of blackness, his arms hanging long and limp-palmed at his sides.

'White mens,' he called.

They moved downward slowly now, without crowding. They could see his head held rigid and high from his drooping shoulders, paler than the night; the face terrific and glistening in the advancing light as if scenting doom too late, as if speared from behind at the very instant of scenting doom, the eyes and nostrils wide, great rippled furrows of fear in his narrow head.

'White mens,' he said.

Slowly, cautiously, they advanced now, forward-leaning and

deliberate and silent, the two Aaron boys in the lead with a gun,
a lantern and the rope.

'White mens,' he said. He didn't move. The stark head and the
hanging arms didn't move as they closed down upon him. 'White
mens,' he said. 'Aw, white mens . . . White mens . . . Aw, men-
folks ——'

IX

And that's the end. I found her next morning on the road — part
way up the red clay hill where the sun hadn't yet come and pulling
behind her the little painted wagon in which sat the child, but I
didn't know yet what had happened. How they had lynched Sylvester the night before and how they had found old Grandma Rust
at the end of her ride. She must have been going mighty fast when
she crossed the railroad tracks and missed the bridge. They traced
her wheel tracks down the embankment and saw where she had
careened across the road and sheared off the other bank and back
onto the road again like a runaway team, and then right down the
middle until she crossed the tracks and missed the bridge. 'She'd
have done been all right if she'd made that turn onto the bridge,'
Bidwell said, 'but I reckon she must have been making fifty miles
an hour when she crossed the tracks.' They found her that night in
Rocky Run with the smashed hind wheels of the Lord around her.

It was a fine morning, crisp and fresh, and you could smell the
chestnuts down in the valleys and you knew the hunting was going
to be fine. That was when I saw the girl.

I remember how we just sat there for a while on the top of that
hill with the little fellow all bundled up and bouncing up and down
between us saying, 'Dubba chabbe yeps?' like me and him was
picking up matters where we'd left off before — and how next she
was crying.

I didn't realize it at first: her making no sound and with her little
mouth shaped in horror like a child's and her eyes sightless with
seeing backwards into the horror and the reality of that valley of
the world. I guess it was the first time she had ever really seen.

THE DOORSTOP[1]

By ROY FLANNAGAN

(From *Story*)

MAJOR TIPTON was Arm Cary's lawyer so the mulatto went to his office shortly before the city newspapers arrived and hell broke loose in Ruffinton. Arm Cary generally looked like a prosperous business man, but he was perspiring like a field hand when he slipped into the lawyer's office. His linen suit hung baggily around his body and, since he was frightened, his yellow face was more Negroid than usual.

He asked Major Tipton for permission to pull down the shades and lock the door. He stood by the attorney's desk twisting his hands, swaying his head and gobbling his words.

The major had difficulty understanding him. The mulatto was trying to tell him something about old Judge King, the drunkard, who once had been a supreme court judge and who had not been seen for some time, and about a Negro undertaker, one Parson Snipes.

'Y'all don't know it,' Arm Cary said, 'but Judge King, he died right here in Ruffinton. Nobody knowed he was dead; nobody but me. Nobody cared 'bout him being dead; nobody but me. Lawdy, Boss!'

'Go on, Arm, what about him?' Major Tipton already had begun to feel creepy because the mulatto generally was a rather steady kind of man.

'I got a lot to tell, sah, and no time to tell it . . .' Arm Cary looked over his shoulder. ' . . . A lot to tell. Judge King, he died right here in Ruffinton, sah, right here in town, and nobody knowed it. Three months before he died I come up Princess Street one night about three o'clock and thar the old judge was, lyin' on 'e sidewalk under the mulberry tree across from 'e postoffice. He was paralysed, Major, paralysed, and he couldn't git up on 'is feet. He had to hang on with his lef' hand to the waterin' trough. He was sober that night, sah, and paralysed and it was awful cold and nobody was around to he'p 'im, not a soul, and so . . .'

The mulatto had taken the old man into his car and put him in an empty flat over the Aaronson store, a flat which Arm Cary owned and had been renting to white people. He had not told anyone the next day or the next and by then he had decided to take care of the old judge without letting anyone in Ruffinton know about it. No one missed the old man except some of the people whose turn it was to lend him money for liquor, and they thought that he had gone away to Macon where he had some relatives.

'You see, Major, I got to thinkin' about what white folks would say if they knowed I was takin' care of 'e old Judge, so I laid low. He was crippled and almost out of his head, but after a while he got so he could enjoy his liquor and cuss. Yes, sah. Sometimes the nurse — I got a nigger trained nurse from Baltimore — sometimes the nurse she had to shut all 'e doors. And I kept out o' sight, cause if 'e old judge had knowed a nigger was payin' for 'is keep, he'd 'a' raised hell sure enough. And I got a doctor from Atlanta. Doctors don't talk, major . . .'

Arm Cary wiped his wet forehead with his sleeve.

'I never thought of 'im dyin', Major, and at last when 'e died, I got scared, proper. Everybody had forgotten 'im by then but I never knowed what to do. I didn't have good sense, sah. I'd been peepin' in at 'e old judge day after day, thinkin' what a fine man he'd been before liquor cut 'im down, thinkin' about 'em fine hosses he used to ride up and down Church Street when I was little. Somebody would holler "Here he come!" and we'd all run out and look. He was handsome even when he was sick, Major, yes, sah, but after he was dead, he looked jus' like a young man again, jus' like he did when he drove 'at tandem team when I was little. After he was dead I went in 'e room and got a good look at 'im, Major . . .'

The mulatto glanced over his shoulder again, but everything still was quiet out in the street. By this time Major Tipton was almost as nervous as his visitor.

'The Atlanta doctor, he sent the death certificate on to the state and there was no trouble about 'at. But I had to git 'im buried, Major. 'At's whar Parson Snipes comes in. I was skeered, Major and I . . . I didn't want nobody to have 'im, Major. I acted like a fool but I don't want nobody to know, nobody to have 'im. It was nigger in me, maybe, but 'at's how it was, sah. So I got me some silver money from 'e bank and I went down to the livery stable

whar Parson Snipes did his undertakin'. I didn't want nobody to
know, so I give Parson Snipes nearly two pounds o' hard money
to he'p me. 'At night we buried Judge King...'

Major Tipton sat, scratching the backs of his hands, trying to
to keep still.

' ... Buried Judge King in Mount Moriah cemetery...'

The major jumped out of his chair at this and walked sideways
over to the door to see if it had been well locked.

'God A'mighty, nigger!'

The gaunt mulatto became calmer now that the lawyer was upset.

'Wait, Major. Don't fly off, sah. I know how it is, but *you* got to
he'p me — got to. We buried 'im thar in 'e nigger cemetery because
I didn't have no place else, and 'e burial plot, it was mine — a whole
half acre in 'at end of Mount Moriah is mine. And I thought I had
'im thar forever under a little stone, a little Georgia marble stone
without no name on it anybody would know, a marble stone I got
from 'e back lot of 'at place on Park Street whar he used to live.
And we smoothed 'e place so it looked like an old grave and nobody
knew 'cept 'at blackmailing nigger, Parson Snipes. Sometimes I had
to pay 'im twenty dollars in one month. He got skeered and he
used to come 'round to my insurance office and pray like 'e devil was
ridin' 'im. And even when I set 'im up in business in 'e big city, he
used to git after me for money. And yestiddy, Major, the big city
police got after 'im, Major...'

Arm Cary wiped his face again.

' ... They got after 'im for switchin' coffins on people. He'd sell
a fine casket to somebody and 'en bury the corpse in 'e grave box
and sell 'e casket over again to somebody else. Them police, 'ey
got after him good, and he talked. He talked about 'is own scalawag
meanness and he talked — he talked about me and 'im burying a
white man, buryin' Judge King, in Mount Moriah cemetery...'

The major was pacing up and down.

'Jesus, Arm!'

' ... And it's in 'e city papers 'is very afternoon...'

The major ran his fingers through his hair.

'Arm, I got to get you out o' the state!'

Within less than an hour after the six o'clock train brought the
papers from the city the whole town was talking. Ruffinton had

a population of about five thousand and half of these were Negroes employed in the lumber mills. Ruffinton was like any other community except for these quiet blacks huddled in their village beyond the ravine south of the business district. This section was called Bucktown and the whites did not go there after dark because over there the streets were not lighted or paved and there were queer noises, barbaric music and strong odors.

The Negro settlement supplied all of the cooks and chauffeurs and nurses, all of the factory hands, laborers and janitors and gardeners for Ruffinton, yet the white people remained in awe of the place. There were too many Negroes there. Individually a cook or a chauffeur was a friend, a member of the family; but collectively the black population hung over the town like a pall.

In one riot Bucktown had been partly destroyed and twenty Negroes killed. In another, fifteen years before, a Negro groom, suspected of having mistreated the daughter of a white carpenter, had been hanged from a beam of the bridge and every man, woman and child in Bucktown had shivered for a week while posses searched their homes for arms which rumor said were in the possession of every Negro family.

Eastward along the ravine where the railroad came into town the poorer white families faced the Negroes across the tracks, and the white slums were as dirty as those of the Negroes although the streets on the white side of the tracks were cobblestoned and lighted because the whites could vote.

It was here, not far from the railroad station, that talk was shrillest after the city papers arrived with their story of the abomination. Young white men gathered.

A white man in a nigger cemetery ... Judge King ... Old Judge King who had been a leading citizen in that part of the state before he became a liquor head, the town drunkard. *Judge King buried in a nigger cemetery!* A white man *in a nigger cemetery!*

By eight o'clock four different gangs were looking for Arm Cary, and a bootlegger was doing big business in the alley behind the junction confectionery. The crowd in the Athletic Center on Main Street stopped bowling and came out. Young men who had dates for the early moving picture show took their girls home and came back downtown with their fathers' pistols in their pockets.

Lemuel Robbins, a railway section hand, was leader of a crowd that assembled in front of the Lincoln garage in Bucktown, a little place one block from the station over which Arm Cary had his office and living quarters. Someone began to throw rocks at the second story windows and the gang grew larger by the minute. The policemen — there were only six on the Ruffinton force — saw what was going on and stayed away.

But the mulatto was not in his rooms over the Lincoln garage. A gang headed by Joe Watts, the tall station bus driver for the Grady hotel, went through Bucktown from end to end hunting for Cary at nine-thirty, but did not find him. This group also threw stones and some of them fired shots into the air to make the Negroes stay in their hovels.

Meanwhile the bunch led by Lem Robbins finished knocking out all of the garage windows and went down to the jail. The sheriff was not there so they sent a detachment after him which got him out of bed and made him lead them through the jail. They thought Arm Cary might have taken refuge there, but they were mistaken. They stamped all through the lock-up and frightened some of the prisoners into praying hysterics.

The two main gangs united at the jail shortly after ten o'clock. By this time there were forty armed men in the mob and more than three hundred people were standing around watching. Many of them were fighting drunk and every few minutes a gun would go off somewhere in the darkness. The wildest stories flew about. Arm Cary now was supposed to have murdered the old judge. This explained why he had buried him secretly in the Negro graveyard.

Doc Thacker, the druggist, tried to disperse the crowd at the jail but without success. Everyone cheered him and laughed at him, but no one would listen. Before he said ten words a boy had him by the coat tails and was pulling him from the horse block he was using for a platform.

The mob roared for action and streamed away up the street to the station and over the tracks to Bucktown again. Here there was a halt at the garage, where Lem Robbins and three others beat in the doors with axes. They shoved out all of the cars in the shop except Arm Cary's Buick, and set fire to the building.

The fire department came, but as fast as a hose was laid to fight the blaze, someone chopped it in two. The drunker ones in the crowd now began looking for Negroes and blazed away at everything that looked like one.

When the fire began to light up that whole end of town, Lem Robbins, long hair flying, face streaked with soot and sweat, and his eyes staring crazily around, held up his hands, and they all started up Mill Street toward the Negro cemetery.

Major Tipton had known that something was going to happen so he had taken Arm Cary through the alley behind the courthouse and over to the home of Sinclair Tuck, president of the Farmers and Merchants Bank. Tipton explained and showed Colonel Tuck the newspaper article. The colonel, like all the other decent people of Ruffinton, had no sympathy for a lynching mob no matter what a Negro had done.

He made sure none of the servants saw Cary and put him inside the house in an unused butler's room. He and Major Tipton then went into the library to take a drink, but by now there was so much shouting down the street and so many automobiles rushing around that Tipton decided to go into town. Colonel Tuck walked back to talk to the mulatto.

Arm Cary was crying and praying. He was lying flat on the cot, fingers gripping the covers. Colonel Tuck went and fetched him a drink with his own hands.

Major Tipton walked down toward the station, noticing the red light in the sky from the burning garage. The streets in the lower end of town were blocked with cars. By the time the major reached the fire, Lem Robbins had led the crowd off toward the cemetery.

Mount Moriah was a small cemetery but one of the oldest in Ruffinton. It was on the hill overlooking the river and it had been the Negro burying ground of the Ruffin place before the town grew up around the lumber mills. In most respects it was as well kept and as pretty as a white cemetery although not all of the graves were marked. Some of the markers were of wood and on some of the graves were mounted old clocks and desk calendars in the belief that on judgment day the dead might want to know the time. A wall surrounded the place and there was a very fine grove of old maples there.

But all that meant nothing to the mob. More than a hundred men and boys swept through the iron gates and began to rage around like loose lunatics. Someone started a big fire to light up things.

They fed the fire with fence palings from a fraternity plot and with rambler roses which they stripped from the walls. One gang pulled down a granite pillar and used it to batter chunks from the old wall. Wooden grave markers were used on the fire.

Major Tipton wanted to go away, but found that he could not. The wild scene hypnotized him. He stood in the crowd on the knoll outside the graveyard. People out there were cursing and crying. The fire grew larger and lighted up the woods beyond the wall. The wall now threw a wide strip of shadow around the blazing burying ground.

Lem Robbins tended the fire, his face glistening red in the glare. People screamed at each other all over the grave mounds as the fire roared and crackled and shot showers of sparks higher than a tall building. Some boys began to cut down the maple trees and a big gang dragged one of the trees all the way across the grave mounds to the fire, sweeping a path through the better part of the place. A drunken man knocked the head from a granite angel with a spade and it rolled out into the road.

It was nearly midnight when someone found the cube of marble which had marked the grave of old Judge King. A big man in overalls brought it over to the fire and showed it to Lem Robbins.

'Git the corpse,' Lem Robbins commanded.

But too many people were trampling around. The man who found the stone could not locate the spot where it had rested. They dug two deep trenches — dug down until they struck water, but they found no new graves — dug until all the whiskey wore off and neither Lem nor anybody else could keep the crowd from melting away. As the fire died into a great mound of orange-colored coals, some people became frightened and ran all the way home from the screaming hell they had created.

When Major Tipton got back to the Tuck house, he found the colonel asleep in his chair and more than half drunk. Together they went down the hall to the servant's room where they had left Arm Cary. The mulatto still was lying on the cot, his head on his arms. He cringed when they touched him, flung out his arms wildly.

'Nobody's here to hurt you, Arm,' Major Tipton said, 'Get up. We got to get you away from here.'

They never did find Judge King's body. Later when the town council had the cemetery restored there was another attempt to find the corpse, but no one ever found it. Judge King still is buried in that Negro cemetery.

On the day after the riot, Ruffinton was a very sober town and there was so much horror over the desecration of the graveyard that folks forgot for a time the thing that caused it all. For more than two weeks there was a crowd of Negroes wailing in the wreckage of Mount Moriah.

The cube of marble which had marked Judge King's grave did not turn up again for more than a month. Major Tipton used to show it to people when he told them how the hoodlums of Ruffinton lynched a Negro cemetery.

He would take them down the street and across to the county courthouse which sat like a Greek temple in the little park on Princess Street. There, against the main door of the courthouse was the lump of Georgia marble. It was about a foot square and a foot high and some pieces had been chipped from it for souvenirs.

Major Tipton would poke at the stone with his cane and then turn it over with his foot and point to the side which had been stained from contact with the ground.

On this side, rudely cut into the surface with a cold chisel, were two words: 'My Father.'

'It's a good thing that crazy coon left town,' Major Tipton would say, 'but I'll have to give him credit for one thing. He paid me and everybody else every cent that he owed — every cent.'

HER OWN SWEET SIMPLICITY[1]

By MARTHA FOLEY

(From *Pictorial Review*)

HAIL to thee, blithe spirit, hail to thee, blithe spirit, hail to thee, blithe spirit. Bird thou never wert.

Emily rocked back and forth over the volume of Shelley open to the 'Ode to a Skylark.'

Fifty cents, fifty cents, fifty cents. Perhaps her father would give her twenty-five cents today if she learned half. Bird thou never wert that from heaven or near it. She'd say that part three times and then go back to the first. If she said each line three times and went back three times over all she had done so far, she was bound to remember it. That from heaven or near it. But she owed that twenty-five cents already to her cousin Louise. For that beaded bag she didn't want. Just because her cousin liked to do beadwork. Her cousin had said don't you like this bag, isn't it pretty? And she, of course, had said yes. And her cousin said would you like one just like it? I'll make you one if you want. And she had said, oh, would you! And her cousin said I'll be glad to. When I go downtown today I'll buy the beads and the silk. They'll cost you only twenty-five cents and you couldn't buy a bag like this in a store for less than a dollar. But she didn't want the bag twenty-five cents worth. She could hardly say no, she didn't want to pay for the beads after saying that she would like a bag. Besides her cousin was grown up, was eight years older than she. If Louise had been the same age, it would have been easy to get out of it. Now she would have to earn all the fifty cents right away to have any for herself.

Unpremeditated art. Unpremeditated art. That was like a criminal when he didn't mean to do what he did. The skylark didn't intend any such art. Shelley intended this poem, though. But she must memorize and not stop and think about Shelley and the poem. If she didn't hurry up, she would never get that fifty cents today. She did wish, though, she didn't have to learn poetry for a living.

[1] Copyright, 1935, by The Pictorial Review Company, Inc.

Other little girls' fathers gave them money and never asked them to
learn or do anything for it.

Higher still and higher into the blue deep, thou soarest.

'Emily! come here!'

Her father was back from downtown.

Emily went into the dining-room where Father was waiting for
her. On the shiny dark table beside the bowl of flowers on the strip
of white embroidery was a big paper bag. The bag was open, and
half in, half out of the bag was a small white straw hat. Separate
from the hat but near it was a tiny wreath of flowers, white cotton
lilies-of-the-valley. Emily's mother stood looking at the array. Her
lips were set tight. Emily knew when her mother's lips were set that
way that she was going to get mad and then cry.

'But you can't make a fool out of the child by having her wear
that!'

Emily felt horrible. This, this was supposed to be her new hat.

'I'm not making a fool out of her. I'm keeping her sweet and
simple as a child should be. It is you who would make a fool out of
her, loading her head down with big bunches of silk and straw.'

'Andrew, can't you understand? She can't wear a hat like this.
It's a pauper's hat.'

'That's what I'm trying to prove. I paid ten cents for the hat and
ten cents for the wreath. Together they make a simple, attractive
hat. No need to go and spend a lot of money on a lot of nonsense.
Emily's own sweet simplicity should be her only adornment.'

Her father wanted her to wear a five-and-ten-cent-store hat! A
five-and-ten-cent-store hat! Oh, oh, how could she ever go to school
or church in a hat like that? Oh, oh. Tears came.

'I don't want that hat, Papa.'

'Because your mother's been putting a lot of nonsense in your
head. What's the matter with that hat?'

'But, please, I can't wear a five-and-ten-cent-store hat!'

'It doesn't matter what it costs. Price is no way to mark good
taste. Put it on and see how it looks.'

Emily lifted the hat to her head as though it were something
burning hot.

'Look at me.'

Emily raised her face. The bare little hat made scrawnier by the
thin wreath of cotton flowers sat high and slightly askew on her

head. Emily's eyes were streaming tears behind her gold-rimmed spectacles and one butter-yellow pigtail hung over a shoulder.

'There! You could go down to a big department store and pay five or ten dollars for one of your pink lace valentines and it wouldn't be as becoming. The minute I saw this hat I knew it would answer the purpose better. I want my daughter to learn that simplicity is good taste.'

'How can you, Andrew! Look at the poor little thing. Can't you see she not only looks simple but a simpleton with that thing on her head?'

Emily put the hat back on the table.

'Please, Papa, please, don't make me wear it. Please, I can't.'

'Because you have been listening to your mother.'

'The other girls will laugh at me.'

'Let them laugh. It shows they do not know any better. Emily, I want you to understand that you mustn't be a parrot, or an ape. You must think for yourself. Think for yourself. Think for yourself.'

Her father's blue eyes went bluer.

'What kind of a hat did you want?'

'I wanted a big pink hat with a big wide brim like this and lace around the edges and roses here.' Emily held her hand up to the side of her head.

'Why do you want a hat like that?'

'Because all the other girls have them.'

'Exactly! That is what I was telling you. You want something because everyone else has it. You want to be part of the mob, a parrot, someone who can't think for herself. By God, I'm going to see that you do think for yourself!'

'But it's a homely hat.'

'Because it hasn't got lace and roses?'

Emily's father took the hat in his hand.

'Now look at this hat and I'll show you why it's a good hat.'

'I can't see. My glasses are all wet.'

'Here's a handkerchief. Wipe your glasses and wipe your eyes and stop trying to grow up into being a fool while I show you this hat.'

Emily wiped her glasses very slowly. She didn't want to look at that terrible hat again. She knew, too, that when her father started explaining like this he went on and on and never stopped.

'Now you take this hat. It cost only ten cents but what has that got to do with it? It's a perfectly good hat, made to wear on the head with a crown to fit the head and a brim to shade the eyes. It has good lines. The brim goes around in an honest way, as it should. It doesn't poke up in front or cock up on the side. The crown doesn't go shooting up in the air. A hat has better balance when it has a little adornment. A band of ribbon or a few flowers. This wreath keeps its place on the hat. It isn't too heavy so it doesn't cover up the hat and it hasn't a lot of gewgaws. It's simple. More things in life should be simple. Now take this room ...'

Emily suddenly transferred her attention from the hat to the room. The first thing she noticed was that her mother was no longer in the room. She must have slipped out while her father was talking. As for the dining-room itself, she was so used to it she hardly saw it. A dark mahogany table, straight-backed chairs, a sideboard with lace cover and silver coffee service, two pictures of vases of flowers, a picture of fruit and vegetables and another of a dead duck lying on a platter. Emily never liked those pictures much. She liked landscapes better, but then, she never thought much about the dining-room anyway.

'You take this dining-room,' her father said again, just as if you could take it under your arm and walk away with it! 'Eight pictures on the wall. One good picture is enough. One good picture. The Japanese have the right idea. They put one picture up in a room and when they want to see another picture, they put that up and take the first one down.'

How did the Japanese put up the nails to hang their pictures on, Emily wondered. The walls of Japanese houses were paper and nails would go right through. Paper would never hold up a nail or wire or a picture. They would all fall down. Like men in the funny papers who always fell down every time they hung up a picture.

'No carpet,' her father was saying. 'No rugs in the house except where you step out of bed. A few chairs and a table. One or two vases for flowers, not all these silly, idiotic gimcracks. That's all and you have a room that is furnished in perfectly good taste.'

Emily wished her father would get through educating her. Yesterday and today he had been educating her all the time. If only he would find a big book he was interested in, he wouldn't be so interested in educating her.

Her father stopped talking for a minute. Emily seized upon the lull.

'Please, Papa, I'm learning "Ode to a Skylark." I want to go back to it.'

'All right. Run along. First, though, have you done your home work?'

'Yes.'

'Perhaps I had better go over it with you.'

'It's all done. The arithmetic and everything.'

'I had better go over it with you anyway. Later.'

Emily was dismayed. It was no use. She had done her home work as soon as she reached home from school, but her father wanted to do it anyway. She might as well have waited and done it with him. Now it was just like having to do it twice, she thought, as she took up her red 'Golden Treasury' from which she was learning the Ode.

No wonder her relatives on her mother's side felt sorry for her. Like her Great-Aunt Kate, her mother's aunt, the old lady whose face was so lined it made Emily think of a jigsaw puzzle.

'You'd think Andrew had enough of studying, wouldn't you?' Emily had heard her great-aunt say one day. 'How many years was it he took going to college?' She had borne down heavily on the word College as if it were a most foolish place.

'Eight. The same as every physician. They all have to go to college four years and then four to medical school.' Emily's mother didn't seem to like her aunt's question.

'Eight years in college. And how many years afterward at the hospital? Two. Then there was his special studies. And now you'd think he'd never been to school the way he goes over all her lessons with that child. I don't want to hurt your feelings, Millicent, but it seems to me you should make your husband get down to some-thing serious. Like getting more patients instead of going to school all over again.'

Her mother had said sharply, 'Andrew is a very brilliant man.'

'But his father is still giving you money to run the house on, isn't he?'

Her mother nodded. 'I guess he can afford it.'

'Well, you would never know Andrew was a rich man's son from the way he wears his hair. You'd think he didn't have fifteen cents to pay the barber for a haircut.'

The listening Emily knew then that Kate had hurt her mother. And herself as well. For as long as she could remember, it seemed, her mother had been telling her father to have his hair cut or his suit pressed or to buy a new overcoat. Her father was tall and thin and his hair and mustache were white. His hair had turned white when he was a very young man and the family was always talking about how strange it was. He wore a soft black hat and, when he needed a haircut, the white hair showed thickly beneath it.

If she got to thinking about her father, though, and what her relatives said about him she'd never know what to do about that terrible hat. And what to do about it! What to do! She couldn't wear that hat to prove her father knew what was simple. She couldn't go up to every girl she saw and say, 'My father thinks my youth should be my only adornment.'

This was terrible. It was worse even than the time she had walked all the way to school in her gym suit and found she had forgotten to put her skirt on over her bloomers. She'd never felt so immodest as that time. Worse even than the time for punishment she had been sent to school wearing one pink hair ribbon and one blue because that time she could take off one ribbon as soon as she got around the corner from the house and pretend without saying it — she didn't want to lie — she had lost it. But she couldn't lose a hat very well.

Or why couldn't she? But there would have to be a reason. Like a tornado. Or an accident. She wished there were hawks in Boston. Then perhaps one would swoop down on her and take the hat right off her head, the way she had heard of them taking chickens and rabbits. She was afraid that even a hawk wouldn't want a hat. Oh, dear, if she could only reason with her father the way he reasoned with her mother! Then he wouldn't know whether he was going or coming. As her mother said she felt sometimes when he got through talking.

No, it wouldn't do. Her father was the only one in the family who could reason. Just think of going up to her father and saying, 'Now be reasonable...' She'd never know how to go on after that.

No, hawks would be better. But there weren't any. No kind of animal that would snatch at anything. Yes, there was, too! She had an idea. Of course, and it would be just like William Tell! She might be afraid but at least today she could stop thinking about that hat and go back to learning her poem. She found the place in her 'Golden Treasury' and she started once more to chant Shelley's lines.

The next morning she woke up feeling that something had happened and something more was going to happen. Of course, the hat! She must be careful not to let her mother think she was nervous about it.

When she was all ready to leave for school she asked, 'Where's my new hat? I want to wear it to school today.'

Her mother was surprised. 'That hat? I thought you didn't like it.'

'Well, I thought I'd wear it to school today so as I could get used to it. Since I have to wear it, anyway.'

'All right. And, Emily, in a few weeks I think I can get you a nicer one. As soon as your father's feelings won't be hurt if you don't wear this one. If any little girls say anything about it, you can tell them you are just wearing it temporarily. And, Emily, you know those nice little bead bags Louise makes? I thought perhaps that while you were wearing this hat you might like to carry one of those bead bags and so I am going to give Louise some money today to buy the beads and silk to make you one. Won't that be nice?'

The bead bag! She'd forgotten about it, thinking of the five-and-ten-cent-store hat. She'd forgotten she'd have to pay Louise out of Shelley. But now it was all right because her mother didn't want her to feel too badly about the hat.

'It will be awfully nice!' She hugged her mother, then remembered something. 'And can I have an apple to take to school today?'

'Of course.'

Swinging her green baize school bag in which the apple made a round bulge and wearing the little white hat perched high on her head from which hung two long yellow braids which almost matched in their shininess the gold rims of her spectacles, Emily set off for school.

'Please, dear God, give me courage. Please, dear God,' she whispered as she hurried along.

As she came to the street where the stable was she slowed down. The horse might not be out in the field this morning. Every morning she had walked on the opposite side of the street from the field because she had been so afraid of that horse and the way he snapped at everybody. She never thought that some day she would be afraid he wouldn't be in the field. But suppose she did have to go right into school wearing this awful hat! That would be much worse than the horse.

The horse was there. She turned both ways before she went close to the fence. There were some people, but they were a long way off. She didn't think they could tell what she was doing.

She put her school bag down on the ground. From it she took out the apple. It looked awfully good. If she took one bite herself perhaps the horse wouldn't notice? No, she'd better use the whole apple. Next she took from under her chin the elastic which kept her hat on and set her hat as lightly as she could on top of her head. Suppose he bit her head? Please, dear God, don't let him do that. Don't let him hurt me. Only the hat!

Standing as close to the fence as she could, she put the apple on top of her hat. It was hard to balance and she had to smash in the crown a little to make a resting place for it. Now if the horse didn't come to get the apple, the hat would look worse than ever! But it couldn't be helped. Just as William Tell couldn't help it if he had missed.

She had better say the Lord's Prayer. So standing carefully so as not to spill the apple off her hat, Emily prayed in a whisper. When she was finished, she called, 'Here, horsey! Here, horsey!' and waited trembling.

At first the animal didn't pay any attention. She called louder and he came slowly over to the fence. 'Oh, dear God, don't let him hurt me, only my hat,' she prayed again.

The horse came closer. He seemed to be studying her, although Emily couldn't see very well because she had to bend her head slightly to keep the apple in place on her hat and because, too, her eyeglasses had become all misty.

'Here, horsey! Here's a nice apple.'

The horse sniffed. He was so close to her now she could see his partly open mouth and white saliva slobbering from it. Was he or wasn't he ever going to take that apple? Just as she thought he was going to turn away, he opened his mouth wide suddenly and bit at the apple. And when he bit into the apple his teeth went into the flimsy crown of the hat. Just as she had hoped! The hat fell off as he galloped away into the field munching the apple. Emily picked up the hat, dusty and slightly moist from the horse's slobbering. It was spoiled, completely spoiled. Well, not quite. She thought he would make a bigger hole. She would have to put her hand through to make it larger. But anyway, he had started the hole. She wouldn't have to lie about it. And anyone could see the hat could never be worn again.

'Thank you, dear God,' she said.

There was great excitement in Emily's class at school. A horse had pulled her hat off! Right off her head! A wild horse. My, but that was terribly dangerous! He might have pulled her head off, too. Wasn't she awfully scared?

Her hat was passed around among all the girls. No one noticed what a dreadful hat it had been. All they thought of was the hole in it. Emily was very proud and felt just like a heroine. Especially when, after the bell rang and the pupils were all seated at their desks, one of the girls raised her hand and said, 'Please, Miss Lavey, did you hear about Emily's hat?' And the teacher said, 'What about it?' And the girl almost shouted, 'A horse tried to eat it!' Then Emily had to stand up and tell all about it and Miss Lavey was very worried and said she would report the man who owned the horse to the police for keeping such a dangerous animal in a public place and that she would write a note to Emily's mother saying she was doing that so she wouldn't be frightened. And, anyway, that the man who owned the horse should be made to pay for a new hat for Emily.

Emily herself was so excited she could hardly study her lessons. When she reached home she rushed right to her mother.

'My hat! My new hat! I can't wear it any more...'

'Oh, dear, it's just as I thought! Did anyone say anything about it?'

'No, no, a horse ate it — I mean, he bit it.'

'A horse!'

'Yes, and I have a note from Miss Lavey telling you not to worry about it.'

Again Emily told the story of the horse and her hat. She made no mention of the apple and how she lured the horse to her hat. Instead, as she told the story, it was of a wild horse that had waylaid an innocent little girl on her way to school and pulled her hat from her head.

'No wonder the horse attacked that hat,' her mother told her father. But her father didn't seem interested. Emily saw with relief that he was turning the pages at the beginning of what seemed a new — and very thick — book. He didn't seem even to worry about how the horse might have hurt her. All he said was, 'And the school authorities are going to see that this animal is no longer a menace to passing children?' Not a word about another hat of the same kind from the five-and-ten-cent store!

And Emily was so glad she didn't even have to hesitate to ask him about getting paid for only half a poem. Just when he was starting to read again she asked, 'Please, Papa, I have learned half of the stanzas in the "Ode to a Skylark" so could I have a quarter now and the rest of the fifty cents when I learn the other half?'

Her father hardly looked up from his book. 'You are sure you know that half thoroughly? Here...' and he gave her a quarter and never asked her to recite the stanzas.

No terrible hat to wear and now she could buy a piece of the double layer chocolate walnut cake in the school lunchroom to-morrow! O hail to thee....

ENEMY COUNTRY[1]

By WALTER GILKYSON

(From *Scribner's Magazine*)

'THE grandeur that is Rome and glory that will be,' Giulio
Manisetti softly repeated to himself, keeping time to the
measure with swinging body and staccato footsteps that expressed
his immense exhilaration. It had been an inspiring evening, the
end of a miraculous five days in New York, and the enthusiasm
of his new-found friends, the Italians assembled at the house of
Cavaliere Aldobrandini in East Forty-Eighth Street, where he had
spent the last three hours, carried him forward through the slow
sauntering crowd on Fifth Avenue in a glowing mist of anticipation
and excitement. At moments, while waiting for the cross-town
traffic, he looked upward, vaguely conscious of the summer wind
that cooled his face. If the tall pale splendor of this city shone in
the sky like the reflection of a crown of empire there was nevertheless no racial depth below the bright arrogance of material conquest,
and no undertone of legend to chant its undying assurance of the
future. Rome the Immortal. Italian eloquence, at long last to be
translated into mighty deeds. Remembering the sublime moment
when, just before his departure, he had stood in the presence of
Mussolini, his dark young face quivered with exaltation. To him,
an engineer of twenty-eight, had been given the task of approving
the purchase of ships that would carry Italian troops to Abyssinia.
The work was done, and now he was free to return to Italy and take
part in the conflict himself.

The Commendatore Manisetti, Podestà of Triano and his father,
had cabled him yesterday in English, as if scorning to conceal his
message, an expression of pleasure at the success of his son, and
a declaration of austere pride in Italian imperial destiny. The
antique concision of his words rang with the single sonorous note
of a carving in stone, reverberating in Giulio's mind above the
clamor of traffic and mutter of voices that marked the huge purpose-

less confusion of the city. His father had spoken of 'my son Alessandro' who had built a city in a desert, dug gold from the bowels of the earth, and pastured flocks upon plains made fertile by his own hands. The words were a paraphrase from Alessandro's letters; he had taken the way of empire nearly ten years ago. In the cable was a suggestion that Giulio visit his brother, if only for a day, and see with his own eyes the children begotten by Alessandro, the city he had founded, and the noble woman of the West who was his wife.

That Giulio intended to do. He would leave on the *Skymaster* — Balbo's magnificent flight to Chicago interrupted his thought — at eleven-forty-five tonight. Alessandro had told them in his letters that the city of Manisetti lay two hundred miles northwest of Albuquerque in the State of New Mexico, and the *Skymaster* reached Albuquerque at one-four P.M. By this time tomorrow night he would be in Alessandro's house, face to face with his brother and hearing again his buoyant confident voice which had always seemed, although not heard for nearly ten years, like a prelude to the opera of Italian glory. Alessandro had been before them, but that was like him, the older one, a torrent of energy pouring itself out in victory over a desolate land. There was nothing that he could not do. There was nothing that any Italian could not do. Time had touched them at one of the apocalyptic moments of history.

He sent a telegram from the office in the Plaza Hotel, just the words, 'I am flying tonight across a continent to greet you,' and then went upstairs and packed his bag. Coming down in the elevator, he stood at the back so as not to be brushed by anyone, feeling a strong desire to preserve his integrity and avoid contact with these large, casual, easy-moving people. He knew he was small, and the propinquity of others made him more reserved and prouder than usual, and yet quite ready to assert himself. One of the men brushed against him, a fat red-faced fellow in a linen dinner coat, and Giulio put out his hand with a murmur and frowned so severely that the man started back in surprise.

After paying his bill, he told the room clerk he would return within four or five days.

'I am going to Albuquerque on the *Skymaster*,' he said in his swift run-together English, 'and thence to the city in New Mexico founded by my brother, and bearing his name.'

'Uh hum,' said the clerk. 'Save you a room Mr. Manisetti four or five days.' He looked up briskly, an irritating impersonal politeness in his eyes.

'The city of Manisetti was founded by my brother.' Giulio repeated with soft insistence. 'My brother Alessandro is one of America's pioneers.'

'Tell you a lot about Indians and cowboys then,' the clerk answered indulgently, as if he were talking to a child. 'The West, they say, is a very entertaining place.'

'Your empire,' Giulio corrected. He waited for the man to understand. He was too dull, too lacking in patriotism and spiritual vigor. 'We Italians are about to win our own West in Abyssinia,' he announced.

'What!' The clerk bent forward as if to examine him closely. 'Oh.' The single toneless ejaculation carried a weight of meaning. 'Pleasant journey and see you in four or five days, Mr. Manisetti,' he said.

Giulio followed the boy to the door, overcome with rage at the insolence of the clerk, which was all the greater for being unconscious and not directed toward him as an individual. The man simply ignored the destiny of race, of all races including his own; it was Anglo-Saxon conceit, the gorged lazy surfeit of indolent men who have swallowed the earth. Giulio got into the taxi and pulled his Panama hat down over his eyes, disgusted at the mere thought of such vast disorder.

As they approached the flying-field at Newark, his self-confidence returned with a sudden visualization of Italian feats in the air, and his own sense of comfortable familiarity with planes. This indeed might be the flying-field at Rome, where order and discipline reigned and morale was upheld by *esprit de corps*. He inspected the ship with the eyes of an engineer, restraining himself from speaking to the pilot, who no doubt had the taciturn disposition toward strangers of one who experienced constant peril. There were five passengers going out, but in the shifting light and darkness of the field they were only figures enveloped in sudden blasts of noise from the motors, receding and reappearing, awaiting the command to embark on the ship. He caught sight of a young girl looking at him with a smile of curiosity that might only be the light moving suddenly across her face. She stood beside a tall man in an overcoat and wide felt hat who had the appearance and the air that Giulio associated with the West. They might know Alessandro, or have heard of his city, or at least be familiar with the State of New Mexico.

When the girl looked at him again, he walked over to her, assuming the privilege of a stranger to her country.

'May you by any chance come from the West?' he inquired, addressing them both. 'I am on mission from my Government in Italy, and I take this opportunity of flying across your continent to visit my brother.'

'We're from Texas,' said the man briefly. 'Amarillo.'

'Which means yellow in Spanish,' Giulio offered with a quick friendly smile.

'That's one on you, Father.'

The girl was very much amused. She had a firm serene disposition, Giulio decided, with the dark eyebrows and startling gray eyes of her father.

'My brother lives in New Mexico,' he explained. 'Is the State of New Mexico near Amarillo?'

'Not so far,' said the man.

'His name is Manisetti and the town where he lives is called by his name.'

He waited, but there was no reply.

'You speak beautiful English,' said the girl, breaking an uncomfortable silence. By her look she gave Giulio to understand that she was interested in him.

'My father, the Podestà of Triano, speaks English as fluently as he does Italian, and it has been a requirement of our early education.' He was among friends again, who would not misunderstand him; the young American girl had touched him with her grave and intelligent sympathy. His enthusiasm for his brother and the destiny of the Italian race, forever ready to burst from his lips, was irrepressible now, and it hurt him to hold it back. 'My brother has turned the wilderness into a city,' he said, 'as so many Italians have done all over the world. We are an expanding race.' The words were magical and potent, spreading the seed of empire before his eyes. 'Like your ancestors of a century ago we are overflowing our boundaries and carrying the light of civilization to the dark places of the earth.'

Eager-faced, trembling with excitement, he waited for the spark of his words to catch fire. But the tall man stood rooted in silence; he chewed on his cigar and looked at Giulio with narrow eyes.

'Most of the men from Texas that settled in New Mexico couldn't read,' he said in a slow, drawling voice. 'They didn't overflow in any way that I ever heard of, and generally they went into the country one by one. I wouldn't say there was even the slightest resemblance between them and the Italians, and I'm sure they wouldn't have thought so if anybody had ever said it. That was a long time ago, son, and best forgotten because the world has moved on since, and nobody down where we live has got any sympathy with the Italian campaign, if they know about it, which most of them don't.'

'We think it's cruel and outrageous,' said the girl, 'although I don't like to say so to Italians because it hurts their feelings.' Her voice was deep and concerned, and she put out her hand as if to shield Giulio from a blow. 'It's a shame to say that to you when you're all alone in a foreign country and going to see your brother, but you're so — eloquent about it that we just have to say something.'

Giulio bowed. 'A frank expression of opinion is better than concealed hostility,' he said. He felt stronger and more able to hide his anger after he uttered that phrase. Holding himself erect, he nodded sharply, then turned on his heel and walked away with a military step.

It was the loose-jointed cynicism of the Yankee who sprawled across a continent and sneered at Europe. The girl reeked of Victor Emmanuel sentiment; she was something out of *I Promessi Sposi*. Thank God, Italian women had passed beyond that and become a glorious crucible for the creation of armies. He smiled ecstatically, letting the iron words of Rome ring in his ears. It didn't matter, not even the opinion of England mattered, to say nothing of two insignificant persons in a country that was dying of peace.

He took his seat in the ship, resolved to have no further words with the passengers, and gave his attention to the take-off, which was managed in a workmanlike fashion. After the landing near Philadelphia, he fell asleep, and awoke as the plane was descending at Pittsburgh. It was two-eighteen, and they had flown four hundred and fifty miles, about the distance between Rome and Vienna. The comparison troubled him and he couldn't stop thinking about

it, although he tried again and again to go to sleep as the plane
continued across the State of Ohio. The flight was longer now than
any he had ever made, and it seemed to stretch out before him
level as night and in a dimension so meaningless that it eluded his
imagination. This ship would fly three thousand miles from coast
to coast above the United States. If a man marched three thousand
miles from Rome he would come to British South Africa, or Iceland,
or Persia, or — halfway across the Atlantic Ocean. The distance
worried him like a problem in physics; he couldn't translate it into
known terms except by assuming that most of America was empty
space. Otherwise such a distance became impossible; it included
his entire world with half of an ocean thrown in. That could not
be. The two terms were incommensurable.

But nevertheless the distance lay before him menacing and repulsive, a huge formless denial that Rome was the center of the
world. He sighed unhappily, feeling lonely and missing the assurance of his friends in this dark duration of unending alien air. It
was better to think of Time, and the Immortality of Rome, and
repeat to himself the warm life-giving phrases that prefigured the
ultimate destiny of his race.

The day began to break as they neared Columbus, and in another
two hours he saw the Mississippi. As the morning wore on, the
land at its farthest reaches took on the color of air, so that sky and
earth seemed to meet in shining distance. His fear of the last few
hours looked thin and phantasmal in the presence of so much light
that flowed over the land with a radiant energy that was benignant,
as if the impersonal splendor of the horizon streamed upward from
the slow turning of the earth. He had seen that once in the desert,
but never before in a fertile populated country, where oil derricks
dotted the landscape and cattle spread like a loose red carpet over
the fields. The ship was late; it was half past twelve, and they were
due in Amarillo at eleven-forty-eight. He watched his acquaintances
of the night before climb down from the side of the ship. It had
been impossible not to return their morning salutation, and now, as
the girl looked up at him, he pulled off his hat and smiled.

In another hour the land below him began to change, piling up
in flat hills with burnt naked sides that grew taller and sharper
every moment. This was Alessandro's country; they were over a
waste of ashy brightness and tortured cliffs. Alessandro — what

courage and what stability of mind he must possess! Giulio drank in
the lunatic beauty of the landscape, half dazed and uncertain of
himself. The dazzling light and the uncouth stony shapes bred a
sort of madness in his brain that turned him into the likeness of
what he saw, and armed him with an illusion of terrible strength
that was veined with cruelty and fear. It lurked silently in the
formidable space where words died stillborn and the clamor of
armies melted away. Here there was nothing but loneliness for
support; loneliness and the awful face of the land.

He drew back from the window, actually frightened by the strange
color of his thoughts.

The city of Albuquerque was like the cities he hoped they would
some day establish in the new province of Abyssinia; modern,
genial, noisy, businesslike, and very sane. When he went to the
Indian Detour office at three o'clock to ask about getting to Manisetti he found that the man in charge knew just where it was.

'They have a post-office there,' he said, 'but I've never seen the
town and I don't think it's very big. You're visiting on a ranch?'

'My brother. My name is Manisetti.'

'Oh, really? Then we don't have to bother about hotels. Now
I would suggest' — he bent over the map — 'that you go up on
Highway 44 to San Isidro, and then on 4 to Jemez Springs where
I'd spend the night.'

'Is it impossible——' Giulio began, but the man interrupted him
with a nod.

'We'd like you to see the country,' he said impressively, 'and
besides I can't send you off until late this afternoon.'

'Very well.' The man wanted him to see the country — *we'd*
like you to see the country. 'I will be ready whenever you are,' he
said.

It was half past four and extremely hot when they started. Giulio
sat on the back seat of the car which the driver had indicated with
a silent gesture, not exactly impolite, but firm, as if showing what
was expected.

After a minute or two Giulio asked him whether he'd ever been
to Manisetti.

'Yes,' he said, without turning around.

'Is it large?'

'No.'

'But you are acquainted with my brother?'

'Who?'

'Alessandro Manisetti.'

'No.'

That was discouraging. Giulio hoped Alessandro had not grown so taciturn in the West, and then remembered the letters.

He saw his first Indian village just as the sun was setting. It looked like a corrugated sand dune on the bank of a dry river. And vacant, although a bridge led over to it from the road. He wanted to ask the driver some questions, but hesitated, and while he was looking the village disappeared between sunlit yellow rocks and the empty bed of the river.

So the land itself seemed to disappear as they went on, becoming gray and insubstantial within the purple ring of the horizon. There were no houses and no people and none of the animals he had expected to see, although there was evidence of them in the countless bodies of small beasts that had been killed by cars. They must live in the blue dusty bushes close to the ground, like everything else in this region of desolation where men seemed lonely growths of the soil, without pride of speech or the noble contagion of spirit that came from association with their kind. He shivered slightly, then coughed and blew his nose. There was dust everywhere and a thin fine smell that kept him from breathing with his accustomed freedom.

On the porch of the hotel in Jemez Springs, after an excellent dinner, he became himself again. The sound of water and the cool presence of trees restored his self-confidence. It was a tender beautiful night, and the guests of the hotel, although apparently mixed in race, were agreeable. He rose as Mrs. Halin, the proprietor, approached and sat down beside him, observing the silence that fell on the little group who were seated nearby.

'I wanted to ask you if you are related to Alessandro Manisetti,' she said.

'My brother,' Giulio answered, sitting down. No more than that in this sardonic country — just the words 'my brother.'

'But you don't live in America,' she suggested, a puzzled inquiring solicitude in her gentle voice. She was a motherly woman with a great deal of feeling, and he liked her.

'I arrived in New York from Italy six days ago,' he answered.

'They're getting excited over there,' she said with a sigh. 'It's a great pity too, because I always think of Italy as the home of art. Your brother ——' She paused. 'I don't like to think of all those nice young Italians going down into Africa.'

'Madam, we must fulfill our destiny,' Giulio said. There was absolute silence now on the porch. 'It may seem to you like an act of aggression on the part of a stronger race, but I assure you the death of a few Ethiopians will soon be forgotten, whereas the spirit of Rome will blossom perennially in that benighted country.'

The silence continued. Giulio rocked to and fro in his chair, smiling to himself and thinking of what he would say next. This was not egotism, it was a vision of mystic adventure offered with all his heart to an elderly home-loving people.

'They'll kill every one of you,' said Mrs. Halin emphatically, 'and those they don't kill are going to die or go crazy in the desert. I think it's terrible, because I like Italians, and Italy is the home of art, and they've no business to send such nice young men down into a country like Africa.' She rose heavily and stood in front of him, then put her hand up to her cheek and sighed. 'My grandfather was a settler and I know what it costs and what it takes, and the less said about such things the better, that's my motto.' She moved away, her steps creaking on the porch, and Giulio heard the screen door slam behind her.

Nobody spoke to him, and in a moment he went up to his room where he undressed and lay down on the bed. There was no understanding this country or its people; they were hostile even in friendliness.

But what she had *not* said about Alessandro returned again and again to keep him awake.

All the next afternoon, as he passed the infrequent little towns that had taken refuge from the encroachment of the desert, Giulio considered his brother with alternating doubt and hope, at moments asking himself whether Alessandro could have suffered an enchantment from too long looking at this country of illusion, where cities rose upon the horizon and disappeared into the shadow of the rock, and light flung the colors of fertility over sterile valleys and infused the wind-shaped creatures of sand and stone with grotesque life. But Alessandro's letters could not lie; they were even more true than this awful reality of the land which denied every syllable he had written and seemed to extinguish the man himself. Alessandro's words lived a spiritual life that was independent of arid physical fact; they created a city and fertile fields that he would see soon, very soon — he closed his eyes — in spite of these unworthy cowardly doubts that interrupted the beating of his heart.

Even when houses did appear, as that gray rickety house far off on the left-hand side of the road, they were marked by desolation. The house overlooked the west and the long low rays of the sun with an air of feeble glamor, as if it had once been an out-post of discovery that was now forgotten. There were tall pointed ovens of earth behind it, and a scarlet gasoline pump stood in front of the door. An Indian with a red blanket over his shoulder crossed the road to the opposite field where a solitary white horse nosed in the bushes. Two children ran down the steps of the house as the car stopped to get gas, and Giulio, stretching his legs, looked at the children and then at the ovens of earth which he saw were some kind of houses.

'An Indian village?' he asked the chauffeur, feeling in his pocket for some coins for the children.

'Manisetti,' the chauffeur said.

Giulio got out slowly. He kept his back to the house while he paid the man. As he approached the steps with his bag, he didn't look up nor speak to the children who were whispering behind him. It would be enough, enough, he repeated firmly to himself, if he found his brother Alessandro alive and well inside that house.

The room he entered was a store, with a partition of post-office boxes that ran halfway to the ceiling. A shadow moved behind the partition and Giulio waited with a stiff smile, knowing he wouldn't even recognize Alessandro if he saw him.

It was a woman who looked out at him through the barred window of the post-office. Her loose red face widened with a genial appreciation of something that Giulio felt must relate to his personal appearance, and he blushed. The woman's warm brown eyes grew moist.

'You're Giulio,' she said. 'Well, to think of it! I'm Irma.' She came out from behind the partition, a voluptuous slatternly creature with yellow hair. 'I declare I ought to kiss my brother!' she exclaimed, moving up on him with eager arms that seemed disgustingly bare and well shaped. He submitted, freezing with anguish, enveloped in soft heavily scented flesh.

'How do you do,' he gulped, touching her cheek with his lips.

'Children, this is your Uncle Giulio come all the way from Italy to see your papa. This is Alec and Frieda, Giulio; they're dirty now, but inside they're sweet and loving like their mama.' She pushed them forward proudly and then stood back to watch.

Giulio kissed the children. 'Where's Alessandro?' he asked.

'Oh now, don't ask me that when you've just got into the house! You come to see us all, I hope!' Her coquettish smile and the bending, swaying motion of her hips as she approached made him retreat involuntarily.

'Alessandro,' he said, but her rich husky voice drowned him out.

'Now, dearie, you just come along and I'll show you where you sleep.'

'Alessandro,' he gasped. That terrible woman might have done anything to his brother.

'I declare I don't know,' she said a little crossly, 'but I reckon he's at his mine as usual. Don't let that worry you because he'll be along soon to get something to eat. That's about all your brother does around here, but he talks so lovely and acts so sweet in the house that I have to keep him on. I declare I don't know which one of us is crazy, but I guess it's me.' She laughed delightedly and her moist brown eyes seemed to overflow. 'That's the Wurtzel in me,' she said. 'We Wurtzels was born kind-hearted.'

Before he could speak, two Indians entered the store, filling it with a sharp saffron smell, and his sister-in-law went behind the counter to wait on them with a seductive readiness that became indecent as she began to talk to them in their barbarous language. Giulio walked to the door and looked out. His niece came up behind him on bare feet and felt for his hand. Her wide dirty toothless face grinned up at him ecstatically. She had Alessandro's eyes.

He wanted to sit down on the doorstep and weep.

A car came along the road, then stopped in front of the house and blew for gas. It was a big car full of nice-looking people who regarded him with friendly reserve. The driver pointed out the collection of huts near the house. 'It isn't a village; the Navajos come here and live while they're trading,' he said. Then the horn blew again and a man came running out from one of the huts and undid the gasoline hose. While he was filling the tank, he glanced at Giulio and then spoke to him.

His long reptilian head and pointed ears and his big clumsy willing body looked like Middle Europe, but his speech had an American accent. The two Indians pushed out beside Giulio, separating him from his niece, and he felt a soft arm laid across his shoulder and a warm breath on his cheek. Irma stood beside him, watching the car move away.

'Cousin Oscar,' she called, 'come up here and meet Brother Giulio.'

Giulio detached himself and advanced to meet Oscar, who held out an immense hand in silence and blinked at him with violet eyes that looked girlish behind his downy yellow lashes. 'It is a pleasure,' Giulio said, drawing himself up straight and shaking hands. However appalling these visitations might be, he was prepared to meet them unflinchingly.

'Cousin Oscar helps out here,' said Irma with a warm vagueness. 'God knows I got to have a man around with your brother away all the time like he is. We couldn't spare Oscar, no indeed we couldn't.' Her rich husky voice sank to a sigh, ruffling the hair on Giulio's neck; it struck Oscar with dumb embarrassment and he looked down.

'Irma,' said Giulio. He had made his decision. 'Where is Alessandro's mine?'

'It's in Chaco Canyon somewhere, about fifty miles. I ain't never seen it myself and I don't want to, because I know it's just a hole in the ground.'

'Can you drive a car to it?'

'There ain't no road beyond Pueblo Bonito, which is thirty miles down there.' She put her hand on Giulio's shoulder and turned him to the south. 'From Pueblo Bonito you ride a horse or walk, and Alessandro walks, all the way.'

'There are horses, then, in Pueblo Bonito?'

'For them as can pay for them, yes,' she said shortly, and then began drumming with her fingers on his arm. 'How would you like it if we went inside and I mixed you two boys up a great big drink?'

'I'd like it better if Oscar and I went to Pueblo Bonito tonight. My brother may not be back for days, so I must go to meet him because I can't wait.'

'Well, for God!' said Irma. 'It's six o'clock, and Oscar can't be spared and he don't know where the mine is either.'

'Do you know anyone who could take me?'

'Nobody lest it be Jesse Colton over beyond the Wash, who helped Alessandro build his house. Now Giulio' — she put her arm around him — 'you just stay here tonight and we'll send Jesse over for Alessandro in the morning.'

'I'd like to go now, so I can bring him back with me tomorrow.'

She scowled, then her face cleared and she laughed with a warm-hearted throaty gurgle. 'He's crazy,' she said to Oscar. 'Ain't he like Alessandro, the little pet! Can't wait for nothing but must go bustlin' off somewhere with a great big idea boiling in his head.' She hugged Giulio, and he yielded, knowing that if he lost command of himself he might never again see Alessandro.

'Could Oscar ask Jesse Colton to take me over there now?' he begged in a soft voice.

'Well, I reckon so. Oscar is easy just like the rest of us Wurtzels. We do anything to please.' She sighed as if in despair at Giulio's obstinacy. 'Oscar, you run over to Jesse's and ask could he take a man down to the Canyon tonight. Say it's Alessandro's brother.'

When Oscar returned in Jesse Colton's car, Giulio felt that the first step out of a terrible situation had been achieved. He was going to meet Alessandro, and the thought of movement relieved his mind and set him free to consider the various possibilities of action. Assuring Irma that he would bring Alessandro back, he got into the front seat beside Jesse Colton, and they started.

Of all the courses that lay before him, to take Alessandro home alone to Italy would be the best. There he could recover and find the reality that he sought, this outrageous dreamer and stranger to them all. Giulio looked fearfully at the still gray plain that sank into the glowing edge of day where a range of mountains stood sharp and black. Alessandro, his brother, had become one with this country which deceived and tortured and exalted, feeding the eager mind with mirage-like images of supernal glory. Alessandro was an alien, not like this grave young Jesse Colton who sat beside him; Alessandro had a fervent imagination and a golden tongue. The land laid the penalty of silence upon its children; they were devout and dreamless, guarding the gift of sanity at the doors of speech.

He asked Jesse Colton whether he knew anything about Alessandro's mine.

'I know where it is,' he answered, 'but that's all.'

It was after dark when they reached the settlement at Pueblo Bonito. The city itself had long been dead, Giulio learned from the man who kept the Lodge, but was living again in history through the labor of archeologists. He was surprised to hear that there were such men in this country, or that human remains could hold anyone's interest amid such vast inhumanity. That field of knowledge belonged to Rome, the Immortal, the Undying, where the buried remembrance of the past gave hope to the living and pointed the way to empire. He dwelt on this thought in the cool rustic privacy of his room, with the desert outside and the rescue of Alessandro very near, allowing himself a flight of imagination upon vigorous wings.

After supper with Jesse Colton in the big log cabin, they went over to the archeologists' camp to see about borrowing some riding-clothes.

There were a dozen or so young people sitting on benches in front of the camp. Giulio felt quieted by the assuring sound of their low, casual, monosyllabic conversation. Jesse Colton introduced him to the director, a tall man with a beard, who had a scholarly voice and the appearance of an engineer. He could fix them up, yes. Alessandro had been in the settlement a week ago, during the evening ——

'Could I speak to you about him?' Giulio asked, turning toward the door.

When they were inside, alone, out of earshot of the others, he paused and took a deep breath. 'Has my brother Alessandro really a mine out there, Mr. Brett?' he asked.

'No,' said the director, 'he has not.'

So much for that. 'You are very kind and I have complete confidence in you, Mr. Brett.' He waited, but the director's face didn't change. 'We are both of us educated men and I want to ask you frankly, what is the condition of my brother? The mental condition, I mean.'

The director looked serious. 'I am not an alienist,' he said. 'I don't want to hurt your feelings, but I think it's the case of a man who comes from a narrow protected environment where everyone lives together, and then finds himself — in this. Your brother has delusions of grandeur that are brought about by loneliness and hardship and disappointment. Frankly, he's not the kind of a man who ought to be out here, and if I were you I'd take him away as soon as possible.'

Giulio bowed. 'Thank you,' he said. 'We have use now for men of imagination in Italy.'

But the director apparently didn't understand, because he walked to the door as if the conversation were over.

As he went back with Jesse Colton to the Lodge, Giulio felt more completely than ever the cold searching hostility of unpeopled space that bore down on the inner weakness of man with an absolute pressure that had no relation to right or wrong, but was natural and self-existent, overcoming prayers, exhortations, and the noble examples of the past, until the whole man as he was stood revealed.

They started early in the morning for Alessandro's mine. The horses picked their way slowly across the dry bed of a river and along a trail that led westward through yellow cliffs. There were caves in the cliffs that looked like dark mouths in a flat yellow face, and the line of the rock joined the faces together in a long winding series under a wedge of blue sky. It grew hot, hotter than Giulio had ever known it could be, with a dark numb weight that lay on the back of his neck and burned into his eyeballs with a feverish ache. They met no one, and there was nothing alive around them except flies and dainty blue lizards with painted necks and birds so far off that they didn't belong to the earth. Giulio imagined his brother toiling for years day by day on foot through this baking hell where even the crumbled rocks shone insanely with the glitter of precious stones, and the caves invited mad discovery, until the whole land became a furnace of wealth to shrivel the mind. Alessandro digging it out with his crazy pitiful hands! He could see how easy it would be for anyone to go mad. It was better to think of Alessandro as he had been long ago, before the bestial print of the land had touched his face, and as he would be soon again, at home in Italy. There was time — there was always time. He closed his eyes to shut out the sight of this dazzling lifeless eternity.

In the afternoon they came to a dry valley that was scattered over with Indian huts.

'Alessandro gets his water here,' Jesse Colton said.

'Is it far?'

Colton nodded at the broad flat cliff in front of them. 'The water's bad,' he said, turning so that he sat sidewise in the saddle. He looked troubled, as if he wanted to say something more; then his hard blue eyes clouded with embarrassment and he pulled in the reins and spoke to his horse.

It was another two hours before they had crossed the valley. As the trail ascended slowly toward the flat cliff, Giulio could see a scar-like trace on the north side where the trail continued. The cliff grew larger by degrees, as if it were rising toward the sun with a mysterious change of shape and color that grew luminous as they approached the black slope of the eastern side. The path emerged into sunlight and a great plain lay below them with an unnatural clearness that upset all Giulio's notions of space. The unnatural clearness terrified him. This was what Alessandro had to look upon day by day when he came out from the darkness of his mine. He prayed that he might find his brother whole in body if not in spirit, and as the words flew upward in his heart he struggled against tears.

The trail came close to the top of the cliff on the western side. A deserted house of sunburned earth stood above him, and in another moment he passed what looked like the shaft of a mine. A little farther on they came to another house built between two big stones with the edge of the cliff just above the roof.

Jesse Colton got down from his horse and looked in the door.

'He's at the mine,' he said. 'I'll stay here.'

Giulio dismounted slowly, and then stood still. It was the first sight of Alessandro that he dreaded, and the sound of his voice. Without looking at Jesse Colton, he started off in the direction that he had indicated. Alessandro was his brother no matter what — he stumbled and almost fell — no matter what he might find in that dark hole beyond him.

It was just high enough for him to stand upright. Through the darkness ahead came a faint tapping sound that continued with a hideous industry. He walked forward, the gritty stone crumbling under his fingers on either side, until the passage turned to the right and the walls became visible forming a corridor that led to a larger space in which was a light. He could hear the rattle of earth at the end of each blow, and as he came nearer he saw the lantern on the ground, and a moving shadow and the flash of steel. Then he stood at the entrance behind a tall gray-haired man in a blue shirt and khaki trousers, who stood with his back to him, swinging a pick.

By the sidewise toss of his head Giulio recognized Alessandro.

'My brother!' he cried out in a loud voice. 'It is I, your brother Giulio, who have come to embrace you.'

Alessandro dropped the pick and put his arms over his head.

'For the love of God,' he moaned, 'why do you torment me?'

Visions. Giulio felt his scalp contract. That man whose face he had not yet seen was his brother.

'Alessandro,' he said, 'do not be afraid because it is I, your brother Giulio, who stands before you.'

'No,' whispered Alessandro. Giulio caught sight of his face, the unfamiliar half-remembered features distorted into a caricature. 'You come to reproach me because I have lied to you, but it is true, it is true I say, because I have said it to you every hour of the day for so many years. It is true, so why do you torment me?'

Giulio struggled to control his voice. 'Alessandro, here, you can see that I am real.' He held out his hand, then came closer and put his arm around his brother.

The long bent fingers touched his sleeve, then his face, with the touch of a tiny child who cannot see.

'It is impossible to believe,' he sobbed.

'You must, because I have come to take you home to our father and the vineyards and pineclad hills of Italy.'

The musical intonation of the words made Alessandro look up as if he were half persuaded from his unreason by their spell. Then his tall gaunt body shook with hysterical relief as he clung to Giulio.

'Never again to see a land like this, and to go home!' he cried in a pitiful voice. 'Not even God in his mercy could work such a miracle!'

TWO WORDS ARE A STORY [1]

By ELIZABETH HALL

(From *Story*)

BECAUSE two words are a story, it is difficult for me to tell this. In the course of time, words have taken on special meanings, a phrase of music has become something personal, and known so well to the mind that it releases all manner of meanings... meanings that are beyond interpretation. I will try to make you see it, for one moment, as it was. Everyone has felt that if he could know completely, for one second, time would not matter, and that knowledge would be eternal. It is impossible, of course. So I will try only to approach it.

There were four people in the room. It was a big room in a country house, and outside it was November. The earth was already resigned to winter. Snow had fallen weeks ago, and lain on the ground, and disappeared, and fallen again. The people — they were two men, and two young girls, just as they should have been — had come to the house only recently, and very soon would leave. That is part of the story. That just for this moment when I try to catch them they were, incredibly, here. And soon would be scattered apart, just as incredibly. Not quite apart, because two of them were married. But they, too, would be gone back into a separate, different life. While they were in the room together, watching the fire that jumped on the hearth they had put off much that was not theirs, and become very much themselves. How were they themselves? That is what I want to know. Through what dangers and escapes had they arrived at this peaceful evening in a warm room, where November beat at the walls and cried in the chimney? What walls had they built against that strange November?

Look at them for a minute. A big burly man on the couch in front of the fire, his feet up comfortably, and a pipe dying and suffering resurrection in his hand. A blonde girl in a chair by the fireplace, little, her hair untidy, her fingers twisted in the rope of beads she wore around her neck. Another girl opposite her, chewing the end of her finger as she bent her dark head over a book, trying to make out the print by the flickering light. Between them, on the floor, a young man with his knees pulled up under his chin, blond wavy hair, a handsome happy face. It was his house. He had invited his friends Tom and Dotty Stewart, and also the dark girl, his friend Love Baker, to stay with him for a week. They had all known each other for a long time, and were much at ease together.

They were silent just now, though they had all been talking passionately before, especially Alec, the host, who sometimes used words solemnly, and with respect, and sometimes talked in a sudden quick spatter, like a little dog, burrowing violently into the earth. They had been talking of technique and content in art, or whether there was soon to be a war in Europe, or some such pyrotechnical subject, where ideas flame up suddenly, and dispute and refutation seem frantically important, and which can descend swiftly into contented silence. They sat, each busy with the secret ritual of thought, telling over familiar scraps of memory and broken bits of ideas, sinking into this firelit room, this quiet picture, assuming, for a moment or two, eternity.

Dotty twisted her beads and thought she must get some sleep, and wished Alec would mix another drink — an impersonal chain of concepts of a kind that often occupied her mind. She was used to them and welcomed them. She could talk and think intelligently, but never trusted her thoughts much, they seemed to shift so alarmingly. Other people were consistent and logical, but logic had very little compulsion for her. She preferred to put her faith in her emotions, which told her with a good deal more authority what she ought to do. They were astonishingly mobile, and rose to her defense swiftly in any crisis, so that she could act with decision while other people tormented their minds for reasons.

At this moment, she was experiencing the calm emotion of marriage that arose from her contemplation of Tom's bulky body sprawled on the couch, and another funny, rather exciting little feeling that jumped and flickered as the fire lit and extinguished lights in Alec's hair. She was very fond of Alec, she thought, but this catalogue did not seem to fit the indefinite little teasing in her brain, and she went on to remember that Alec had, after all, been very much in love with her at one time. Why, he had even left college because he couldn't stand being away from her. She had a sudden clear vision of a big room at some dance, and the excitement that came from watching Tom and Alec, best friends, being scrupulously polite to each other, with their eyes turning involuntarily toward her. Heavens, said her mind, what a fool you are to think of that! You were a child then. You've been married three years, and you love Tom, and you know he's the better man. It was quite true. Alec was very unstable. He began and left colleges and jobs with a remarkable regularity, until he had one day discovered the efficacy of cutting down trees as a wearying and steadying occupation, and had since lived in the country, where much forest was available for his exorcisms. Dotty knew all this very well. She tried to stimulate the responses that came from 'Tom,' 'My Husband,' but the firelight jumped on Alec's hair, and she watched it.

Alec twisted on the floor into a better position to watch Love's face as she bent inexorably above her book. He wanted very much to pull her away from it, turn on the victrola, and bring their bodies together into the swaying conventional embrace of a dance. He refrained, because he was aware that Love was highly intellectual, and his awe of wisdom overcame him at the thought of interrupting her concentration. He lay back, and the restless demon that lived behind his good-looking boyish face awoke to start again its worn, fingered questioning: 'What are you doing here?' said its well-known voice. 'It's just an escape. You've run away from things all your life — oh, always from the best of motives, I grant you that. You're running away now. What right have you to live out here comfortably, in your big house, with your servants, while millions of men wake every morning to walk the streets and tighten their belts against another day? Who are you to be given privileges? It's only your father's industry and hard work that places you here instead of as a clerk in an office — and he hated you for your weakness, and you hated him for his hardness — but you took his money when he died. You broke your mother's heart, because she tried to understand you, and you were afraid to love her, and only grew irritated by her sympathy. You coward!' Alec laughed. My God, I'm getting dramatic, he thought. I'm a perfectly normal soul, really, he said to Love's bent head, and I could make you very happy if you'd ever look at me instead of at a book, or a piano, or

Tom, or the view through the nearest window. How can you tell someone you love her when she's always walking away from you? Look, he said, we could live out here gloriously all year round — you'd love it. And we wouldn't be badly off — I have money —— That's what you ought to say, said the demon, you coward. Your money's the only argument you dare advance. Why don't you show her, instead of sitting and yearning? Why don't you go back and get another job? This time you'd stick — really you would. Or write a book. Make them all respect you. What do they think of you now? Alec, in the grip of his private torture, achieved deliverance for a moment by noticing that Love's eyebrows, as she wrinkled them over the page she turned, were the most beautiful in the world.

She was thinking that she couldn't go on reading this book mechanically forever. Pretty soon she'd have to look up, and Alec's eyes would jump to meet hers, and Tom's would continue to stare at the fire. Soon she would have to admit the collapse of this frail defense and return to the stresses of companionship. Just for one moment more she would hold herself aloof, listening to the weather. She was one of those people to whom wind at the eaves and rain streaming on the window-pane seem to be beating against their naked bodies. They lack the normal complement of skins, or their insensibility has failed them in one important aspect (being perhaps, alas, concentrated in some other region). Love, being unfortunately possessed of a sense of humor — a factor precluding much happiness in women — would never have admitted to being sensitive, but she was none the less exalted by wind, high bright skies, and speeding clouds, while steady rain could reduce her to gloom and hysterical reaction. She was, just now, walking in the wet wild woods by her wet wild lone, shrieking in the tops of the trees, or lifting suddenly a drift of sodden leaves into a brief whirlpool. She was indulging in a pastime in which she did not often allow herself to relax — going primeval, she called it. Because if she did not, she knew she would do something worse. She would think of Tom.

She was obviously not in love with him. He, of course, was by no wild stretch of the imagination enamored of her. But they had only to meet for something to waken. Something that had brought them together for one crazy year, when she was eighteen and he was twenty-two. Something that had been compounded of wild rides through quiet streets and countrysides — evenings spent solemnly dancing together, to part and sit solemnly across from each other at a little table, and as solemnly rise to dance again. Childish humor that delighted in meeting-places like the south library lion, the oldest mummy in the Metropolitan, the birth-control speaker in Columbus Circle. Something that had been love-making ending in tears and quarrels ending in kisses, and, always, laughter that broke through sacred moments, and turned the top of a bus to a carnival. Then she tore off to Paris to study, and forgot him completely, and he got married, and they were just good friends — as everyone said. Only — some enchantments can be broken, and broken, and still catch hearts on their jagged edges.

They weren't friends — they met just by chance — and the things that were important to them were miles apart. They certainly weren't lovers — but Love knew how easily and familiarly she could slip into his arms. And she knew, too, that she was going to lie awake tonight, and shiver in bed, and think of Tom and Dotty whose bodies lay together in warm contentment, or aroused to some more dramatic action. She bent her head over her book.

Tom dozed on the sofa and thought that he'd like to go to bed pretty soon, and wished Dotty would keep her hands still and that Alec wasn't such a fool, and that Love was more get-at-able. It was nothing or everything with her — and he was surprised by a sudden violent wish that it might be everything. He had never slept with her, and in that moment he regretted it very much. He thought of it, not as an experience that he might go through, but rather could see himself thinking of it in the past. He decided that it would make a very nice memory to live his life with. She was the kind of woman that fits best into a man's past, rather than his present. You certainly couldn't imagine marrying Love. She was something extra — something that life had created some fine day as a little work of supererogation. She wasn't anything that could belong to you, the way Dotty could — Dotty who was little and sweet and his own. This was a truly lamentable error, for Love wanted to belong to someone more than anything else in the world — but was too proud to show her desire, too proud to do anything but fight bitterly against an attempt at possession, though she longed for it.

Do you see them for a moment? Do you see an approximation of what they were? It is the last time they will ever be like this — but this bitter or cheerful knowledge is, of course, withheld from them. For a moment that holds and stretches and does not break yet — yet — yet. Look! They are there! Four private souls busy with matters that will be forgotten as completely as a dream — unexplainable — so individual that there is nothing to compare them to, and words are only clumsy fists. For one moment the thread of this precarious reality, swung over the abyss, tightens and holds. Then ——

'Lord, what a merry group!' said Dotty. 'Alec — Tom — turn on the vic. Let's dance. Why in heaven's name don't you have a radio, Alec?'

'He has to deny himself luxuries in his frugal existence,' said Tom. 'Another drink around, and then beddy? Love?'

'Are you offering her a drink or a bed, dear?' asked Dotty over her shoulder. She knew she shouldn't appear to be overhearing conversations, but she couldn't help jumping briskly into them at times.

'Whichever she'd prefer,' said Tom, with automatic gallantry.

'I think just now I'll have the drink,' replied Love. 'Don't think I don't appreciate the full extent of your offer, though, Tom. I'll put it in my files.'

'It'll be in distinguished company, I'm sure,' he said politely, and went into the kitchen. Love leaned back and watched Alec and Dotty dance, in close artificial passion. The music was artificial, and wickedly lecherous, making you think of naked shoulders, hands moving on warm bare flesh — everything that goes by the fascinating name of adultery. Highly conventional thoughts fitted into an expected pattern, evoked by a conventional stimulus. A throaty voice sang of parting and betrayal and true love found and lost, and she marveled at the least common denominator of love, and its extreme potency.

Tom came back with highballs and asked her to dance, but Love was aroused to defiance of response to stimuli, and said no, she was tired. She yawned tremendously and wandered over to the window to cool her forehead on the pane, and see if it rained still. Outside the night dripped quietly down and a dim stain of light showed where the moon should be. Quite suddenly, Love had to go out into it or go screaming crazy inside four walls and a roof. She went out the door to the hall and was slipping the bolts that held her in when Tom caught her.

'Are you mad?' he said. 'Where are you going?'

'Out,' said Love briefly.

'Artistic temperament must be a strain on the possessor,' he observed. 'Here — have my coat. I'll take you out for ten minutes. That'll have to do. You mustn't be spoiled, you know.'

The wind swept them up as soon as they came out the door, and Love shrieked and ran down the lawn, to jump up on the stone wall and teeter for a minute, before she lost her balance and landed ignominiously in damp mud. Tom pulled her up philosophically.

'I suppose if you haven't killed yourself yet, you never will,' he said. 'Come on in. You'll get gout.'

'Oh, no, it's heavenly, it's too grand! Look, you can see lights over there — you can never see a house in the daytime. Darling, feel the wind!'

'Uhuh,' said Tom, and having put his arms around her to stop her shivering, he fell to kissing the back of her neck.

Love jerked away in a cold fury. What damn fools men were! If he was going to kiss the back of her neck, he ought to have done it five years ago. They never seemed to have a sense of proportion. This wasn't going to turn into anything — it was just silly and futile, and didn't mean a thing. Tom, guessing that she was in one of her 'nothing or everything' moods, walked her briskly back to the house, but detained her on the doorstep. After all, memories were rather pale realities.

He took her in his arms again, and she stood against him, looking bored and sulky.

'Listen,' he said, 'Liebchen, are you going to put me irrevocably in your files? Must I stay there forever?'

'Yes,' answered Love uncertainly.

'I don't believe it,' he said.

She kissed him back, and they went in both a little surprised, and dimly expectant.

Alec, who had been visible to any normal eye during this strange conversation, stepped into the light from the transom and looked at the door that had closed behind them. He was, quite simply, stunned. His mind that suffered such agonies on some points had

been quite clear on this one. Some day he would manage to make
Love see how desirable it would be to love him and marry him.
He loved her in a peculiar chivalric fashion, abnormal in this day
and age, and he had regarded her old affair with Tom as on a par
with his schoolboy interest in Dotty. Tom was, of course, his best
friend. There they were, fitted neatly into their pigeonholes — but
they wouldn't stay! They jumped out, and upset his mind and
set his hands to clutching at each other, and his eyes to watering.

Love! Love! he said. How could you! How can you hurt me so,
he meant, and how can you be such a fool! You're going to wreck
yourself over Tom — he'll never leave Dotty. I know how intense
you get — you mean things too hard. You'd never love Tom unless
you loved him too much. Oh, Love — his pain couldn't be altruistic
any longer — don't you see what you're doing to me? I thought if
I could ever catch you, you'd be my safety. If I have to run away
again, I thought I could run to you. Oh, Love, how could you leave
me so alone? You're kind — you've always been kind to me, damn
you — I'll accept even that now, if you just won't leave me all
alone. Leave me some hope — don't take yourself out of my life
altogether!

He ranged up and down the walk, hitting his hand against the
big elm as he passed it. After a while, Dotty came to the door,
and called 'Alec!' And Love said behind her, 'Is he outside? I
didn't see him. He's gone to bed.' At her voice he clutched the tree
and clung to it till the door closed. Then he ran down the lawn, and
crossed the muddy road, and got into the trees that climbed the
tilting land beside the house.

It was pitch-black in the woods and he bumped into things, and
branches caught his clothes, but he wouldn't be turned back, and
struggled on, swearing and sobbing. He never knew how far he
went. He just stumbled along, saying her name over and over, as
the Penitentes glory in the beatings of their cactus whips. A bitter
wind arose, and tried to lift the trees out by their roots, and sudden
showers from the wild branches soaked him, and everything in the
world was horrible, a roaring pit of hell that shouted around him.
This night didn't really belong in the year at all. It was a little bit
of the time after the world ended, got loose early by mistake.

Everything had left him. He was demonstrating the truth of
that well-mouthed phrase, 'He is not himself.' All personality and

the small identifying marks that civilization had left on him were stripped away — by the wind — by the brambles that tore at him — by the necessity of not thinking, since thought would only worry and snap at his heels like a little angry dog. What was left was nothing that could have been recognized by anyone who knew him — it was only something frightened that had been threatened and had to escape — had to run with bursting lungs and hammering heart up a hillside into a wild autumn night.

He staggered out into a bare pasture on the summit that had once been inhabited by sheep, and fell full length onto the slippery earth. Getting up wasn't worth the tremendous effort, and he lay gasping, wondering doubtfully if it were true that one might draw strength from the earth. It hardly seemed possible that anything so palpably disintegrating could help him. This silly conjecture was the first sign of returning personality and for a while he was content just to lie and say calmly, 'What an utter fool I am.' The frightened thing that he had become was moving farther and farther away — and he watched it go with relief and shame that it should overcome him so easily. Still he could not yet face two people in each other's arms — such a meaningless gesture — and see them as his friends, not his enemies.

Which were they? They had betrayed him — but if he knew why, he might be able to forgive them. Love — Love, he said, why did you do such a thing? How much did you mean? Would you have done it if you had known that it was to me a knife in the breast, a noose at the throat? No, he reminded himself, that's not fair — don't talk of yourself — ask her only 'Why?'

In all his searching as he sat unconscious in the wet and spatter, twisting a twig between his fingers, he could find no answer that seemed to belong to the girl he knew so well. What reason would she give? Love — he drew little pictures of her in his mind — Love walking, and dawdling, and watching people that passed. Love talking — too fast — and the laughter that answered her — Love always with a defense of wary eyes, that would spring between him and the truth he had to know.

He got up and walked shivering about. He kicked stones, and stumbled, and thought, I'm a sentimental fool. I'm a coward. There's something wrong, something terribly wrong that I should always meet danger with a gasp and an urge to get out of that place.

Here is something I must find out — because I am I — to anyone else it would not matter. And that, too, is part of why I ran. I have read in so many books that to be different is a fine thing, a thing to be proud of. I don't believe it. I don't believe it, he said with a horrible desolation sweeping over him. What am I going to do? You have a chance, he told himself, to do something that is not running away. Instead of creeping back and forgetting that you saw them together — denying the fact — refusing to answer the question, instead of this, you can know. Be brave. That's really a very simple thing, he said, and it gets easier as you go on. Just do what you are afraid to do. Look, he said, nothing can be as hard as this; go back and find out.

Because it was part of the system of beliefs that he had been using as texts, he plunged into the trees again without thinking any more, and all the way down the hill as he slipped precariously on, grasping branches and squatting to slide better, he managed to believe that the only thing he could do was the one he was going to do. There is nothing else to do, he repeated firmly. Not one other thing. I must ask her. Tomorrow morning at the first opportunity. I will make an opportunity and find out the truth. It is the only thing to do.

But when he got to where the road should have been, he was lost. He had wandered so far, with so little thought, that he could not say at what point, in whose thinning woodland, he stood. It was appalling. He realized suddenly how tired he was — how cold — how soaked. He held firmly onto the thing that wanted to run, and walked with infinite effort out of the trees toward some shape of darkness that showed ahead of him. Perhaps it was a place where he could sleep — that was all he asked — to be able to sleep and forget and never bother to feel anything, never want to know anything again. He made a bargain with his mind — his frightened mind that had been surprised and shocked at his new determination. I won't try to change you, he said. I'll let you stay as you are. I'll let Love go. Just let me get out of this terrible shrieking night to some place where I may be myself again, some warm small place where I am important. I was wrong to think I could change myself. If I am a coward, I shall accept that fact — but rationalization was too much bother, and he sank back into apathy and the moving of one foot in front of the other, knowing Love lost to him, all things that he might reach for forever beyond his grasp.

He looked again at the bulky shape he was approaching, and then he began to run toward it, and stopped because he was too tired. It was the house. He was home. The back door was unlatched, and he let himself in clumsily because his hands wouldn't seem to obey him very well. He found a chair and sat down. Heaven could have done no more than give him a chair to sit on.

At last he began to come alive again. He knew at once that nothing was settled. He had made two opposite determinations and something would have to be done about them — at once. If he waited until morning, he knew he would never ask Love what that fugitive embrace had meant, and if, in her mind, he, Alec, played any other part than that of 'someone I know, rather amusing, rather to be pitied, unimportant.' And his fine decision in the wild windy night should be treated more considerately than just by being ignored. He felt the two courses of action before him, balancing them one on each palm — knowing the force of each so well, because he had yielded himself completely to both of them. He had accepted each, and seen himself moving down each path with all intention of following it. Now he was suddenly whirled about, back at the crossroads. Which — which — said his mind helplessly.

Then he realized that he was on the stairs and he was going to do something — and he knew what — but he mustn't admit it yet. He reached Love's door and opened it.

She was sleeping with one arm thrown up over her head, he could see in the dim light. He closed the door very quietly behind him and walked slowly over to the bed. 'Love,' he said, and shook her. 'Love.' He felt her move, and shook her again. 'Love, are you awake? It's Alec. Are you awake?'

'Alec,' she said stupidly.

'Yes. Listen to me. I've got to ask you something. And you've got to tell me the truth. Do you hear me? You've got to tell me. Are you Tom's mistress?'

'No. What on earth...'

'Are you going to be?'

'Alec, you're crazy! Why...'

'Answer me!'

'No.'

'Love, I know I'm crazy. Won't you please believe I've got to know? I saw you kiss him. Why did you? I've been walking and

walking. Love, you've got to tell me. I can't stand it any longer.
I've loved you so long, and you've never cared whether I did or not.
But I always thought maybe you would some day. I thought maybe
some day you'd be glad ...'

'Alec, you're soaked. Have you been out in this rain? You're
absolutely mad. You've got to get to bed at once or you'll have
pneumonia, and ...'

'Do you love Tom?'

'No, I don't. Now, will you ...'

'Do you mean it? Darling, do you? Are you just saying it because you don't want to hurt me? If you lie to me, I'll kill you,
Love, I mean it.' He was crying, and Love sat up and put her arms
around him. She didn't really believe any of this was happening,
she decided, but she clung to Alec, and her head whirled with the
strangest mixture of feelings. Out of them all, she managed to know
that she must comfort this man who loved her. Something had
taken all his strength away, and she must give it back to him.

'Love,' he said, 'will you marry me?'

She knew what she had to say, though it surprised her. 'Of
course I will.'

So it wasn't just once. For always and always, she saw, she would
be comforting him, strengthening him, accepting his need for her,
and never again admitting that it existed. She had wanted to belong to someone. That was wrong. Alec belonged to her, but she
must not let him. People should not belong to one another. It was
terribly important that if you yielded up your strength, by loving
someone, you should not just give it to them. That was what Alec
had done. But she must never let him know. She must never
assert the strength he had given her against him. Both of them together was the important thing, not one of them subservient to the
other. Could she do it? Could she bend his agonies to the produc-
tion of strength and beauty of companionship? Could she give him
such a sure refuge in life that he would not need to use it? Could she
never, never, betray him by seeing herself apart from him? She
was the only one who could help him — and he needed help so. He
was worth helping. Tom would say she was silly — sentimental
— that these wierd problems did not really exist. He would say,
as she had heard him before, 'Alec's a child — an adolescent.'
Whatever he was, Love knew he had a claim on her she could not

deny. He needed her so terribly — and she, how she needed to be needed! She was better able to camouflage her loneliness than Alec, but they were alike in their sad apartness. They had got along without other people in their self-sufficiency, and she thought now that Alec was wiser than she. He had been unhappy — had known something was wrong. She had been proud of herself for her independence. Now it was over. They would be together. And who, of the two, needed this most? Love could not answer.

'Darling,' she said, 'go to bed now, you're tired and cold. To-morrow we'll tell Tom and Dotty. I love you, Alec.'

'Good night, Love, sweet.' He stood and looked down at her, and she knew that he was already surer of himself, heard it in his voice. 'Dream of me,' he said.

The breakfast table was bright with sun that winked off handles and the silver cream pitcher. Love was late for breakfast. Alec looked at the empty chair and looked away again, telling himself he was a fool to let his mind quiver uncertainly over her absence, imagining betrayal. 'Of course I will,' she had said, and 'I love you.' Love was always late. She was sitting absent-mindedly brushing her hair, or whatever women did in the mornings. He saw her suddenly, sitting in warm sunlight, her dark hair forward hiding her face, her bare arms moving rhythmically. The vision gave him a sudden brief pain. Love — his. It was the first time he had really believed it possible. He felt a new strength, something solid bracing him, seeing before him days and years illumined by the simple incidents of their life together. He saw a thousand little pictures of intimacy. They would not be trivial, those tiny future episodes. They would be strong rope to hold on to. They would mean an integrity in his life that he had never found before. He knew consciously now what Love meant to him. He looked again at the empty chair, and because of his knowledge, was shaken by a worse anxiety than before. If something happened now, he would know what he lost. You're crazy, he kept telling himself, and Why doesn't she come down? he asked.

'This has got to stop,' said Alec, and looked firmly at Dotty, not seeing her.

She smiled brightly, met blank eyes, and raised her coffee cup as an instant shield. He's vague this morning, she thought a trifle resentfully, feeling his preoccupation as a small stimulating obstacle that she would enjoy overcoming, in a little while. No need to be precipitate. She could take her time with Alec. He never changed. That was, of course, if she decided to do anything about Alec at all. She didn't know yet. He was an amusing thought to turn her mind to whenever she felt dull. But not awfully real. Tom was real, now. Only — reality was boring sometimes. She sighed. Oh, well. The coffee was good.

Tom, always imperviously silent till breakfast was over, also stared at Love's empty place. He, too, was in no hurry. The pleasurable anticipation of a game to be played held him. His thought went no farther than that. He did not consciously consider the moves the two opponents would use, the stages to be skillfully entered and fulfilled till the proper termination should arrive. The simple knowledge of something left unfinished so long ago, between Love and him, something revived last night, was enough. He waited patiently for her to come down this morning. Their eyes would meet, and he would see the consciousness in hers of something going to happen. Expectation held him like a warm bath.

'Isn't it a lovely morning?' said Dotty. 'Such a change from last night.'

'Yes,' Alec answered in a doubtful tone. Love's heels clattered on the bare floor, and she stood in the door for a second, smiling right across at him. 'Yes,' said Alec, with conviction. 'Hi, Love. How are you?'

Tom watched her, amused at her coquetry. She wouldn't look at him.

'I'm fine,' she answered, smiling again at Alec. 'I'm wonderful.'

She sat down, and grapefruit became her chief concern. She was realizing this morning how surprised she was. Because in a moment of nostalgia for her youngest, gayest lover, she had kissed the man he had become, she was now caught inexorably into a new pattern of life. It was a place that had been waiting for her. She turned it over in her mind a little, testing, trying it, behind the barrier of the grapefruit. It was not too unfamiliar. She could feel how accustomed it would become, how it would fit her. But how many other places might she have found? How many had she just missed, how many were waiting for her five years away around the corner if she did not do this? What compulsion in the fine-spun fabric of her life had led her to this bright young day, set her pondering on her engagement to Alec?

In what way had this unforeseen fact been implicit in them — just last night, for instance, as they sat before the fire? So soon was it to come out of the future that you would have thought she would have felt it — and yet there had been no murmur. They had been just the same. Now there would be a new same for them to be. Tom and Dotty and Alec and Love — they would sit before a fire again, silent, entertaining their thoughts — but they would be different. She was confronted with the passage of time and change, and knew she must accept it, but could not yet quite admit its power. She sat very still, unwilling for a moment to change the pattern, feeling the old one still firm and accustomed about her, seeing Tom's eyes reaching for hers, Dotty quietly watching both men, Alec waiting for her to speak. She had the power to break it all — to make a new pattern. She was going to, too. But before she spoke, before she reached across for Alec's hand and said gaily, 'We have an enormous shock for you,' she must sit here just a second, clutching the strings of the old relationship tighter and tighter to her. 'Never again,' she whispered, 'never again.' Then she looked up and spoke.

WITH SOME GAIETY AND LAUGHTER[1]

By FRANK K. KELLY

(From *Story*)

COLD came in with him, and a breath of sterile whiteness without, but no snow except that which clung to the scuffed shoes on his feet, because the wind had died an hour before and there was no snow now driving from the sky. Old Berger, his short-ranging eyes peering from behind the glass walls that hung before his face, went to his counter and stood teetering on his toes.

The young man — he was young, though his face was marked with the shadow of unsweetened bitterness — almost laughed to see the old man waiting amiably for him to speak. It was warm in Berger's shop, and crowded with the presences of many quiet things, and the old man looked so rosy and happy with his apple cheeks and his bright eyes in cozy pockets of flesh, that the young man could not speak for a time, his throat was so choked with tender envy. He stood, taking big breaths of this warm air around him; it sank down with soft hissing into his lungs, and the fragrance of it was sweeter to him than the satisfaction he had once taken in tobacco smoke.

Berger waited patiently, with the expectant quietude of an old man, and didn't press him for facile speech. It might have been that Berger could see how it was with him.

Suddenly he put his hands down on the smooth, shining pane of the showcase. Old Berger's hands were spread up on the counter also, and the young man nearly laughed again looking at the difference between them: Berger's hands were so knotted and old, and still they were well-fed, while good young hands could starve. Good clever hands could find nothing for them to do. Tears did come sourly to the young man's eyes, but he wasn't sure whether this was because of his sudden warmth after great cold, or because he had only now remembered some terrible injustice.

The young man was proud of his hands. They were fine hands, even Berger through his dusty glasses had seen that; but long and slim and clever and strong as they were — and they could do many things well — yet for all that, there was no work for them anywhere in the world.

The young man slowly opened his mouth. Old Berger was frugal with light as with all things, and the loan shop had only what small glitter came of a lamp hanging from the ceiling: in the dimness the young man's mouth was heavy and hard. Berger somehow began to feel a tension about the young man; his head was set too firmly on his neck.

'Yes, what is it, eh?' Berger asked. 'A distinguished medal to sell, eh?'

'No.'

'Then what do you want here, eh?' Berger said. 'It isn't a medal, eh?'

'No, not a medal.'

The young man's voice was as unshaken as he looked himself, standing there planted squarely on the soles of his feet. Yet his feet went down through the scraps of leather he had bound them in, and when he walked he felt nothing, whether he walked on stone or on soft ground. The outer skin of him had thickened to a scale over his inner skin. The snow had worked into his dirty shoes; he had known for a long time that his feet were frozen. Yet nothing so real and sharp as that seemed able to reach the cords behind his eyes, and travel up to his brain to tell him what had happened.

It was a long time before he spoke any more after his first five words. At last he said gently:

'I'll tell you how it is with me, friend.'

Old Berger nodded in a sort of exasperated patience.

'My name is Gorman. Ray Gorman. I've been an American citizen twenty-seven years. I'm twenty-seven years old. I haven't eaten anything in four days.'

Berger made a slow gurgle in his throat.

'Yes, I hunted work, but I could not find any work. There was none of the kind of work I could do.'

'Now you're begging,' Berger muttered, with just a slight twist to the words.

'Once I begged for a few scraps, but there were not many scraps to be given away in these times. I beg no longer.'

'How have you been living, then?' Berger asked, softly.

'I've sold things.'

'Your own possessions, of course,' Berger said.

'Yes. I've sold all I own, except this one thing I have here. I've brought that to you.'

'Yes, let me see it,' Berger said, nodding. 'Perhaps I'll buy it, eh?'

Berger saw for the first time that the other carried something under his arm. It was a package of some sort, a small flat bundle, carefully wrapped up in soft white paper with a green string tied in a good knot at the middle. The young man carried it very gently, as if it were a thing so valuable to him that he would have walked quietly with death rather than let it be taken from him against his will.

He put it down slowly, on old Berger's counter, as one would handle a precious thing, and left it there a little while, without making any move to open the coverings.

'Ach, I'm glad you haven't brought me any medals,' Berger said comfortably. 'I have already so many medals.'

He pointed one fat old finger and the young man followed the line of that sausage with his eyes, and saw that it was true: Berger had a great number of fine medals, all in one big box divided up into sections to hold them. They were classified according to distinction. The box had contained jewelry once, and there was still some plush to cover the bottom. In a slow way the light of Berger's lamp gleamed on the medals, so that they gave a brave bright shine, and in their rich shiningness seemed to belong there on the plush. It was Berger's best box, because he thought that the medals should be with the plush — being worthy of the good things.

'So,' the young man said, clipped. 'Fortunately I am not a war veteran.'

He smiled, but his eyes in their burning vacancy didn't in the least alter. 'My father had one of the best medals, I think. He lived with me till just a short while ago; then he left ... I have no bitterness like his bitterness.'

Berger coughed in his throat.

'Why did he leave, eh?'

The young man jerked up his head. Now his eyes changed: they took a polish.

'He had somewhere else to go. We were pretty poor, you understand. But he had been honorably to a war and back, and they let him go and enter a Soldiers' Home. There were guns fired at his funeral.'

'Then he is dead,' Berger said, and held his voice low.

The young man lifted up his wild head again.

'Yes, yes. I thought you'd understand that. I told you, they fire the guns morning and night at the Home. He stays at the Home now. He is not lonely.'

'Eh?' old Berger said. 'Eh?'

'He has company there. They are all dead where he is.'

Berger drew back a little, though it was usually his inclination to approach his customers too closely, and peer at them almost with offensiveness out of his near-sighted eyes.

'Ach, I see,' Berger said.

The young man's fingers began to fumble with the string of his package. Berger saw that his fingers had been so cold that even the first blue tinge had gone away from them, and they were left like long sticks of white punk lying loose on the counter. Berger had known the fingers of a few dead men, and this was just the same. He turned his eyes at another angle.

When he looked again, the other had unlaced the knot, and was pushing the wrappings from a round object. Berger stared at what lay on the glass top of the showcase, a circular dark blob shifting under the lamplight in a steady black glow. The thing was a phonograph record of standard size. It seemed in good condition yet, the glaze of the heavy surface still almost unscarred, as if the owner had taken care about the manner of its playing.

'Will you give me a little something for this?' the young man asked softly.

'Well, I don't know where I'd have use for it,' old Berger said.

'Even a little money would be good to feel in my hand,' the young man whispered. 'I've been hungry so long now.'

Berger noticed then that when the young man spoke, he kept his lips pressed close together until just before he opened his mouth to let the sound out, as if he used his speech in fear that he had not strength enough to form every syllable that should give his words full meaning. His language progressed on stilts, heavily placed down, perhaps because he thought that unless he took care he would lose footing in his mind, and stumble headlong into a labyrinth of incoherence.

Berger's thick blunt fingers brushed the record slowly, and he bent down to peer at it with his old eyes. There was no title printed on the white inner strip that curled in a circle of stiff paper around the center of the disc. The white ring lay blank.

'What is this, eh?' Berger asked, his glance rising in bewilderment. 'It does not say here what kind this record is.'

'There is no music on it,' the young man said softly. 'And no words. It is better than that. You see, it will help you to keep the beast back.'

He took a breath, and after the passing of a little time, added:

'It has helped me, when I had need of it.'

Berger hesitated, looking at him sidewise.

The young man waited two minutes, and then very slowly began to wrap the round black disc in the paper which had held it before; there was something terrible about the stoop of his shoulders that shook old Berger's brain.

'Wait,' Berger muttered. 'Did I say I would not buy? Tell me what the record plays, and I will see.'

'The record plays nothing. It laughs.'

'This beast you speak of — what about that, eh?'

'It laughs,' the young man said. 'That is all.'

'Please,' Berger stammered. 'I do not understand.'

'I've found that if you laugh at the Beast, he won't be so sure you're afraid of him; of course you really are afraid, sick to your guts, but if you put a good laughing face on, with no solemn hollow stuff in you, he'll rage, and charge at you, but he will not overcome you. Only if you flee, he'll turn and follow you to the world's ends . . . I have no need of laughter to help me now; I am a little beyond that. Do you understand?'

Berger asked slowly: 'This beast — where do you find him, eh?'

'He is within you,' the young man said. 'Oh, and within me. Someone has spoken these fine words: "With subtlety we can get our hands round the throat of the Beast, and so destroy him." Wrong, wrong. I have used this record so many times that I know what is right and what is wrong. Laughter is right and sadness is wrong.

you cannot think how good it is sometimes to hear the sound of laughter; it will help you when you think there can be no more help ... Wait, I'll show you what I mean. Do you have a phonograph here?'

Berger raised his bony shoulders and let them fall, in the old German way of shrugging that he had kept through these long years in a raw country; he smiled.

'Yes. I think there is everything here. You have seen how many things I have bought that I cannot sell. I am an old man with the heart of a fool. If your record amuses me ...'

'Perhaps it will not amuse you,' the young man said; a kind of muscular contortion leaped the lines of his face, crossing from one side to the other with such speed that it seemed to vanish in shadow like a thought repulsed. Berger saw that he had struggled a while with some great memories.

'Perhaps it will not amuse you,' the young man said again, very softly. 'It will do so much more than that. How can I tell you what it has meant to me? I do not think you could know what it means to a man who has not laughed for so long himself, except by forcing a kind of vomit, to hear good laughter when he has need. This is good laughter you'll hear. You couldn't be sad, hearing the voice of it. Nobody could be sad, after such laughter ...'

He followed the old man behind the counter. There was an ancient gramophone in one corner of the crowded room. They went to it together. The young man put the record down on the green felt slowly, lifted a needle, set the point on the edge of the black disc; he released the catch that held the voice of the machine to silence.

The black disc hummed, and the light winked back in a moving shimmer from its middle. An echo of all the laughter that had washed the world since it had been shaped out of chaos ... rose to them now. There was madness in it, of a kind, and more than madness: it was born to rebirth in a quivering fullness of being that mocked the destiny and the damnation and the death of the Beast. A clean spirit sang in it ... A clean spirit singing ...

The young man stood as if incapable of lifting the weight of his head while he drank the music of this mirth into him; old Berger couldn't stop looking at him. The laughter rose like smoke leaping into an empty sky.

'Please, that is enough,' Berger said. 'Shut it off, eh?'

The young man put down one finger and pressed the latch that had power to choke the life from the disc. Now it was quiet again all around them and through them. But the room was not the same room, and the silence was not the same silence: there were remembrances and fragments remaining from the lilt of that laughter.

Old Berger had long ago shut up his soul against these things, and they hurt him now in their renewal of meaning, they were so fresh in their newness and gentle in their cruelty. He put his hands together in the long sleeves of his jacket.

'Will you buy?' the young man said, after a minute.

'Yes,' Berger said.

'How much?' the young man asked.

'Five dollars I'll give you for the record.'

'Five dollars?' the young man whispered. 'That's so little for a priceless thing.'

'No more,' Berger said. 'I can give no more.'

The blood ran in a tide into the young man's face.

'Then I'll go now. Good afternoon, friend.'

He waited a little time, as if he thought perhaps Berger might have something more to say; but when the old man did not speak, he began to wrap the record again in its coverings. He took it up carefully in his hands, and put it under his arm.

'With some gaiety and laughter,' the young man said, 'I'll take my leave of you.'

He went out. Old Berger watched awhile, and saw the long shadow of that tall body pass by his windows: it dwindled finally into a dim outline against the snow, and at last that too was gone.

'Well,' old Berger said. 'Well...'

A queer thing, he thought. A queer thing to happen to him of all men; he'd led a quiet life and never harmed a soul.

TINKLE AND FAMILY TAKE A RIDE

By KARLTON KELM

(From *International Literature*)

THERE comes, you see, a time when a fellow faces the futility
of saving what there'll never be enough of to ever matter
anyway — skinching on what of itself is a skinch — then with a
god-swell gesture he says, oh, hell, and gets what he wants — or
tries to.

I suppose that is why Mr. Tinkle got the Ford.

It was a very old model, black worn blue with the iridescent
shadings of oil on water. A touring car, five-seater, with the isin-
glass knocked out of two of the three window-lights in back, and the
black leather seats blistered open in places, like cracked fingers that
won't heal, and the stuffing coming out. Mr. Tinkle said it cost him
twenty dollars, though, and the tires were in pretty fair shape. It
had a sick once-used-now-unused look as it stood all day, all night,
in the blazing stuffy street outside the Tinkle flat, third-floor rear,
its front wheels twisted painfully into the curb. Mr. Tinkle said it
had performed very decently that first day he had driven it home on
the complimentary gallon of gasoline the used-car man had put in it
to get-it-the-hell-out-of-here.

Mr. Tinkle had not driven it since. But I did not know this till
I stopped to talk to him on my way home from work. Before I only
knew what I seen. I would walk home from work and see him tinkering with the thing, his head in the engine, his backsides looming upward, or simply his long oil-smeared legs jutting out like stovepipes
from in-and-under it. It was only the one time I seen his face that
I stopped to talk.

Every evening that summer I walked back to town after supper to
shoot pool with some of the boys and perhaps pick up a date later.
Past the Tinkles' again I'd go and there as sure as anything would
be the whole family sitting in that car, sitting in rags, talking and

looking around nice as you please, just like they was moving along a fine country road. It's true I saw Mr.'s face then, but there was the five faces to see, six with the baby, so I just kind of see 'em all as a whole, not sorting out any one at the time. It's only now as I look back that I do that.

Mr. was always at the wheel with the little boy aside him except sometimes when the two little girls kicked up a fuss and scrambled over into the front seat and made the little boy go in back. But the mother, Mrs., was always in back with the baby in her lap. She just flopped there and seemed so kind of still while the rest kept up a holler that you guessed it was the only time in the day she ever really took a moment to rest. I remember now noticing once her eyes were a nice blue and kept blinking softly as if she were trying to see everything for the first time, trying to believe everything was new and different and worth looking at. Now it's our turn, the little girls would say, and over they'd plop into the front seat with little squeals.

Mr. never seemed to notice the noise they made, but kept looking straight ahead at the road, all hunched up over the wheel, and answered all their questions. Once in a while he smiled, as if the idea of their not budging an inch had suddenly hit him full in the face all over again.

Now we're going up a hill, said the little boy. More gas, Papa, more gas, and he pounded on the tinny footboard with his thin little sandals.

Papa's giving it all the gas he's got, said Papa, and then that kind of smile of his.

Or:

Oh, see the cow, Mama, see the big fat cow, said the bigger little girl, clutching her scrawny body excitedly.

It's not a fat cow, it's a very thin cow, corrected the smaller little girl with a forlorn little face. It's a very thin cow and it can't give any milk and all the farm babies are crying for their milk.

No, no, no, cried the first little girl more and more excited. It's ever so fat and it gives ever so rich cream and it's all nice brown like in the picture-book except one little white patch between its ears.

It's black and white and not brown, said the second little girl. It's black and white like on the magazine cover, only its bones stick out very and all the little babies are crying. Hear them cry, Mama.

Hush, said their mother, looking out where there was only hot pavements, high hot tenements, screaming, filth.

Nuts! muttered a dirty little neighbor boy listening from the curbing; and I passed on.

Or:

Papa, is it cool in the country and are there lots of trees and can you walk in grass? Can you pick little flowers and roll up your pants and wade in real water instead of what comes from the hydrant, can you, Papa? Is it all like in the book?

Yes, son, all like in the book.

When are we going there, Papa?

Why, we're there now, son. See that little brook over there? See all the bright green things? Smell the fresh clean smells, son?

The little boy's eyes shone, his thin little chest expanded, the small black nostrils dilated — but just for an instant, then he sat back very far in his seat, sighed like a little old man exhausted, and meekly said, Yes, Papa.

Yes, said Papa looking straight ahead, Yes.

Nuts! said the dirty little beggar on the curb.

Then the day I stopped to talk. What seems to be the trouble? I asked. He was sitting on the running-board, his head in his hands. He looked up and squinted at me for a moment, then he drawled, Why, nothing special — thinking I meant his car. You know how it is when they get old. And then a feller has to be doin' something. — Then, brightening, Oh, it's in fine shape right now, but it'll be even better when we finally get goin'.

He had a fine long sensitive face, and a violin would have fit nice under his chin, but his hands were maimed flat toil-hands and seemed in the way of the rest of him. The work had not touched his face, only the emotion of it, but his hands were the made hands of his place in the world. His face could do nothing about his hands now, it was too late. Like he told me after we got to jawing a while: I got tunes in my head. All the time I got tunes in my head. If someone could take them down, he said. Where does one take these tunes to? Would you know where I could get someone to listen to them and take them down, would you?

His eyes were alight for a moment, very black-bright light, but then there was those hands, and all that shabbiness, and a beaten-dog look, so I was ready with my answer. No, I said, I wouldn't know where.

Maybe he knew what I meant.

Maybe they were lousy tunes anyway. But just the same they were in his head.

But first:

He said, Maybe you think like the others I shouldn't have the car. No, it wasn't before but after I was laid off that I bought it. I don't suppose you can understand that. I just had the twenty bucks left, that was all. When you don't know where the next twenty's coming from, well, the twenty you got don't matter so much. And we'd been planning on it so, the car — just getting out in the country of a Sunday. Really for the first time since we got married we could see a little fun ahead. We figured it wouldn't take so much gas if we diluted it up with kerosene like some of our neighbors does.

You see, I kept saying I'd have another job in a few days, but I knew I wouldn't. I just said that so I wouldn't have to think about what I was going to use for gas. Food? Oh, my little girls go with a basket to a convent every day. Whatever is left over they give us. You see the charities won't give us help unless I sell the car. Our landlord says I must sell it too to help pay what I owe him. My wife says it's the only thing to do now, but I won't do it. I bought that car and paid for it and I'm going to keep it. That's the last hope and I'm going to hang on to it. Why, that car's freedom, it's a way out, the only way out I can see. Why, I couldn't give it up before the wife and kids even had a ride in it, could I?

Listen, if I can hold on to it a little while longer, I'll get hold of some money somehow, see? And then what do you think I'm going to do? buy food? pay the rent? No! I'm going to buy gas, lots of gas. It's better than food or lodging, is gas. A feller can get somewhere with gas, see something. A feller has to get *some*where before he dies, don't he?

Yessir, I'm going to fill 'er up with gas and oil and go far into the country. We'll just keep going, me and the wife and kids, until all the gas is gone, then we won't have to come back, ever. We can get along then. Animals do. But here, this ain't a fit place for an animal!

Well, why don't you say something? I guess you think I'm an awful guy. But it all seems fair enough to me, Mr.

Nuts! said the little roughneck on the curb, and I said, Fair
enough, and went home.

Well, the next night Tinkle wasn't tinkering around his car, when
I went home, and after supper on my way down to the poolhall
there was only the little boy in the car foolin' around with the
steering-wheel. Mama's sick, he said when I asked him where
everybody was, and then he went right on playing, kind of mumb-
ling to himself about how he was a racer and going a hundred miles
an hour, *Whew! just made that corner on two wheels, whew!*

The next night it was the same, then the night after that even
the little boy wasn't there and the car stood empty and forlorn,
twisted into the curb. There was a big-fat woman sitting out on
the second-floor stoop rocking away with her arms folded high on
her stomach and I yelled up to her and she said, Mrs. Tinkle died
last night, she's always been poorly, and this ptomaine she got from
the old food sent in just done her, that's all. Yes, the whole family's
down at the undertaker's with her, Ward's, funeral tomorrow afternoon, two o'clock, you're very welcome I'm sure.

I swallowed that and went home.

Next morning on my way to work the Tinkle car was not at the
curb, and the big-fat woman leaned over the railing of her stoop,
a kind of balcony, and without my even asking her, said, He come
with a gallon of gas and druv it off this A.M. They're going to use
it in the funeral procession instead of the regular mourner's car to
cut down expenses. — Then she laughed — I shouldn't say procession because there'll just be the hearse and their car, they were
never people to neighbor much, always stuck to themselves, but
they have a cousin at the other end of town, and I guess it's him
that's buryin' her and that bought the gallon of gas. Mr. says the
kids is all excited about the ride to the cemetery. I says the cousin
might of filled it up while he was at it, but Mr. says he's been laid
off too, and the gallon will just do it out there and back.

It was Saturday and in the afternoon I didn't work and I thought
several times of going over to Ward's and talking to Tinkle, but
hell, I couldn't, just couldn't, and then first thing I knew it was after
two o'clock and they'd be on their way to the cemetery, and what
the hell anyway. But I might as well of gone because all afternoon
I saw it all anyway, just like it was happening. The long dull black-
solemn hearse moving with not too disrespectful haste through the

bright-glittering afternoon. Then the Tinkle flivver, the worn color of oil on water, struggling along behind.

I didn't want to see more than that, but I had to. I had to see Mr. and the cousin from the other side of town, whom of course I'd never seen, sitting together stiffly in the front seat, Mr. hunched over the wheel just a bit and his eyes straight ahead. I had to see those kids, the two girls and the little boy (the baby'd been left somewhere, of course), bouncing about the back seat, looking at everything, having the time of their life, clapping their hands and even yelling in their excitement, *See the cow, Papa. See the beautiful white cow. — And the flowers, Papa, all the bright little flowers. — Oh, doesn't it all feel good, Papa, doesn't it smell good ! Isn't it fine to ride in the country, Papa ?*

And Papa letting them make all the noise they want, *what the hell no one's around out here, and they've been quiet so long.* And Mama, so cold and still in the dull black hearse ahead. Was Mama seeing the flowers and the cow and nice bright air? Was Mama having a nice ride too?

And now the crude black box is going down, down, but the little girls and the little boy are so busy watching a beautiful yellow butterfly fluttering high above it in the bright sun-lazy air, that they forget to look down, forget to say good-bye to Mama, until the dull black box is out of sight, gone! And then the cousin is bustling them away, while Papa keeps standing there, looking, looking, looking where the black box is no more!

Nuts! I said like the little roughneck. Nuts! and went home. I didn't go past the Tinkles'. After all, it was a short cut and I most always had time for the longer way.

THAT BLOWZY GODDESS FAME[1]

By MANUEL KOMROFF

(From *Esquire*)

'EVERY dog has its day,' I said, 'and your day is sure to come.'
But my words were hardly consoling.

'Yes! That's the bunk I've been hearing for years. If you don't
mind, I'll have some of it now. My hair is gray from waiting.' A
smile crept over his face. He smiled as though he himself was his
own best joke.

'Well, some fellows are lucky and some ... You are really due
for a break and ...'

He did not let me finish.

'Yes, I am due for a break and maybe it is coming to me and
maybe not. But I don't believe in luck. When I am dead my pictures may bring high prices. Yes, I know all the stories about
Rembrandt and Van Gogh and Gauguin and all the poor suffering
geniuses and how the dealers bought up the pictures for a song and
raked in the cash. I've heard all the stories and if you think I give
a damn about being great after I am dead you are mistaken. I want
to eat something now.'

'Well, Ben, I've known you for twenty years and you always
managed somehow or other.'

'Sure I managed. But I'm damned sick of that existence stuff.
I'm sick of the lousy ten-dollar-a-month studio on Fourteenth
Street. I'm sick of smoked fish that I keep in the sketch box. I'm
damn sick of painting on old canvases and wearing the cast-off
clothes of my friends. And who the hell wants to buy a picture
these days anyway? Say, you know a good joke. Listen to this one.
Every year for over fifteen years I sent a picture to the Pennsylvania
Academy. Yes, sir. I sent them and they sent them back just as
certain as rejection is a word in the dictionary. Well, I don't claim
I sent them masterpieces, but, by golly, my stuff is better than a lot
of the junk that they hang. Well, the story is a good one. Every

year I fill out the blanks and mark down the value of the painting at one thousand bucks. Sure, I'd take less, but how often does a fellow sell a picture? Then the Artists' Express Company, comes around and collects the picture and two-dollars-and-fifty cents from me. They are a good company and reliable and careful and I have no kick. Well, for fifteen years I sent and was rejected and I wasn't discouraged; but last year things were pretty bad and I couldn't afford the two-fifty and I said to myself, what the hell. Supposing this year the damn jury has one picture less to reject. And supposing I don't send and don't get it back and don't pay out the two-fifty, is my art any worse for it? Not at all. So the hell with them, and I didn't send. And what do you know, the damn train wrecked on the Horseshoe Curve and the box car that looks like a padded cell for lunatics got all smashed and the insurance company paid for each picture in full, and the boys have been living on it all year. Well, I suppose you think that is bad luck. Sure it's bad luck, but I don't believe in luck. That's all the bunk. Robert Henri used to tell his pupils: "Don't come to me and tell me that you have no luck. Use the luck you have, good or bad, and use it over again and keep on painting and soon you will discover that you have more luck than you imagined. And what is true for luck is also true for talent. Use what you got and keep on using it." That man Henri was certainly the wisest teacher an art school ever had. And J. P. Wicker in Detroit was another. These two men turned out some real artists. Where would Bellows have been without Henri? And remember that fellow Charlie Lister? He was sure one of the rattiest painters in our class, a good slick commercial broadstroke fake technique. Well, today Charlie Lister sells everything he does and he only has to do a half-dozen canvases a year. The museums gobble them up. And would you believe me if I told you I could paint a better Lister than Lister can; and no joke about it. In fact I am doing the fourth copy now of that piece of cheese of his that hangs in the Metropolitan.'

'Who do you do them for?' I asked.

'An interior decorator. He sells them with his modern rooms all framed in a dirty white chalk frame, French style, for seventy-five bucks. He gives me forty. And my landlord takes ten for that hole of a studio. Figure it out for yourself. Yep. I climb up the marble steps of the Metropolitan Mausoleum of Art and set up my copying easel in the Modern American room and I look around and there they all are: Kroll, Speicher, Karfiol, Poor, Luks, Sloan, Bellows, and all the rest. And I knew them all when . . . You know how the saying goes. Bellows was certainly a real fellow and if Henri could only have painted half as well as he spoke, he would have been the greatest of the lot. But the magic he had with words did not quite get down into his brush. But anyway he was somebody, and when he spoke to you he made you feel that you too were somebody and that you had something; and when you left you would carry your pictures home in the cold and you felt warm. That's how he was and he made all his pupils feel they were all right and the world be damned! That's the way an artist ought to feel. That's the whole secret. The joy of the whole business comes from such a feeling. Glad to have seen you. I'm sending another picture to the Pennsylvania this year. Hope the train wrecks again. What a break! But it couldn't happen twice. Besides, I don't believe in luck, anyway. Good-bye.'

Well, that is how he was and that is how he spoke. His name was Ben Ross. I had known him for years and what he said was true. He was an old pupil of the Independent Art School and he did know Robert Henri and Bellows and Sloan and all the rest; and twenty years had slipped by noiselessly and quietly and without much fuss.

Twenty years of hand-to-mouth existence. And now Henri is dead and Bellows is dead, and Luks also, and the memory of them alone was enough to warm his chilled nature. And that old stink-hole of a studio on Fourteenth Street has survived and the cracks in the walls are quite something. The gas comes through from next door every time . . . There were three suicides in the twenty years and Ben pasted strips of old canvases over the cracks and when he did so he remarked very cheerfully to a friend who happened in: 'Gee, a fellow is never safe, for when they kill themselves next door they want to kill you too.' And with that he slapped the paste on good and heavy and sealed up another crack.

Now, about that dried fish that he kept in a sketch box, that is also true and ten years from today that sketch box will still give off a lingering odor of smoked fish rather than turpentine. The fish and the turpentine and the old hole were all part of him and this you can multiply by twenty years. Twenty years of a meager existence. Twenty years of living with the expectation of a sudden glory to come. Twenty years with stretcher-frames, carpet-tacks, turning old canvases over, scraping off the palette. Twenty years of that demon temptation that attacks every poor painter. The demon that whispers in the artist's ear: 'Go easy on that Cadmium Yellow, it's two dollars a tube. There's a substitute for thirty-five cents a tube, but then it might turn black. It's not permanent. Don't you dare! How about posterity!'

Ah, yes. Posterity, the great future after life. Yes, that is the glowing coal in the heart of the poor artist. And he tries to cover it up and act indifferent to it. He is modest. He waves his hand in a let-the-future-take-care-of-itself manner, but secretly he sees his name engraved on the great tablets of all time and he may starve and not feel the hunger and outside he may be cold, but inside he is warm.

And you probably noticed when Ben Ross referred to the Museum he called it a mausoleum. But that was not quite what he really thought. There was also a note of bitterness when he spoke of Charlie Lister and the fact that he had to copy 'that piece of cheese' that now hangs in the Metropolitan.

And so twenty years have gone and some of the boys — he named them — have come forward in a big way and are recognized and hang in the Metropolitan. And there is no doubt about it, when you hang in the Metropolitan then you have arrived. And no jokes about the 'mausoleum' or the 'cheesy stuff' can brush aside this popular recognition.

And so Ben Ross, who did not believe in luck, went on year after year with a conviction that both he and his paintings were great and recognition was just around the corner. But in the meantime it was ten dollars a month for the studio, and dried fish, and two-fifty once a year for the express company and some copying work in the museum for an interior decorator. Well, try it yourself for twenty years and you will forgive Ben Ross his crime. Twenty years of industry should count for something. And not all crimes are guilty ones.

Soon after he spoke to me and told me about the wreck of the freight car going to the Pennsylvania Academy and his bad luck at not having sent anything that year, he conceived a plan to bring himself proudly to the front rank. He got out an old canvas, dusted it off and gave it a coat of retouching varnish. It was a little picture of a dish and some apples done in the modern woolly Cézanne manner; a small study about twelve-by-sixteen inches, not any larger than his sketch box.

Well, the varnish was soon dry and he nailed it back into its frame and wrapped it up in a paint rag and strapped it to his paint box. In this manner his picture entitled 'Sad Apples' arrived at the Metropolitan Museum and into the copying room. Then he got his easel and climbed the steps to the Modern American section and went to work copying 'that cheesy' picture of Charlie Lister's. And all the time he was copying, he was looking around the room at the pictures of the boys he knew in the old days and also at the spaces between the pictures.

At last, about five o'clock in the afternoon, the great moment had come. He watched for his chance and at a time when the guard was in the other room, quick as a flash, he unwrapped 'Sad Apples' and, with a little hook that penetrated the cloth of the wall, he hung up his picture in the space between two large paintings of his contemporaries. Then he closed down his work for the day and put his stuff back into the copying room and left the museum with a step livelier than his old shoes had known for years.

He obtained an advance of five dollars from the interior decorator and with this he bought wine and sandwiches for a party.

'Well, a fellow has got to have a party once in a while,' he said.

'Did you sell a picture?' he was asked.

He smiled broadly. His face glowed. 'Sell a picture!' he said with contempt. 'Any nut with money can buy a picture, but ... Come along about eight o'clock and you will hear the good news.'

And the good news rang out from one end of Fourteenth Street to the other.

Ben Ross hangs in the Metropolitan! Our own Ben Ross hangs with the masters in the Metropolitan!

'Which one did they get, Ben?'

He smiled: 'A funny thing. You know the little study of apples. The one the Pennsylvania jury rejected, well, it wasn't good enough for Pittsburgh, but it's good enough ... Well, I don't believe in luck.'

'Well, Ben, you were due for a break. Congratulations old man.'

'Sure,' he said proudly. And in that moment he forgot all about those long bitter twenty years that went before. It all did not matter, for now ... Now there was a seal of approval on all Ben Ross canvases. And on himself also there was the stamp of glory, the hall mark of posterity. And his life was justified and the dried fish O.K., and the use of Cadmium Yellow at two dollars a tube instead of chrome, that also was justified.

'And where does it hang?'

'Well, you know as you come upstairs and then you turn to the right and you walk in and you see the big Winslow Homer and then on the other wall are the . . .' here he named the pictures on the wall.

'Well, right there you will find my little study. Size don't make any difference. You don't measure art with a yardstick.'

It was a good party and everyone promised to go up to the Metropolitan and see how Ben's picture looked on the wall.

At night before he closed his eyes he smiled contentedly. He reasoned with himself: 'Where is the crime? Sure it's a crime to steal a picture like the 'Mona Lisa' once was stolen. A rich man like Morgan gives a picture to the Metropolitan and it's no crime. Well, and so I give them a Ben Ross and it's no crime. And isn't my picture as good as some fake old master that is presented by a rich man? Sure it is. And does it hurt the museum any? No, not a bit of it. It's no crime to be where a fellow belongs to be. In fact it's no crime to be if you have a right to be. And every man has a right to be. Think of some of the cheesy pictures that hang on the walls. Well, maybe I'm not a Renoir or a Rubens, but . . .'

And so he closed his eyes and fell asleep in the little ten-dollar-a-month studio and he was warm and slept as though he were in the soft comforting lap of that fickle goddess Fame. And I believe that Fame is a cock-eyed bitch without much reason or judgment and without much regard whom she embraces or whom she casts aside. She's just a giddy blowzy blonde. And now if she wants to lift up Ben Ross and raise him to dizzy heights — well, I can't say I care so much for his pictures — but it's all right with me. Twenty years should count for something.

That night Ben slept in the warm lap of Fame, but in the morning when he got back to his work copying in the Metropolitan he took a quick glance about the room and alas! the apples were gone. His little picture had been taken down. Removed. Rejected. Not even the little brass hook remained in the wall.

'Well, the hell with it,' he said to himself. 'I don't believe in luck.'

A KIND OF A SUNSET[1]

By ERLING LARSEN

(From *The Frontier and Midland*)

THE fields south of the farm were soaked black in the spring with the rains and they shone glossy black and gray and swept away to the southern hills which were green shiny in the rain with the first spring growths. And on the hills you could see her walking in the high places where the wind blew so she doubled against it while her wet skirts blew tight around her legs and her hair plastered to her face as wet leaves plaster against tangled tree-roots in the woods in the rain. But as she walked the wild screaming wind died with the light dying toward evening and the rain became a drizzle coming softly down like a heavy mist in the air and breathing she could almost breathe the rain.

Coming down from the hills walking north to the farm, she could see the buildings of the farm and one light in the barn and one in the house yellow in the fading day. She left the grass of the hills and came through the new-plowed fields with the mud catching on her shoes, and in the big field south of the barn she stopped to watch the flickering light in the barn window. It was almost dark now and she watched the light from the oil lantern and saw how it came from the window and caught on one big clod turned up beside the stone foundation of the barn. She leaned over to touch the clump of earth, but when she did the light went from it and when she stood up the light came back. She tried again, but when she leaned the least bit the light was gone from the clod and the earth was shiny oil black with no yellow light at all.

She stayed there in the field south of the barn watching the window until the night came on and the two lights, the one in the barn and the one in the house, were bright yellow in the black of night, and there was no more rain and the air stood, not moving but damp and cool against her hot face. And when it was dark, she pulled her feet from the mud and walked around to the gate in the fence leading into the yard. Her feet squashed in the mud and made sucking sounds in the dark, and when she reached the gate, she could see only the light in the house, but she could hear sounds from the barn of milk spurting into a pail and of animals moving now and then and the sound of a young boy's voice talking to the animals and then singing or humming a little while he milked.

The girl stood a moment by the gate and then lifted her wet skirts and climbed between the rails. On the other side her feet slipped on wet grass and she put her hands into the grass to help herself and felt it cool in her hands. The boy was still singing in the barn. The light from the house shone bright reflecting in the wet grass and lighting up one circle of muddy flower-beds by the sagging front porch. A shadow passed across the window and the front door creaked and the girl saw her mother pass by the flower-beds with a black shawl wrapped about her head. She could see her mother in the light by the flower-beds walking stooped over in the back, but with her head high. The girl moved toward the barn.

'Helen,' the mother said.

The girl stopped.

'Where you been?'

'I went down to the pasture hill,' the girl said.

'And no hat.'

The girl passed a wet hand over her forehead and pushed the soaking hair back on her head.

'The rain feels cool,' she said.

'It ain't right your gallivanting ways,' the mother said. 'It ain't right you carrying on this way.'

'I'm a good girl otherwise,' the girl said. 'I ain't sinning overmuch except as natural man is sinful by nature.'

'And I don't want you in the barn with him there.'

The wind was coming up a little now again and it began to rain again, a fine cold rain blowing easily with the wind through the light by the flower-beds and the two women stood together there in the yard in the rain looking at one another, the mother bent, but with her head high so her neck came from her back at an odd upsticking angle, and the girl straight, bareheaded, with her face to the heavy mist blowing through the yard. High above them a wire on the windmill squeaked and rattled in the wind.

'I ain't seen a man on this here farm yet that wouldn't of been glad to have his way with you,' the mother said.

'None has,' the girl said.

'Your own father even.'

'You chased him off for nothing. He was good. God don't like for us to take punishment in our own hands.'

'I didn't. And times we nearly have to. But he wanted off, he always wanted off somewhere, and I said to him to go and he went. He was a blasphemer he was and an evil man.'

The boy in the barn was singing again, and once his voice talking low to the animals came to them in the yard.

'Why don't you tell him?' the mother said.

'What?'

'There ain't no use him hanging around.'

The girl did not answer.

'I ain't being hard on you,' the mother said. 'I only want you kept the way you are for God.'

The girl stood very straight listening to the rattling in the windmill high in the dark.

'I had evil desires tonight, ma,' she said.

'I knew it when I see you walking in the rain.'

'Ma, is God as hard as you say he is?'

'He hates sinners. That's why I say to forget your father.'

'He hates all sinners,' the girl said repeating in a singsong voice.

'Come on in and get yourself dry,' the mother said.

They walked together toward the house, the mother with her arm around the daughter's waist.

'It's very hard to understand how God is the way he is,' the girl said.

They went around the muddy flower-beds and up the steps to the porch where the door stood open an inch and light spilled in a long finger over the wet wooden flooring, making deep shadows in the inch-wide cracks. The mother opened the door wide and they went in closing their eyes against the light for a moment.

'It's kind of different when he ain't here,' the girl said, opening her eyes.

An oil lamp burned on a table in the middle of the room and shone in a gold cross on a Bible cover under it. A pair of glasses lay folded on the Bible cover.

'There's no tobacco smell,' the girl said.

The old woman walked around the room. The girl watched her

thin face that looked as though she shivered all the time with cold and her small tight mouth tight shut to keep her teeth from chattering.

'You ought to pray more,' the mother said.

The girl stood by the window now, seeing nothing but the wet pane streaming water outside catching the gleam of the lamp.

'It was nice on the pasture hill,' she said. 'There was a kind of a sunset even with all the rain.'

'You had evil thoughts,' the mother said.

'I think they was evil.'

'You ought to pray more.'

'I will,' the girl said, watching the water on the window. 'I want to now. I felt all afternoon I wanted to, but I didn't. I want to now. I will alone up in the barn, alone.' She opened the door and the sound of water dripping in the trees came into the room.

'Alone,' the mother said.

'Yes.'

'All right. You need to pray.'

The girl went slowly through the yard. The boy was in the milk-house now. She could hear the separator whining, now high, now low, as the boy's weight went on the crank. The light from the milk-house window shone on the front of the dark red barn so she could see the name painted in white — Meadowbrook Holstein — and her great shadow lessening as she came nearer and nearer the barn. The door was open a very little and she squeezed through into the silent dark inside, where she leaned against the beams of the door until she could see the white forms of the cows down the long aisle and the shapes of the stalls in the dark. The animals moved a very little in the dark now and then, and their breathing was heavily irregular in the heavy air. She could smell the cows wet with the rain and the fresh milk smell in the air and the hay and straw. It was warm in the barn.

She turned and looked out the small opening of the door and saw the light still in the milk-house. The whine of the separator came to her even here in the barn. A drift of cool air came through the door and she walked out into it into the rain again toward the light. Standing in the milk-house door, she saw the lantern hung on a nail and the boy bending up and down over the crank

of the separator so shadows came and went along his back where
the muscles showed through his wet blue shirt.

'Can I have a drink?' she said.

The boy looked up. He was young and the light caught in the
fine yellow hairs along his jaws.

'I didn't hear you with the machine going,' he said.

'I want a drink.'

'Sure.'

He poured the warm frothy milk from a pail into the cup he
took from the wire hanging on the pump handle. He watched
her drink.

'I never could do that,' he said.

'I always could.'

'I grew up in the city.'

She tilted the cup high and drained the last warm drops.

'I never knew there was pretty girls like you in the country.'

The girl dropped the tin cup on the cement floor and went through
the rain again to the barn. When she had climbed the ladder into
the hayloft, she closed the trapdoor after her and lay down panting in the dusty hay. There was not much hay now that it was
spring and the animals had been eating all the winter through and
it was very dusty, but she lay in it panting and smelling the dry
earthy smell of it. The rain drummed on the roof of the barn and
echoed through the big loft. She lay listening to it until she was
breathing easily again, lying on her back, feeling the wet soaking
through her dress to her skin and feeling the water in her shoes
like a warm foam working between her toes when she moved them.
The sound of the rain was loudly insistent in the dark and almost
buried under it the little sounds of moving beasts in the barn below; but suddenly through the dreamlike monotony of humming
rain she heard a new strange sound of feet swishing through the
straw below and then she heard the ladder creak.

She sat up, stiff-backed, listening. Her hands opened and closed
clutching at the dry hay. And just as she saw the dim shape of the
trapdoor lifting in the dark and his head coming level with the
floor, she jumped to her feet and slammed the trapdoor shut.
She heard him yell and then hit the floor, and after that there
was no sound as she sat on the trapdoor shivering with a sudden
cold that ran through her body making her legs twitch and her

neck muscles go tight and loose quickly like the muscles flexing in a horse's shoulder when you whip it.

For a long time she did not hear even the rain. She prayed aloud in the loft so her words echoed back to her, and she asked God for forgiveness for evil thinking and thanked him for delivering her from evil, and after a long time she heard the rain again and her muscles went smooth again and she felt all warm as she had felt before when standing in the milk-house door drinking the frothy milk.

Slowly she lifted the trapdoor and went down the ladder. It was very dark in the barn where the ladder came down behind the stalls and in the dark her feet went against his body lying there and she moved carefully across his legs stretched out in the narrow passage and groped toward the dull glow of a lantern turned very low over by the big door. She took the light and turned it up and came back to find the boy lying with a small smile on his face. She touched his curly hair and his head moved and fell toward one side on his neck with the neck bent strangely sharply near where it came from his shoulders. His shirt was torn loose at the throat and his chest was dead white contrasting with the brown red which sun and wind had made his throat. She put her hand into his open shirt, but could not feel his heart beating and she put her head down on his chest listening and kneeled that way listening with one hand inside his shirt, and after a while she buttoned the shirt and arranged it around his throat and ran her fingers through his hair again, pushing it from his forehead. She straightened his bent knees and put an arm under his shoulders and laid him straight in the dusty hay that had fallen from the too full mangers, and when her arm came from under him, her hand brought dusty hay with it and she put a wisp of it in his hands crossed on his chest. The light made deep shadows in his eye-sockets and under his chin as she set the lantern carefully in the hay by his head, and once again she touched his hands and the hay in them and brushed the hay and dust from his body before she walked to the door and out into the rain.

The wind had come up again and it whistled through the trees rustling the fresh young leaves and made a strange screaming noise in the windmill stays. It was very dark in the yard now and raining hard again, and the only light was that in the house

shining on the muddy flower-beds. The girl stood in the rain looking at the light and twisting a wisp of hay she held in her hand
until it broke into small pieces with the twisting and with the
rain falling on it soaking it.

ANNUNCIATION[1]

By MERIDEL LE SUEUR

EVER since I have known I was going to have a child, have I
kept writing things down on these little scraps of paper. There
is something I want to say, something I want to make clear for
myself and others. One lives all one's life in a sort of way, one
is alive and that is about all that there is to say about it. Then
something happens.

There is the pear tree I can see in the afternoons as I sit on this
porch writing these notes. It stands for something. It has had
something to do with what has happened to me. I sit here all afternoon in the autumn sun and then I begin to write something on
this yellow paper; something seems to be going on like a buzzing,
a flying, and circling within me, and then I want to write it down
in some way. I have never felt this way before, except when I
was a girl and was first in love and wanted then to set things down
on paper so that they would not be lost. It is something, perhaps,
like a farmer who hears the swarming of a host of bees and goes
out to catch them so that he will have honey. If he does not go
out right away, they will go, and he will hear the buzzing growing
more distant in the afternoon.

My sweater pocket is full of scraps of paper on which I have
written. I sit here many afternoons while Karl is out looking for
work, writing on pieces of paper, unfolding, reading what I have
already written.

We have been here two weeks at Mrs. Mason's boarding-house.
The leaves are falling and there is a golden haze over everything.
This is the fourth month for me and it is fall. A rich, powerful
haze comes down from the mountains over the city. In the afternoon I go out for a walk. There is a park just two blocks from
here. Old men and tramps lie on the grass all day. It is hard to
get work. Many people besides Karl are out of work. People are
hungry just as I am hungry. People are ready to flower and they
cannot. In the evenings we go there with a sack of old fruit we

can get at the stand across the way quite cheap, bunches of grapes and old pears. At noon there is a hush in the air and at evening there are stirrings of wind coming from the sky, blowing in the fallen leaves, or perhaps there is a light rain, falling quickly on the walk. Early in the mornings the sun comes up hot in the sky and shines all day through the mist. It is strange, I notice all these things, the sun, the rain falling, the blowing of the wind. It is as if they had a meaning for me as the pear tree has come to have.

In front of Mrs. Mason's house there is a large magnolia tree with its blossoms yellow, hanging over the steps almost within reach. Its giant leaves are motionless and shining in the heat, occasionally as I am going down the steps toward the park, one falls heavily on the walk.

This house is an old wooden one that once was quite a mansion, I imagine. There are glass chandeliers in the hall and fancy tiles in the bathrooms. It was owned by the rich once and now the dispossessed live in it with the rats. We have a room three flights up. You go into the dark hallway and up the stairs. Broken settees and couches sit in the halls. About one o'clock the girls come downstairs to get their mail and sit on the front porch. The blinds go up in the old wooden house across the street. It is always quite hot at noon.

Next to our room lies a sick woman in what is really a kind of closet with no windows. As you pass, you see her face on the pillow and a nauseating odor of sickness comes out the door. I haven't asked her what is the matter with her, but everyone knows she is waiting for death. Somehow it is not easy to speak to her. No one comes to see her. She has been a housemaid all her life tending other people's children; now no one comes to see her. She gets up sometimes and drinks a little from a bottle of milk that is always sitting by her bed covered with flies.

Mrs. Mason, the landlady, is letting us stay, although we have only paid a week's rent and have been here over a week without paying. But it is a bad season and we may be able to pay later. It is better, perhaps, for her than having an empty room. But I hate to go out and have to pass her door and I am always fearful of meeting her on the stairs. I go down as quietly as I can, but it isn't easy, for the stairs creak frightfully.

The room we have on the top floor is a back room, opening out onto an old porch which seems to be actually tied to the wall of the house with bits of wire and rope. The floor of it slants downward to a rickety railing. There is a box perched on the railing that has geraniums in it. They are large, tough California geraniums. I guess nothing can kill them. I have watered them since I have been here and a terribly red flower has come. It is on this porch I am sitting. Just over the banisters stand the top branches of a pear tree.

Many afternoons I sit here. It has become a kind of alive place to me. The room is dark behind me, with only the huge walnut tree scraping against the one window over the kitchenette. If I go to the railing and look down, I can see, far below, the back yard which has been made into a garden with two fruit trees and I can see where a path has gone in the summer between a small bed of flowers, now only dead stalks. The ground is bare under the walnut tree where little sun penetrates. There is a dog kennel by the round trunk, but there doesn't ever seem to be a dog. An old wicker chair sits outdoors in rain or shine. A woman in an old wrapper comes out and sits there almost every afternoon. I don't know who she is, for I don't know anybody in this house, having to sneak downstairs as I do.

Karl says I am foolish to be afraid of the landlady. He comes home drunk and makes a lot of noise. He says she's lucky in these times to have anybody in her house, but I notice in the mornings he goes down the stairs quietly and often goes out the back way.

I'm alone all day so I sit on this rickety porch. Straight out from the rail so that I can almost touch it is the radiating frail top of the pear tree that has opened a door for me. If the pears were still hanging on it, each would be alone and separate with a kind of bloom upon it. Such a bloom is upon me at this moment. Is it possible that everyone — Mrs. Mason who runs this boardinghouse, the woman next door, the girls downstairs — all in this dead wooden house have hung at one time, each separate, in a mist and bloom upon some invisible tree? I wonder if it is so.

I am in luck to have this high porch to sit on and this tree swaying before me through the long afternoons and the long nights. Before we came here, after the show broke up in S. F., we were in an old hotel, a foul-smelling place with a dirty chambermaid and

an old cat in the halls, and night and day we could hear the radio
going in the office. We had a room with a window looking across
a narrow way into another room where a lean man stood in the
mornings looking across, shaving his evil face. By leaning out and
looking up, I could see straight up the sides of the tall building
and, above, the smoky sky.

Most of the time I was sick from the bad food we ate. Karl
and I walked the streets looking for work. Sometimes I was too
sick to go. Karl would come in and there would be no money at
all. He would go out again perhaps to borrow something. I know
many times he begged, although we never spoke of it, but I could
tell by the way he looked when he came back with a begged quarter.
He went in with a man selling Mexican fleas, but he didn't make
much. I lay on the bed bad days feeling sick and hungry, sick too
with the stale odor of the foul walls. I would lie there a long time
listening to the clang of the city outside. I would feel thick with
this child. For some reason I remember that I would sing to myself and often became happy as if mesmerized there in the foul
room. It must have been because of this child. Karl would come
back perhaps with a little money and we would go out to a dairy
lunch and there have food I could not relish. The first alleyway
I must give it up with the people all looking at me.

Karl would be angry. He would walk on down the street so
people wouldn't think he was with me. Once we walked until
evening down by the docks. 'Why don't you take something?'
he kept saying. 'Then you wouldn't throw up your food like that.
Get rid of it. That's what everybody does nowadays. This isn't
the time to have a child. Everything is rotten. We must change
it.' He kept on saying, 'Get rid of it. Take something, why don't
you?' And he got angry when I didn't say anything, but just
walked along beside him. He shouted so loud at me that some
stevedores loading a boat for L. A. laughed at us and began kidding
us, thinking perhaps we were lovers having a quarrel.

Some time later, I don't know how long it was, for I hadn't any
time except the nine months I was counting off, but one evening
Karl sold enough Mexican jumping beans at a carnival to pay our
fare, so we got on a river boat and went up the river to a delta
town. There might be a better chance of a job. On this boat
you can sit up all night if you have no money to buy a berth.

We walked all evening along the deck and then when it got cold we went into the saloon because we had pawned our coats. Already at that time I had got the habit of carrying slips of paper around with me and writing on them, as I am doing now. I had a feeling then that something was happening to me of some kind of loveliness I would want to preserve in some way. Perhaps that was it. At any rate, I was writing things down. Perhaps it had something to do with Karl wanting me all the time to take something. 'Everybody does it,' he kept telling me. 'It's nothing, then it's all over.' I stopped talking to him much. Everything I said only made him angry. So writing was a kind of conversation I carried on with myself and with the child.

Well, on the river boat that night after we had gone into the saloon to get out of the cold, Karl went to sleep right away in a chair. But I couldn't sleep. I sat watching him. The only sound was the churning of the paddle wheel and the lap of the water. I had on then this sweater and the notes I wrote are still in the breast pocket. I would look up from writing and see Karl sleeping like a young boy.

'Tonight, the world into which you are coming' — then I was speaking to the invisible child — 'is very strange and beautiful. That is, the natural world is beautiful. I don't know what you will think of man, but the dark glisten of vegetation and the blowing of the fertile land wind and the delicate strong step of the sea wind, these things are familiar to me and will be familiar to you. I hope you will be like these things. I hope you will glisten with the glisten of ancient life, the same beauty that is in a leaf or a wild rabbit, wild sweet beauty of limb and eye. I am going on a boat between dark shores, and the river and the sky are so quiet that I can hear the scurryings of tiny animals on the shores and their little breathings seem to be all around. I think of them, wild, carrying their young now, crouched in the dark underbrush with the fruit-scented land wind in their delicate nostrils, and they are looking out at the moon and the fast clouds. Silent, alive, they sit in the dark shadow of the greedy world. There is something wild about us, too, something tender and wild about my having you as a child, about your crouching so secretly here. There is something very tender and wild about it. We, too, are at the mercy of many hunters. On this boat I act like the other human beings, for I do not show that I have you, but really I know we are as helpless, as wild, as at bay as some tender wild animals who might be on the ship.

'I put my hand where you lie so silently. I hope you will come glistening with life power, with it shining upon you as upon the feathers of birds. I hope you will be a warrior and fierce for change, so all can live.'

Karl woke at dawn and was angry with me for sitting there looking at him. Just to look at me makes him angry now. He took me out and made me walk along the deck, although it was hardly light yet. I gave him the 'willies,' he said, looking at him like that. We walked round and round the decks and he kept talking to me in a low voice, trying to persuade me. It was hard for me to listen. My teeth were chattering with cold, but anyway I found it hard to listen to anyone talking, especially Karl. I remember I kept thinking to myself that a child should be made by machinery now, then there would be no fuss. I kept thinking of all the places I had been with this new child, traveling with the show from Tia Juana to S. F. In trains, over mountains, through deserts, in hotels and rooming-houses, and myself in a trance of wonder. There wasn't a person I could have told it to, that I was going to have a child. I didn't want to be pitied. Night after night we played in the tent, and the faces were all dust to me, but, traveling, through the window the many vistas of the earth meant something — the bony skeleton of the mountains, like the skeleton of the world jutting through its flowery flesh. My child, too, would be made of bone. There were the fields of summer, the orchards fruiting, the berry fields and the pickers stooping, the oranges and the grapes. Then the city again in September and the many streets I walk looking for work, stopping secretly in doorways to feel beneath my coat.

It is better in this small town with the windy fall days and the sudden rain falling out of a sunny sky. I can't look for work any more. Karl gets a little work washing dishes at a wienie place. I sit here on the porch as if in a deep sleep waiting for this unknown child. I keep hearing this far flight of strange birds going on in the mysterious air about me. This time has come without warning. How can it be explained? Everything is dead and closed, the world a stone, and then suddenly everything comes alive as it has for me, like an anemone on a rock, opening itself, disclosing itself, and the very stones themselves break open like bread. It has all got something to do with the pear tree, too. It has come about some way as I have sat here with this child so many afternoons, with the pear tree murmuring in the air.

The pears are all gone from the tree, but I imagine them hanging there, ripe curves within the many scimitar leaves, and within them many pears of the coming season. I feel like a pear. I hang secret within the curling leaves, just as the pear would be hanging on its tree. It seems possible to me that perhaps all people at some time feel this, round and full. You can tell by looking at most people that the world remains a stone to them and a closed door. I'm afraid it will become like that to me again. Perhaps after this child is born, then everything will harden and become small and mean again as it was before. Perhaps I would even have a hard time remembering this time at all and it wouldn't seem wonderful. That is why I would like to write it down.

How can it be explained? Suddenly many movements are going on within me, many things are happening, there is an almost unbearable sense of sprouting, of bursting encasements, of moving kernals, expanding flesh. Perhaps it is such an activity that makes a field come alive with millions of sprouting shoots of corn or wheat. Perhaps it is something like that that makes a new world.

I have been sitting here, and it seems as if the wooden houses around me had become husks that suddenly as I watched began to swarm with livening seed. The house across becomes a fermenting seed alive with its own movements. Everything seems to be moving along a curve of creation. The alley below and all the houses are to me like an orchard abloom, shaking and trembling, moving outward with shouting. The people coming and going seem to hang on the tree of life, each blossoming from himself. I am standing here looking at the blind windows of the house next door and suddenly the walls fall away, the doors open, and within I see a young girl making a bed from which she had just risen, having dreamed of a young man who became her lover... she stands before her looking-glass in love with herself.

I see in another room a young man sleeping, his bare arm thrown over his head. I see a woman lying on a bed after her husband has left her. There is a child looking at me. An old woman sits rocking. A boy leans over a table reading a book. A woman who has been nursing a child comes out and hangs clothes on the line, her dress in front wet with milk. A young woman comes to an open door looking up and down the street waiting for her young husband. I get up early to see this young woman come to the door in a pink wrapper to wave to her husband. They have only been married a short time, she stands waving until he is out of sight, and even then she stands smiling to herself, her hand upraised.

Why should I be excited? Why should I feel this excitement, seeing a woman waving to her young husband, or a woman who has been nursing a child, or a young man sleeping? Yet I am excited. The many houses have become like an orchard blooming soundlessly. The many people have become like fruits to me, the young girl in the room alone before her mirror, the young man sleeping, the mother, all are shaking with their inward blossoming, shaken by the windy blooming, moving along a future curve.

I do not want it all to go away from me. Now many doors are opening and shutting, light is falling upon darkness, closed places are opening, still things are now moving. But there will come a time when the doors will close again, the shouting will be gone, the sprouting and the movement and the wonderous opening out of everything will be gone. I will be only myself. I will come to look like the women in this house. I try to write it down on little slips of paper, trying to preserve this time for myself so that afterwards, when everything is the same again, I can remember what all must have.

This is the spring there should be in the world, so I say to myself: 'Lie in the sun with the child in your flesh shining like a jewel. Dream and sing, pagan, wise in your vitals. Stand still like a fat budding tree, like a stalk of corn athrob and aglisten in the heat. Lie like a mare panting with the dancing feet of colts against her sides. Sleep at night as the spring earth. Walk heavily as a wheat stalk at its full time bending towards the earth waiting for the reaper. Let your life swell downward so you become like a vase, a vessel. Let the unknown child knock and knock against you and rise like a dolphin within.'

I look at myself in the mirror. My legs and head hardly make a difference, just a stem my legs. My hips are full and tight in back as if bracing themselves. I look like a pale and shining pomegranate, hard and tight, and my skin shines like crystal with the veins showing beneath blue and distended. Children are playing outside and girls are walking with young men along the walk. All that seems over for me. I am a pomegranate hanging from an invisible tree with the juice and movement of seed within my hard skin. I dress slowly. I hate the smell of clothes. I want to leave them off and just hang in the sun ripening ... ripening.

It is hard to write it down so that it will mean anything. I've never heard anything about how a woman feels who is going to have a child, or about how a pear tree feels bearing its fruit. I would like to read these things many years from now, when I am barren and no longer trembling like this, when I get like the women in this house, or like the woman in the closed room — I can hear her breathing through the afternoon.

When Karl has no money, he does not come back at night. I go out on the street walking to forget how hungry I am. This is an old town and along the streets are many old strong trees. Night leaves hang from them ready to fall, dark and swollen with their coming death. Trees, dark, separate, heavy with their down-hanging leaves, cool surfaces hanging on the dark. I put my hand among the leaf sheaves. They strike with a cool surface, their glossy surfaces surprising me in the dark. I feel like a tree swirling upward too, muscular sap alive, with rich surfaces hanging from me, flaring outward rocket-like and falling to my roots, a rich strong power in me to break through into a new life. And dark in me as I walk the streets of this decayed town are the buds of my child. I walk alone under the dark flaring trees. There are many houses with the lights shining out, but you and I walk on the skirts of the lawns amidst the down-pouring darkness. Houses are not for us. For us many kinds of hunger, for us a deep rebellion.

Trees come from a far seed walking the wind, my child, too, from a far seed blowing from last year's rich and revolutionary dead. My child budding secretly from far-walking seed, budding secretly and dangerously in the night.

The woman has come out and sits in the rocker, reading, her fat legs crossed. She scratches herself, cleans her nails, picks her teeth. Across the alley lying flat on the ground is a garage. People are driving in and out. But up here it is very quiet and the movement of the pear tree is the only movement, and I seem to hear its delicate sound of living as it moves upon itself silently, and outward and upward.

The leaves twirl and twirl all over the tree, the delicately curving, tinkling leaves. They twirl and twirl on the tree and the tree moves far inward upon its stem, moves in an invisible wind, gently swaying. Far below straight down the vertical stem like a stream, black and strong into the ground, runs the trunk; and invisible, spiraling downward and outward in powerful radiation, lie the roots. I can see it spiraling upward from below, its stem straight and from it spiraling the branches season by season and from the spiraling branches moving out in quick motion the forked stems and from the stems twirling fragilely the tinier stems holding outward until they fall the half-curled pear leaves.

Far below lies the yard, lying flat and black beneath the body of the upshooting tree, for the pear tree from above looks as if it had been shot instantaneously from the ground, shot upward like a rocket to break in showers of leaves and fruits twirling and falling. Its movement looks quick, sudden, and rocketing. My child when grown can be looked at in this way as if it suddenly existed ... but I know the slow time of making. The pear tree knows.

Far inside the vertical stem there must be a movement, a river of sap rising from below and radiating outward in many directions clear to the tips of the leaves. The leaves are the lips of the tree speaking in the wind or they move like many tongues. The fruit of the tree you can see has been a round speech, speaking in full tongue on the tree, hanging in ripe body, the fat curves hung within the small curves of the leaves. I imagine them there. The tree has shot up like a rocket, then stops in midair and its leaves flow out gently and its fruit curves roundly and gently in a long slow curve. All is gentle on the pear tree after its strong upward shooting movement.

I sit here all the afternoon as if in its branches, midst the gentle and curving body of the tree. I have looked at it until it has become more familiar to me than Karl. It seems a strange thing that a tree might come to mean more to one than one's husband. It seems a shameful thing even. I am ashamed to think of it, but it is so. I have sat here in the pale sun and the tree has spoken to me with its many-tongued leaves, speaking through the afternoon of how to round a fruit. And I listen through the slow hours. I listen to the whisperings of the pear tree, speaking to me, speaking to me. How can I describe what is said by a pear tree? Karl did not speak to me so. No one spoke to me in any good speech.

There is a woman coming up the stairs, slowly. I can hear her breathing. I can hear her behind me at the screen door.

She came out and spoke to me. I know why she was looking at me so closely.

'I hear you're going to have a child,' she said. 'It's too bad.' She is the same color as the dead leaves in the park. Was she once alive too?

I am writing on a piece of wrapping-paper now. It is about ten o'clock. Karl didn't come home and I had no supper. I walked through the streets with their heavy, heavy trees bending over the walks and the lights shining from the houses, and over the river the mist rising.

Before I came into this room, I went out and saw the pear tree standing motionless, its leaves curled in the dark, its radiating body falling darkly, like a stream far below into the earth.

THE SHROUD[1]

By DOROTHY McCLEARY

(From *Story*)

NOW you know, Jenny, deep down in your heart, we don't rightly know how to make a shroud,' said Miss Emma.

'Sh. Tell her yes,' said Jenny.

'No, we'd botch it sure,' said Miss Emma, shaking her head. 'I'll say no such thing.'

'Give me that receiver!' Jenny cried. She pulled it out of her sister's hand. 'Yes, indeed, Mrs. Tidball,' she said brightly into the telephone, 'we'll be *so* happy to ——'

'Mercy, Jenny!' said Miss Emma, close to her ear. 'Don't sound so ——'

'Oh, yes, we'll make it just lovely for her,' exclaimed Jenny, her face radiant. 'Yes, ma'am.... Yes, ma'am. Oh, we *will*. Over her princess slip, yes, ma'am ——'

'Gracious,' said Miss Emma. '*Now* what?'

'She's going to send over some satin,' Jenny whispered in excitement.

'Dear me suz! Satin!'

'Oh — before evening?' said Jenny weakly, putting her hand to her heart. 'Well, I don't know as ——'

'Now — you see, miss?' warned Miss Emma. 'Tell her no and be done with it! Tell her plain sewing only! Goodness knows we don't profess to ——'

'Yes,' said Jenny resolutely. 'Yes, ma'am. Don't you worry one bit about it. We'll make it just beautiful, oh, indeed we will!' She hung up the receiver.

'*Before evening!*' said Miss Emma, sinking down onto a chair, and covering her face with her hands; '*us*, to make a real shroud before evening! We'll be the laughing-stock, you mark my words, Jenny Pitney.'

'Well, she wants her to look nice, she says, when their cousins get here from the West, and all that,' said Jenny. 'But before evening — you could have knocked me over with a look ——'

'You'll rue this, Jenny Pitney!'

'Oh, shoot!' said Jenny. 'If we never tried we'd never do anything. Look at Mabel Louise's confirmation dress — you said we'd never ——'

'Well, yes, but a *child's* dress, I don't feel ——'

'How do you make a shroud, I wonder? What does a shroud look like?' Jenny got out the big Star-Elite pattern book from under the table.

'A pretty time to think of that!' moaned Miss Emma.

'Well, only the top part shows much on a shroud — where the lid lies open, you know.'

'Oh, mercy, no, we'll never live this down. "A fine fist the Pitney sisters made of that shroud," they'll say, around amongst themselves — oh, dear!'

'I'll bet we get five dollars for this job, if we get a nickel,' said Jenny, eagerly turning over the pages of the pattern book. 'Shroud,' she said, looking in the index. 'Shroud —— Now, here's Shirts — Shirtbands — Shirtwaists — Tam o'Shanter — there's no shrouds here!' she cried out, panic-stricken.

'Look under Burial Garments,' suggested Miss Emma.

'No, Em,' said Jenny, running her eyes over it. 'No. Oh, this old pattern book! Why couldn't we have a new pattern book?'

'New?' asked Miss Emma tartly. 'Shrouds are as old as the hills, miss.'

'Well, they certainly do keep it a secret, the making of them,' grumbled Jenny.

'And she's a stout woman, Sadie Cudlip is,' said Miss Emma plaintively. 'That'll make work around the bosom — so you see!'

'I'll bet Sadie's a 44, the big thing!' said Jenny.

'Oh, dear, yes,' said Miss Emma. 'Every bit of it.'

'A-a-a-h,' came a low cry from the couch in the corner.

'Oh, pshaw,' said Miss Emma, putting on her glasses to examine the pattern book. 'Just at this time of all things! Go see what he wants. If it's the commode ——'

'What is it, Eben, dear?' asked Jenny, running to the couch.

'Bo ——' said Eben, licking around his lips.

'Tell Jenny,' she said. She smoothed his sparse hair. 'Tell sister.'

He worked his mouth-muscles violently. 'Box!' he managed to get out.

'Box?' asked Jenny. 'What box?'

Sweat appeared on his forehead. '*Box*,' he said again, frowning and closing his eyes, to rest after his exertion.

'Oh, you rascal!' Jenny shook her finger at him. 'I know what you want. All right, Jenny'll get it!' She came, laughing, over to Emma. '"Box," he says. Do you know what he's after, Em? Cousin Madge's candy!'

'Oh, for any's sake!'

'Pretty cute, isn't it? "Box," he said.'

'Don't let him throw his stomach out, now, of all things,' said Miss Emma. 'We've got enough on our hands ——'

'These are awful rich, dear,' said Jenny, setting a big box on his chest, where he could see into it. 'Oh, don't they look just *lovely!*' She sighed. 'Oh, they're so fine!' French bonbons, the lid said; and inside the box each chocolate sat in a little gold-colored frilled cup. 'Cousin Madge must have spent an awful lot on these,' said Jenny.

'Tsch, I should think so,' murmured Miss Emma. 'Such a thing to pitch good money away on! And I suppose she had them blessed by the Pope, did she?'

'Oh, Em, let Cousin Madge be!'

'Hm.'

'Well, *we* like them, don't we, Eben?' said Jenny. 'Now, which?'

Eben lay turning his eyes slowly from one piece to another.

'They're all the same inside, dear,' said Jenny, 'just the top's a little different. How about this one, with the little hat on it?' She pointed.

He shook his head.

'Not big enough — is that it?' She tapped him on the cheek. 'I know *you*. Well, this one?'

He smiled, showing cavernous depths of gum, with here and there a dark tooth.

'Here — take.' Jenny held it to his mouth and he took it in whole, closing his eyes to blot out everything but the bliss of dissolving it.

There came a ring at the doorbell.

'Oh, mercy on us!' said Emma, getting up. 'There's your satin for you! Oh, dear, now we're in for it, Jenny.'

'A *shroud!*' said Jenny to Eben, selecting him another candy.

'Ah?' he grunted, opening his eyes wide.

'We have to make a shroud,' said Jenny. 'Sadie Cudlip's dead, and ——' She put into his mouth the largest piece in the layer. 'Is it good?' she asked, taking his handkerchief from under the pillow, and wiping chocolate off his lips.

He nodded, deeply absorbed in eating.

'Tiptop, isn't it?' said Jenny.

'Well, here it is,' said Miss Emma, coming in with a white tissue-paper bundle. 'Casper's boy brought it, with his roller-skates on, if you please — all up over our front porch ——'

Jenny tore open the paper wrapping. 'Oh, fathers above!' she breathed. 'And a bolt of lace too — Em, it's double-faced satin.'

'Yes — we'll make no shroud of that!' declared Miss Emma, folding her lips tight together. 'That's a hundred dollars the yard.'

'Feel of it, feel of it!' said Jenny; 'oh, the soft feel of it!' She put her cheek down against the satin. 'Oh, merciful fathers above! *That* for Sadie Cudlip?'

'Now you see what you've got us into!'

'Spread newspaper. Spread out the whole *Bugle.*' She unrolled the goods, measuring from her nose to her outstretched hand. 'Six and a half to seven yards, I make it,' she said, 'of pure double satin.'

'You cut into that and I'll never speak to you again in this world, Jenny Pitney!'

'All right, here goes my doom!' cried Jenny, picking up her big shears and brandishing them over the satin.

'Don't you dare!' said her sister.

'Look, I know how we can make it,' said Jenny excitedly. 'Look here, we'll fold it right over in half, see? Then I'll cut out a little hole, big enough to put her head through, and cut holes for the arms — and there'll be loads off the bottom to make up a couple of flowing sleeves, sort of, and a sash around the middle ——'

'No, you don't,' said Miss Emma firmly. 'We'll put no doll-dress on any poor dead body! No, I'll never let it be said that ——'

'Well, then, how?' asked Jenny impatiently. 'We've got to cover her up, don't we? *Somehow.*'

'"Cover her up!"' said Miss Emma, sitting down helplessly.

'Oh, a nice way to talk! Why, poor Sadie Cudlip. What would she think if she was alive to hear you ——'

'Poor Sadie Cudlip nothing!' said Jenny, folding the satin over double. 'Rich Sadie Cudlip, that's what. Oh, my, Sadie and her rings and her bracelets and her eyeglasses on a stick — it's enough to ——'

'Have you no Christian charity, Jenny? And the poor woman lying dead?'

'All right, let her lie dead,' Jenny jerked out. 'I'm not stopping her.'

'Indeed, Jenny, sometimes I wonder at you,' Miss Emma said sadly. 'If I didn't know you had such a good heart at base, indeed ——'

'Some people have everything!' cried Jenny, stroking the satin. 'And some people have nothing — just the bare bones to live, that's all.'

'The first shall be last, and the last shall be first,' said Miss Emma, tying on her black work-apron.

'I'll bet not,' said Jenny. 'We'll come out the little end of the horn there, too. Sadie Cudlip'll lord it up in heaven, the same as anywhere else, just you watch! She'll have her fine house and her fine clothes and her automobile with a bunch of flowers in it — and the rest of us'll ride shanks' mare.'

'There'll be no riding in heaven,' said Miss Emma quietly. 'No rich or poor.'

'Then the first won't be last,' said Jenny sharply. 'Yes, our turn — that'll never come, just mark what I say!' She held the goods up against her. 'Well, there's fullness here and to burn,' she said, 'and thousands at the bottom.' She took the folded end, folded it once again, and grabbed up the scissors.

'What? Without pattern or *nothing?*' demanded Miss Emma.

'Just a tiny little wee hole at the first,' said Jenny coaxingly, 'then we'll see ——'

'Oh, no, Jen. Oh, I can't bear to look. Oh, I won't look!' Miss Emma covered her eyes. 'Merciful Father,' she prayed aloud, 'please, if it be Thy will, grant Sister not to spoil it; oh, if Thou knewest ——'

'Open!' Jenny cried. 'See?' She wormed her head softly into the hole she had cut. 'Now, then, we've got something to go on. I'll make it into a V on myself, and then ——' She held up the satin, and made her way to the full-length mirror. 'Em, this'll be a stunner,' she said, 'before we're through with it.'

Miss Emma followed her anxiously. 'Do be careful, Jen,' she begged. 'So far, all right, but it's only by a miracle. Don't get rash now, don't get headstrong.'

'Thread the basting-needles,' called out Jenny, snipping at the neck. 'I'll just give this neck a baste-up and get it out of harm's way; first come, first served,' she said gaily, admiring the effect in the glass. 'See that? In a sharp V, how's that?'

'Not too low, now,' said Miss Emma. 'A dead person, remember ——'

Eben sneezed. 'Oh, wipe him, will you, Em?' said Jenny. 'Under the pillow.'

Miss Emma found his handkerchief and held it to his nose. 'Blow!' she told him sternly.

'Oh,' he said, sneezing again. He sneezed terrifically, time after time.

'My poor darling,' said Jenny.

'It's from when I opened the door to Casper's boy,' said Miss Emma. 'Just the least little draught, and you see —— Now don't do it again, Eben. Hold in. You'll damage yourself.'

He turned his eyes and looked wistfully at Jenny.

'Give him a little kiss, Em,' said Jenny. 'That's what he wants, after a big sneeze. So he won't feel lonesome,' she whispered. 'Jenny can't come just this minute,' she called to him. 'Jenny's very busy with her shroud.'

Miss Emma bent down and brushed her lips against his forehead.

'One grand thing about sewing for a corpse,' said Jenny, 'we don't need to bother our heads about how the skirt hangs — any old way'll go.' She laughed.

'But the *stitching*, Jenny, that must be of the very finest,' said Miss Emma.

'Oh, the stitching,' said Jenny carelessly, 'that's the least of my worries.'

Miss Emma picked up an edge of the goods and studied it. 'It's just off white,' she said. 'It's not the eggshell, nor it's not the oyster —— Our Letter E ivory-white ought to do it — and our number Naught needle.'

'Yes, it's the bridal shade,' said Jenny, holding out her arms at her sides to see how far the goods would reach. 'Look, Em, there's enough for kimono sleeves — only they call 'em raglan sleeves now, or some, the dolphin — all the same thing. We'll tell Mrs. Tidball raglan — and lace all around the edge, oh, my! Give me the thing of pins.'

'Kimono sleeves,' said Miss Emma dubiously, bringing the pin-bowl, 'no, Sister, I don't know if that's just the thing or not. Kimono sleeves, is that respectful enough — of the dead, I mean?'

'All right, then,' Jenny broke out angrily, 'if you think I'm going to burst a blood-vessel trying to cut arm-holes and fit sleeves to them, when I don't have to —— Don't forget Miss Jebb's shirt-waist!'

'Oh, dear, Jenny!' A flush spread over Miss Emma's face. 'Oh, Jenny, how can you bring that up at such a time?'

'*Well!*'

'Well, I do think the kimono sleeves maybe would look soft and nice — the kimono sleeve is a restful-looking sleeve ——'

'I wonder if they'll bury all her bracelets and stuff on her?' said Jenny, marking off the line of sleeve with pins. 'There's enough of them to fill the casket just in themselves.'

'Oh, I wouldn't think so,' said Miss Emma. 'Just the one bracelet is more likely, to look pretty and graceful. And the wedding ring.'

'One of the bracelets, Em, and you and Eben and I could live on the cream of the earth,' said Jenny bitterly.

'Covet not that which is thy neighbor's,' said Miss Emma.

'*Neighbor*,' said Jenny. 'Sadie Cudlip's no neighbor of mine. She'd pass me right by on the street this minute as smooth as smooth, and never say boo.'

'Oh, so you may say, Jenny. But I always thought Sadie Cudlip was a nice civil-spoken girl. On the stout side, of course; and plenty to come and go on — but you can't hold that against her. She was born into it.'

'She shamed me once,' said Jenny, looking down darkly at the white satin. 'And now she'll never shame me again, that's one thing!'

'*Shame* you? Why, Jenny Pitney!'

'No, she didn't!' said Jenny with fire. 'I was too spunky for her.

"My dress is just as good as yours," I told her. "My dress is changeable silk," I said. "What's yours?" And she didn't know what her dress was!' Jenny laughed derisively. 'Stood there, twelve years old, and couldn't say what her own dress was made of!'

'Oh, at that party, you mean,' said Miss Emma. 'Mercy, so many years ago. But if we'd known, dear, we'd never have sent you in the dark dress, poor child.'

'The rest weren't silk!' cried Jenny defiantly.

'No, but they were all white,' said Miss Emma compassionately. 'I know.'

'She said to me, "Haven't you got a party dress?"'

'Oh, the little minx! If her mother'd heard her, she'd have got a good paddlewhacking.'

'Yes, Mrs. Tidball treated me just fine,' said Jenny. 'Mrs. Tidball said out big and loud, "Oh what a lovely little dress, Jenny!" And she gave me two helpings of ice-cream — hearts, it was, made of fresh strawberry ice-cream, all fancy.'

'Well, there you are,' said Miss Emma.

'I'd do anything in this world to please Mrs. Tidball,' said Jenny. 'But not Sadie!' Jenny slipped the satin off over her head and laid the two outer edges together. 'Now, I've only got to follow the pins, and both sleeves will be cut in.'

'Oh, dear, my heart's in my mouth!' said Miss Emma, watching the shears plunge through. 'Oh, if it shouldn't be right, Jenny!'

'I could cut into this satin all day!'

'How you can do it beats me,' said Miss Emma. 'Why, I wouldn't cut into that satin, no, not if I was offered my choice, that or ——'

'Oh, I like to feel it, soft under my shears,' said Jenny. 'All cutting I like, but oh, this *satin* — I wouldn't give you a thank-you for voile or gingham, if I can get my shears on satin.'

'Jen, I declare you do get the funniest face on you when you cut out,' said Miss Emma, watching. 'Why, you'd scare a person, if a body didn't know you.'

'Funny? How do you mean?'

'Oh, gracious, just as if you were going to eat the goods right up. Your mouth kind of goes funny — and look at your eyes! They get all whichway.'

'They do? Well,' said Jenny savagely, 'I like to cut! When I

cut I think, "Now I've got you. Now you can't get away from me."
Why, when I get started, I could cut up a whole tiger, and never
notice it!'

'Oh, Jenny, such talk!'

'What's that we used to say, back when we were little — what
was that, now, Em? "Me to cut ——"'

'"You to cut,"' recited Miss Emma, '"me to sew ——"'

'Oh, yes, "Me to cut, and you to sew, that's the way the dresses
grow!"'

'That was just doll-dresses,' said Miss Emma, threading needles
with basting-thread, 'back in those days.'

'Well, we're still at it, though, aren't we?'

Miss Emma sighed. 'Dear, dear,' she murmured. 'Give here.
Let me baste those sleeves up.'

'No, I can do it quicker,' said Jenny. She took up needle and
thread, and basted, down on her knees.

'Such basting, Jen!'

'Anything just to hold it together,' said Jenny. 'I haven't the
patience to ——'

The cat walked in and smelled at the front door.

'Can't we let Minnie out?' asked Jenny.

'Oh, no, not yet a while, I think,' said Miss Emma, looking at the
cat over her glasses. 'Or what do you think, Sister? Best to wait.'

'The poor thing.'

The cat rose up on its hind legs and howled.

'Just see that,' said Jenny.

'Ps, ps, ps, ps, ps,' said Eben, turning his eyes to the door.

The cat went and leaped onto Eben's chest, turning about and
settled down with one paw under its chin.

'Little did I think I'd ever be making on any shroud of hers,'
said Jenny, violently biting off a thread.

'It's a great pity,' said Miss Emma, 'a young woman like that
to be taken ——'

'Two years older than me!' said Jenny.

'Well, that's young,' said Miss Emma, 'as people go.'

'She's had her fill,' said Jenny sharply. 'Let her go.'

'Why, *Jenny!* When a person has everything in this world to
live for — a good husband, two dear little girls ——'

'I'm not wishing *them* any harm, am I?' Jenny snapped out.

'Then don't talk so.'

'Now,' said Jenny, jumping up, 'how long ought it to be, would you think?'

'A good modest length,' said Miss Emma. 'Say to the feet?'

'Eben's just the thing, now, isn't he?' said Jenny. She picked up the satin and went over to the couch. 'Jump off, Kittie-poots,' she said, giving Minnie a push. 'Now, let's see ——'

'Jenny!' cried Miss Emma in horror. 'You wouldn't dare to measure that shroud on Eben!'

'Oh, Eben won't mind; will you, dear?' asked Jenny. 'See the pretty goods. Feel of it.' She laid it against his cheek. 'Soft?'

'If anything should happen, Jen, I wouldn't thank you to be in *your* shoes!'

'Ah,' said Eben, opening his eyes in alarm.

'There, you see?' said Miss Emma.

'Well, I measured it on myself, too, didn't I? Where's the harm?'

'Yes, a very different thing — you up and about like a jumping-jack, and poor Eben, there he lies ——'

'All the better,' said Jenny. 'I can see how it'll look.'

'Well, don't you dare to take the tape-line to him,' said Miss Emma. 'Just measure with the eye, that's all ——'

Jenny arranged the sleeves out across Eben's shoulders and spread the rest of the goods down his length. 'Oh, there'll be loads left,' she said.

Miss Emma crept closer to view the measuring.

'Look — to here,' said Jenny, 'and a nice roomy hem; that'll leave almost a yard and a half, double, to do with as we please!'

'Yes, and every jot and tittle that's left over of that goods, Jenny Pitney, is to go right back where it came from!'

'No,' said Jenny. 'Not all, maybe.'

'*Yes*, I say.'

'Not if I say not!' said Jenny, coloring in anger. 'I'm no thief, but ——'

'No, I should say not,' said Miss Emma. 'We're none of us thieves around here. We've never taken hide nor hair of a customer's goods as yet, no, not so much as a thimbleful's worth, and we will not start today — on the trappings of a poor dead woman.'

'Well, then, what do they have to go and bury her in this fine satin for?' asked Jenny. 'Put it under ground — such beautiful, lovely satin —— She's got dresses enough! Why do they have to bury this satin?'

'That's for others to decide and us to obey,' said Miss Emma.

'Now, just look at this,' said Jenny. She laid the goods on the floor and put in pins along a straight line at the bottom. 'This will give her a good five-inch hem — and then all this, over. That ought to satisfy her, don't you think?' She picked up the shears and cut along the pins viciously. 'A satin shroud with a five-inch hem, that'll let them know up in heaven who's coming in at the front gate!'

'I don't like to hear you speak so, Jenny,' said Miss Emma.

'Here comes Sadie Tidball Cudlip,' announced Jenny in mock solemnity.

'Jenny!'

'All right, well, all I say to Sadie is, "Here's your dress, Sadie — what's your hurry?"'

'Jenny, before I would utter any such words as that, I'd sooner wash my tongue out with lye,' said Miss Emma.

'Well, I don't mean anything by it, I guess,' said Jenny. She brought a chair and set it close to her sister's, and they each took a side of the shroud to work on, beginning the long French seams. 'Only ——'

'Oh, these gold-eyed needles!' sighed Miss Emma contentedly, beginning to trip the fine stitches along under her broad thumb. 'When it comes to the *sewing* end of it! These gold needles — this was always Mama's idea of a needle, too ——'

'When it comes right down to it,' said Jenny, 'I wouldn't want to be her at this minute — dead. I'd rather be me, alive. Wouldn't you?'

'Are you speaking to me, Jenny Pitney?' asked Miss Emma with severity. 'Are you asking *me* that question?'

'Well, wouldn't you?'

'To that I can only say,' said Miss Emma, sewing steadily, 'that I *am* myself, and how could I be anybody else? We've all got to answer for our sins at the mercy-seat, Jen, and though I wouldn't care to say I'm anywhere near perfect, still I'd a good deal sooner have my own life on my conscience than to have a stranger's I know nothing about. No, I'm not ashamed of my life, I can tell you that. I joined earlier than most, I've never missed but four

Sabbaths in all my life — and those times I had sickness and death as my reasons to give to the Lord.'

'Yes,' said Jenny, 'I remember.'

'And what's more to the point,' said Miss Emma, 'I never, so long as I've lived, took up needle on the Sabbath day, no, nor ever will! Though we've lost money by it, that I will not deny. But it's been money well lost, say I. Satan's money.'

'Oh, I'm not so sure about that,' said Jenny, frowning over her needle. 'Money's money, once you get your hands on it. Who can remember where it came from, once it gets in your pocketbook?'

'So the Tempter says!' said Miss Emma, tightening her lips.

'I wish I had a hundred dollars right this minute,' said Jenny. She took a glance at Eben, who had fallen asleep and begun to snore, the cat back on his chest. 'I wish I had a million!' she added.

'You'd be no better off,' said Miss Emma brusquely, 'if as well.'

'With a million dollars?' laughed Jenny, pausing to stretch wide in her chair.

'Sew, sew, sew!' commanded Miss Emma, 'or we'll not get five dollars, even.'

'First thing I'd do,' said Jenny, 'I'd get some double satin like this, and I'd make myself a dress with a train to it.'

'Vanity, saith the Preacher.'

'Well, soon I'll be too old to look nice in one,' broke out Jenny, digging her needle into the goods. 'Do I have to go on *all* my life like this? Do we have to go on, forever, without ——'

Miss Emma raised her eyes from her needle long enough to look at Jenny hunched over her work, her cheeks burning with resentment, her left thumb darting in angry leaps ahead of her sewing-hand. 'Don't fret, Jen,' Miss Emma said kindly. 'We might be worse off, the three of us.'

'Oh!' Jenny spun out a long line of stitches. 'It's only when I get stuff like this into my hands, that I —— It's only at times like this ——'

'If we get five dollars from Mrs. Tidball,' promised Miss Emma, 'we'll have a little treat, dear. Indeed we will. Maybe one of those little plum-cakes, or if Hellersens' are still making their nice lemon sherbet ——'

'I don't want plum-cake!' cried Jenny, tears coming to her eyes.

'Gracious! All right, then.'

'She gets a dress like this, just to be buried in, that's all — nothing but a shroud, but oh, my, it must be just so! Yes, and all her life it's been the same way. Why, when she wasn't more than eight years old, didn't she have a muff and a nice little fur-piece of *ermine*, Em, as sure as I sit here! Real ermine — and on the likes of her, the big fat —— And take Cousin Madge ——'

'Oh, Cousin Madge!' exclaimed Miss Emma impatiently. 'Get along with your Cousin Madge!'

They both glanced furtively at the big crayon portrait over the mantel.

'Cousin Madge lives what I would call an ideal life,' said Jenny. 'Go anywhere she wants, eat what she wants, clothes to burn, nothing to do if she doesn't want to do it —— That's my idea of the way to live!'

'Yes, she can go and get herself blessed by the Pope!' put in Miss Emma, snapping off her thread.

'Well, let her, if she wants to do it,' said Jenny.

'And her Methodist Episcopal born, as ever was!' muttered Miss Emma. 'Hurry up. I'm through mine.'

Jenny finished off her side, trimmed the seams, and turned the shroud. Miss Emma started the pressing-down of the seam with thumb and forefinger.

'These two fine pieces,' said Jenny, fondling the goods that was left, 'I could make a blouse ——'

'Put those pieces right straight over on the tête,' said Miss Emma sharply, 'out of temptation's way.'

'Take that poor little McCandless baby,' said Jenny, back at the stitching, 'buried in one of his mother's shirtwaists. I'll bet he'd have liked a nice piece of this satin on him ——'

'Yes, indeed,' said Miss Emma. 'Well, he and Sadie Cudlip will be equal in the eyes of the Redeemer, never fear! Yes, when they face their Maker ——'

'This satin was never in the world made for putting underground,' said Jenny. 'It's a sin to put this down under ground. This is wedding-dress satin.'

'Wedding-dress!' scoffed Miss Emma.

'If it was a wedding-dress,' said Jenny, 'those extra pieces would make into a lovely train!'

'Well, alack, it's far from a wedding-dress,' said Miss Emma. 'The poor woman, that's over and done with.'

'And a little bouquet of orange blossoms right in the front,' said Jenny, dreamily. 'Oh, couldn't I fix it, though!'

'Hush that, now!' said Miss Emma sternly.

The cat jumped down, stretched herself and approached the satin to smell it.

'Now I'll try it on,' said Jenny, fastening her thread, 'and we'll see.'

'Oh, indeed, I hate to see you put it on you again,' said Miss Emma. 'Dear me, first on poor Eben, then on you ——'

'Well, that's it —— If we only had a dummy!' burst out Jenny passionately. 'Like other dressmakers —— But no, of course we'll never have one. We'll never have *anything!*'

'I s'pose a body could hardly even call us dressmakers,' said Miss Emma sadly. 'Not in the real sense, I mean.'

'Oh, I don't know,' said Jenny stoutly.

'Oh, no, they couldn't, if the truth must be told,' said Miss Emma, staring disconsolately as Jenny pulled off her skirt and waist, then put the shroud over her head. 'Pantie-waists and petticoats, and suchlike, we're right at home there; but when it comes to the fancy doings ——'

'Oh, look, Em!' cried Jenny, holding out her arms in the sleeves. 'That looks just like real sleeves. Nobody could say a *word* about those sleeves.'

'No, praise God,' said Miss Emma.

'And, oh, that V-neck is simply ——' Jenny looked at herself rapturously. 'Oh, Em, it becomes me like paper on the wall!'

'Is it going to be roomy enough, there across the bosom?' asked Miss Emma anxiously — 'for Sadie?'

'Oh, I wish Cousin Madge could see this!' cried Jenny. 'She'd think this was pretty fine.'

'Well, if it was anything else but what it is,' said Miss Emma bitterly, arranging the sleeves, 'I'd say you look as sweet as a rose in it.'

'This is a wedding-dress!' said Jenny. 'That's what this is. This is no shroud! And when we get the lace on it ——' She cut off a length of satin and twisted it into a girdle. 'Why, we've made a wedding-dress!' she cried out triumphantly. 'A complete wedding-dress! Maybe we don't know when we start out, do we, what'll make of it? But ——'

'Hush,' said Miss Emma. 'You've got Eben looking at you. Stand still till I turn up this hem now.'

'This is how I'd have looked,' said Jenny, edging closer to the glass, 'if I'd ever ——'

'Will you stand still!'

'Oh, no — the *veil!*' cried Jenny. 'Just let me see, Em, just let me try it on ——' She held up her skirts and ran into the bedroom.

'Jenny, are you gone crazy?' called Miss Emma.

'Turn Eben's head around,' said Jenny, 'so he can see me, I want him to get the full benefit ——'

'Oh, I'll do no such thing,' grumbled Miss Emma. But she took Eben by his cheeks, and turned his head on to its side.

'Look at me, Eben,' said Jenny, coming out with Cousin Madge's veil pinned to her hair. '"Here comes the bride!"' she sang. 'Dah, dah, da, dah ——'

'Take that trumpery off your head,' said Miss Emma.

'Don't I look nice, Eben?'

Eben shut his eyes, and a sweat appeared all over his face and hands. 'Um ——' he groaned.

'Oh, dear,' said Miss Emma. 'The ammonia! Quick, Jen.'

They poured him out a spoonful in water, opened his mouth, and poured it down.

'Eben, my poor darling,' said Jenny, wiping his face dry.

'If it's an attack,' moaned Miss Emma, 'oh, I don't know what we'll do in this world ——'

'Eben,' said Jenny, 'open your eyes, dear.'

He opened them, looked at her bridal veil, and shut them again. 'No!' he said with all the force of his jaw muscles.

'Oh, he doesn't like *this!*' said Jenny, pulling off the veil. 'The poor darling! Look, Eben, open up — look at Jenny. Jenny's taken off the veil. Jenny isn't going to get married.'

Eben opened his eyes.

'Give him another spoonful,' said Miss Emma.

'Jenny's *never* going to get married,' said Jenny, twining her fingers with his. 'Jenny'll always be here, with Eben.'

'A-ah,' said Eben, a look of satisfaction coming into his eyes. He smiled. 'Box,' he said.

'No,' said Miss Emma firmly. 'First the commode — don't you

think so, Jen? Yes, let's get it over with. Duty first,' she added,
'then comes pleasure.'

'*Pleasure*,' said Jenny, fingering at Cousin Madge's veil. Suddenly she picked up her shears and cut a big gash in the veil. 'Now
I've got you,' she said savagely. 'See, Eben?'

MAN ON A ROAD[1]

By ALBERT MALTZ

(From *The New Masses*)

AT ABOUT four in the afternoon I crossed the bridge at Gauley, West Virginia, and turned the sharp curve leading into the tunnel under the railroad bridge. I had been over this road once before and knew what to expect — by the time I entered the tunnel I had my car down to about ten miles an hour. But even at that speed I came closer to running a man down than I ever have before. This is how it happened.

The patched macadam road had been soaked through by an all-day rain and now it was as slick as ice. In addition, it was quite dark — a black sky and a steady, swishing rain made driving impossible without headlights. As I entered the tunnel a big cream-colored truck swung fast around the curve on the other side. The curve was so sharp that his headlights had given me no warning. The tunnel was short and narrow, just about passing space for two cars, and before I knew it he was in front of me with his big, front wheels over on my side of the road.

I jammed on my breaks. Even at ten miles an hour my car skidded, first toward the truck and then, as I wrenched on the wheel, in toward the wall. There it stalled. The truck swung around hard, scraped my fender and passed through the tunnel about an inch away from me. I could see the tense face of the young driver with the tight bulge of tobacco in his cheek and his eyes glued on the road. I remember saying to myself that I hoped he'd swallow that tobacco and go choke himself.

I started my car and shifted into first. It was then I saw for the first time that a man was standing in front of my car about a foot away from the inside wheel. It was a shock to see him there. 'For Chrissakes,' I said.

My first thought was that he had walked into the tunnel after my car had stalled. I was certain he hadn't been in there before. Then I noticed that he was standing profile to me with his hand held up in the hitch-hiker's gesture. If he had walked into that tunnel, he'd be facing me — he wouldn't be standing sideways looking at the opposite wall. Obviously I had just missed knocking him down and obviously he didn't know it. He didn't even know I was there.

It made me run weak inside. I had a picture of a man lying crushed under a wheel with me standing over him knowing it was my car.

I called out to him 'Hey!' He didn't answer me. I called louder. He didn't even turn his head. He stood there, fixed, his hand up in the air, his thumb jutting out. It scared me. It was like a story by Bierce where the ghost of a man pops out of the air to take up his lonely post on a dark country road.

My horn is a good, loud, raucous one and I knew that the tunnel would redouble the sound. I slapped my hand down on that little black button and pressed as hard as I could. That man was either going to jump or else prove that he was a ghost.

Well, he wasn't a ghost — but he didn't jump, either. And it wasn't because he was deaf. He heard that horn all right.

He was like a man in a deep sleep. The horn seemed to awaken him only by degrees, as though his whole consciousness had been sunk in some deep recess within himself. He turned his head slowly and looked at me. He was a big man, about thirty-five with a heavy-featured face — an ordinary face with a big fleshy nose and a large mouth. The face didn't say much. I wouldn't have called it kind or brutal or intelligent or stupid. It was just the face of a big man, wet with rain, looking at me with eyes that seemed to have a glaze over them. Except for the eyes you see faces like that going into the pit at six in the morning or coming out of a steel mill or foundry where heavy work is done. I couldn't understand that glazed quality in his eyes. It wasn't the glassy stare of a drunken man or the wild, mad glare I saw once in the eyes of a woman in a fit of violence. I could only think of a man I once knew who had died of cancer. Over his eyes in the last days there was the same dull glaze, a faraway, absent look as though behind the blank, outward film there was a secret flow of past events on which his mind was focused. It was this same look that I saw in the man on the road.

When at last he heard my horn, the man stepped very deliberately around the front of my car and came toward the inside door. The least I expected was that he would show surprise at an auto so dangerously close to him. But there was no emotion to him whatsoever. He walked slowly, deliberately, as though he had been expecting me and then bent his head down to see under the top of my car.

'Kin yuh give me a lift, friend?' he asked me.

I saw his big, horse teeth chipped at the ends and stained brown by tobacco. His voice was high-pitched and nasal with the slurred, lilting drawl of the deep South. In West Virginia few of the town folk seem to speak that way. I judged he had been raised in the mountains.

I looked at his clothes — an old cap, a new blue work shirt and dark trousers, all soaked through with rain. They didn't tell me much.

I must have been occupied with my thoughts about him for some time, because he asked me again.

'Ahm goin' to Weston,' he said. 'Are you a-goin' thataway?'

As he said this, I looked into his eyes. The glaze had disappeared and now they were just ordinary eyes, brown and moist.

I didn't know what to reply. I didn't really want to take him in — the episode had unnerved me and I wanted to get away from the tunnel and from him too. But I saw him looking at me with a patient, almost humble glance. The rain was streaked on his face and he stood there asking for a ride and waiting in simple concentration for my answer. I was ashamed to tell him 'no.' Besides, I was curious.

'Climb in,' I said.

He sat down beside me, placing a brown paper package on his lap. We started out of the tunnel.

From Gauley to Weston is about a hundred miles of as difficult mountain driving as I know — a five-mile climb to the top of a hill, then five miles down and then up another. The road twists like a snake on the run and for a good deal of it there is a jagged cliff on one side and a drop of a thousand feet or more on the other. The rain and the small rocks crumbling from the mountain-sides and littering up the road made it very slow going. But in the four hours or so that it took for the trip, I don't think my companion spoke to me half a dozen times.

I tried often to get him to talk. It was not that he wouldn't talk, it was rather that he didn't seem to hear me — as though as soon as he had spoken, he would slip down into that deep, secret recess within himself. He sat like a man dulled by morphine. My conversation, the rattle of the old car, the steady pour of rain were all a distant buzz — the meaningless, outside world that could not quite pierce the shell in which he seemed to be living.

As soon as we had started, I asked him how long he had been in the tunnel.

'Ah don' know,' he replied. 'A good tahm, ah reckon.'

'What were you standing there for — to keep out of the rain?'

He didn't answer. I asked him again, speaking very loudly. He turned his head to me.

'Excuse me, friend,' he said, 'did you say somethin'?'

'Yes,' I answered. 'Do you know I almost ran you over back in that tunnel?'

'No-o,' he said. He spoke the word in that breathy way that is typical of mountain speech.

'Didn't you hear me yell to you?'

'No-o.' He paused. 'Ah reckon ah was thinkin'.'

'Ah reckon you were,' I thought to myself.

'What's the matter, are you hard of hearing?' I asked him.

'No-o,' he said, and turned his head away looking out front at the road.

I kept right after him. I didn't want him to go off again. I wanted somehow to get him to talk.

'Looking for work?'

'Yessuh.'

He seemed to speak with an effort. It was not a difficulty of speech, it was something behind, in his mind, in his will to speak. It was as though he couldn't keep the touch between his world and mine. Yet when he did answer me, he spoke directly and coherently. I didn't know what to make of it. When he first came into the car I had been a little frightened. Now I only felt terribly curious and a little sorry.

'Do you have a trade?' I was glad to come to that question. You know a good deal about a man when you know what line of work he follows and it always leads to further conversation.

'Ah generally follows the mines,' he said.

'Now,' I thought, 'we're getting somewhere.'

But just then we hit a stretch of unpaved road where the mud was thick and the ruts were hard to follow. I had to stop talking and watch what I was doing. And when we came to paved road again, I had lost him.

I tried again to make him talk. It was no use. He didn't even hear me. Then, finally, his silence shamed me. He was a man lost somewhere within his own soul, only asking to be left alone. I felt wrong to keep thrusting at his privacy.

So for about four hours we drove in silence. For me those hours were almost unendurable. I have never seen such rigidity in a human being. He sat straight up in the car, his outward eye fixed on the road in front, his inward eye seeing nothing. He didn't know I was in the car, he didn't know he was in the car at all, he didn't feel the rain that kept sloshing in on him through the rent in the side curtains. He sat like a slab of moulded rock and only from his breathing could I be sure that he was alive. His breathing was heavy.

Only once in that long trip did he change his posture. That was when he was seized with a fit of coughing. It was a fierce, hacking cough that shook his big body from side to side and doubled him over like a child with the whooping cough. He was trying to cough something up — I could hear the phlegm in his chest — but he couldn't succeed. Inside him there was an ugly, scraping sound as though cold metal were being rubbed on the bone of his ribs, and he kept spitting and shaking his head.

It took almost three minutes for the fit to subside. Then he turned around to me and said, 'Excuse me, friend.' That was all. He was quiet again.

I felt awful. There were times when I wanted to stop the car and tell him to get out. I made up a dozen good excuses for cutting the trip short. But I couldn't do it. I was consumed by a curiosity to know what was wrong with the man. I hoped that before we parted, perhaps even as he got out of the car, he would tell me what it was or say something that would give me a clue.

I thought of the cough and wondered if it were T.B. I thought of cases of sleeping sickness I had seen and of a boxer who was punch drunk. But none of these things seemed to fit. Nothing physical seemed to explain this dark, terrible silence, this intense, all-exclusive absorption within himself.

Hour after hour of rain and darkness!

Once we passed the slate dump of a mine. The rain had made the surface burst into flame and the blue and red patches flickering in a kind of witch glow on a hill of black seemed to attract my companion. He turned his head to look at it, but he didn't speak, and I said nothing.

And again the silence and rain! Occasionally a mine tipple with the cold, drear, smoke smell of the dump and the oil lamps in the broken down shacks where the miners live. Then the black road again and the shapeless bulk of the mountains.

We reached Weston at about eight o'clock. I was tired and chilled and hungry. I stopped in front of a café and turned to the man.

'Ah reckon this is hit,' he said.

'Yes,' I answered. I was surprised. I had not expected him to know that we had arrived. Then I tried a final plunge. 'Will you have a cup of coffee with me?'

'Yes,' he replied, 'thank you, friend.'

The 'thank you' told me a lot. I knew from the way he said it that he wanted the coffee, but couldn't pay for it; that he had taken my offer to be one of hospitality and was grateful. I was happy I had asked him.

We went inside. For the first time since I had come upon him in the tunnel, he seemed human. He didn't talk, but he didn't slip inside himself either. He just sat down at the counter and waited for his coffee. When it came, he drank it slowly, holding the cup in both hands as though to warm them.

When he had finished, I asked him if he wouldn't like a sandwich. He turned around to me and smiled. It was a very gentle, a very patient smile. His big, lumpy face seemed to light up with it and become understanding and sweet and gentle.

The smile shook me all through. It didn't warm me — it made me feel sick inside. It was like watching a corpse begin to stir. I wanted to cry out 'My God, you poor man!'

Then he spoke to me. His face retained that smile and I could see the big, horse teeth stained by tobacco.

'You've bin right nice to me, friend, an' ah do appreciate it.'

'That's all right,' I mumbled.

He kept looking at me. I knew he was going to say something else and I was afraid of it.

'Would yuh do me a faveh?'

'Yes,' I said.

He spoke softly. 'Ah've got a letter here that ah done writ to mah woman, but ah can't write very good. Would you-all be kind enough to write it ovah for me so it'd be proper like?'

'Yes,' I said, 'I'd be glad to.'

'Ah kin tell you-all know how to write real well,' he said, and smiled.

'Yes.'

He opened his blue shirt. Under his thick woolen underwear there was a sheet of paper fastened by a safety pin. He handed it to me. It was moist and warm and the damp odor of wet cloth and the slightly sour odor of his flesh clung to it.

I asked the counterman for a sheet of paper. He brought me one. This is the letter I copied. I put it down here in his own script.

My dere wife ——

i am awritin this yere leta to tell you somethin i did not tell you afore i lef frum home. There is a cause to wy i am not able to get me any job at the mines. i told you hit was frum work abein slack. But this haint so.

Hit comes frum the time the mine was shut down an i worked in the tunel nere Gauley Bridge where the govinment is turnin the river inside the mounten. The mine supers say they wont hire any men war worked in thet tunel.

Hit all comes frum thet rock thet we all had to dril. Thet rock was silica and hit was most all of hit glass. The powder frum this glass has got into the lungs of all the men war worked in thet tunel thru their breathin. And this has given to all of us a sickness. The doctors writ it down for me. Hit is silicosis. Hit makes the lungs to git all scab like and then it stops the breathin.

Bein as our hom is a good peece frum town you aint heerd about Tom Prescott and Hansy McCulloh having died two days back. But wen i heerd this i went to see the doctor.

The doctor says i hev got me thet sickness like Tom Prescott and thet is the reeson wy i am coughin sometime. My lungs is agittin scab like. There is in all ova a hondred men war have this death sickness frum the tunel. It is a turible plague becus the doctor says this wud not be so if the company had gave us masks to ware an put a right fan sistem in the tunel.

So i am agoin away becus the doctor says i will be dead in about fore months.

i figger on gettin some work maybe in other parts. i will send you all my money till i caint work no mohr.

i did not want i should be a burdin upon you all at hum. So thet is wy i hev gone away.

i think wen you doan here frum me no mohr you orter go to your grandmaws up in the mountens at Kilney Run. You kin live there an she will take keer of you an the young one.

i hope you will be well and keep the young one out of the mines. Doan let him work there.

Doan think hard on me for agoin away and doan feel bad. but wen the young one is agrowed up you tell him wat the company has done to me.

i reckon after a bit you shud try to git you anotha man. You are a young woman yit.

Your loving husband

Jack Pitckett

When I handed him the copy of his letter, he read it over. It took him a long time. Finally he folded it up and pinned it to his undershirt. His big, lumpy face was sweet and gentle. 'Thank you, friend,' he said. Then, very softly, with his head hanging a little — 'Ahm feelin' bad about this a-happenin' t'me. Mah wife was a good woman.' He paused. And then, as though talking to himself, so low I could hardly hear it, 'Ahm feelin' right bad.'

As he said this, I looked into his face. Slowly the life was going out of his eyes. It seemed to recede and go deep into the sockets like the flame of a candle going into the night. Over the eyeballs came that dull glaze. I had lost him. He sat deep within himself in his sorrowful, dark absorption.

That was all. We sat together. In me there was only mute emotion — pity and love for him, and a cold, deep hatred for what had killed him.

Presently he arose. He did not speak. Nor did I. I saw his thick, broad back in the blue work shirt as he stood by the door. Then he moved out into the darkness and rain.

THE GRAVE[1]

By KATHERINE ANNE PORTER

(From *The Virginia Quarterly Review*)

THE grandfather, dead for more than thirty years, had been twice disturbed in his long repose by the constancy and possessiveness of his widow. She removed his bones first to Louisiana and then to Texas, as if she had set out to find her own burial place, knowing well she would never return to the places she had left. In Texas she set up a small cemetery in a corner of her first farm, and as the family connection grew, and oddments of relations came over from Kentucky to settle, it contained at last about twenty graves. After the grandmother's death, part of her land was to be sold for the benefit of certain of her children, and the cemetery happened to lie in the part set aside for sale. It was necessary to take up the bodies and bury them again in the family plot in the big new public cemetery, where Grandmother had been recently buried. At long last her husband was to lie beside her for eternity, as she had planned.

The family cemetery had been a pleasant small neglected garden of tangled rosebushes and ragged cedar trees and cypress, the simple flat stones rising out of uncropped sweet-smelling wild grass. The graves were lying open and empty one burning day when Miranda and her brother Paul, who often went together to hunt rabbits and doves, propped their twenty-two Winchester rifles carefully against the rail fence, climbed over and explored among the graves. She was nine years old and he was twelve.

They peered into the pits all shaped alike with such purposeful accuracy, and, looking at each other with pleased adventurous eyes, they said in solemn tones: 'These were graves!' trying by words to shape a special, suitable emotion in their minds, but they felt nothing except an agreeable thrill of wonder: they were seeing a new sight, doing something they had not done before. In them both there was also a small disappointment at the entire

[1] Copyright, 1935, by The University of Virginia.

commonplaceness of the actual spectacle. Even if it had once contained a coffin for years upon years, when the coffin was gone a grave was just a hole in the ground. Miranda leaped into the pit that had held her grandfather's bones. Scratching around aimlessly and pleasurably, as any young animal, she scooped up a lump of earth and weighed it in her palm. It had a pleasantly sweet, corrupt smell, being mixed with cedar needles and small leaves, and as the crumbs fell apart, she saw a silver dove no larger than a hazel nut, with spread wings and a neat fan-shaped tail. The breast had a deep round hollow in it. Turning it up to the fierce sunlight, she saw that the inside of the hollow was cut in little whorls. She scrambled out, over the pile of loose earth that had fallen back into one end of the grave, calling to Paul that she had found something, he must guess what.... His head appeared smiling over the rim of another grave. He waved a closed hand at her: 'I've got something too!' They ran to compare treasures, making a game of it, so many guesses each, all wrong, and a final show-down with opened palms. Paul had found a thin wide gold ring carved with intricate flowers and leaves. Miranda was smitten at sight of the ring and wished to have it. Paul seemed more impressed by the dove. They made a trade, with some little bickering. After he had got the dove in his hand, Paul said, 'Don't you know what this is? This is a screw head for a *coffin!* ... I'll bet nobody else in the world has one like this!'

Miranda glanced at it without covetousness. She had the gold ring on her thumb; it fitted perfectly. 'Maybe we ought to go now,' she said; 'maybe one of the niggers'll see us and tell somebody.' They knew the land had been sold, the cemetery was no longer theirs, and they felt like trespassers. They climbed back over the fence, slung their rifles loosely under their arms — they had been shooting at targets with various kinds of firearms since they were seven years old — and set out to look for the rabbits and doves or whatever small game might happen along.

On these expeditions Miranda always followed at Paul's heels along the path, obeying instructions about handling her gun when going through fences; learning how to stand it up properly so it would not slip and fire unexpectedly; how to wait her time for a shot and not just bang away in the air without looking, spoiling shots for Paul, who really could hit things if given a chance. Now and then, in her excitement at seeing birds whizz up suddenly before her face, or a rabbit leap across her very toes, she lost her head, and almost without sighting she flung her rifle up and pulled the trigger. She hardly ever hit any sort of mark. She had no proper sense of hunting at all. Her brother would be often completely disgusted with her.

'You don't care whether you get your bird or not,' he said. 'That's no way to hunt.'

Miranda could not understand his indignation. She had seen him smash his hat and yell with fury when he had missed his aim.

'What I like about shooting,' said Miranda, with exasperating inconsequence, 'is pulling the trigger and hearing the noise.'

'Then, by golly,' said Paul, 'whyn't you go back to the range and shoot at tin cans?'

'I'd just as soon,' said Miranda; 'only like this, we walk around more.'

'Well, you just stay behind and stop spoiling my shots,' said Paul, who, when he made a kill, wanted to be certain he had made it. Miranda, who alone brought down a bird once in twenty rounds, always claimed as her own any game they got when they fired at the same moment. It was tiresome and unfair and her brother was sick of it.

'Now, the first dove we see, or the first rabbit, is mine,' he told her. 'And the next will be yours. Remember that and don't get smarty.'

'What about snakes?' asked Miranda idly. 'Can I have the first snake?'

Waving her thumb gently and watching her gold ring glitter, Miranda lost interest in shooting. She was wearing her summer roughing outfit: dark blue overalls, a light blue shirt, a hired-man's straw hat, and rough brown sandals. Her brother had the same outfit except his was a sober hickory-nut color. Ordinarily Miranda preferred her overalls to any other dress, though it was making rather a scandal in the countryside, for the year was 1903, and in the back country the law of female decorum had teeth in it. Her father had been criticized for letting his girls dress like boys and go careering around astride barebacked horses. It was said the motherless family was running down, with the grandmother no longer there to hold it together. Miranda knew this, though she could not say how. She had met along the road old women of the kind who smoked corncob pipes, who had treated her grandmother with most sincere respect. They slanted their gummy old eyes sideways at the granddaughter and said, 'Ain't you ashamed of yo'self, Missy? It's aginst the Scriptures to dress like that. Whut yo' pappy thinkin' about?' Miranda, with her powerful social sense, which was like a fine set of antennae radiating from every pore of her skin, would feel ashamed because she knew well it was rude and ill-bred to shock anybody, even bad-tempered old crones; though she had faith in her father's judgment and was perfectly comfortable in the clothes. Her father had said, 'They're just what you need, and they'll save your dresses for school....' This sounded quite simple and natural to her. She had been brought up in rigorous economy. Wastefulness was vulgar. It was also a sin. These were truths; she had heard them repeated many times and never once disputed.

Now the ring, shining with the serene purity of fine gold on her rather grubby thumb, turned her feelings against her overalls and sockless feet, toes sticking through the thick brown leather straps. She wanted to go back to the farmhouse, take a good cold bath, dust herself with plenty of her sister's violet talcum powder — provided she was not present to object, of course — put on the thinnest, most becoming dress she owned, with a big sash, and sit in a wicker chair under the trees.... These things were not all she wanted, of course; she had vague stirrings of desire for luxury and a grand way of living which could not take precise form in her imagination, being founded on a family legend of past wealth and leisure. But these immediate comforts were what she could have, and she wanted them at once. She lagged rather far behind Paul, and once she thought of just turning back without a word and going home. She stopped, thinking that Paul would never do that to her, and so she would have to tell him. When a rabbit leaped, she let Paul have it without dispute. He killed it with one shot.

When she came up with him, he was already kneeling, examining the wound, the rabbit trailing from his hands. 'Right through the head,' he said complacently, as if he had aimed for it. He took out his sharp, competent Bowie knife and started to skin the body. He did it very cleanly and quickly. Uncle Jimbilly knew how to prepare the skins so that Miranda always had fur coats for her dolls, for though she never cared much for her dolls, she liked seeing them in fur coats. The children knelt facing each other over the dead animal. Miranda watched admiringly while her brother stripped the skin away as if he were taking off a glove. The flayed flesh emerged dark scarlet, sleek, firm; Miranda with thumb and finger felt the long fine muscles with the silvery flat strips binding them to the joints. Brother lifted the oddly bloated belly. 'Look,' he said, in a low, amazed voice. 'It was going to have young ones.'

Very carefully he slit the thin flesh from the center ribs to the flanks, and a scarlet bag appeared. He slit again and pulled the bag open, and there lay a bundle of tiny rabbits, each wrapped in a thin scarlet veil. The brother pulled these off and there they were, dark gray, their sleek wet down lying in minute even ripples, over pink skin, like a baby's head just washed; their unbelievably small delicate ears folded close, their little blind faces almost featureless.

Miranda said, 'Oh, I want to *see*,' under her breath. She looked and looked — excited but not frightened, for she was accustomed to the sight of animals killed in hunting — filled with pity and astonishment and a kind of shocked delight in the wonderful little creatures for their own sakes, they were so pretty. She touched one of them ever so carefully. 'Ah, there's blood running over them,' she said, and began to tremble without knowing why. Yet she wanted most deeply to see and to know. Having seen, she felt at once as if she had known all along. The very memory of her former ignorance faded, she had always known just this. No one had ever told her anything outright, she had been rather unobservant of the animal life around her because she was so accustomed to animals. They seemed simply disorderly and unaccountably rude in their habits, but altogether natural and not very interesting.

Her brother had spoken as if he had known about everything all along. He may have seen all this before. He had never said a word to her, but she knew now a part at least of what he knew. She understood a little of the secret, formless intuitions in her own mind and body, which had been clearing up, taking form, so gradually and so steadily she had not realized that she was learning what she had to know.

Paul said cautiously, as if he were talking about something forbidden: 'They were just about ready to be born.' His voice dropped on the last word.

'I know,' said Miranda, 'like kittens. I know, like babies.' She was quietly and terribly agitated, standing again with her rifle under her arm, looking down at the bloody heap. 'I don't want the skin,' she said, 'I won't have it.'

Paul buried the young rabbits again in their mother's body, wrapped the skin around her, carried her to a clump of sage bushes, and hid her away. He came out again at once and said to Miranda, with an eager friendliness, a confidential tone quite unusual in him, as if he were taking her into an important secret on equal terms:

'Listen, now. Now, you listen to me, and don't ever forget. Don't you ever tell a living soul that you saw this. Don't tell a soul. Don't tell Dad because I'll get into trouble. He'll say I'm leading you into things you ought not to do. He's always saying that. So now, don't you go and forget and blab out sometime the way you're always doing.... Now, that's a secret. Don't you tell.'

Miranda never told; she did not even wish to tell anybody. She thought about the whole worrisome affair with confused unhappiness for a few days. Then it sank quietly into her mind and was heaped over by accumulated thousands of impressions, for nearly twenty years.

One day she was picking her path among the puddles and crushed refuse of a market street in a strange city of a strange country, when, without warning, in totality, plain and clear in its true colors as if she looked through a frame upon a scene that had not stirred nor changed since the moment it happened, the episode of the far-off day leaped from its burial place before her mind's eye. She was so reasonlessly horrified she halted, suddenly staring, the scene before her eyes dimmed by the vision back of them. An Indian vendor had held up before her a tray of dyed-sugar sweets, shaped like all kinds of small creatures: birds, baby chicks, baby rabbits, lambs, baby pigs. They were in gay colors and smelled of vanilla, maybe.... It was a very hot day and the smell in the market, with its piles of raw flesh and wilting flowers, was like the mingled sweetness and corruption she had smelled that other day in the empty cemetery at home: the day she had remembered vaguely always until now as the time she and her brother had found treasure in the opened graves. Instantly upon this thought the dreadful vision faded, and she saw clearly her brother, whose childhood face she had forgotten, standing again in the blazing sunshine, again twelve years old, a pleased sober smile in his eyes, turning the silver dove over and over in his hands.

THANKS FOR NOTHING[1]

By ROALDUS RICHMOND ✓

(From *Story*)

W E WENT into the office and Grascha looked up at us. He was sitting behind his desk, a big cigar sticking out of his round dark face. His eyes were hard and mean. He smiled at us from in back of that cigar, but his eyes didn't smile.

'How'd it go?' Grascha said. 'How'd it go this time?'

'Not so good,' Jigger said.

'What you mean, "not so good"?' Grascha demanded, the cigar bobbing up as his teeth tightened. 'How much you collect?'

'Forty-five bucks,' Jigger said.

'Forty-five bucks!' Grascha snarled. 'What the hell is this, huh? You mugs gettin' fresh, aintcha? Forty-five bucks! Listen, don't give me that stuff. You oughta got forty-five outa one or two slots.'

'Sure,' Jigger said. 'Sure, and we woulda, only your slots aren't on location no more. We only found three slot-machines and they was ruined.'

Grascha got up and leaned over the desk, his eyes looking crazy. He hammered the desk with a huge fist.

'Who knocked 'em off, huh? Who lifted my machines?'

'Who'd yuh think?' Jigger said.

'You mean Halloran? Halloran . . . he wouldn't dare to.'

'Who else would dare to?'

Grascha sat back in his chair. The cigar waved up and down as he chewed it. I felt like laughing. I wanted to laugh, but I was afraid of Grascha. We were all afraid of Grascha but Jigger.

'All right,' Grascha said. 'All right, all right, all right. Halloran, huh? All right, Mister Halloran, all right. Irish bastard!'

'The Irish aren't afraid of anybody,' Jigger said.

'You're Irish, aintcha?' Grascha looked up quick.

'Sure, I'm Irish.'

'I don't like the Irish,' Grascha said.

[1] Copyright, 1935, by Story Magazine, Inc.

Jigger shrugged his slim shoulders and grinned.

'Last month it was the cops,' Grascha said. 'This month it's Halloran's mob. This ain't no racket to be in. This slot-machine business ain't no good. No good, see? How can a guy make dough in this racket? No good.'

I lit a cigarette and offered one to Jigger. He shook his head and picked a cigar off the desk. He was grinning when he lit it.

'Forty-five bucks,' Grascha mumbled. 'That won't even pay off you punks. That won't begin to pay for the dress my old lady bought yesterday.' He shook his big black head. 'How can I send my girls to Smith's College, huh? How can I, answer me that?'

'Send 'em to City College,' Jig said.

'Yah-h! City College. With all the kikes. They wouldn't go, they wouldn't hear of it. All I hear is Smith's College, Smith's College. Whatsa difference, one college or another, huh?'

'I'm a Harvard man myself,' Jigger said.

The Greek looked up quick. 'You're a pretty smart fella, huh?'

'Sure,' Jig said. 'Right.'

'Don't get too smart. I like you still less, you get too smart, see?'

'Okay,' Jig said. 'Okay, chief. Where do we go from here?'

'Where's the chicken feed you collect? Where's the forty-five?'

Jigger pulled out some crumpled bills. 'Here's thirty-five,' he said. 'Ten went for expenses.'

'You're pretty expensive guy, too,' Grascha said slowly. 'You get too expensive an' too fresh, I think. I get sick of havin' you around.'

My throat was dry and tight and the insides of my hands felt warm and wet. But Jig was easy and cool as ever.

'You're so smart,' Grascha went on in that slow flat voice, 's'pose you go get me some of Halloran's machines. What you say?'

'Okay.'

'Get me all his machines you find, see? You know his spots?'

'Yeah, I know 'em.'

'Take a coupla the boys. Don't have no trouble, see? Unless you gotta have it, see? After you got 'em, go see Halloran. Tell him he's all done in this town. Tell him, get out right away. Tell him he oughta know better, try to chisel on Grascha. Understand?'

'Nice little evening you got mapped out for us,' Jigger said. 'Want to come along?'

Grascha came out of his chair fast.

'Listen,' he said, 'come here, huh? Before you go.' Jigger stood facing him, slim and straight against Grascha's bulk. 'You like my cigars, no?' Grascha said, smiling, whipping the cigar out of Jigger's mouth to the floor.

Jigger's eyes narrowed and his lips tightened, but he didn't move. Grascha reached out a big hand and cuffed Jigger's lean cheek, playfully. Grascha laughed, down in his throat.

'You still know who is the boss, huh?'

'Sure,' Jigger said.

When we were outside in the dim hallway, Jigger broke loose, cursing, his long arms jabbing out at the shadows.

'Sometime when he does that,' Jigger said tightly, 'he's goin' to get it, *plenty*!'

I laughed nervously. 'Then your girl will be an orphan.'

'She'll be better off,' Jig said. 'She'll still have a mother.'

'The old lady don't count. All she knows is to spend dough.'

'I'll get that sonofabitch,' Jigger said.

'Ann might not like it if you bumped her old man.'

'Ann likes anything I do.'

'She won't after she's been at Smith,' I said.

'She ain't going to Smith,' Jig said.

'Well, all I hope is that Grascha don't find out about you and Ann.'

'To hell with Grascha,' Jig said.

Redeye and Dilly were in the front room with the boys playing five-and-ten and drinking gin. They were the two we wanted.

'How'd yuh like to go for a joy-ride, Redeye?' Jigger asked. 'You and Dilly.'

'Where's our cut?' Redeye said.

'Ha, ha, ha,' I said. 'There ain't no cut.'

'That's why we're goin' ridin',' Jig said.

'Whatsamatter, no cut?' Dilly said. 'What the hell is this? Somebody chiselin'?'

'Ask the Greek,' I told him, laughing.

'Who wants to play?' Redeye said. 'Prince Hal?'

'Right,' Jig said. 'Let's go. You lugs ask too many questions.'

'Hell of a sweet note,' Dilly mumbled. 'I'm gittin' sick o' this no-cut stuff.'

'Come and earn your cut,' Jig told him.

'Earn it!' Dilly said. 'I been punchin' the clock here every day for a month, ain't I?'

'Yeah, sittin' on your tail an' drinkin' the Greek's gin!' Jigger said disgustedly. 'You comin'?'

Redeye and Dilly pushed back their chairs and got up. Redeye took one of the gin bottles. Dilly said, 'I'm owin' you one fish, Mac.'

'One an' a quarter yuh mean,' Mac said. 'Just my luck you get rubbed out tonight.'

'There's a chance o' that, too,' Jigger said. 'Let's be on our way.'

We went outside and paused on the sidewalk.

'Big car,' Jigger said. 'You drive, Dilly.'

Dilly slid in behind the wheel and Jigger got in beside him. Redeye and I crawled in the back.

'Where we goin'?' Dilly said.

'I don't know,' Jigger said. 'Head for Halloran's territory.'

'Hal been gettin' fresh?' Redeye asked.

'Yeah,' I said. 'Lemme see that gin.'

We didn't know just what spots Halloran had his machines in, but we knew his territory and we knew what places were likely to carry slot-machines. I took three or four stiff jolts of the gin to key me up a little. You never could tell what might pop. Halloran must be getting pretty cocky to muscle in like that on the Greek. Cocky or crazy.

'You got that dick's badge, Redeye?' Jigger asked. 'Give it here, will yuh?'

'What the hell yuh goin' to do, pinch somebody?' Redeye said, handing the badge up to Jigger.

'Pinch Hal's machines, you cluck.'

'Oh, just a little fun, hey?' Redeye said, grabbing for the gin bottle.

'We gotta make some hay,' Jigger said grimly. 'Grascha's gotta send his girls to college.'

'I thought you had Ann all educated,' Dilly said, snickering.

'Drive the car and shut up,' Jig said.

Everything went pretty smooth, at first. We'd spot a joint, park the car handy, and walk in to look the machines over. There were usually two or three machines in each place, but sometimes only one. Jigger would flash his badge and say, 'Sorry, boys. We got orders to pick these things up all over town.' The rest of us would grab machines and carry them out to the car, with Jig keeping his eye on the proprietor and covering our exit. Then we'd hop in the crate and beat it. It was duck soup.

One place, I was the first one out with a machine and I almost ran over a flatfoot. I damn near swallowed the machine. Dilly was right behind me and I heard his breath whistle through his teeth.

'Hey, you!' yelled the bull. 'Where you goin' with those?'

Just then Jigger came out and showed his badge to the copper. 'Surprise raid,' Jig said. 'It's okay, officer.'

'Funny I didn't hear nothin' about it,' muttered the flatfoot.

'Lots of things *you* don't hear about,' Jig said. 'Come on, boys.'

We got away with it, all right. When we landed in the back seat, Redeye and I dove for the bottle.

After we got a load, we took the machines back to the Greek's, got another bottle of gin, and started out again. Mac and the rest thought they ought to trail us in another car, but Jigger said there was no need of it. I was getting to feel brave myself on account of the gin. We began loading up once more and everything went smooth and easy. It got to be almost monotonous.

In one joint we were just lifting the machines when some guy yells out, 'Them ain't coppers!'

I set my machine down and reached for my pocket, but there was no need of it.

'No, but we shoot a lot straighter,' Jigger said, showing them an automatic.

We went out with the slots and Jigger backed out after us. He was laughing when we got in the car. 'Hadda play my ace that time,' he said.

But most of the time there was nothing to it. We just walked in and walked out with the machines, and beat it. It was like stealing milk off the doorstep of an empty house.

'This is gettin' awful dull,' complained Redeye. 'An' them machines are gettin' awful heavy. I thought this was a racket, not a laborin' job.'

'Cheer up, we gotta call to make on Prince Hal before the night is over,' Jigger said.

'Gimme the badge an' *you* play stevedore for a while,' Dilly said.

'I work with my head, not my hands.'

'An' you're goin' to marry the boss's daughter, too,' Redeye said.

'Won't the boss be tickled?' I joined in.

'Betcha he'll give you a slot-machine for a weddin' present,' Redeye said.

We were all laughing except Jigger.

'You guys ain't funny,' Jigger said.

'I wouldn't mind ownin' a slot,' Dilly said. 'In a good spot, you know. Make a nice day's pay.'

'Plenty o' suckers shove coin into 'em, all right.'

'Didja read in the papers?' Redeye said. 'Some big shot says that slot-machines was robbin' the poor women and children. Says the workmen put their money in machines insteada buyin' food an' stuff for their families.'

'They'd waste it some way,' Jigger said. 'What difference how they waste it? Might's well be in slots as in liquor an' whores an' like that.'

'Oughta have a drink on that,' Redeye said. 'Jig's a smart boy.'

'The Greek thinks he's too smart,' I said.

'If the Greek only knew!' Dilly said.

'—— the Greek!' Jigger said.

After a while it got harder to find any machines. We'd strike a likely looking location, drop in, and no machines in sight. That meant the word was going around ahead of us and they were ducking the slots. We had no way of knowing whether they had us tagged as coppers or the Greek's boys.

In one lunchroom Jigger says to the proprietor, 'Didn't you used to have some nickel-machines in here? I feel lucky tonight.'

'No, never had any,' the guy said. 'Don't believe in 'em, myself.'

'*I* like 'em,' Jigger said. 'And *you* lie like hell.'

'What? Whatta hell you mean, fella?'

'What I said.'

'Wise guy, huh? Wise guy?'

'And tough,' Jigger said, looking right through the man.

'Listen, you want somethin' here?' the guy said, rubbing his hands on his apron.

'If I did I'd take it,' Jig said.

'Cut it out, Jig,' I said. 'What the hell, let's blow.'

When we got back in the car, Dilly said we ought to go home. 'We gotta 'nough machines,' Dilly said.

'I'm runnin' this show,' Jigger said. He was feeling ugly and hard. When he felt like that, hell was to pay. You couldn't hold him in a straitjacket. 'Drive to Horton's,' Jigger said.

Horton's was one of Halloran's strongholds. I reached for the gin, but Redeye beat me to it. When he put the bottle down, it was empty. I threw it on the floor and swore. Redeye laughed, and I rammed my hand into my pocket to feel the gun and slip off the safety. My mouth was dry as Kansas.

'The party's just beginnin',' Redeye said.

We parked across the street from Horton's.

'Stay in the car, Dill,' Jigger said. 'An' don't go to sleep.' I wished I had been driving.

Jig led the way across to Horton's, walking fast. Redeye was whistling. I kept spitting from my dry mouth.

There was a big gang in Horton's, and a whole row of slot-machines against one wall. Jigger looked the crowd over and then made for the machines, Redeye and I following him. Nobody was playing the machines. I could feel the crowd watching us. It wasn't a nice feeling. Jigger started putting nickels in one of the slots, and a few guys drifted over to watch.

'Don't this goddam' thing ever pay?' Jigger said. Redeye was still whistling.

The crowd was getting thicker around us, I could feel them massing up around our backs. We had a swell chance of getting out of that joint. We were on the spot for fair. Then the crowd split and one guy came through. I saw him out of the corner of my eye. It was Halloran. Halloran was a dude, a dresser and a ladies' man. He liked to be called Prince Hal. Most people didn't spell Prince that way when they spoke of him behind his back.

'Hullo, boys,' Halloran said.

Jigger turned around. 'Hiyah, Hal. Nice lotta machines you got here.'

'Yeah, oh, yeah,' Halloran said. 'Glad you like 'em, Jigger. Go right ahead an' play.'

'I'm all through,' Jigger said.

'Don't let me stop you.'

'I wouldn't,' Jig said.

Halloran laughed. 'I hear you been out collectin'. I hear you turned copper.'

'Just lookin' for strays.'

Halloran laughed again. It sounded like when you pour oil.

'Have a drink?' Halloran said. 'I'll buy a drink.'

'Sure.' We followed Halloran to a table. Two other guys came along and sat down with us. The rest of the gang broke up and straggled off. The two guys were Kicker Kane and Mopey Lutz. We knew them, all right, just like they knew us. Hal ordered the drinks and we drank.

'Where's the big fella tonight?' Halloran asked.

'He don't get out much. Too busy,' Jig said. 'Sent his regards.'

'What's he doin', countin' his profits?' Halloran said. 'Or checkin' up on his daughter Ann?'

'Both, maybe. You know his daughter?'

'No, but I've heard of her. They say she's a looker. Kinda wild, but a swell looker.'

Halloran was smooth and smiling all the time. I waited for the blow-up to come. Kicker and Mopey were laughing, watching Jigger. Jig's face was tight and cold and hard, like a mask.

'I like you, Jigger,' Halloran said. 'How'd you like to work for a real guy?'

'Too busy.'

'The Greek's no good,' Halloran said. 'The Greek's all washed up. I know how you feel, his daughter and all, but ——'

'The Greek's still runnin' this town,' Jigger said.

'Maybe,' Halloran laughed. 'But how long would *you* be workin' for the Greek if he knew about you and Ann?'

'Leave her out of it, see?'

'Sure, sure, sure. Don't get sore. But everybody knows about it, everybody but the Greek. An' he's sure to find out pretty soon. You know ——'

'The Greek wanted me to tell you to blow, Halloran,' Jigger said. 'He ain't kiddin' either, he means it. Either you blow, or else ——'

'He'd tell you to blow, too, if he knew about you and his girl ——'

'How do *you* know so much?'

'Hell,' Kicker Kane said, 'it was in Winchell's column the other day.'

Jigger stood up. All of us stood up.

'Along with the crack that all pansies wear spats!' Jigger said.

Everybody looked down at Halloran's spats. Halloran's smile faded and he looked down, too. Crack! Jigger swung one off his chin, and Halloran folded up. Kicker reached under his arm, but Redeye cut loose shooting through his pocket, and Kicker fell face down across the table. I had Mopey covered and he just looked at me and backed away. We cut for the door and they were shooting before we cleared it. I was out first, and Redeye came through, stumbling and swearing. Jigger came out on the jump, and we grabbed onto each side of Redeye. Dilly was on his toes, and swung the car around with squealing tires, and we piled in. Dilly slammed the gear shift through and gave her the gun. It was a snappy getaway.

Redeye was sprawled out on the rear seat. 'My leg,' Redeye moaned. 'My leg, my goddam' leg. Oooh, my goddam' leg!'

'Is it bad?' I said.

'I don't know. It feels bad.' We hit some trolley tracks. 'Jeeesus! I wisht we had that gin.'

'Shoulda shot Halloran, too,' Jigger muttered.

'Who didja shoot?' Dilly asked.

'Kicker Kane. Redeye got him.'

'I thought you was all dead,' Dilly said. 'All them fireworks.'

'Get to the doc,' Jigger said.

'This'll ruin the slot-machine racket,' I said.

'It'll blow over,' Jigger said. 'What the hell? They's other rackets.'

'S'pose Kicker croaked?' I said.

'I *know* he croaked!' Redeye said. 'Oh, *Jesus*, this leg ...'

We took Redeye to our regular doc and hung around smoking cigarettes while the doc fixed him up. It was nothing serious, but it was painful. The slug had ripped some ligaments off Redeye's knee and he would be laid up a long time and never be so fast on the getaway again. But he was lucky it hadn't been a direct hit on his knee. The doc was nervous and shaky as usual and kept asking if there'd been anyone bumped off. Jigger told him there was three guys and one broad killed, and he thought a little kid was knocked off by a stray bullet. Redeye kept cursing the doc because his leg hurt so like hell, and that made the doc all the more nervous. We smoked cigarettes and wisecracked and laughed at them. Jigger was feeling pretty good now, only he was sorry he hadn't plugged Halloran instead of just smacking him down.

'We done a nice job of work for the Greek tonight,' Jigger said. 'I hope he'll be grateful to us.'

'I hope he kicks through with some coin,' Dilly said. 'I'm a guy who can't stand empty pockets.'

When Redeye's knee was fixed up, we carried him out to the car and drove to our rooming-place and got Redeye up to bed. The doc was going to send around some crutches in the morning. Jigger took the car to go down and report to the Greek, and Dilly and I stayed with Redeye. I had some gin in the room, and Dilly and I sat around drinking Redeye to sleep. Redeye was a great man for his liquor and it sure took a lot of it to put him to sleep. He claimed the pain in his leg kept him sober, but I seen him when he didn't have any pain.

'How 'bout in the morning, Red?' Dilly said. 'I should think it would be painful enough to wake up with that leg, let alone a hangover.'

'Hangover, hell!' Redeye said. 'I don't have hangovers no more. Just leave me a little o' this for a mouthwash in the mornin', an' I'll be okay.'

When Jigger came back, he had fifty bucks apiece for us.

'Them machines was loaded,' Jigger said. 'The Greek was happy as hell, you shoulda seen him, smilin' all over the place. 'Course he crabbed a little 'bout bumpin' Kicker, but that was just for show. I think he'll give Redeye a bonus for it, on the level.'

'I hope he at least gives him a case of gin,' I said. 'Mine ain't going to last forever.'

'Did Halloran think we was goin' to take it layin' down?' Dilly said. 'Leavin' them slots around like that full of jack.'

'Halloran don't think,' Jigger said. 'He ain't got a thought in the world beyond dames.'

'Well, whadda we do now?' Dilly said.

'We might get drunk,' I said. 'We got a swell start.'

'Let's hit the bed,' Jigger said. 'We can get drunk in the mornin'.'

'It's damn near mornin' right now, kid.'

'That's right. Well, I'm for sleep. C'mon, Chick.'

'I s'pose I'll hafta sleep on the floor,' Dilly said, 'so's not to disturb this goddam' cripple.'

'You've done it before,' Jigger said. 'Good night, boys.'

We left them there and went across the hall to our room to get undressed. It was starting to get daylight already, and I yanked the curtains down.

'Well, did the Greek box your ears to show his appreciation?' I asked, as we stripped off our clothes.

'Aw, the Greek ain't a bad guy,' Jigger said.

'He'll make you a nice father-in-law, all right.'

'Go to hell,' Jigger said, flopping into the bed.

In the morning Jigger got a call, and I knew it must be from the girl. It was, and he started dressing right away, saying he had to go and meet her, and he thought something must be up or she wouldn't 'phone at this ungodly time. I asked him where I could get hold of him in case something big showed or the bulls were after us or something, and he said I couldn't, but he'd be back soon as he could. I knew he and Ann Grascha had an apartment some place where they went and stayed together, but Jigger never would say anything about it. I was too sleepy to think much about anything right then. I only wanted Jigger to hurry up and get out so I could go back to sleep.

It was early afternoon when Dilly woke me up, and we got dressed and started for the Greek's, stopping for coffee and sinkers on the way. The usual deadwood was laying around the front room of the Greek's, and they looked at us in a funny, surprised sort of way.

'Thought you birds had scrammed,' Mac said.

'Why?' I said.

'Why!' Mac said. 'Holy Jeeze, you ask me why! Where you been?'

'Sleepin',' Dilly said. 'Whatsamatter, the coppers after us?'

'Not much!' Mac said. '*Not much!*'

'Listen,' I said. 'Quit stallin' an' give us the stuff, will yuh?'

'Where's Jigger?' Dilly said.

'Jigger's dead,' Mac said. Just like that.

Dilly and I looked at him. He didn't look like he was kidding. I grabbed Mac by the neck.

'God damn you,' I said. 'If you ——'

The rest of the boys flocked around. 'That's right, Chick,' somebody said. 'Mac gave it to yuh straight.'

I let go of Mac and he rubbed his throat. 'I wouldn't kid about *that*,' Mac said.

Dilly and I looked at each other.

'Who got him, the Law?' I said. 'Where's the Greek? Where's Grascha?'

'You won't see the Greek around here today,' Mac said grimly.

'Who got Jigger? Christ Almighty, can't you talk?'

'Don't know. Nobody knows.'

'Where was he? Where'd it happen?'

'In an apartment somewheres. Jigger walks in an' somebody lets him have it. With a submachine gun. Shot him all to hell. No trace of anybody. They figger it was Halloran's mob, gettin' even for Kicker Kane.'

I looked at Dilly, and he was looking at me with a sick, awful look. A knowing look. We both knew. We knew, all right.

'C'mon, Dill,' I said, and we went out.

'Grascha,' Dilly said, looking like a hypnotized man.

'Sure,' I said. 'Halloran tipped him off.' I felt all sick and gone inside.

Dilly shook his head slowly from side to side. There was nothing left in me but an awful empty sickness. Like when you want to vomit and you can't.

'That bastard of a Greek,' Dilly said, still shaking his head.

I couldn't say anything.

Dilly and I blew town. It was the only thing for us to do. That town was too hot for us. Halloran could have it. All I hoped was he would get the Greek, and somebody would get him. That town was no place for us. We had to blow. There was nothing we could do for Jigger. All we could do was lam out of there. We couldn't take Redeye with us, but I left him all my gin.

Dilly and I grabbed a street-car to go to the outskirts, and then we were going to jump on a bus. It was hot and crowded on the car, and we didn't do any talking. We just sat there and sweated and felt sick. A couple of average-looking guys in front of us were talking about slot-machines.

'I got a jackpot this morning,' one of them said. He sounded real proud and happy. 'Four bucks and a half,' he said, 'and I only put in three-four nickels. I'm pretty lucky on those things. I crack 'em every once in a while.'

'I almost hit the jackpot coupla days ago,' the other guy said. 'I played this machine for half an hour, not losin' too much. Then I quit. An' I'll be damned if some fella didn't walk up and drop a nickel and cop the jackpot. With *one* nickel!'

'That's the way it goes,' said the first guy. 'Funny things, these machines.'

I looked at Dilly, but he was looking out the window.

FUGUE FOR HARMONICA[1]

By ALLAN SEAGER

(From *Vanity Fair* and *Lovat Dickson's Magazine*)

EVERY afternoon they came up to the village green to wait, the unemployed, a few men sagging limply against the wall of a barn, with large soft hands, caps on their heads, and their necks swathed in scarves knotted and held sometimes with brummagem pins. They spoke little, watching the vapors lift or sink on the Downs, and hearing, before the cottage across the road, an old man's parrot squawking in the sun, a gray bird with a red crest. Or, to escape the sudden rains, they sat on the bench beneath the big elm on the green, watching for the newsboys to bring the *Mail*, which would tell them if their horse had won the four-thirty at Newmarket and their shilling bets turned into five; or they waited until the pub, the Greyhound, should open at six.

From the green they could just see the large botany cross of limestone in the churchyard, gray against the yews, a memorial with a graven base, bearing the legend, 'For God, King, and Country.' It was erected by small subscriptions in the village to commemorate the bravery, and the deaths, of their friends with whom they had gone out to war. Few of the unemployed ever looked at it, because there was always the mist to watch above the distant summit of the Downs and the parrot's curses to listen to.

Jack Haines was unemployed, living on twenty-eight shillings a week dole, and supporting his wife and his son, Cyril. He never went to the green to wait out the day, but in fine weather dug in a small garden patch, or if it rained, stayed in his cottage teaching his five-year-old Cyril how to play the mouth-organ.

Out of such a dole you would not expect much of a house. There are two willows in front, a flagged walk, and the garden beside it. The cottage itself has a thatched roof, and in summer there is wistaria climbing up the side. There are also rats in the thatch that will face a terrier down, and in one room, the bricks of the floor are laid on the earth which spurts up mud in wet weather.

The pump is outside, and there is a fireplace in one room only. On the mantel are cigarette cards with pictures of fish, flowers, and racehorses on them. 'I was on him when he won the Autumn Cup at Newbury,' Jack says, pointing to Loosestrife, a handsome bay horse. 'Won a fiver. Coo, I didn't half have a night out.'

Tea at the Haines's is bread, bacon dripping, and a poached egg, but if you are a guest Jack's wife will buy three of the baker's best little cakes — 'Get down, Cyril, there's none for you. Shame on you' — with icing colored violet, red, and a brilliant malachite. After tea, Jack offers a twopenny packet of Woodbines to smoke.

When Cyril has played the newest piece he has learned on the mouth-organ, Jack will tell, while his wife smiles a set and patient smile, of the high point in his life. This is not the three years he was a company runner in France, and often carried sacks of Mills bombs in the open when the support trenches were blown, but the halcyon evening that he won the South Berks shove-halfpenny championship. 'On the Bell board at Wantage 'twas. Landlord had it polished till it shone like glass.'

The recital takes an hour, with gestures, while Cyril squeaks on the mouth-organ, and as a climax, Jack brings out from under the bed a huge photograph of himself, looking very sheepish, with a huge cup. 'We had to sell it. Only fetched seven and six. Man at the jeweler's said it was lead.'

It had been very bad with Jack before Cyril was born and while he was a baby too young to talk. There had been no work much since the War, and until Cyril began to ask questions and to run about, Jack had gone every day to the village green with the rest of the workless. They had not talked against the Government nor about the War nor their officers. They simply had not talked, but leaned and sat in apathy, waiting for the day to go over their heads, sunshine or mist.

But when Cyril began to grow a little bit, Jack could see that he was very bright and quick. If he saw the baker with the back of his wagon full of fresh loaves, he wanted to see how bread was made, and often on rainy days they watched the baker, with flour in his hair and eyebrows, moulding the dough and putting it in pans for the ovens. Or when they passed a farmer working in a garden, Cyril had to know why he dug, what he planted, and how it grew.

Jack started his own garden at that time, and Cyril helped him. And once a gentleman gave Jack three huge trees to cut down on his estate, and told him he could have the wood to sell in return for the cutting down. Jack borrowed a long, two-handed saw, and Cyril was just large enough to guide one handle and keep it from wiggling. At night Cyril walked into the cottage, struck his cap on his thigh to shake out the sawdust and shouted, 'What's for tea?' in the same manner as his father.

Every evening at six Jack and Cyril came along by the row of pollards to the pub. Jack is very tall and Cyril came up to the middle of his thigh. But Jack never walked slowly so the boy could keep up, and Cyril never hung on to his father's coat. He trotted breathlessly beside, gasping, 'Yes, Dad,' to Jack's remarks.

When they got to the doorway of the Greyhound, George, the landlord, standing with his hand on the lintel waiting for custom, would say, 'Hello, artful,' to Jack, and always, 'Yer sprouting up like a weed,' to Cyril. Jack and Cyril answered, 'Evening, George,' together. Then the three would go in, and the landlord would draw a pint of ale for Jack and give Cyril a chocolate biscuit.

As champion of the district, Jack always took the shove-half-penny board into the sitting-room, a small chamber with piano and aspidistra, and on the wall a picture of the landlord's son in uniform at Poona. The bar-room is too small to play in, because the bar itself and the four barrels behind it, two of ale and two of beer, the domino table and the space before the dart board take up the room. The sitting-room is usually reserved for occasional transient gentry and the wives of the men in the bar, who sit in chairs around the walls, gossiping and drinking stout in small bottles, and when they laugh they hold their hands genteelly up before their mouths.

If no one would play Jack at shovers, he would take on Cyril, whose chin just reached over the table top. There were no concessions. Jack was quite as polite when Cyril made a good shot, and as scornful of a bad as he was with a man. When Jack got another partner, Cyril sat in an armchair gravely watching the game.

He was a fat little boy with cheeks the color of raw liver and he kept his cap on indoors like his father. He would comment, 'Well done, Dad,' or 'Bad luck, Dobbin,' impartially. When he thought Jack was not looking, he climbed down from the chair and nipped a drink out of his father's pint. If Jack caught him, he would shout, 'Stay outa me beer, me son, or I'll smack your head.'

Often Jack would take Cyril on the bike to the more distant pubs, as far as the Fox at Steventon or the Noah's Ark, and Cyril would sit on the bar singing while Jack played the mouth-organ, with the farmers and working-men joining in the choruses. Occasionally Cyril got drunk from too many nips into his father's pint, and the women of the neighborhood often said that they were going in a body to Mrs. Haines to speak sharply to her about her dear little boy drinking in public-houses.

They should have spoken, even though Jack would have cursed them out of the place for meddling, for one day Jack noticed that Cyril looked too fat. It was three days later that he saw it was not fat round the boy's chin but a swelling. The backs of his hands were puffed. He put the child to bed, where he sang songs and jumped about for a week. He did not feel any sickness, but the swelling grew until his legs were as big around as a quart pot. At last, with the rustic's fear of all officials, Jack called the charity nurse, who packed Cyril off to hospital in Wantage, and when Jack came to see his son the first time, the matron, an old woman in a hooded cap, told him it was Cyril's kidneys, and that it was very serious.

When Jack told his wife, she suggested timidly, 'Perhaps you shouldn't have fed him beer.'

A bewildered man, seeing his little mainstay broken, and knowing no way to answer but in anger, he said, 'Don't speak to me of that. He shall have beer if he wants it. Gallons of it.'

Every day for weeks that spring Jack rode his bike the five miles to Wantage, where King Alfred was born, and stopped at the confectioner's in the market place by Alfred's statue to buy chocolate biscuits to take his son, as if he would wheedle him back to life with songs and little gifts.

And every night he was in the bar at the Greyhound drinking old beer, black and musty, because it was strong and he could sleep if he drank enough.

One day the matron met him at the door of the ward, and whispered: 'He's very bad. He won't last the day out. I'm sorry,

Mr. Haines. He was a dear little boy,' And, Jack, turning his cap around in his hands, could only answer, 'Yes, madam.'

He entered the ward softly, a long room full of bedridden old women with iron-gray braids, who began to nod and whisper when they saw him. In the corner was Cyril in a crib. When he heard his father's step, he rolled back his head so he could see under his swollen eyelids. 'Hello, Dad,' he said weakly.

Jack talked to him very cheerfully and rapidly a long time telling over all the things they would do together as soon as he was well again. A terrier, certainly, and perhaps a little bike of his own, and Newbury for the races. As if he were begging the child a favor, Jack spoke, and then pulled out the mouth-organ and wiped it on his trouser leg. 'What'll it be, me son?'

'The Old Rustic Bridge by the Mill,' whispered Cyril.

Jack played it, making one hand flutter at the end of the mouth-organ to give expression, and some of the old women sang in cracked voices.

He asked Cyril again, and one of the women said, with false encouragement, 'Play "Gandhi" so Cyril can sing it.'

Jack played the tune, and Cyril's lips moved with the words:

> Gandhi, Gandhi, they're coming after you.
> When they catch you, they'll give you a month or two.
> They'll bind you up with wire
> And tickle your Black Maria,
> And you'll look sweet upon the seat
> Of a bicycle built for two.

'Now what, Cyril?' Jack said.

But Cyril had closed his eyes and turned his head away.

Jack said, 'Tell me a song to play fer ye, son.'

Cyril did not answer.

'Tell me a song, son,' Jack said again, and the tears ran down his cheeks.

'Tell me a song, Cyril, tell me a song.'

The old women had begun to cry noisily.

'A song, son.'

The day after the funeral, the little group of idle men on the green saw Jack coming towards them along the road, head down, walking hard. As he passed, one called, 'Where be going, then, Jack?'

Jack stopped short, and looked up startled, 'Why — no place, Tom. There be no place I'm going.' And he looked at the barn, plastered with advertising posters, and the line of men sagged against it in the sun, and he turned slowly with resignation and leaned against the barn.

'Too bad about the little chap,' one said.

Jack answered, 'Aye.'

And, after an hour or two of staring at the grass, with the cackling of the gray, caged parrot in his ears, Jack took from his pocket the mouth-organ and threw it into the ditch.

A LIFE IN THE DAY OF A
WRITER[1]

By TESS SLESINGER

(From Story)

O SHINING stupor, O glowing idiocy, O crowded vacuum, O privileged pregnancy, he prayed, morosely pounding X's on his typewriter, I am a writer if I never write another line, I am alive if I never step out of this room again; Christ, oh, Christ, the problem is not to stretch a feeling, it is to reduce a feeling, *all* feeling, all thought, all ecstasy, tangled and tumbled in the empty crowded head of a writer, to one clear sentence, one clear form, and still preserve the hugeness, the hurtfulness, the enormity, the unbearable all-at-once-ness, of being alive and knowing it too...

He had been at it for three hours, an elbow planted on either side of his deaf-mute typewriter, staring like a passionate moron round the walls that framed his life — for a whole night had passed, he had nothing or everything to say, and he awoke each morning in terror of his typewriter until he had roused it and used it and mastered it, he was always afraid it might be dead forever — when the *telephone* screamed like an angry siren across his nerves. It was like being startled out of sleep; like being caught making faces at yourself in the mirror — by an editor or a book-critic; like being called to account again by your wife. His hand on the telephone, a million short miles in time and space from his writing-desk, he discovered that he was shaking. He had spoken to no one all the morning since Louise — shouting that she could put up with being the wife of a non-best-seller, or even the wife of a chronic drunk with a fetich for carrying away coat-hangers for souvenirs, but not, by God, the duenna of a conceited, adolescent flirt — had slammed the door and gone off cursing to her office. Voices are a proof of life, he explained gently to the angry telephone, and I have not for three hours heard my own; supposing I have lost it? Courage, my self! he said, as he stupidly lifted the receiver and started

[1] Copyright, 1935, by Story Magazine, Inc.

when nothing jumped out at him. All at once he heard his own voice, unnaturally loud, a little hoarse. *I wish to report a fire*, he wanted to say, but he said instead, roaring it: *Hello*. The answering *Hello, sunshine*, came from an immeasurable distance, from America, perhaps, or the twentieth century — a rescue party! but he had grown, in three long hours, so used to his solitary island! And though he was a writer and said to be gifted with a fine imagination, it was beyond his uttermost power to imagine that this voice addressing him was really a voice, that since it was a voice it must belong to a person, especially to the person identifying herself as Louise.

Ho, Louise! he said, going through with it for the purpose of establishing his sanity, at least in her ears if not actually in his own: he spoke courteously as though her voice were a voice, as though it did belong to her, as though she really were his wife; *now, darling, don't go on with* —— But then he discovered that she was not going on with anything but being a wife, a voice, an instrument of irrelevant torture. *How goes the work*, she said kindly. What in hell did she think he was, a half-witted baby playing with paper-dolls? *Oh, fine, just fine*, he answered deprecatingly. (I'm a writer if I never write another line, he said fiercely to his typewriter, which burst out laughing.) *Well, look*, she was saying, *Freddie called up* (who in hell was Freddie?), and then her voice went on, making explanations, and it seemed that he was to put away his paper-dolls and meet her at five at Freddie's, because Freddie was giving a cocktail party. *Cocktail party*, he said obediently; *wife; five*. Cocktail party, eh — and a dim bell sounded in his brain, for he remembered cocktail parties from some other world, the world of yesterday; a cocktail party meant retrieve from typewriters, rescue from desert islands; and it might also mean Betsey — he cocked a debonair eye at his typewriter to see if it was jealous — Betsey, who, along with half a dozen coat-hangers, had been the cause of this morning's quarrel! *Yes, your wife for a change*, came the off-stage tinkle over the telephone again; *and you might try taking her home for a change too, instead of someone else's — and by the way, my treasure, don't bring those coat-hangers with you, Freddie has plenty of his own. — Right you are, my pet*, he said, feeling smart and cheap and ordinary again, *right you are, my lamb-pie, my song of songs, ace of spades, queen of hearts, capital of Wisconsin, darling of the Vienna press* —— But she had got off somewhere about Wisconsin.

He looked, a little self-conscious, about his now twice-empty room; aha, my prison, my lonely four-walled island, someone has seen the smoke from my fire at last, someone has spied the waving of my shirt-tails; at five o'clock today, he said, thumbing his nose at his typewriter, the rescue plane will swoop down to pick me up, see, and for all you know, my black-faced Underwood, my noiseless, portable, publisher's stooge, my conscience, my slave, my master, my mistress — for all you know it may lead to that elegant creature Betsey, whom my rather plump Louise considers a bit too much on the thin side ... ah, but my good wife is a bit short-sighted there, she doesn't look on the *other* side, the bright side, the sunny side, the side that boasts the little, hidden ripples that it takes imagination, courage, to express; the little hiding ripples that the male eye can't stop looking for ...

He seated himself again before his typewriter, like an embarrassed schoolboy.

Black anger descended upon him. It was easy enough for her, for Louise, to put out a hand to her telephone where it sat waiting on her office desk, and ring him up and order him to report at a cocktail party — Louise, who sat in a room all day surrounded matter-of-factly by people and their voices and her own voice. But for him it was gravely another matter. Her ring summoned him out of his own world — what if he hadn't written a line all morning except a complicated series of coat-hanger designs in the shape of X's? — and because he couldn't really make the crossing, it left him feeling a little ashamed, a little found-out, caught with his pants down, so to speak — and a little terrified, too, to be reminded again that he was not 'like other people.' He was still shaking. She had no right, damn it, no damn right, to disturb him with that sharp malicious ringing, to present him with the bugbear, the insult, the indignity, of a cocktail party — she, who was proud enough of him in public (Bertram Kyle, author of *Fifty Thousand Lives*, that rather brilliant book), although at home she was inclined to regard him, as his family had when he refused to study banking, as something of a sissy.

Still, when you have accepted an invitation to a party for the afternoon, you have that to think about, to hold over your type-

writer's head, you can think of how you will lock it up at half-past
four and shave and shower and go out with a collar and a tie around
your neck to show people that you can look, talk, drink, like any of
them, like the worst of them. But a party! Christ, the faces, the
crowds of white faces (like the white keys of the typewriter I had
before you, my fine Underwood), and worst of all, the voices.....
The party became abnormally enlarged in his mind, as though it
would take every ounce of ingenious conniving — not to speak of
courage! — to get to it at all; and as he fell face downward on his
typewriter, he gave more thought to the party than even the party's
host was likely to do, Freddie, whoever the devil 'Freddie' was...

O degrading torture, lying on the smug reproachful keys with
nothing to convey to them. He remembered how he had once been
afraid of every woman he met until he kissed her, beat her, held her
captive in his arms; but this typewriter was a thing to master every
day, it was a virgin every morning. If I were Thomas Wolfe, he
thought, I should start right off: O country of my birth and land I
have left behind me, what can I, a youth with insatiable appetite,
do to express what there is in me of everlasting hunger, loneliness,
nakedness, a hunger that feeds upon hunger and a loneliness that
grows in proportion to the hours I lend to strangers... If I were
Saroyan I should not hesitate either: But I am young, young and
hungry (thank God), and why must I listen to the rules the old men
make or the rich ones, this is not a story, it is a life, a simple setting
down in words of what I see of men upon this earth. No, no, I am
not Saroyan (thank God), I am not Thomas Wolfe either, and I am
also not Louise's boss (ah, *there's* a man!). And I cannot write an
essay; I am a natural liar, I prefer a jumbled order to chronology,
and poetry to logic; I don't like facts, I like to imagine their implications. O to get back, get back, to the pre-telephone stupor, the
happy mingled pregnancy, the clear confusion of myself only with
myself...

And so Bertram Kyle opened up his notebooks. He felt again that
the story he had outlined so clearly there, of the 'lousy guy' whom
everyone thought was lousy including himself, but who was so only
because of a simple happening in his childhood, might be a fine
story; but it was one he could not do today. Nor could he do the
story (which had occurred to him on a train to Washington) of the
old lady, prospective grandmother, who went mad thinking it was

her own child to be born. Nor could he do the story — partly because he did not know it yet — which would begin: 'He lived alone with a wife who had died and two children who had left him.' Perhaps, he thought bitterly, he could never do those stories, for in the eagerness of begetting them he had told them to Louise; too often when he told her a story it was finished then, it was dead, like killing his lust by confiding an infidelity.

And so, desperately, he turned to those thoughtful little flaps in the backs of his notebooks, into which he poured the findings in his pockets each night; out came old menus, the torn-off backs of matchbooks, hotel stationery that he had begged of waiters, ticket-stubs, a time-table, a theatre program, and odd unrecognizable scraps of paper he had picked up anywhere. The writing on these was born of drinking sometimes; of loneliness in the midst of laughing people; of a need to assert himself, perhaps, a desire to remind himself — that he was a writer; but more than anything, he thought, for the sheer love of grasping a pencil and scratching with it on a scrap of paper. 'If I were a blind man I should carry a typewriter before me on a tray suspended from my neck by two blue ribbons; I think I *am* blind' — he had written that on a tablecloth once, and Louise was very bored.

'It is always later than you think, said the sundial finding itself in the shade' — from the back of an old match-box, and undoubtedly the relic of an evening on which he had strained to be smart. A night-club menu: 'Dear Saroyan: But take a day off from your writing, *mon vieux*, or your writing will get to be a habit...' Another menu — and he remembered the evening well, he could still recall the look of tolerance growing into anger on Louise's face as he wrote and wrote and went on writing: 'Nostalgia, a nostalgia for all the other nostalgic nights on which nothing would suffice... a thing of boredom, of content, of restlessness, *velleities*, in which the sweetness of another person is irrelevant and intolerable, and indifference or even cruelty hurt in the same way... linking up with gray days in childhood when among bewilderingly many things to do one wanted to do none of them, and gray evenings with Louise when everything of the adult gamut of things to do would be the same thing...' (At that point Louise had reached down to her anger and said, 'All right, sunshine, we come to a place I loathe because you like to see naked women and then, when they come on, you don't even watch them; I wouldn't complain if you were Harold Bell Wright or something ...') 'In order to make friends,' he discovered from another match-box, 'one need not talk seriously, any more than one needs to make love in French' — and that, he recalled tenderly, was plagiarized from a letter he had written to a very young girl, Betsey's predecessor in his fringe flirtations. 'A man's underlying motives are made up of his thwarted, or unrealized, ambitions,' 'The war between men and women consists of left-overs from their unsatisfactory mating.' 'But the blinking of the eye' — this on a concert program — 'must go on; perhaps one catches the half-face of the player and sees, despite the frenzied waving of his head, a thing smaller than his playing, but perhaps the important, the vital thing: like the heart-beat, at once greater and smaller than the thing it accompanies ...' 'We are not so honest as the best of our writing, for to be wholly honest is to be brave, braver than any of us dares to be with another human being, especially with a woman.' *'At bottom one is really grave.'*

He was pulled up short by that last sentence, which was the only one of the lot that made sense. 'At bottom one is really grave.'

Suddenly he raised his head and stared wildly round the room. He was terrified, he was elated. Here was his whole life, in these four walls. This year he had a large room with a very high ceiling; he works better in a big room, Louise told people who came in. Last year he had worked in a very small room with a low ceiling; he works better, Louise used to tell people, in a small place. He worked better at night, he worked better in the daytime, he worked better in the country, better in the city, in the winter, in the summer ... But he was frightened. Here he was all alone with his life until five o'clock in the afternoon. Other people (Louise) went out in the morning, left their life behind them somewhere, or else filed it away in offices and desks; he imagined that Louise only remembered her life and took it up again in the late afternoon when she said good night to her boss and started off for home — or a cocktail party. But he had to live with his life, and work with it; he couldn't leave it alone and it couldn't leave him alone, not for a minute — except when he was drunk, and that, he said, smugly surveying the scattered coat-hangers, relic of last night's debauch, that is why a writer drinks so much. Hell, he thought, proud, I'm living a life, my own whole life, right here in this room each day;

I can still feel the pain I felt last night when I was living part of it and Louise said . . . and I can still feel the joy I felt last week when Betsey said . . . and I can feel the numbness and the excitement of too many Scotch-and-sodas, of too perfect dancing, of too many smooth-faced, slick-haired women; I can remember saying *Listen — listen* to anyone who would or would not, and the truth of it is I had nothing to say anyway because I had too much to say . . . Hell, he thought, my coat-hangers lie on the floor where I flung them at three this morning when Louise persuaded me that it was better not to sleep in my clothes again, I have not hung up my black suit, I have not emptied yesterday's waste-basket nor last week's ashtrays (nor my head of its thirty years' fine accumulation) . . . everything in my room and in my head is testimony to the one important fact, that I am alive, alive as hell, and all I have to do is wait till the whole reeling sum of things adds itself up or boils itself down, to a story . . .

There seemed now to be hunger in his belly, and it was a fact that he had not eaten since breakfast and then only of Louise's anger. But the turmoil in his insides was not, he felt, pure hunger. It came from sitting plunged in symbols of his life, it came because he did not merely have to live with his life each day, but he had to give birth to it over again every morning. Of course, he thought with a fierce joy, I am hungry. I am ravenously hungry, and I have no appetite, I am parched but I am not thirsty, I am dead tired and wide awake and passionately, violently alive.

But he lifted his elbows now from his typewriter, he looked straight before him, and he could feel between his eyes a curious knot, not pain exactly, but tension, as though all of him were focused on the forefront of his brain, as though his head were a packed box wanting to burst. It was for this moment that, thirty years before, he had been born; for this moment that he had tossed peanuts to an elephant when he was a child; that he had by a miracle escaped pneumonia, dropping from an airplane, death by drowning, concussion from football accidents; that he had fallen desperately and permanently in love with a woman in a yellow hat whose car had been held up by traffic, and whom he never saw again; that he had paused at sight of the blue in Chartres Cathedral and wept, and a moment later slapped angrily at a mosquito; that he had met and married Louise, met and coveted Kitty Braithwaite, Margery, Connie, Sylvia, Elinor, Betsey; for this moment that he had been born and lived, for this moment that he was being born again.

His fingers grew light. The room was changing. Everything in it was integrating; pieces of his life came together like the odd-shaped bits of a puzzle-map, forming a pattern as one assembles fruits and flowers for a still-life. Listen, there is a name. Bettina Gregory. Bettina is a thin girl, wiry, her curves so slight as to be ripples, so hidden that the male eye cannot stop searching for them; she drinks too much; she is nicer when she is sober, a little shy, but less approachable. Bettina Gregory. She is the kind of girl who almost cares about changing the social order, almost cares about people, almost is *at bottom really grave.* She is the kind of girl who would be at a cocktail party when someone named Fr — named Gerry — would call up and say he couldn't come because he was prosecuting a taxi-driver who had robbed him of four dollars. She is the kind of girl who would then toss off another drink and think it funny to take old Carl along up to the night-court to watch old Gerry prosecute a taxi-man. She is the kind of girl who will some-how collect coat-hangers (I give you my coat-hangers, Betsey-Bettina, Bertram Kyle almost shouted in his joy) — and who will then go lilting and looping into the night-court armed to the teeth with coat-hangers and defense mechanisms, who will mock at the whores that have been rounded up, leer at the taxi-driver, ogle the red-faced detective, mimic the rather sheepish Gerry — all the time mocking, leering, ogling, mimicking — nothing but herself. Frankly we are just three people, she explains to the detective, with an arm about Gerry and Carl, who love each other veddy veddy much. She must pretend to be drunker than she is, because she is bitterly and deeply ashamed; she must wave with her coat-hangers and put on a show because she knows it is a rotten show and she cannot stop it. It is not merely the liquor she has drunk; it is the wrong books she has read, the Noel Coward plays she has gone to, the fact that there is a drought in the Middle West, that there was a war when she was a child, that there will be another when she has a child, that she and Carl have something between them but it is not enough, that she is sorry for the taxi-driver and ashamed of being sorry, that *at bottom she is almost grave.* In the end, Bertram Kyle said to any-body or nobody, in the end I think ...

But there was no reason any more to think. His fingers were

clicking, clicking, somehow it developed that Gerry had muddled things because he was drunk so that the taxi-man must go to jail pending special sessions, and then Bettina and Gerry and Carl take the detective out to a bar some place; explaining frankly to waiters that they are just four people who love each other veddy veddy much ... and, perhaps because they all hate themselves so veddy veddy much, Carl and Gerry let Bettina carry them all off in her car for a three-day spree which means that Gerry misses the sub-poena and the taxi-driver spends a week in jail, earning himself a fine prison record because he stole four dollars to which Carl and Gerry and Bettina think him wholly and earnestly entitled, and perhaps in the end they give the four dollars to the Communist Party, or perhaps they just buy another round of drinks, or perhaps they throw it in the river, or perhaps they frankly throw themselves ...

And is this all, Bertram Kyle, all that will come out today of your living a life by yourself, of your having been born thirty years ago and tossed peanuts to elephants, wept at the Chartres window, slapped at mosquitoes, survived the hells and heavens of adolescence to be born again, today — is this all, this one short story which leaves out so much of life? But neither can a painter crowd all the world's rivers and mountains and railroad tracks onto one canvas, yet if his picture is any good at all it is good because he has seen those rivers and mountains and puts down all that he knows and all that he has felt about them, even if his painting is of a bowl of flowers and a curtain ... And here, thought that thin layer of consciousness which went on as an undercurrent to his fingers' steady tapping, here is my lust for Betsey, my repentance for Louise, my endless gratitude to the woman who wore a yellow hat, my defeatism, my optimism, the fact that I was born when I was, all of my last night's living and much that has gone before ...

The room grew clouded with the late afternoon and the cigarettes that he forgot to smoke. His fingers went faster, they ached like the limbs of a tired lover and they wove with delicacy and precision because the story had grown so real to him that it was physical. He knew that his shoulders were hunched, that his feet were cramped, that if he turned his desk about he would have a better light — but all the time he was tearing out sheet after sheet and with an odd accuracy that was not his own at any other time, inserting the next ones with rapidity and ease, he typed almost perfectly, he made few mistakes in spelling, punctuation, or the choice of words, and he swung into a rhythm that was at once uniquely his and yet quite new to him.

Now each idea as he pounded it out on his flying machine gave birth to three others, and he had to lean over and make little notes with a pencil on little pieces of paper that later on he would figure out and add together and stick in all the gaping stretches of his story. He rediscovered the miracle of something on page twelve tying up with something on page seven which he had not understood when he wrote it, the miracle of watching a shapeless thing come out and in the very act of coming take its own inevitable shape. He could feel his story growing out of the front of his head, under his moving fingers, beneath his searching eye ... his heart was beating as fast as the keys of his typewriter, he wished that his typewriter were also an easel, a violin, a sculptor's tools, a boat he could sail, a plane he could fly, a woman he could love, he wished it were something he could not only bend over in his passion but lift in his exultation, he wished it could sing for him and paint for him and breathe for him.

And all at once his head swims, he is in a fog, sitting is no longer endurable to him, and he must get up, blind, not looking at his words, and walk about the room, the big room, the small room, whether it is night or day or summer or winter, he must get up and walk it off ... *Listen, non-writers, I am not boasting when I tell you that writing is not a sublimation of living, but living is a pretty feeble substitute for art. Listen, non-writers, this is passion. I am trembling, I am weak, I am strong, pardon me a moment while I go and make love to the world, it may be indecent, it may be mad — but as I stalk about the room now I am not a man and I am not a woman, I am Bettina Gregory and Gerry and the taxi-driver and all the whores and cops and stooges in the night-court, I am every one of the keys of my typewriter, I am the clean white pages and the word-sprawled used ones, I am the sunlight on my own walls — rip off your dress, life, tear off your clothes, world, let me come closer; for listen: I am a sated, tired, happy writer, and I have to make love to the world.*

Sometimes it was night when this happened and then he must go to bed because even a writer needs sleep, but at those times he went to bed and then lay there stark and wide awake with plots weaving like tunes in his head and characters leaping like mad chess-men, and words, words and their miraculous combinations, floating about on the ceiling above him and burying themselves in the pillow beneath him till he thought that he would never sleep and knew that he was mad ... till Louise sometimes cried out that she could not sleep beside him, knowing him to be lying there only on sufferance, twitching with his limbs like a madman in the dark ...

Louise! For it was not night, it was late afternoon, with the dark of coming night stealing in to remind him, to remind him that if he were ever again to make the break from his life's world back to sanity, back to normalcy and Louise, he must make it now, while he remembered to; he must leave this room, stale with his much-lived life, his weary typewriter, he must shake off his ecstasy and his bewilderment, his passion, his love, his hate, his glorious rebirth and his sated daily death — and go to meet Louise; go to a cocktail party ...

He was shocked and terrified when he met his own face in the mirror because it was not a face, it was a pair of haggard, gleaming eyes, and because like Rip Van Winkle he seemed to have grown heavy with age and yet light with a terrible youth. He managed somehow to get by without letting the elevator man know that he was crazy, that he was afraid of him because he was a face and a voice, because he seemed to be looking at him queerly. On the street Bettina appeared and walked beside him, waving her drunken coat-hangers and announcing, 'Frankly there is nothing like a coat-hanger,' while Gerry leaned across him rather bitterly to say, 'If I hear you say frankly again, Bettina, frankly I shall kill you.' But they walked along, all of them, very gay and friendly, despite the taxi-driver's slight hostility, and then at the corner they were joined by Carl with the detective's arm about him, and Carl was saying to anybody and nobody that they passed — 'Frankly we are veddy veddy mad.' And they came at last to Freddie's house, and there Bertram Kyle stood for a moment, deserted by Bettina and Carl and Gerry — even the detective was gone — hiding behind a collar and a tie and frankly panic-stricken. The door opens, he enters mechanically — good God, is it a massacre, a revolution, is it the night-court, a nightmare? ...

But he pushed in very bravely and began to reel toward all his friends. 'Hello, I'm cockeyed!' he roared at random. 'Hell, I've been floating for forty days, where's a coat-hanger, Freddie, frankly, if there's anything I'm nuts about it's coat-hangers, and frankly have you seen my friends, some people I asked along, Bettina Gregory, Gerry, and a detective?' He saw Louise, ominous and tolerant, placing her hands in disgust on her soft hips at sight of him. Frankly, he shouted at her, frankly, Louise, I am just three or four people who love you veddy veddy much, and where's a drink, my pearl, my pet, my bird, my cage, my night-court, my nightmare — for frankly I need a little drink to sober down...

TRAVELING SALESMAN[1]

By ELISABETH WILKINS THOMAS

(From *Pictorial Review*)

YOU might say I haven't any story to tell. Nothing has ever happened to me that anybody could write a piece about. And here I am over forty. I'll never be made a director of anything, either, the way I keep changing my line just when I might be promoted. One year it's dolls; another year it's hosiery; right now it's hairbrushes, bristles guaranteed.

That's where the story is, I guess.

But it started with Tom Leadbitter, not with me. When I think of his family as I first knew them ——

Tom Leadbitter was a florist, a nurseryman in a small way. Funny thing, too: nobody would think, to meet him, he was the sort to care for flowers. A large, broad-shouldered fellow, not saying much, he seemed glum at first, and gave the impression he was only temporarily in the business. All the time, even in his house when he wasn't working, his thoughts seemed somewhere else, as if (though he never said any such thing) when he found something better he would change. But those Scotch eyes of his could smile; his folks were in Edinburgh, he had come over; and once he knew a person he was friendly enough, though never outgoing.

He had a neat little place on Spring Road just out of Fieldtown: a hothouse filled mostly with carnations and Boston ferns, a few acres of shrubs and evergreens, and a two-story frame house for his wife and children. It looked good to me, a single chap working in a real-estate agency, selling homes to other folks, no home of my own. It still looks good, as I recall it.

Myrtle Leadbitter was the finest woman I ever knew. It wasn't so much her looks I remember, though they were all right — she had a rope of brown hair, and clear gray eyes, and quick hands — but her quiet womanly ways. She was capable, and everything was always easy around her.

They were raising a family: couple of boys, twins, just beginning

[1] Copyright, 1935, by The Pictorial Review Company, Inc.

high school, and a little girl named Gladys. Many's the evening I spent in their house with them. Just quiet and comfortable, you know; no parties, they weren't that kind. Some folks wouldn't have cared for it; too slow, they would have thought. But it suited us. Winter evenings, sitting there, the boys getting their lessons at the table, Tom and me talking, Gladys on her mother's lap having her hair brushed — well, they seemed to me the grandest family.

We would talk about the news in the paper, or about my future in real estate. 'When you get yourself a wife,' Tom would say, for he knew I had piled up a little. But I couldn't see how there was another woman as fine as Myrtle. I figured I'd rather do without than be satisfied with less, and I said so. They used to joke me about it.

To hear me tell all this! You're saying to yourself: an American family, as like the next one as two pods of peas. And you're right. They were usual folks enough; though Tom did not drink or smoke. Yet, as events turned out, not anything about them was the way you think.

First of all was that evening in November. It was more than ten years ago, but I remember it as clearly as yesterday from thinking it over so long. There we sat as usual; I can see the room, and Tom in his armchair by the fireplace. There had been a mizzling kind of rain all day, 'a regular Scotch mist,' Tom said. Then a few minutes later he excused himself, to see to the temperature in the greenhouse for the night. Whatever his private feelings might be, he was always careful and particular on the job. We heard him rustling into his waterproof (though it wasn't but a step from the house), then the door shut behind him.

Pretty soon Myrtle finished brushing the little girl's hair and sent her upstairs to bed. Then she took some sewing. We were all surprised when the clock struck eleven.

'It can't be that late, can it?' Myrtle exclaimed. 'What's keeping Tom? He's been out there more than two hours.' So the boys ran out to see what was keeping him.

Now I might as well make a long story short by mentioning at once that Tom Leadbitter was not in his greenhouse. He was gone. He did not come back that night nor any night. He had cleared out. Though you understand, we did not guess it as quick as that. For a long time we were hopeful.

We tried to think he had gone into town on an errand; maybe some accident had happened to him and we'd soon hear. Better that than nothing. However, nothing it was to be. We asked everybody, we tried all sorts of leads that didn't come to a thing. Finally we had to face the fact that he had simply cleared out.

The way we knew it was this. Myrtle ran short of money. She tried to make a joke of it. 'We're out of petty cash,' she said one morning when I stopped in there for news. She smiled, but I could see she was afraid to go to the bank. So I said I'd go at noon and find out how she might draw on Tom's account. The chance made me glad. It was in my mind that if Tom had got into the red somehow and had to run off, I could fix up a little account, and no one but old Stearns need be any the wiser.

The one thing that comforted me in all this was the way Myrtle turned to me for help. Simple and natural she was with me. And I respected it, understand. Jealousy never drove Tom away. He himself could swear to that, then or now.

Well, I don't know why we hadn't thought of the bank before. As soon as I began to ask questions, old Stearns brought out his lists. Tom was solvent, though he had less than I thought. A pretty good savings book, but no income except from sales; and those had fallen off since he disappeared, there being no one to run the business properly and boss the helper. Tom had drawn out money the morning of the day he left. What was more, Stearns told me that a few days before he had brought in his wife's signature and had a joint account made.

So Myrtle had money to draw on, and it was plain Tom had planned to go. Everything was fixed up. It began to look as if Myrtle had been in on it, though. I was afraid to go back to her for fear of what she might tell me.

That was a crazy notion. She stood in the kitchen, arranging apples in a baking-pan. I remember how Gladys sat on the floor piling up blocks like a baby for all she was a good-sized little girl. But I did not think of Gladys then. When I told Myrtle how it was at the bank, she stared at me. She tried to speak, but her mouth twisted up funny, and she laid her face and hands against the door. Her tears fell on the linoleum. 'Oh, Tom.'

'Yes, I did that,' she said in a few minutes, and turned around quiet again, and wiped her face with her apron. In all that hap-

pened then or later, in all she went through, that was the only time
I ever saw Myrtle give way. 'I did that. He asked me to sign a
paper for him, and brought the pen to me. I was busy, never ques-
tioned him. He always took care of such things.' She wrung her
hands together like a dishrag. 'Oh, Fred, what shall I do now?
How am I going to bring up the children?'

She managed, though. She brought up the children. She'd be
comfortable among them today, if those boys —— But we haven't
come to that yet.

The first thing she did was to take Tom's helper on shares. Tom
had always said he was a good worker; now he began to feel more
responsibility. She had the twins working there after school hours;
and she took a hand at selling and at keeping the books. It was
hard work for them. It meant skimping and drudgery; but they
made enough to pay their bills and keep their home over their
heads. Things would go easier, Myrtle said, when the boys got
through school.

They were all so busy, there was no time to mope or brood about
Tom. Which was just as well, I guess. He was gone and they were
there.

Things went along, fair to middling, for a couple of years. Nearer
three, I guess. I used to drop in evenings as usual; everything would
be much the same. But there was no use pretending; though we
never said a word, we did feel the queerness of Tom's being gone.
It made us all nervous — doorbell, you know, or the clock striking,
or a car suddenly stopping. I used to sit there looking at Myrtle,
or the fire, or nothing at all, and try to figure out what kind of fellow was that Tom we thought we knew. What made him do such a
thing? Glum, steady-going Scot, too canny to get tangled up with
women, or to speculate in wildcat schemes. What could have been
in his mind, making him want to break everything clean off that
way without saying a word?

'If he had only told me,' Myrtle said, 'only talked it over, whatever it was. I would have tried to understand.' There was never
any answer to our thoughts about him.

It was no surprise then, when Myrtle told me they were going to
give up the place and move into Fieldtown. As long as there had
seemed a chance of Tom's coming back, she had wanted to stay
right there. But, now that it seemed clear he was not coming back,

she had made up her mind. She had talked it over with the boys;
and Craley, Tom's helper, had made them a proposition. He
wanted to buy the business. He could pay a small sum down and
the rest in mortgage.

They would be poor, they knew that, but they had planned.
The twins were more than willing to find jobs in Fieldtown and go
to continuation school. Just so they were together, they liked any
work. Smart, freckle-faced youngsters they used to be when I
first knew them. Myrtle had trained them to be self-reliant and
obliging. Yet, as they grew up, it seemed to me they became offish
like their father. They had the same way of acting as if their jobs
were only temporary until some change should come. No more
than Tom, they never said anything, beyond the little asides and
understandings twins always have with each other. It was just an
impression I got; and maybe I'm imagining, after events, what I'd
never have noticed otherwise.

Anyhow, they got clerk-jobs together at one of the chain stores.
Myrtle took one side of a two-family house I found for them in
Fieldtown; new, with all modern improvements, a good furnace,
gas stove in the kitchen, everything fresh and sweet. Close to Front
Street, it was; trolley cars, shops, and moving pictures handy
(though Myrtle never learned to care for these), and decent neighbors in the other half.

When I think of that first evening there, and the supper, I could
cry like a baby. Myrtle asked me to come and help them celebrate,
a kind of housewarming. None of them had ever been long on
sociability. They had acquaintances out Spring Road, but they
felt sensitive now, and there was no one in Fieldtown they cared to
invite to a party. So there were only the five of us in the new dining-
room.

It was March, I remember, and we were glad to hear the radiators
clacking. We had a fire too, though it was of gas logs instead of
wood. Some people don't think much of gas logs, but it seemed to
me they were always ready and clean, and would save Myrtle a
good deal of housework.

The dinner was like Myrtle herself, simple and comfortable. She
asked me to carve. It was a cut of beef, and I gave them dish gravy
on the pieces of bread they sent up. We all had appetites that evening, and we sat and joked — even the boys. As if we five were a

fort against the world. If I live to be a hundred I'll remember how a weight was lifted off us for a little while, at that dinner table in the new house.

For a little while, I say.

After we'd eaten, Joe and Junior went down to the corner for cigarettes. Those boys never came back. They never were seen, they never were heard of, by any of us, again. Gone, cleared out, without a sign, same as Tom. Myrtle's face aged years that night. I began to feel —— But there's no use; a fellow can't find words for his feelings when he is up against queerness like that.

We waited for them until morning. We walked around; I went down to Front Street twice, and back and forth to the corner a dozen times. But everything was shut. Each time I came back to the stoop, Myrtle would be waiting in the doorway, and I could only shake my head. She wouldn't go to bed and I wouldn't leave her that way, before daylight at least. Daylight might help.

But it didn't. Nor anything we could do. We turned to the police. You may have read about the case in the papers at the time. Folks helped us all they could. I even wrote to Tom's people in Edinburgh; though as I had only a very old address Myrtle had saved, my letter did not reach them and was returned.

Well, we go on living, don't we? Things dragged along for some months. By the end of May an idea had come to me, which I wanted to put up to Myrtle. Her affairs were beginning to look shaky. She had lost the boys' wages. Craley's payments came in on the dot, but they couldn't carry her. Neither would she let me help. She talked about taking a job.

Maybe I've said it before, but Myrtle Leadbitter is the finest woman I ever met, bar none. And if I ought to be saying 'was' instead of 'is' — well, nobody has proved it to me, and I won't until I have to.

Where was I? Oh, yes, she was talking about taking a job, when I got this idea. So I went around, one evening in May. There she sat on the front steps. It was warm and a bush of lilacs was in bloom, I remember. I don't often notice those things, but I had a kind of homesick feeling for her that evening.

What she told me made it worse.

I sat down beside her, and Gladys came along. Some children

were playing ball in the street, but she was not playing with them. She carried her doll for me to admire. 'See my doll,' she kept repeating. The old doll was dirty, and I said so — said I should have to get her a new one. But she did not answer; just looked at me the way she generally did, and said, 'See my doll.'

Now I never knew much about children, but it struck me lately that Gladys was getting pretty big to be such a baby. Myrtle hadn't even sent her to school, that I knew of.

'Gladys, how old are you?' I asked her. But she would not answer. She leaned on her mother's knees and peeked up sidewise. Her curls fell over her face, and Myrtle smoothed them back. She was always gentle with the child.

'Gladys is nearly nine,' she spoke for her. 'She will be nine on her birthday.... Fred,' she said then slowly in another tone, 'I know what you're thinking, and I might as well tell you the truth. Gladys isn't right. She never will be; she'll never be any more than five years old in her head.'

I didn't know what to say. I couldn't say anything but just look at her. All the time she kept on smoothing the child's hair, and Gladys rested her head, never heeding a word. I couldn't believe she didn't understand.

But Myrtle went on speaking. 'For a long time I had been suspecting. Just little things you come to notice. She was always good enough, no trouble, but she didn't catch on the way the boys did. I kept hoping she was only slow.'

'Did Tom know?' I had to ask her.

'No. She was too young then. It was after we came to town, when I wanted to send her to school, I found out. They sent me to a doctor; he told me.'

Myrtle couldn't say any more, and I didn't want her to. If I felt sorry for her before, I felt so more than ever now. Myrtle was so good, sensible, active, strong — with all the cards stacked against her. And there was nothing I could do about it. What could anybody do, even she herself?

The evening grew dark, and street lamps suddenly shone out. I remember the gold band on her finger, gleaming a little soft and dull in the reflection, and the pain I felt seeing it there.

Gladys got sleepy, and Myrtle pulled her on to her lap for a few minutes. Then she unfastened the child's clothes and sent her into the house to bed. I just sat there, dumb as a clam, thinking about that first dinner in the new house. I was remembering how the dining-room had looked to me like a fort, five of us there against the world, unbeatable. Now here were just two of us, Myrtle and me. We two were allied now, I felt; against what, I didn't know. Darkness, fate, more than just the world, I thought.

So I told her what I wanted to do. I wanted to go to Edinburgh and hunt up Tom's folks. Somehow I had a notion Tom might have gone back there — Lord knows what for, or why I thought it. I wanted to go in all friendliness; it seemed to me there was nothing would make me happier than to have that family together again the way it used to be in the old days.

'But if I can't find him, Myrtle —— After all, it's over three years now.' I never was able to say what I meant, that minute least of all. There I sat stammering and gulping like a kid. 'Oh, Myrtle, Myrtle,' I kept repeating, as if the word were something I could hold in my hands. It was her name, her nearness to me, her quiet, and her warm brown hair. Though no other words would come, it seemed to me I was saying something when I said her name.

I guess she understood, for she turned to me and smiled. Then she said, 'You're a good friend to me, Fred; nobody could have a better. But I've told you how it is; and I wouldn't wish Gladys on anyone.'

'Why, Myrtle, she's nothing but a baby.' I'd have taken on ten Gladyses for Myrtle's sake.

'I know. And she's good. The doctor says she may never be troublesome. But she'll always be a care, Fred; she'll have to be looked after as long as she lives. And it isn't only Gladys.'

Myrtle stopped. Then she began to talk again.

'Fred, I've said you're a good friend to me. I haven't said all I mean, either; but ——' She had trouble finding her words. 'Don't you see how it is? We don't know anything. I can't rest easy one way or the other. Tom and my boys —— Here I sit, on these steps. Maybe if I saw Tom face to face, and spoke with him, I could understand. Even if I was to turn away from him for good, that would be a clear thing forever, between the two of us. But as it is, I don't see how I could be happy, nor make you happy.' Tears began to shine in her eyes. 'Oh, my poor Fred, I'm wasting your life,' she said. 'Better for you if I were swallowed up like the others. But I don't know where they are.'

'Myrtle!'

She reached out her hand to my fist on my knee. I took her hand and held it hard.

We neither of us said any more, just sat there close together. Though there was no promise between us, I fancied there was a kind of understanding. That was as much as I dared ask for.

Then we came to plans. We talked hard enough over those. At first Myrtle raised objections because she couldn't pay my expenses. That made me angry. I asked her if she thought I was a detective agency. As if Tom hadn't been like a brother to me while I had known him. And a vacation was coming to me; and so on. She got the point and gave in gracefully. That was all I needed. My trip was as good as begun.

The next day I made my bookings and gave Myrtle my forwarding address, just in case; though I planned to be back in a month.

There is only a bit more to this story. At least, there is only a bit more that I know of. There may be a whole book known to folks somewhere else.

I suppose anyone but me might have guessed the Edinburgh trip would be useless. Tom's folks turned up, right enough, after a little searching. But they were an old couple, innocent as pigeons. They knew nothing about Tom or the boys, and were shocked at my news. Having little, they couldn't help Myrtle; though they were kindness itself and offered her a home if I'd pay her passage. What I saw of their home — a dreary, narrow flat in a dark street — told me it would be no place for my poor hard-working Myrtle. They said they had always wanted a daughter, and I knew they felt like making it up to her for Tom's trick. But they lived in a pinched way, and I feared burdens would fall on her.

Why should I go over all this, since none of it was of any use? I came home again to tell Myrtle what I had and had not learned.

Home, did I say? I have never had a home. It just doesn't seem as if I know how to tell this last bit. But it's the nub of my story; it explains me now. When I got off the train that evening at Fieldtown straight from the boat, and took the trolley-car out to her

street, I imagined I could see her waiting in the doorway. I had
not heard from her while I was away, but I had sent her word how
things were and when I would sail.

The doorway was dark. What's more, her half of the house was
dark; not only dark, but closed up. I tell you my hands turned cold
as ice. When I rang the door-bell, I could hear it echoing in the
rooms. The back door, too. I walked around and tried to look in
the windows. Wherever I could see in, where the street light shone
through a crack, there wasn't a stick of furniture. Finally I grew
desperate, and though I knew it was no use, I stamped up the porch
steps again, knocked on the front door — I couldn't bear the jang-
ling of that bell — and called Myrtle's name.

At that, a window opened in the other half of the house, and a
woman stuck her head out. 'Who is it you want?' 'Mrs. Leadbitter,' I told her, and she said, 'Mrs. Leadbitter's gone away. She
had an auction and sold everything. There's no one there now. . . .
No,' she said, 'I don't know where they went. She took the little
girl; about a week ago, it was. . . . No, I'm sorry, I don't know anyone who could tell you. They went very quietly, just the two of
them.'

Well, I guess you know that was the end.

Look for her! What else have I been doing all these years? And
planning for her, too. Even though she ran away from me. You
see, I knew why she went. 'Better for you if I were swallowed up
like the others. My poor Fred, I'm wasting your life,' she said.

Nobody in town could tell me anything about her. There was
nothing left at the bank. Craley had paid off his mortgage some
time ago. As I figured it, my giving up the real-estate business
there in Fieldtown, and going off to hunt for her, wouldn't bring
me any money. And I asked myself, How are you going to take care
of Myrtle when you find her, if you have no money?

So I turned salesman — nearly ten years ago, it was — and that's
what I am now. Do you know what I do?

I get myself hired, and I go to house doors selling things I think
Myrtle or Gladys might care for. One year it's dolls; another
year it's hosiery; right now it's hairbrushes, bristles guaranteed.
I'm a pretty good salesman, you see, because I've got no other
interests to distract me, and I'm thorough. All the companies are
glad to get me. When it looks as if there's danger of promoting

me into an office, I change my line. Wanderlust, I tell them. A different town each time.

She hasn't answered the doorbell yet; but I haven't covered the country yet. She'll open the door to me some day, somewhere. I'm making quite a little for her, too. Salting down my commissions, you know. No expenses, practically.

So there's an American family for you. As like the next one as two pods of peas. What has become of them, Lord only knows. You may say there isn't any point to all this, now I've told it to you. But they lived; it happened; it had a point for them. They knew more about it than I did.

But you've had the story. As I said in the beginning, it all started with Tom Leadbitter. Nothing has ever happened to me.

THE MUSTYDINES WAS RIPE[1]

By HOWELL VINES

(From *The Atlantic Monthly*)

I

ONE Thursday fifty years ago this September I was walkin'
a little sandy road through the woods. It was in '77, and I
always remember that the mustydines was ripe when I found Patsy.
The sun was goin' down fast and I had a crokersack on my shoulder
with all my belongin's in it, and I was a little blue and dead tired
of strollopin' around. I remember just as well how the sun looked.
It was like a ball of fire. I was dressed in homespun and home-
made from top to bottom, had a few dollars in my pocket, and had
strolloped on foot all the way from the Savannah River in Georgia.
I'd been gaddin' about workin' as a hireling since I was sixteen,
and I was twenty-one then. I had started to Toadvine, and some
men in Birmingham had directed me. Birmingham was a wide
place in the road then — just six years old.

I was thinkin' about a place to stay all night and draggin' the
sand beds when I seed some young squirrels cuttin' hickernuts
up a little bitty hickory tree. I took a red flint rock about the size
of a Dommer hen egg from my pocket and throwed it at the bunch
of squibs. I killed one of 'em — but I hadn't expected to — and
I picked it up thinkin' as how I'd give it to the madam of the house
where I stayed all night that night. I thought to myself that they
was plenty of game and lots of timber and some good land in this
country, and I said to myself that I'd like to settle here and live.

I set down by a bank spring on the side of the road and took
out my knife and gutted my squirrel. It was a little boar just
big enough to kill. You know and I know what good eatin' that
is. It was a good spring of water. It tasted good. And it was
cold. That spring made me think more about livin' in this country.
It minded me of a spring back home in Georgia. A good spring
of water in one country the good Lord made makes that country
kin to any other country He made with good springs of water

in it. A spring'll do that more'n most anything else. I've studied that out. You just notice it and you'll see that that's the way it is.

The sun was gone and it was gettin' dusty and I got up and started on. Old Darkus would catch me in the timber if I didn't move on, I thought to myself. But I just had to stop at a big mustydine vine up some pines before I'd made many steps. I shook the vine and they peppered to the ground. They was dead ripe and black as bess bugs. They's nothin' better in this world, I figgered to myself, as I eat a dog's bait of 'em. This made me think more good thoughts about the country I had strolloped to. When you eat a bait of good mustydines in a place, you never do get over it. You always do love that place after that. So I walked on thinkin' as how if I could find me a good nice young woman I wouldn't mind endin' up here bein' buried in the same hole with her. I wasn't feelin' much blue if any, and I had forgot that I was so tired.

II

I got to a house just ahead of Old Darkus and stopped to see if I could get to stay all night. It was a comfortable-lookin' place. The livin' house was a big log house most hid in a cluster of big white oaks, and all the outbuildin's showed that this was a good farm. A big yaller cur dog ran out at me and barked and took on. He like to a bit me. Somebody said, 'Hush your mouth, Cæser,' and the madam of the house come to the door. I muched the dog and he smelt of me good all over and then sidled off. I axed the madam if a body could get to stay all night there. She said, 'My old man's out at the lot feedin' his oxen. Go see him about it.' I walked out to the lot and the man of the house was seein' to his beasts and talkin' to 'em. He called 'em Buck and Ball. They's big black-and-white spotted steers. I axed him could a body get to stay all night at his house. He sized me up and said I could stay. I told him my name and where I's from, and where I'd started to.

A grown girl was milkin' a red cow in a big gourd. Her pap spoke to her and called her Patsy. She was barefooted and was just makin' the milk talk in the gourd with both hands. By the time I took her in, the milk had 'come witched and was singin' a

tune in the gourd. I didn't know the difference. I didn't know
what it was all about any more'n I knowed what the katydid
song all around us and over us was all about. It would a took a
Solomon to have 'splained all them mysteries. But everything
was laughin' with me. I knowed that much. I told the girl that
I could milk good and to let me help her. She was shy, but she
smiled at me and said I could if I wanted to. She said Pied wouldn't
care for me milkin' her. She give me a rope to rope Pied's calf;
and I roped the bull calf and he tried to butt me and the girl
laughed. But I let him suck to get Pied to give down her milk,
and then I milked with one hand while I held the gourd she give
me with the other hand. I didn't mean for the cow to turn the
gourd over, so I milked as hard as I could with one hand to make
the girl see that I was a good milker. The girl finished her cow
and roped Heifer's calf and started to milk, and by then I'd finished. She said Heifer wouldn't let me milk her, and while she
was milkin' Heifer I skinned my squirrel and told her I killed it
for her to eat, but didn't know it at the time. She smiled at me
and thanked me when she took it and put it in her apron, and then
I walked to the house with her pappy.

A strong wild varment of a somethin' got hold of me and made
me want Patsy. It got in me and jumped and urged me to stay at
the lot with the girl. I never in all the days of my life had wanted
anything half as bad. And no wonder. The way she was built
up and the way she moved minded me of a well-pastured filly.
I knowed she was the she-un I would like to be buried in the same
hole with. I was sick all over for Patsy. She could a took a little
bran in her apron and a tolled me to the jumpin'-off place. All
the things that made Patsy a woman had got to me and was
makin' me grown and take on to myself.

At the supper table we begin to get acquainted and everything
they was hummed to the tune of Patsy. I'd catch her castin'
sheep's eyes at me. Her pappy told me that he needed a hand
and that he wanted to hire me. Then if we suited each other I
wouldn't need to go on to Toadvine at all. We'd make a trade
in a day or two. I knowed we could satisfy each other, I told him.
He said yes, he thought we'd suit.

The supper was a good one and hit the spot. They had plenty
to eat at this house. I seed that. They had flour bread and corn

bread raised on the farm and plenty of garden stuff at a time when garden stuff was sca'ce, and good meat from the smokehouse. They had milk and butter from the spring and fried peach pies. The squirrel had been salted and put in a pan in the spring for breakfast.

I told 'em about the dog's bait of mustydines I had had, and the girl said she eat a bait of 'em somewhere every day. She said she had her lots of vines nobody else knowed where was. I believe that's all she said at the supper table that night. Well, in spite of the mustydines I had put down, I eat a hearty supper that night. It was fun to eat a bite when Patsy did and look across the table at her and catch her lookin' at me. I seed by the fat-lighten'd torch that Patsy was purty in the face and that she had long dark purty hair. I seed this better than I could out at the lot. I thought she had blue eyes and I was right. She had that purty hurt look that all girls has that makes a decent boy want to be kind to 'em and take good care of 'em. Even girls that ain't purty has that look. And it makes them purty. But when a purty girl that's well built up has that look it's a sight for sore eyes. When I got older and knowed more about women I understood that that purty hurt look all girls has is callin' for a mate. Patsy, she was seventeen then, and that look of hern seemed to be askin' me to be her mate.

Patsy's pappy and mammy told me things about theirselves that night at supper and I told 'em things about myself. Since I was goin' to stay with 'em I axed 'em not to call me Mr. Freeland, but to call me Benny. And they did. They had two other girls, they said, who had married their cousins and was homesteadin' now — one of 'em over on Lick Creek and the other one down on Mud Creek. They said Patsy's pap was jerked up by the hair of the head down in Canebrake near the river and strolloped off up to the Piney Woods and hired out to her pap and married her. They married five years before the war and homesteaded their place on Rock Creek adjoinin' her pap's place. They'd just got the title to it when Patsy's pappy went off to the war. Patsy's pappy told me how her mammy kept the place goin' and looked after her three babies while he was away. She was just a girl herself, he said; and he was just a boy three years older, his wife put in. She had a hard time in more ways than one, he said, but he come back from the war and found everything all right. When I got older I heard men talk about how Wed Tucker come back and found his true-blue Minnie waitin' with open arms and no secrets and somethin' to eat at the house and in the ground. It made 'em sympathize with me when I told 'em how the war 'stroyed my pappy's and mammy's worldly goods and broke us up, and how pappy never did come back. And when I told 'em of how mammy had died and how all of us children had strolloped over Georgia and Alabama ever since, Patsy's mammy looked tender-like toward me. She said I's just the age of her oldest girl. But best of all I could see that Patsy had tender feelin's toward me.

Soon after supper I went to bed in a good bed in a side room and lay awake thinkin' that Patsy would be worth her weight in gold to me there in the bed with me. There was just a wall between us, but I went to sleep thinkin' that that wall was mighty big. I meant to sleep with Patsy by Sunday night if I could work that fast. I didn't think I could stand it any longer than that.

III

The next mornin' after we eat a hearty breakfast of eggs and cured meat and coffee and flour bread Patsy's mammy cooked over the big fireplace in the kitchen, and I'd watched Patsy gnaw the squib's bones and wouldn't touch it myself, I went to the field to pick cotton, and glory be if Patsy didn't go with me. Her pappy yoked Buck and Ball up to the plough and went to ploughin' in his wheat patch by the cotton patch. He was fixin' to sow his wheat.

Patsy was shy, but she'd talk when I talked to her. I axed her if she had a sweetheart and she said she didn't have — that they was no boy around she wanted for a sweetheart. Her sisters growed up with their cousins and went to lettin' 'em kiss 'em for pleasure, and the first thing she knowed they upped and married and went off to homestead some land of their own. But there was no boy for her. I said I's glad of that and she axed me why. I told her cause I wanted to be her sweetheart. She axed me if I left a sweetheart in Georgia and I told her that I didn't, but that I had my mind set on her. She smiled at me, but didn't say nothin' to that. We picked more cotton and carried our rows on a little fudder, and I axed her if she'd ever been kissed. She said she didn't know nothin' about that kissin' business, but that her sisters said it was the very thing. She said good girls wasn't supposed to go to kissin' before they found 'em a husband. I axed her if she wanted a husband and she laughed, but didn't answer me. She axed me if I wanted a wife and I told her yes, that I did, and that I wanted her to be it. She laughed, but didn't say nothin', and I couldn't get her to give her 'sponse to that. She'd just laugh when I'd try to get her to say somethin'. Well, that laughin' of hern made things like a tune to me, and I picked cotton to that tune. And she picked on, keepin' her row about up with mine, and played that tune. She seed she had me eatin' out of her hand, and pickin' the cotton wasn't hard for her. She just smiled and looked at me, and her hands went from stalk to stalk like little song birds.

Every time we'd see a little old bird we'd speak to each other about it. I found out that she liked birds and knowed as much about 'em as I did. We had a lot of fun tryin' to catch a mole, and she told me all she ever had heard about a mole. We seed some field mice and she knowed all about them, too. I said to myself that here was a purty female that was as stout as I was and liked the ground and everything on top of the ground as good as I did. We'd even as much as talk about a lizard or a scorpion when we seed one. When a body's interested the way we was, even a little old butterfly is enough to get up excitement. When I'd try to get her to talk about love she wouldn't do nothin' but smile or laugh; but when we seed anything alive or looked out over the timber toward Rock Creek she was all tongue. She said she sometimes waded in Rock Creek when she's by herself, and I don't guess she knowed how such a purty sight in my mind made me nearly jump out of my skin. I just picked cotton and thought about that sight. I wanted to see that sight.

She said she sometimes seed little fawns down in the creek field when she'd be lookin' for the sheep, and she told about how her pappy loved to deer-hunt. I told her all I knowed about deer and little deers. She told me she liked to go fishin' down on the creek. She said she knowed how to catch 'em and I told her I knowed all about fish. Then she said she's goin' down on the creek the next week and gather mustydines to make wine. I axed her if she'd let me climb the trees for her and she said she could climb 'em herself and that her pappy and mammy wouldn't let her go off down there with me by herself. That wasn't the way good girls acted. I said they wouldn't care for it if we got married Sunday, would they? She laughed and said no, they wouldn't care for her goin' off in the timber with me if that was to happen, but that to get married Sunday was somethin' else.

By the time we'd filled our sacks we got us some guinea watermelons in the cotton patch and I busted their hearts out on a stump. Some was red-hearted and some was yaller-hearted and they all tasted sorter like the fall of the year and was as cold as the dew and shade could make 'em. Well, from then on till dinner time we picked cotton and talked about things the good Lord made and what we liked to do, and eat watermelons and emptied our cotton in the pen. Her pappy was right close so we could hear all his words to Buck and Ball every time he spoke, and we never did get out of his sight 'cept when we'd go in the cotton pen. I talked love mighty hard and she listened good, and I soon got to touchin' her with my hands when we'd go in the cotton pen. Then I got her to puttin' her hand on me when she'd smile.

Before dinner I made a believer out of her by fast work on how I didn't have nobody but myself, and how I wanted her to take what I did have and let me take her and us make the best out of it. And the last time or two when we's emptyin' our cotton I got to huggin' and kissin' of her, and we worked up a weddin' for Sunday if her pappy and mammy would give in. She said she loved me and liked to look at me and for me to hold her and kiss her. Enough said. I'd won a wife. Back in them days when a girl got to lettin' a boy hug and kiss her and handle her it meant a weddin' would soon take place. On the way back to the house for dinner I watched her climb over the rail fence and I seed her leg above her knee. It was somethin' to see a good nice young girl's leg back then. And it was more good luck than hardly ever come to a young buck to get to see a purty girl's leg 'bove her knee. Then it'd be a accident like this was. Well, that sight made me crazy. She axed me if I seed her knee. I 'fessed up that I did and she cried. Nice girls was like that way back then. She said I oughtn't to a done it. I told her I knowed I oughtn't to, but I just couldn't help it. But as we walked on to the house ahead of her pap I made her believe it wasn't a sin and didn't matter much, and had her smilin' as we entered the yard gate.

IV

Well, she smiled all through dinner that day and laughed with me all that evenin' in the cotton patch. She said she's as happy as a little old bluebird in April and let me kiss her every time we could catch her pappy not lookin'. All that evenin' I'd pick cotton and help her fill her apron when we'd get the sacks full, and she'd just stand there between the rows and let me hold her hand and feel of her arms. Sometimes some tears would come in her eyes and she'd tell me she's just so happy she couldn't keep from cryin'. That hurt look that stays in every girl's eyes kept me busy bein' good to her and sayin' kind words to comfort her. Girls is funny that way. They're not at all like boys. I felt duty-bound to that girl. I didn't mean for a thing to harm a hair of her head as long as I could help it. And that feelin' for Patsy never did leave me.

I broke the news at the supper table and Patsy stuck it out with me. The old folks axed us if we was certain sure we knowed our minds. We both made 'em believe we did. Her mammy said that it minded her of her own sparkin' days 'cept that I had worked faster. Her pappy said they both liked my 'pearance and that they seed at first that me and Patsy liked each other's looks, but that he's afraid we didn't know one another well enough. But me and Patsy kept to our side, and by the time we'd finished supper they both 'greed with us that this way of waitin' about gettin' married after a weddin' had been worked up was not to their way of thinkin'. They'd been through the same mill together that me and Patsy was goin' through together then, and that helped us win 'em to our side. It didn't matter much if I had worked faster than Patsy's pap did. The cases was similar. You know a good catch didn't come to girls often in them times. The boy mostly had to grow up with the girl and be kin to her. And Patsy had been left out that way. Not many girls got to marry strange boys back then. And strange boys fascinate girls. The old folks said my pappy's Irish blood and my mammy's Dutch blood ought to mix well with Patsy's English and Scotch-Irish blood and that if nothin' else would do us we could go on and get married Sunday. But they would have to make one request of me. They'd have to axe me not to never take Patsy away from 'em, but to let her live on with 'em or always in hollerin' distance of 'em, and me be one of 'em. Their other girls didn't live by 'em and they'd lost their two youngest children, and they wanted to keep Patsy with 'em. We closed our bargain that way.

That night after supper I sparked Patsy on the porch and made no secret of it. But we didn't leave the porch. Girls was modest way back in them times and didn't go away from the house with boys much to do their sparkin'. The old folks went to bed inside and lay on their bed with the wall between us and the door standin' open. We could hear 'em talkin' about us and about the ways of a man with a maid. They could hear some of our words and some of 'em they couldn't, for lots of our words didn't need a audience. When a hog or somethin' would come up, Cæser he'd run out and bark at it. One time he barked terrible at Patsy's sheep when they come up behind the smokehouse.

That night we didn't feel much need for King David or somebody to be there with us and 'splain the hollerin' of the katydids and everything like that. It just drawed us closer together and made us kiss and hug and handle one another more, and the world didn't need 'splainin' then. A old whoo owl down about the spring made her want me to hold her tighter. All that was needed was for Patsy to say somethin' like, 'Listen at that little old cricket,' and I'd think that was Bible wisdom. Everything 'splained itself that night. But people knowed all about the mysteries and feelin's of the timber back in them times anyhow. Everybody knowed a lot about everything like that. The good Lord was on the fur side of it and people was on the near side and that 'rangement kept the good Lord and the people purty close together after all. Everything Patsy'd say that night I'd think she's the smartest girl that ever was and the cutest little trick that ever lived. Like when she said, 'I try to catch every purty thing I see that's alive and I know won't hurt me.' She said them very words. I mind 'em just as well. And she said somethin' else I mind well. She said, 'I love the wild flowers lots better'n I do the tame ones, but mammy she don't.' Finally me and Patsy went to bed in different beds that night, but it was mighty hard on both of us. Patsy had found her a mate that would stay with her, and she couldn't foller out the good Lord's best design for a grown girl that night, but had to go to bed by herself,

v

The next mornin' we had company from Toadvine for breakfast. Uncle Jake Smith was riding his horse to Birmingham and
had made it there in time to set down at the breakfast table with
us. Patsy's pappy introduced us and 'splained that me and Patsy
was goin' to get married the next day. Uncle Jake said that I
looked like I'd be all right and that he knowed Patsy was above
an average, and that they was no use in puttin' off even if it was
fast work. He was goin' to town so he could see some friends
there that Saturday night and stay with a friend and be on the
jury Monday mornin'. He said I could ride his horse part of the
time and walk 'longside him and up about Hueytown or Rutledge
Springs I might catch a ride on a wagon. 'You help him fix everything up with Judge Mudd, Jake,' Patsy's pappy said. Uncle
Jake give his word and said he'd be as good as his word, and we
got up from the table and left the house together with me walkin'
'longside the horse.

Me and Uncle Jake had a big time talkin' and gettin' acquainted
that mornin'. His pappy and mammy had come to the Warrior
River from the Savannah River in Georgia and I had to tell him
lots of things about Georgia. But he told me a lot more about
Alabama. I caught a ride with a man drivin' a team of mules at
Rutledge Springs and rode on into town and Uncle Jake rode his
horse 'longside the wagon. The first thing when we got in town
we went around to the courthouse and he helped me get the license.
Then we went to a restaurant and ordered two big beef stews and
coffee. After that we went to a saloon and had two good drinks
and separated.

I walked all the way back to Piney Woods. I walked mostly
in the night and got to the roof over Patsy's head at the first blue
crack of day. Patsy was still in the bed asleep, but her pappy hit
the floor about the time I walked up on the porch and her mammy
went to the kitchen by the time I got in the house good. I went
to Patsy's bed and as I looked at her lyin' there asleep I thought
she was too purty and too sweet for any man but me. A man'll
think that. You just notice and you'll see that he'll think that
about the girl he's sparkin' and goin' to marry. When I woke
her up and showed her the license she looked at it and at me in
such a way with that hurt female look in her eyes that I thought

to myself that grown girls was not supposed to sleep by theirselves. It was not natural and was not intended to be that way. The good Lord made it the most natural thing in the world for them to bed up with a mate. I went on to the big kitchen and set down by the fireplace till her mammy got breakfast on the table. Then Patsy come in with the license and we all set down to breakfast and looked at the license.

I got up from the breakfast table and went to bed and went to sleep, and slept till nearly the middle of the day. Patsy spent that mornin' lookin' through quilts she had quilted and the blankets she had wove 'ginst the day she got married. And she worked with her best dress and looked at it and handled it and got out her shoes and stockin's and talked to her mammy about the weddin' that was about to take place. After that she told me how she'd walk to my bed and gaze down at me and think of how we was about to give ourselves to one another for keeps. I'd brought her stick candy of all flavors and she sucked on that while I was sleepin'.

VI

While I was asleep Patsy's pap walked up to Uncle Tillman Salter's, who didn't live far away, to gas off with Uncle Till and Squire Joe Lisper. Squire Joe was the justice of the peace and we called him the country lawyer. Him and Uncle Tillman spent most of their Sundays together talkin' law and politics. They was goin' to start to town together sometime in the night hours of Monday and be on the jury with Uncle Jake Smith the next week. And all the people in the country said that Squire Joe and Uncle Till had to be in town on such occasions to help Judge Mudd run his court. Patsy's pap went on up to the house early to tell Squire Joe to wait till we got there right after dinner to get married. He would eat dinner there and wait for us.

Right after dinner me and Patsy walked up to Uncle Till's. I don't believe any man ever got to feelin' close to a new country as quick as I did this country. It seems like I was already feelin' my roots in the place while me and Patsy walked along armed up goin' to get married. But Patsy — she was the cause of this. It takes love for a woman to make a man feel at home in a place. Without that a man never can be nothin' much more'n a stranger on top of the ground in any country. I don't care how much a man loves to be on top of the ground. He needs to have a woman on top of the ground by his side. Saint Paul didn't love no woman and no woman loved him, else he couldn't a talked so about bein' a stranger on earth. It'll do that to any man. You just notice it and see if I ain't right. No man's ever been won to a place 'cept by some woman. No man's goin' to be won to life at all 'cept by some woman.

Well, we got married and that's enough to say. I had a jovial time with the older men in the time of it and always did feel close to them and Uncle Jake after that. Patsy, she had a bashful time amongst 'em. She blushed a lot and talked to Uncle Till's girls while we was there gettin' the knot tied. We walked back towards home by ourselves. It was gettin' dusty when we got to the big mustydine vine up the pines, and I led Patsy through the timber to it and shook the vine till the ground was covered. And Old Darkus caught us in the timber together not far from the mustydine vine. From then on to now it's been me and Patsy.

AMERICAN NOCTURNE[1]

By ROBERT WHITEHAND

(From *American Prefaces*)

IT WAS their last night.

Neither Carl nor Irene had mentioned it, yet all afternoon the thought had lain between them with sweet, muted sadness. As they were eating their picnic lunch, she had almost alluded to it. Although she caught herself in time and began spreading a film of butter over her sandwich, Carl looked up intently, and she knew that he had read the thought in her eyes. Then, after rolling up blanket and tablecloth, they burned the paper plates and wandered through the park, oblivious to a few September stragglers who strolled gratefully in the languid warmth of these last days of summer.

It wasn't until sunset, when Irene coaxed Carl down to the dock, that the thought again bubbled in their minds. This time it was Carl. He balanced the canoe while she stepped into it to lie back against some cushions packed into the prow. Watching her, he suddenly leaned forward and said, 'Irene...'

'What?'

But when her eyes met his, he straightened up on his knees and began paddling. 'Shall we go to a dance?' he asked.

'Do you feel like dancing?'

'Not if you don't,' he answered eagerly.

'Let's not.'

They cruised about the lake, watching shadows grow out of the sunset to stretch across the water and become silhouettes of jagged, undulating shade on the ruffled water. After a while Irene saw that Carl was steering up 'Lovers' Lane' where low-hanging trees dangled mossy hair in the lake and clasped their branches above the narrow headwaters in a long arch of matted leaves.

Sitting upright, she breathed deeply of air that was fragrant with the promise of autumn. 'Carl! It's all so pretty!'

'Isn't it!'

She lay back on the pillows again, careful to set her head at the angle Carl liked. Her hands dropped over the sides to let her fingers comb the soft, warm water. She knew that Carl was watching. 'Maybe he's thinking how much he likes me.' The thought lingered in her mind, pleasantly, as a kind of solace, and through occasional openings in the interlaced branches she saw a cauldron of burning clouds in the west.

Finally her eyes turned back toward him, met his gaze, and turned hastily away again. But after a moment she was looking at him once more. Twilight had softened the angles of his face into dim lines, and she liked them that way. It seemed as if all the sadness of her life were gathered into this moment. 'He's my own,' she thought. 'He may go away tomorrow, but he'll always be my sweetheart — my first love!'

But she mustn't make this farewell hard on him; she must be brave. She smiled a bit. Sadly. Then she spoke:

'Carl, this is our last night.'

'Yes.' He laid the paddle across his thighs.

'Tomorrow you'll be gone to the university, and I'll be getting ready for that silly finishing school.'

'I wish we were going to the same place.'

'Dad wouldn't change his mind, though, once he gets it set.'

'And I can't go to a finishing school.'

'Will you miss me, darling?' While she was speaking, she kept singing over and over to herself: 'He's good-looking! He's the best-looking boy at school!'

'You know I will,' he answered.

'We've just known each other six months.'

'It seems like longer.'

She laughed. 'You'll never know how jealous the other girls were when you began taking me to dances and parties.'

'I don't want to know. What do I care about them?'

Her hands floated upward and lay quivering against her breast. 'I could write a sonnet like Rossetti now,' she thought. Her heart began to swell.

'Will you study hard?' Carl asked after a moment.

'Yes.' Her hands unclasped and settled in her lap. 'Will you?'

'I guess so.'

'And lots of pretty girls will flirt with you.'

'I won't like any of them.'

'We'll both have to learn fast so that we can make enough money to get married on right after we graduate.'

Still drifting slowly, the canoe bumped against the grassy shore. Irene raised her head to peer over the gunwale.

'Carl, let's get out and go for a walk!'

He jumped to the bank to help her step ashore. They went up the hillside to a spot where a circular opening, scalloped with a fringe of leaves, revealed a disk of evening sky. Carl spread the blanket and they sat down.

'Do you want to put your head on my lap?' she asked. He crept to her and lay back, looking up into her face. With her fingers she felt the smoothness of his cheeks and laid her palms against them.

'Your hands are cool and nice,' he said.

She tickled the corners of his mouth with her fingertips, smiling down at him. Then she traced the line of his cheek. 'I hate to see you leave.'

'We'll be home again Thanksgiving.'

'But that's so long.' Reaching up to take the hairpins from a pliant knot on the nape of her neck, she tried to laugh. 'Now we're getting sad on our last night.' As her head shook backward, the fine, yellow hair streamed over her shoulders.

Fascinated, Carl watched it. 'Your hair's prettier and longer than any girl's at school.'

'What if I should get it cut?' she teased.

'You do, and I'll shave my head.'

She flipped his nose with a finger. 'Did you think I really would?'

Twisting around, he poked his fingers lightly between her ribs. 'You devil!' They wrestled for a moment, tickling, pulling hair and trying to blow into each other's ears. After a while Irene sat up, laughing. 'You'll get me all grass-stained and mussed up,' she said. 'Then what'll mother think?'

Subsiding for the while, she wriggled her dress back into place. Everything was going fine. Carl wasn't being gloomy and she had kept from crying. Now if only something momentous would happen, something which she could recall each night as she lay in the solitude of her room at school. When she had finished smoothing herself, Carl asked, 'Did you ever sleep "hobo"?'

'Hobo?'

'Sure. Lie on your back and put your head on my shoulder, and I lie on my back and put my head on your shoulder. Like this...' She listened carefully. Then both lay on their backs, legs stretching out in opposite directions and their heads, cheek to cheek, resting on each other's shoulder.

'I'm not going to sleep, though,' Irene said.

'Do you like it?'

'It's fun. I can hear your heart beating.'

Her hair was spread over Carl's shoulder, and she knew that some of it was caressing his cheek as softly as a breeze so light that you feel only its coolness and never its passage. 'You've got the prettiest hair in the whole world,' she heard him say. Her heart floundered with the sudden thrill. Rolling over quickly, she rose to her elbows, leaned over him and showered his face with its softness.

'That tickles,' he said.

'I meant for it to.'

As she lay down again, one of her slender arms pointed toward an opening in the leaves. 'There's the moon coming up.'

'It's pretty.'

'Let's go up the hill and watch it.'

'It'll come to us in a little while.'

'Well, lazy, we *could* go up and meet it.'

'All right.'

She lay still until Carl arose, grinning, lifted her up to her feet and helped her over the rough places in their path. From the hilltop they watched the moon float up into the blue darkness, turning whiter and whiter and growing smaller and smaller, until it was like a plate of glowing chinaware tossed among the stars. Irene's hand slipped up against Carl's breast. 'He's mine,' she thought. 'He'll always be mine.' She looked out across the mist which lay in the small valley. The distant city was a glittering jewel, and shadowy trees about her became huge vases of spreading ferns.

Her head bent to his shoulder and her eyes closed. 'I wish we could get married before you go.'

'So do I.'

'Then we'd always belong to each other.'

'It would be swell.'

'And we'd be sure of our love.'

'Aren't we now?'

'Of course, silly. But I mean *more sure.*'

While they strolled back to the blanket, arm in arm, she kept thinking over and over to herself: 'He's mine and nobody else's. He's all mine.' She wondered if any other woman had ever felt this way — as if something kept growing inside you until you were about to burst. But you didn't want to because the thing growing was so nice you wanted to feel that way always.

Arriving at the blanket, they lay down again, stretched out full length, with their hands folded behind them, pillowing their heads. The sound of waves slapping the sides of the canoe came up the hillside. 'I'm in love,' Irene kept repeating to the rhythm of an artery pulsing in her breast. 'I'm in love ... I'm in love ...'

'What's that star?' she asked after a while, pointing toward a bright planet, hanging motionless and unblinking, where the western sky gleamed with its myriad flecks of light.

'Which one?'

'The one over that tall tree there.'

Carl looked for a moment. 'I don't know. Evening Star, I guess.'

Then they were quiet for a long time. Irene listened to the lisping of the grass as it undulated with each breeze. Finally she said, 'I tell you what let's do.'

'What?'

'If you wouldn't be afraid,' she went on, and added hastily, 'Wouldn't be ashamed, I mean.'

'Ashamed of what?'

She turned her head away from the cone of moonlight shining through the opening in the branches and kept her eyes in the shadow of her forehead. Her hands unfolded and she followed a seam of her dress with a finger. Then her answer came, almost a whisper: ' ... of taking off our clothes.'

His startled 'What!' made her smile.

'If we saw each other that way, neither of us could ever love anyone else; could we?'

His answer was lost somewhere in a sudden rustling of wind among the leaves.

'And we'd really be married then — just as if we had gone to a minister.'

'Do you think we ought to?' he asked.

'We love each other; don't we?'

'Sure. But...'

'Then it's all right.' Standing up, she unsnapped her dress. It slipped back over her shoulders and fell around her feet. Glancing down at Carl who still sat, rigid, staring up at her, she asked, 'Aren't you going to?'

He stood up then and began undressing.

After a moment their bodies glistened white. The moonlight streamed like milk over Irene's young breasts and poured down her long, slender legs into the shadows about her feet. She stood, motionless, looking at Carl's browner body and trying to hide the wonder in her eyes. The tip of his tongue slipped between his lips before he spoke.

'You're beautiful!'

A rapturous, tingling wave flowed through her heart and away from her body filling the whole world with its ecstasy. 'He thinks I'm beautiful...., He thinks I'm beautiful....' The thought hummed in her mind like the purl of water in slow rapids above a roaring falls. But it seemed to her that of all the people who had mated since the beginning of time, only her love for Carl was real.

Everything around them was etched by the moon and the moment into brilliant clarity — at the foot of the hill a scimitar of water glistened between the curved shores, two leaves coasted downward from the trees, a bird twinkled somewhere overhead.... And directly in front of her stood Carl. Above the tumult of her thoughts she heard him whisper:

'Irene! You're wonderful!'

She crossed the space between them. 'And you're like a Greek god.' She leaned forward and kissed him lightly. Her body warmed at the touch of his dry lips. 'Now we'll always love each other; won't we?'

'Yes!'

'Forever and ever.'

He nodded.

'We'd better dress now.'

They turned their backs to each other as they lifted their clothing from the ground, but after a few minutes she called to him: 'Help me with this. I can't get it fastened.' She stood with her back still toward him, holding the ends of her unclasped brassiere against her shoulder blades. His steps sounded loud on the brittle grass, then she felt him fumble with the snaps and heard his breathy words:

'You're beautiful! I love you!'

She laughed quietly.

When they were dressed, Carl picked up the blanket, and Irene slipped a hand through his arm. She looked around once more before they left, memorizing every detail of the spot. 'This is where I gave my heart away,' she said to herself. 'My heart that's his for always. This is our shrine.' After a final glance at the well of moonlight, she followed Carl down the hill, without speaking, without wanting to speak, and it wasn't until they arrived at the canoe that either spoke. Lying back once more in the prow, Irene said, 'I'll always remember it just like this.'

'It was wonderful.' Carl knelt in the stern.

'You'll write to me often; won't you?'

'Every day,' he promised.

She watched the paddle slip into the water, then glanced back toward the hill. 'Love is beautiful.' Turning around, she asked aloud, 'Isn't love beautiful, Carl?'

His quiet nod was her only answer.

The canoe swerved about, pointed toward the dock across the water, then glided out onto the lake which was an upturned sky with a galaxy of pin-point stars and the reflection of Venus, clearer than all the others, shifting back and forth among the small waves like a bright light swinging in the wind.

ON THE SIDEWALK[1]

By CALVIN WILLIAMS

(From *Saplings* and *New Stories*)

THE street was deserted. The tall man was sitting at the only table left on the sidewalk, and with him sat the short man. The former wore a long, loose topcoat, with the collar turned up. The lights were out, so his face was invisible as to features. He was probably Mexican, maybe French. It doesn't matter.

The other man, the short one, was sitting at the other side of the little round table. He wore no coat, but seemingly did not mind the cold. It would soon be spring, and then he would not need an overcoat; he wouldn't need one when he was dead, either, he reflected. His legs were encased in blue serge that shone in the light reflected from the stagnant water in the gutter.

'Works in a night club?'

'Yes, he's pretty good, though,' answered the short one.

'Works in a night club.'

'Yes, the one on the road east of Blountil.'

'He left school in twenty-three, huh?'

At this query, the short one inclined his head as if for better recollection, then righted it and said,

'Yes, twenty-three or four.'

'Singing in a dump like that.'

'Yes, he's pretty good, though,' reiterated the short one.

'How long has he been working there?' asked the tall one.

'Four months.'

'In a dump like that.'

'He's pretty good, though.'

A door opened somewhere, and a streak of light crossed the table and was obliterated as the door closed again. The two at the table sat unmoved.

'Tell him to come to see me sometime,' the tall one said, turning the collar of his coat still higher about his neck.

[1] Reprinted from 'Saplings,' 9th Series, 1934. Copyright, 1934, by Scholastic Corporation. publishers of *Scholastic, The American High School Weekly*.

'I never see him to speak to,' said the short one.

'Oh, high hat, huh?'

'No, but he works at night and sleeps in the day, and I work in the day and sleep at night.'

'Works at night — sleeps at day — you work at day — sleep at night,' mumbled the tall one.

The short one shivered, not from cold. The waiter frightened him as he came up beside him.

'Your check, *señor*,' mumbled the waiter in a flat, sleepy voice.

'Have you ever been without a *centavo*?' asked the short one.

'*Si*,' came the answer.

'Hah, so you know the feeling?'

'*Si*,' the waiter replied.

'And the feeling of hunger, have you known that?'

'*Si*, in Zacualpam I was hungry.'

'Ah, what a feeling is the feeling of hunger! I do not see how one endures it.'

The waiter left.

'We do, though,' said the tall one.

'Do what?'

'Endure it.'

'Endure what?'

'Hunger.'

'Oh!'

Silence. The street was quieter than ever now. More quiet than either had ever known. The silence was broken soon, however, by someone blaring *Tu Quiero Dijiste*. The voice was a harsh, pinched tenor, and the singer's throat must have ached when he was through.

'Does he sing like that?' asked the tall one.

'No, his voice is sweet and clear.'

'He sings jazz, though.'

'Yes, but he's pretty good, though.'

'Does he sing in English?'

'Yes, and in French and in Spanish,' said the short one.

'Can he sing better in English than in French?'

'Yes.'

'Ahah.'

'Does he still stay at the same place?' asked the tall one, after a pause.

'Yes.'

'I should hate to stay there.'

'I, too, should hate to stay there,' said the short one.

'Doesn't he mind?'

'Yes.'

'Then why doesn't he leave?'

'Where would he go?'

'There are other places.'

'Yes, there are other places.'

Silence again. Suddenly the short one shook himself, and his face brightened with a new thought.

'But at the other places he would have to pay,' he said.

'Doesn't he pay where he is?'

'No, that is part of his salary arrangement.'

'Oh,' sighed the tall one.

'The woman keeps it clean for him,' said the short one.

'Keeps what clean?'

'The room, the place where he stays, the place he sleeps in.'

'Oh, yes. What woman?' asked the tall one, suddenly aware that they were no longer alone. The waiter was again standing beside the table with another tray in his hand, and on the other tray was another check.

'The one he lives with,' said the short one, oblivious of the waiter standing beside him.

'The American?'

'She's not American.'

'What is she, then?'

'I don't know, but she's not American.'

'She speaks English.'

'So do you.'

'And you.'

They sat in silence for fully two minutes. The tall one had allowed his coat to fall open. There were no buttons on it, and the cloth was torn where the buttons had been. They must have been pulled off to have made such rents in the cloth. The waiter left them without presenting the check.

'Where is the place?' asked the tall one.

'What place?'

'The place where he stays.'

'O, yes, the place where he stays. Ummm. Why, it is on a street in back of the place where he sings.'

The way the tall man was sitting made his shadow look like that of a vulture. His black coat was stretched taut across his hunched shoulders.

'On the road to Cuatla?' he asked.

'No, on the road to Blountil.'

'Who lives in the place besides him and the woman?'

'The *mozo.*'

'What does he do?'

'He waters the plants.'

'What plants?'

'The plants in the *patio.*'

'Is that all he does?'

'So I hear.'

THE LONE PIONEER[1]

By WILLIAM E. WILSON

(From *Literary America*)

WELL, sir, I had an experience on my last trip. You know, I usually try and get down to Crescent City by Thursday night. That gives me all day Friday here and part of Saturday, if I don't happen to get around to all my customers. Then I can start back to Chi and be home for the next weekend, or I can lay over here if I want to. It's a good town to lay over in. You boys all been out to Bertha's place, I guess.'

The broad man's suspenders creaked as he leaned forward to drop his cigar ash on the dusty brown corolla of the art-metal ash-stand. His two listeners sat solidly in the leather chairs of the hotel lobby, looking out at the lighted street through the wide sheen of a plate-glass window. Although they had just come in from the dining-room and had only begun their cigars, they were wearing hats, pushed back on their heads. One was an oldish man, stumpy and square. He sat with his short legs uncrossed, two rolls of long cotton underwear showing below trousers that were hitched almost to his knees. The other was younger, broad, rosy, and well-dressed, like the speaker. He had eaten too much, and from time to time his deep belly quivered in the spasm of a belch.

'Yes, sir, it was an experience,' the speaker repeated, leaning back and examining his cigar, which he held by the tips of his four fingers and his thumb, as if it were a piccolo which he was about to play. 'I was driving in on 41 about 5 P.M. in the afternoon, and I'd had a good day in Vincennes and Princeton, so I was riding along easy, smoking a cigar and listening to the radio in my car which the wife gave me last Christmas. There was some dinner music on from one of the big hotels in New York, coming in on a national hookup. It was kind of classical stuff—you know the kind they play in those hotels. Then once in a while they'd change over and play a dance tune. Usually I'd rather hear a good comedian or one of these here Kentucky hill-billies with a guitar. You see, I come from Kentucky originally — Christian County. But that day this music suited me just right. It had been hot and was beginning to cool off a little and the country all around was kind of peaceful and, like I said, I'd had a good day.

'You all know that stretch north of here, straight as an arrow almost all the way down from Vincennes, and flat, too, although I always feel like you're coming downhill a little all the time. I don't know, but it always seemed to me like you could put your car in neutral in Vincennes and just coast down here. Well, just the same, there is a hill on that stretch, and a curve, too, about eight miles north of the city limits. You come up over a rise of ground and then you swing a little to your left as you come down. There's a farmhouse about half a mile to your left with some whiteoaks around it and straight ahead you can see that dirt track they built awhile back. You know the place I mean.

'Well, when I come down that grade on my last trip, there was one of these hitch-hikers on the road just ahead of me. Usually I don't stop for those fellows. There's been so many stories in the papers about murders and like of that. Even figuring the company's trademark on the door of my Chevvy was protection, I never liked to take chances. But this time I stopped. It was my mood, I guess, like I said about that music and the peaceful way those wide flat fields looked and the smell of clover, too. It might of been I had a hunch he was a Kentuckian, like myself — they always say you can spot a Kentuckian a mile away if you've ever known any — because that was what he turned out to be, a fellow from down near Christian County, as I learned later.

'He was a thin little chap about thirty or thirty-five, I'd of said, and not like the usual run of hitch-hikers. I mean, he had on a dark double-breasted suit that fit him pretty tight and was squared out in the shoulders, and he had on a felt hat and tan shoes that were as shiny as if he'd never set foot off of a city street. He was carrying a tan leather suitcase with stickers on it.

'"Goin' to town?" I said to him; and he hopped in beside me.

'"How far is it?" he asked.

'"'Bout ten miles," I said.

'"Well, it's lucky I got a lift," he said; and then, after I got the car going, he said, "I got to take care of my feet."

'That sounded funny somehow, a hitch-hiker talking about his feet, like these ads for soap talking about a woman saving her hands. I turned around and looked at him. He didn't seem to notice me. He just sat there in a queer limp sort of way and at first I thought maybe he was sick. He wasn't very strong-looking. His face was thin and he had a sharp nose and black eyes that bulged out like his collar was too tight. His complexion wasn't very good either, what you could see of it. His beard was close-shaved, but it was so heavy that it made his face look black. I started to say something about maybe him being sick, and then I noticed his hands. I've got the habit of looking at people's hands from selling this new fingernail enamel my company puts out. Well, I could tell by his hands he wasn't sick. He had 'em spread out on his knees as limp as he could make 'em and I could see it was all something he had studied and practiced.

'He didn't seem to want to talk, so I leaned back in the seat and relaxed a little myself and we drove on quite a piece without saying anything. I began to listen to that dinner music again, and every once in a while I took a deep breath of that clover smell. I guess I almost forgot he was beside me, because I was kind of startled when he sat up a little and said,

'"That tune always makes me think of June."

'It was the *Wabash Blues*. You know how it goes. It come out quite a while ago, but you still hear it once in a while.

'"Well," I said, "only two more days and it'll be June."

'"No," he said. "That ain't what I mean. June was a girl."

'"Oh," I said, and then, kind of laughing, I said, "the girl you left behind you."

'He didn't say anything for a minute, and when he finally did speak, it made me feel real ashamed of myself. He said, "She's dead. She was my first partner."

'I told him I was sorry, I didn't understand. I said I was sorry he'd lost his wife, and so on. But that wasn't it either. He turned around and looked straight at me.

'"I guess you didn't notice my suitcase, did you?" he said.

'I'd noticed it, but I didn't pay much attention to it. I noticed there were stickers on it, but I didn't read them.

'"I'm a marathon dancer," he said. "I'm the Lone Pioneer."'

The salesman stopped to look up at a man who came to join them. He, too, was a drummer, heavy and complacently dyspeptic.

'Sit down, Bert,' the speaker said. 'I was just telling Tom and Haskell here about a hitch-hiker I picked up on my last trip. He was a marathon dancer that called himself "The Lone Pioneer."'

The newcomer sat down and the speaker studied his cigar for a moment before he went on. His broad pinkish face was without expression when he was not talking. His three listeners waited, apparently self-absorbed.

'You-all ever seen a marathon dance?' he said finally. 'Well, sir, you ought to see one. I tell you, it's part of your education. I went out to see this Lone Pioneer the next Saturday in a dance just outside of town that he told me he was going to enter. Well, sir, I never would of believed it was such a business. There must of been a thousand people in the audience, and they had reserved ringside seats and everything, just like a prize-fight or a theatre. On the dance-floor they had about fifty couples in the contest. And it's a real thing, I tell you. They got it down to a science. These couples dance forty-five minutes and rest fifteen minutes. They give them eight meals a day and cod-liver oil every day. And they've got a complete staff working there night and day, two judges and a master of ceremonies, and a trainer and a foot specialist and two trained nurses. And a doctor and a dentist come out twice a day to give the marathoners a free examination. It seems they have a lot of trouble with their teeth. I tell you, it's a big concern. They even publish a daily newspaper. *The Marathon News*, they call it. Every once in a while they get these dancers up before a microphone and have 'em sing, and afterwards the crowd throws pennies and nickels on the floor for them. And some of them have books they pass around that you can look at, telling all about their past histories and like of that. You're expected to put a little money in an envelope at the back after you've finished looking at it. These dancers pick up quite a bit of money that way even if they don't win a prize, and of course they get their room and board free as long as they're in the contest. I wouldn't of missed it for anything.

'But I was going to tell you about this Lone Pioneer.

'It seems this Lone Pioneer started out in the marathon dancing business about ten years ago. He was younger than I thought at first, because he said he was only seventeen when he entered his first contest. They were just beginning the business then, and I guess, from all he said, conditions were pretty crude. They didn't have it down to a science yet, you see. They didn't have nurses and trainers and like of that, and the beauty parlors and clothing stores weren't signed up for the advertising they'd get out of it. Of course it wasn't such a good proposition for them then, because they didn't broadcast the dances on the radio. He said the dancers didn't get much attention and they went in their own clothes and after they wore out their shoes they put on bedroom slippers and sometimes the winners ended up barefooted. He said he supposed it was just like the beginning of any other profession. "Profession" was the word he used, and he talked about his "career," just like it was grand opera or something. I thought it was kind of funny at first, but after I saw this dance, I could see his point.

'Well, he and this girl named June that he'd run around with a lot in his home town saw in the papers about a dance up near Louv'lle and they went up there. They started out thinking it was just a lark, kind of. He said they didn't have technique or like of that. But after you get started at it, he said, it kind of gets you, like any other business, I suppose, just like us being on the road all the time and getting restless if we tried anything else. He and this June started out that way, but pretty soon they began to take their dancing seriously. They began to develop technique, like not using any muscles that weren't necessary and learning how to dance in their sleep, one leaning on the other, and studying how to relax during their rest periods.

'And, along with that, they began to take each other seriously, too. He said dancing with a girl like that for two or three weeks, with only fifteen minutes apart out of every hour, you get to know her pretty well. He meant it in a nice way. Well, it seems they got pretty fond of each other, and he said finally in those fifteen minute rest periods his arms got to feeling funny without her, just like a finger you'd take a ring off of that you'd been wearing a long time, and she told him she felt the same way when she was away from him. He didn't tell me much about her, except that she was kind of thin and not very strong. It seems her dad had died of the t.b. I saw her picture when I looked at his book out at the dance, and she was a real pretty little thing.

'Like I said, they fell in love with each other, and they began to make plans for the future. They had the marathon fever, as he called it, by this time, and their idea was to work their way up and become the champion marathon dancers of America. He made it sound real inspiring, the way he described what the two of them planned. He said they talked a lot about dancing through life together. It's a kind of beautiful idea, when you come to think about it, "dancing through life together."

'Well, the manager of the dance finally caught on that they were sweet on each other and he suggested a marathon dance wedding. It would of been the first one in the world, this fellow said. So they started to make their plans. Their idea was to do it right away, but the manager said they ought to work up a little publicity first. They saw his point and agreed to wait a week or so.

'Up to that time, he said, this June was getting pretty tired. He said he was holding her up most of the time, and sometimes she'd even sleep right through the whole forty-five-minute stretch. But when the plans for the wedding was made, she pepped right up. He said her cheeks took on a lot of color, and he never saw her so pretty.

'A lot of people came out to the dance-hall to watch them. The papers were full of the plans for the wedding, and the crowd could pick them out easy enough, because the manager put them off by themselves in a little space that was covered over by artificial orange blossoms that had an arch of lights over it that said, "Bride and Groom." This fellow said he never was so proud in his life as he was then, with the people all crowding up against the ropes to look at them and this June would put her head down on his shoulder and he'd kiss her cheek now and then just to show them how proud he was.

'They began to get all kinds of presents, too. It's funny how a wedding kind of gets people, you know, especially women. He said the girl got all kinds of fancy underwear and people sent him a lot of money. Then the stores began to realize the possibilities of the thing. A bakery made a five-hundred-pound wedding cake for them. He said you should have seen it. And then some clothing stores fitted them out in a tuxedo and a complete wedding gown and a going-away suit, which he said they laughed about a lot, because there were still ten couples in the dance and it looked like they wouldn't be going away from there for a long time yet. And a jewelry store gave this June a ring and gave him a watch. He showed me the watch. He carries it with him everywhere he goes.

'Well, sir, everything was going along beautifully, and he thought this June was kind of getting her second wind and maybe they would win the hundred-dollar first prize in addition to all these presents. And then, the night before the ceremony was to take place, the girl just collapsed in his arms. The orchestra was playing the *Wabash Blues* at the time. That's why the *Wabash Blues* always makes him think of this June he was in love with, see.

'He said he was scared at first and started to carry her off of the floor, but the manager ran out and said she'd only fainted and they'd make it all right and he should go on dancing by himself. "Solo," he called it. Well, he did, but when his rest period came, he rushed right over to the women's room. He said the manager kept saying he'd make it all right but the doctor looked pretty serious. He was good and scared then and he went over to this June and asked her how she felt. He told me he never would forget the way she looked up at him when she opened her eyes.

'"Carry on, Jim," she said to him. Jim was his real name. "Remember what we planned. Go out there and win for both of us."

'There was a kind of tremble in his voice when he told me what she said to him. It was real heroic the way she said, "Carry on, Jim." He said he nearly broke down and cried, but he did go back and dance by himself. During the next rest period, he went to the women's room again, but they'd taken her away somewhere and the manager didn't give him much satisfaction. So he went back to the dance, remembering what she said to him about carrying on.

'Well, of course the newspapers got hold of it, and a few days later the authorities made 'em close the dance. In the meantime, he said, he got all kinds of presents from the crowds that come out to see him dancing all by himself under those artificial orange blossoms. One of the presents, he said, wasn't worth anything, but it kind of touched his heart. It was a poem that a little cripple girl wrote for him, about this lonely young lover dancing with sadness in his heart and like of that. It was printed in the paper and she gave him a copy of it in her own handwriting. But the crowd gave him money, too, and he said when the dance was finally closed up, he figured he'd made more in presents and cash than if he'd won all the prizes.

'As soon as he could, he got back to his home town to see how this girl was, and — would you believe it? — he got there on the day they were burying her. It seems nobody in her family could write, so they didn't let him know. Well, sir, I guess that pretty near killed him, from what he said. The worst part about it was the girl had been so brave up to the minute she passed on. She kept telling her mother things to tell him — how he should go on with their dreams and she'd be watching him from heaven and giving him strength and so forth. You all ought to of heard him tell it. I darn near cried myself.

'Well, sir, he went and did just like she told him to. And that's how he got his name, "The Lone Pioneer." The next contest he entered was up in Ohio somewhere. He got him one of these photograph albums and wrote "The Book of the Lone Pioneer" on the back of it in white ink, and inside he put all the newspaper clippings about his first dance and the marathon wedding they planned and how she took sick and what she said to him. And he copied out the poem the cripple girl wrote for him and put it in. Then at the end he put a picture of this June and under it was the newspaper article about her funeral down in Kentucky. Inside the back of the book he pasted an envelope and wrote on it, "Won't you help the Lone Pioneer of the Marathon Dance construct a fitting memorial for that plucky little loved one buried in the cold, cold ground of Old Kentucky?"

'This Lone Pioneer told me he had competed in more than twenty marathon dances since that time, and he's won three first prizes, one second, and five thirds. But the most of his money comes from this book. He bought a tombstone for this June. I know, because he had a snapshot of the tombstone in his book when I saw it and the newspaper article about how he paid for it. And he sent half of his income home to the girl's widowed mother for the upkeep of the grave and the support of the family, until about a year ago when the girl's mother died. He's got the clippings right there in the book to prove it.

'Of course he had to get new books all the time because the number of the clippings kept growing, and he said the crowds had worn out almost a hundred of his books handling them. He finally ordered them by the dozen because it was cheaper. He said he had a kind of pride in keeping a clean and tidy book. It made a better impression on the crowd, of course, and then, too, he liked to think he was doing it for this June that died. His book sure is interesting. It reads just like a book — I mean, like a book you'd buy somewhere.'

The salesman stopped, removed a moist brown strip of tobacco from his mouth, and spat into a cuspidor.

'But, you know,' he went on, 'when I saw this Lone Pioneer he was having a hard time. That was why he was hitch-hiking. He'd lost all his money and kind of got himself into trouble. I felt real sorry for him.

'It seems, after the girl's mother died, he got the idea of building a mausoleum for this June down in Kentucky, because a lot of people who'd seen him in marathons all over the country had visited this June's grave. He had letters from some of them, telling him they'd found everything just like it was described in the book. So he had the notion of building a mausoleum and making a kind of shrine out of her grave for people to see when they went there. Well, in order to double his capital, he got to gambling a little, and pretty soon he'd lost everything he'd saved.

'Well, sir, that fellow had nerve. He swore off gambling and kept right on carrying on, but just about when he'd begun to get on his feet again, he got himself into trouble.

'It was at the last dance he was in before he came down here. He said it was in a place he'd danced in before and he was a little worried for fear he wouldn't do so well, since all the people had seen him before. So he went into debt and bought himself an outfit, a set of fancy pioneer's suits made out of silk with an imitation of a coonskin cap. You know, the kind you see in pictures.

'Well, the manager of this dance didn't want him to enter, because the last time he had gotten more contributions than any of the others and the manager thought he might scare off a lot of the contestants that was in the profession just for the money. He finally had to let him in, but he made him dance with a girl that he picked out for him. On top of that, the manager decided to collect all the contributions himself and divide them equally between all the dancers at the end of the contest, with a big percentage for himself. You can see for yourself how that would cut down this Lone Pioneer's income.

'But that wasn't all.

'It seems the girl the manager picked out for him looked a whole lot like this June. The Lone Pioneer said he tried not to think about it for a long time, and they danced together about four weeks before he did anything. Then one day, he said, it got to be too much for him and, while she was asleep and he was carrying her, he kissed her. He was thinking of this June all the time, see.

'He said he didn't know the girl had woke up until the next day when the manager came up to him and said,

'"You're disqualified!"

'This Lone Pioneer said you could of bowled him over with a feather.

'"Get off of the floor!" the manager said.

'The Lone Pioneer asked him why he was disqualified, and the manager said,

'"Your partner reports to me you been making improper advances to her."

'He said he was flabbergasted. He said he hadn't intended to make improper advances to the girl, it was just because she looked so much like this June that he couldn't help kissing her. But the manager called a cop and they made him get off of the floor, and he wasn't even able to get his share of the contributions or anything. And the girl stood up for the manager and said it was true, he'd made improper advances to her. He said he felt pretty bad. He said it wasn't so much because he'd lost all that money, but because he felt like he'd done something to this June's memory.

'He was all cut up over it, and I felt real sorry for him. There wasn't much I could say to him, but I told him I thought he hadn't done wrong and maybe after all he was really in love with this girl and like of that. Sometimes it happens that way, I told him. I tell you, it made me feel real bad the way he let it upset him. You could see it was the principle of the thing that bothered him.'

Leaning forward, the speaker dropped the glowing butt of his cigar down the long neck of the ash-stand. There was a hiss at the bottom of the stand and a little white puff came up through the mouth like the smoky belch of a volcano's crater. The three other men did not move.

'The Saturday night I was out at the dance, he pointed out the girl he'd kissed at the last dance, and when I saw her, I didn't blame him at all. She was a pretty little thing with black hair and black eyes and she did look something like the pictures of this

June. I'd of kissed her myself, and I wouldn't of waited four weeks to do it.'

The men did not move and the speaker dug a newspaper from under himself in the leather chair.

'If you-all would like to come along, we could go out there and watch them for a while tonight. I want you all to meet this Lone Pioneer. He's a real fellow, and right now he's the most important dancer out there. You probably didn't read it in the paper, but it says that this Lone Pioneer and this girl that looks like June are going to have a marathon wedding. They're going to call it an Honor Wedding. It tells here about his kissing her at the last dance and getting put off of the floor for it and how his conscience began to hurt him. Her name is Mary Frances and now he's going to marry her and make everything o.k. It tells, too, about the June he used to love and how this Mary Frances looks a whole lot like her, and how this Mary Frances understands and has forgiven him.

'It don't say anything about how she happened to forgive him, but I know the answer to that. I don't like to brag, but when I was out to this dance on my last trip, I went right up to her and told her all the things this Lone Pioneer had told me. She didn't want to listen to me at first, but I made her listen. I showed her just what a fine fellow this Lone Pioneer was.'

The speaker paused and surveyed his audience, sure of his effect. His face was glowing.

'I tell you,' he said, 'it was a real experience to be able to help a fellow like this Lone Pioneer. I got room in my Chevvy, if you'd like to come. They're having a knockout grind tonight, too. A knockout grind is where they make them dance for four hours steady with only three minutes out for hygienic purposes. I think we ought to go out and give this Lone Pioneer a big hand.'

ONLY THE DEAD KNOW BROOKLYN[1]

By THOMAS WOLFE

(From *The New Yorker*)

DERE'S no guy livin' dat knows Brooklyn t'roo an' t'roo, because it'd take a guy a lifetime just to find his way aroun' duh goddam town.

So like I say, I'm waitin' for my train t' come when I sees dis big guy standin' deh — dis is duh foist I eveh see of him. Well, he's lookin' wild, y'know, an' I can see dat he's had plenty, but still he's holdin' it; he talks good an' is walkin' straight enough. So den, dis big guy steps up to a little guy dat's standin' deh, an' says, 'How d'yuh get t' Eighteent' Avenoo an' Sixty-sevent' Street?' he says.

'Jesus! Yuh got me, chief,' duh little guy says to him. 'I ain't been heah long myself. Where is duh place?' he says. 'Out in duh Flatbush section somewhere?'

'Nah,' duh big guy says. 'It's out in Bensenhoist. But I was neveh deh befoeh. How d'yuh get deh?'

'Jesus,' duh little guy says, scratchin' his head, y'know — yuh could see duh little guy didn't know his way about — 'yuh got me, chief. I neveh hoid of it. Do any of youse guys know where it is?' he says to me.

'Sure,' I says. 'It's out in Bensenhoist. Yuh take duh Fourt' Avenoo express, get off at Fifty-nint' Street, change to a Sea Beach local deh, get off at Eighteent' Avenoo an' Sixty-toid, an' den walk down foeh blocks. Dat's all yuh got to do,' I says.

'G'wan!' some wise guy dat I neveh seen befoeh pipes up. 'Whatcha talkin' about?' he says — oh, he was wise, y'know. 'Duh guy is crazy! I tell yuh what yuh do,' he says to duh big guy. 'Yuh change to duh West End line at Toity-sixt',' he tells him. 'Get off at Noo Utrecht an' Sixteent' Avenoo,' he says. 'Walk two blocks oveh, foeh blocks up,' he says, 'an' you'll be right deh.' Oh, a *wise* guy, y'know.

'Oh, yeah?' I says. 'Who told *you* so much?' He got me sore because he was so wise about it. 'How long you been livin' heah?' I says.

'All my life,' he says. 'I was bawn in Williamsboig,' he says. 'An' I can tell you t'ings about dis town you neveh hoid of,' he says.

'Yeah?' I says.

'Yeah,' he says.

'Well, den, you can tell me t'ings about dis town dat nobody else has eveh hoid of, either. Maybe you make it all up yoehself at night,' I says, 'befoeh you go to sleep — like cuttin' out papeh dolls, or somp'n.'

'Oh, yeah?' he says. 'You're pretty wise, ain't yuh?'

'Oh, I don't know,' I says. 'Duh boids ain't usin' my head for Lincoln's statue yet,' I says. 'But I'm wise enough to know a phony when I see one.'

'Yeah?' he says. 'A wise guy, huh? Well, you're so wise dat someone's goin' t'bust yuh one right on duh snoot some day,' he says. 'Dat's how wise *you* are.'

Well, my train was comin', or I'da smacked him den and dere, but when I seen duh train was comin', all I said was, 'All right, mugg! I'm sorry I can't stay to take keh of you, but I'll be seein' yuh sometime, I hope, out in duh cemetery.' So den I says to duh big guy, who'd been standin' deh all duh time, 'You come wit me,' I says. So when we gets onto duh train I says to him, 'Where yuh goin' out in Bensenhoist?' I says. 'What numbeh are yuh lookin' for?' I says. *You* know — I t'ought if he told me duh address I might be able to help him out.

'Oh,' he says, 'I'm not lookin' for no one. I don't know no one out deh.'

'Then whatcha goin' out deh for?' I says.

'Oh,' duh guy says, 'I'm just goin' out to see duh place,' he says. 'I like duh sound of duh name' — Bensenhoist, y'know — 'so I t'ought I'd go out an' have a look at it.'

'Whatcha tryin' t'hand me?' I says. 'Whatcha tryin' t'do — kid me?' *You* know, I t'ought duh guy was bein' wise wit me.

'No,' he says, 'I'm tellin' yuh duh troot. I like to go out an' take a look at places wit nice names like dat. I like to go out an' look at all kinds of places,' he says.

'How'd yuh know deh was such a place,' I says, 'if you neveh **been** deh befoeh?'

'Oh,' he says, 'I got a map.'

'A *map*?' I says.

'Sure,' he says, 'I got a map dat tells me about all dese places. I take it wit me every time I come out heah,' he says.

And Jesus! Wit dat, he pulls it out of his pocket, an' so help me, but he's *got* it — he's tellin' duh troot — a big map of duh whole goddam place wit all duh different pahts. Mahked out, you know — Canarsie an' East Noo Yawk an' Flatbush, Bensenhoist, Sout' Brooklyn, duh Heights, Bay Ridge, Greenpernt — duh whole goddam layout, he's got it right deh on duh map.

'You been to any of dose places?' I says.

'Sure,' he says, 'I been to most of 'em. I was down in Red Hook just last night,' he says.

'Jesus! Red Hook!' I says. 'Whatcha do down deh?'

'Oh,' he says, 'nuttin' much. I just walked aroun'. I went into a coupla places an' had a drink,' he says, 'but most of the time I just walked aroun'.'

'Just walked aroun'?' I says.

'Sure,' he says, 'just lookin' at things, y'know.'

'Where'd yuh go?' I asts him.

'Oh,' he says, 'I don't know duh name of duh place, but I could find it on my map,' he says. 'One time I was walkin' across some big fields where deh ain't no houses,' he says, 'but I could see ships oveh deh all lighted up. Dey was loadin'. So I walks across duh fields,' he says, 'to where duh ships are.'

'Sure,' I says, 'I know where you was. You was down to duh Erie Basin.'

'Yeah,' he says, 'I guess dat was it. Dey had some of dose big elevators an' cranes an' dey was loadin' ships, an' I could see some ships in drydock all lighted up, so I walks across duh fields to where dey are,' he says.

'Den what did yuh do?' I says.

'Oh,' he says, 'nuttin' much. I came on back across duh fields after a while an' went into a coupla places an' had a drink.'

'Didn't nuttin' happen while yuh was in dere?' I says.

'No,' he says. 'Nuttin' much. A coupla guys was drunk in one of duh places an' started a fight, but dey bounced 'em out,' he says, 'an' den one of duh guys stahted to come back again, but duh bartender gets his baseball bat out from under duh counteh, so duh guy goes on.'

'Jesus!' I said. 'Red Hook!'

'Sure,' he says. 'Dat's where it was, all right.'

'Well, you keep outa deh,' I says. 'You stay away from deh.'

'Why?' he says. 'What's wrong wit it?'

'Oh,' I says, 'it's a good place to stay away from, dat's all. It's a good place to keep out of.'

'Why?' he says. 'Why is it?'

Jesus! Whatcha gonna do wit a guy as dumb as dat? I saw it wasn't no use to try to tell him nuttin', he wouldn't know what I was talkin' about, so I just says to him, 'Oh, nuttin'. Yuh might get lost down deh, dat's all.'

'Lost?' he says. 'No, I wouldn't get lost. I got a map,' he says. A map! Red Hook! Jesus!

So den duh guy begins to ast me all kinds of nutty questions: how big was Brooklyn an' could I find my way aroun' in it, an' how long would it take a guy to know duh place.

'Listen!' I says. 'You get dat idea outa yoeh head right now,' I says. 'You ain't neveh gonna get to know Brooklyn,' I says. 'Not in a hundred yeahs. I been livin' heah all my life,' I says, 'an' I don't even know all deh is to know about it, so how do you expect to know duh town,' I says, 'when you don't even live heah?'

'Yes,' he says, 'but I got a map to help me find my way about.'

'Map or no map,' I says, 'yuh ain't gonna get to know Brooklyn wit no map,' I says.

'Can you swim?' he says, just like dat. Jesus! By dat time, y'know, I begun to see dat duh guy was some kind of nut. He'd had plenty to drink, of course, but he had dat crazy look in his eye I didn't like. 'Can you swim?' he says.

'Sure,' I says. 'Can't you?'

'No,' he says. 'Not more'n a stroke or two. I neveh loined good.'

'Well, it's easy,' I says. 'All yuh need is a little confidence. Duh way I loined, me older bruddeh pitched me off duh dock one day when I was eight yeahs old, cloes an' all. "You'll swim," he says. "You'll swim all right — or drown." An', believe me, I *swam!* When yuh know yuh got to, you'll do it. Duh only t'ing yuh need is confidence. An' once you've loined,' I says, 'you've got nuttin' else to worry about. You'll neveh forget it. It's somp'n dat stays with yuh as long as yuh live.'

'Can yuh swim good?' he says.

'Like a fish,' I tells him. 'I'm a regular fish in duh wateh,' I says. 'I loined to swim right off duh docks wit all duh odeh kids,' I says.

'What would yuh do if yuh saw a man drownin'?' duh guy says.

'Do? Why, I'd jump in an' pull him out,' I says. 'Dat's what I'd do.'

'Did yuh eveh see a man drown?' he says.

'Sure,' I says. 'I see two guys — bot' times at Coney Island. Dey got out too far, an' neider one could swim. Dey drowned befoeh anyone could get to 'em.'

'What becomes of people after dey have drowned out heah?' he says.

'Drowned out where?' I says.

'Out heah in Brooklyn.'

'I don't know whatcha mean,' I says. 'Neveh hoid of no one drownin' heah in Brooklyn, unless you mean a swimmin' pool. Yuh can't drown in Brooklyn,' I says. 'Yuh gotta drown somewhere else — in duh ocean, where dere's wateh.'

'Drownin',' duh guy says, lookin' at his map. 'Drownin'.' Jesus! I could see by den he was some kind of nut, he had dat crazy expression in his eyes when he looked at you, an' I didn't know what he might do. So we was comin' to a station, an' it wasn't my stop, but I got off anyway, an' waited for duh next train.

'Well, so long, chief,' I says. 'Take it easy, now.'

'Drownin',' duh guy says, lookin' at his map. 'Drownin'.' Jesus! I've t'ought about dat guy a t'ousand times since den an' wondered what eveh happened to 'm goin' out to look at Bensenhoist because he liked duh name! Walkin' aroun' t'roo Red Hook by himself at night an' lookin' at his map! How many people did I see get drowned out heah in Brooklyn! How long would it take a guy wit a good map to know all deh was to know about Brooklyn!

Jesus! What a nut *he* was! I wondeh what eveh happened to 'm, anyway! I wondeh if someone knocked him on duh head, or if he's still wanderin' aroun' in duh subway in duh middle of duh night wit his little map! Duh poor guy! Say, I've got to laugh, at dat, when I t'ink about him! Maybe he's found out by now dat he'll neveh live long enough to know duh whole of Brooklyn! It'd take a guy a lifetime to know Brooklyn t'roo an' t'roo. An' even den, yuh wouldn't know it all.

THE YEARBOOK OF
THE AMERICAN SHORT STORY

JANUARY 1 TO DECEMBER 31, 1935

ABBREVIATIONS

I. PERIODICALS

```
A.B.C. ............... American Book Collector.
A. Crit. .............. American Criterions.
A. Fed. ............... American Federationist.
A.L. ................. American Literature.
A. Merc. ............. American Mercury.
A. Sp. ............... American Spectator.
A.W. ................. All's Well.
Adv. ................. Advance.
Adven. ............... Adventure.
Am. P. ............... American Prefaces.
An. .................. Anvil.
Ar. .................. Arise.
Argon. ............... Argonaut.
Asia. ................ Asia.
Atl. ................. Atlantic Monthly.
Av. .................. Avenue.
Books. ............... Books (New York Herald Tribune).
Boz. ................. Bozart-Westminster.
Br. E. ............... Brooklyn Eagle.
C. For. .............. Canadian Forum.
C.G. ................. Country Gentleman.
C.H.J. ............... Canadian Home Journal.
C.S.M. ............... Christian Science Monitor.
Can. ................. Canadian Magazine.
Cath. W. ............. Catholic World.
Chat. ................ Chatelaine.
Chic. Trib. .......... Chicago Tribune (Syndicate Service).
Col. ................. Collier's Weekly.
Col. R. .............. Columbia Review.
Colum. ............... Columbia.
Com. ................. Commonweal.
Cos. ................. Cosmopolitan.
Del. ................. Delineator.
Dick. ................ Lovat Dickson's Magazine.
Dir. ................. Direction.
Dub. ................. Dubuque Dial.
E.T.H.S.P. ........... Eastern Tennessee Historical Society Publications.
Eng. J. .............. English Journal.
Esq. ................. Esquire.
Essex. ............... Essex Institute Historical Collections.
Fan. ................. Fantasy.
For. ................. Forum.
Frontier. ............ Frontier and Midland.
G.H. (N.Y.). ......... Good Housekeeping (New York).
Gall. ................ Galleon.
Gol. ................. Golden Book.
H.A. ................. Harvard Advocate.
Hai. ................. Hairenik.
Harp. B. (London). ... Harper's Bazaar (London).
Harp. B. (N.Y.). ..... Harper's Bazaar (New York).
Harp. M. ............. Harper's Magazine.
Hin. ................. Hinterland.
```

House..............Household Magazine.
Husk................Husk.
Hyg.................Hygeia.
I.L.................International Literature.
Kos.................Kosmos.
L.H.J...............Ladies' Home Journal.
L.H.Q...............Louisiana Historical Quarterly.
L.L.................Life and Letters To-day.
L. Merc.............London Mercury.
Lan.................Lance.
Lit. A..............Literary America.
Ly..................Liberty.
M.L.N...............Modern Language Notes.
McCall..............McCall's Magazine.
Maclean.............Maclean's Magazine.
Mad.................Mademoiselle.
Mag.................Magazine, The.
Man.................Manuscript.
Manu................Short Story Manuscripts of 1935.
Mod. M..............Modern Monthly.
N.A. Rev............North American Review.
N.E.Q...............New England Quarterly.
N.M.Q...............New Mexico Quarterly.
N. Mass.............New Masses.
N. Rep..............New Republic.
N.S.................New Stories.
N. State............New Statesman.
N.T.................New Talent.
N.Y.................New Yorker.
N.Y.H...............New York History.
N.Y. Her............New York Herald Tribune.
N.Y. Times..........New York Times Book Review.
Nat.................Nation.
Opp.................Opportunity.
P.M.L.A.............Proceedings of the Modern Language Association of America.
Part. R.............Partisan Review.
Pers................Personalist.
Pict. R.............Pictorial Review.
Plow................Plowshare.
Pr. S...............Prairie Schooner.
Q.Q.................Queen's Quarterly.
R.H.................Rocking Horse.
R.N.L...............Richmond News Leader.
R.T.D...............Richmond Times-Dispatch.
Red Bk..............Red Book Magazine.
S.C.H.G.M...........South Carolina Historical and General Magazine.
S.E.P...............Saturday Evening Post.
S.W.................Southwest Review.
S.W.J...............Southwestern Journal.
Sat. R. (N.Y.)......Saturday Review of Literature.
Scan................American-Scandinavian Review.
Scr.................Scribner's Magazine.
Sky.................Skyline.
So. R...............Southern Review.
Spa.................Space.
Stan................Year Book of Stanford Writing.
State...............State (North Carolina).
Sto.................Story.
T.T.................Time and Tide.
T.W.................This Week.
Tan.................Tanager.

```
Tex................University of Texas Studies in English.
Transit.............Transition.
Trend..............Trend.
U. Mo. S...........University of Missouri Studies.
V.F................Vanity Fair.
Va.................Virginia Quarterly Review.
Ver................Vernier.
Vil................Village Press.
W.H.C..............Woman's Home Companion.
W.M.Q..............William and Mary College Quarterly.
W.W................Woman's World.
Wauk...............Waukon Republican Standard.
Westm..............Westminster Magazine.
Wind...............Windsor Quarterly.
Work...............Literary Workshop.
World..............New York World-Telegram.
Yale...............Yale Review.
(161)..............Page 161.
(2:161)............Volume 2, Page 161.
```

II. BOOKS

```
Barker.............Barker. Janus. (English edition.)
Bates P............Bates. Duet. (English edition.)
Bates Q............Bates. Cut and Come Again. (English edition.)
Beachcroft.........Beachcroft. A Young Man in a Hurry.
Bell...............Bell. Mixed Pickles. (English edition.)
Bentley............Bentley. The Whole of the Story. (English edition.)
Blackwood D........Blackwood. Shocks. (English edition.)
Bolitho............Bolitho. The House in Half Moon Street. (English edition.)
Bunin E............Bunin. The Elaghin Affair.
Burke F............Burke. Night-Pieces. (English edition.)
Byrne G............Byrne. The Hound of Ireland.
Calder B...........Calder-Marshall. A Pink Doll. (English edition.)
Caldwell D.........Caldwell. Kneel to the Rising Sun.
Canby..............Canby and Dashiell, editors. A Study of the Short Story.
Chamberlain........Chamberlain. What the Sweet Hell?
Chesterton H.......Chesterton, editor. A Century of Detective Stories. (English
                    edition.)
Chesterton J.......Chesterton. The Scandal of Father Brown.
Collier B..........Collier. Variation on a Theme. (English edition.)
Coppard P..........Coppard. Polly Oliver. (English edition.)
Crime C............Sayers, editor. The Third Omnibus of Crime.
Cross B............Cross, editor. A Book of the Short Story.
Dane E.............Dane. Fate Cries Out.
Davis B............Davis. Love Among the Ruins.
Derleth B..........Derleth. Place of Hawks.
Dingle.............Dingle. Pipe All Hands!
Dobie..............Dobie. San Francisco Tales.
Dobrée.............Dobrée. To Blush Unseen. (English edition.)
Douglas D..........Douglas. Strangers Come Home.
Drus...............Drus. Hexenboo.
Farrell B..........Farrell. Guillotine Party.
Feuchtwanger.......Feuchtwanger. Marianne in India.
Fifty..............Fifty Years of Ghost Stories. (English edition.)
Fitzgerald C.......Fitzgerald. Taps at Reveille.
Footman............Footman. Half-Way East. (English edition.)
Frankau............Frankau, editor. A Century of Love Stories. (English edition.)
Freund.............Freund. The Snow.
GK.................GK's.
```

ADDRESSES OF MAGAZINES
PUBLISHING SHORT STORIES

I. AMERICAN AND CANADIAN MAGAZINES

Adventure, 161 Sixth Avenue, New York City.
America, 329 West 108th Street, New York City.
American Criterion, 148 West 23rd Street, New York City.
American Magazine, 250 Park Avenue, New York City.
American Mercury, 730 Fifth Avenue, New York City.
American Prefaces, University Hall, Iowa City, Iowa.
American-Scandinavian Review, 116 East 64th Street, New York City.
American Spectator, 132 West 31st Street, New York City.
Anvil and Partisan Review, 54 Barrow Street, New York City.
Argonaut, 544 Market Street, San Francisco, Cal.
Argosy, 280 Broadway, New York City.
Asia, 40 East 49th Street, New York City.
Atlantic Monthly, 8 Arlington Street, Boston, Mass.
Bozart-Westminster, Oglethorpe University, Georgia.
Canadian Forum, 6 Manning Arcade, 24 King Street West, Toronto, Ont., Canada.
Canadian Home Journal, Richmond and Sheppard Streets, Toronto 2, Canada.
Canadian Magazine, 345 Adelaide Street West, Toronto, Ont., Canada.
Catholic World, 401 West 59th Street, New York City.
Chatelaine, 143 University Avenue, Toronto, Ont., Canada.
Chicago Tribune (Syndicate Service), 220 East 42nd Street, New York City.
Collier's Weekly, 250 Park Avenue, New York City.
Columbia, New Haven, Conn.
Columbia Review, 415 John Jay Hall, Columbia University, New York City.
Commonweal, 386 Fourth Avenue, New York City.
Cosmopolitan, 57th Street and Eighth Avenue, New York City.
Country Gentleman, Independence Square, Philadelphia, Pa.
Crisis, 69 Fifth Avenue, New York City.
Delineator, 161 Sixth Avenue, New York City.
Direction, Box 555, Peoria, Ill.
Dubuque Dial, 75 West 17th Street, Dubuque, Iowa.
Elks Magazine, 50 East 42nd Street, New York City.
Esquire, 919 North Michigan Avenue, Chicago, Ill.
Exchange Quarterly, 807 E. Broadway, Sweetwater, Tex.
Fantasy, 950 Heberton Avenue, Pittsburgh, Pa.
Fiction Parade, 220 East 42nd Street, New York City.
Fight, 112 East 19th Street, New York City.
Forum, 441 Lexington Avenue, New York City.
Frontier and Midland, University of Montana, Missoula, Mont.
Galleon, P. O. Box 705, Reading, Pa.
Good Housekeeping, 57th Street and Eighth Avenue, New York City.
Harper's Bazaar, 572 Madison Avenue, New York City.
Harper's Magazine, 49 East 33rd Street, New York City.
Hinterland, 624 Third Avenue, S.E., Des Moines, Iowa.
Holland's Magazine, Dallas, Texas.
Home Magazine, 55 Fifth Avenue, New York City.
Household Magazine, Topeka, Kansas.
Hub, 1730 Second Avenue, S.E., Cedar Rapids, Iowa.
Husk, Cornell College, Mount Vernon, Iowa.
Jewish Frontier, Room 404, 1225 Broadway, New York City.
Kansas Magazine, Kansas State College, Kansas.
Ladies' Home Journal, Independence Square, Philadelphia, Pa.

Latin Quarterly, 11 Barrow Street, New York City.
Left Front, 1475 South Michigan Avenue, Chicago, Ill.
Liberty, 1926 Broadway, New York City.
Lion and Unicorn, 151 Fifth Avenue, New York City.
Literary America, 175 Fifth Avenue, New York City.
McCall's Magazine, 230 Park Avenue, New York City.
Maclean's Magazine, 481 University Avenue, Toronto, Ont., Canada.
Manuscript, 17 West Washington Street, Athens, Ohio.
Modern Monthly, 52 Morton Street, New York City.
MS., 2960 Broadway, New York City.
National Home Monthly, Bannatyne and Dagmar, Winnipeg, Manitoba, Canada.
New Masses, 31 East 27th Street, New York City.
New Mexico Quarterly, University of New Mexico, Albuquerque, N.M.
New Quarterly, Box 434, Rock Island, Ill.
New Republic, 40 East 49th Street, New York City.
New Talent, 24 West 20th Street, New York City.
New Yorker, 25 West 45th Street, New York City.
North American Review, 587 Fifth Avenue, New York City.
Opinion, 122 East 42nd Street, New York City.
Opportunity, 1133 Broadway, New York City.
Pictorial Review, 222 West 39th Street, New York City.
Prairie Schooner, Box 1232, Station 'A,' Lincoln, Nebraska.
Queen's Quarterly, Queen's University, Kingston, Ont., Canada.
Redbook Magazine, 230 Park Avenue, New York City.
Rocking Horse, 820 Irving Place, Madison, Wis.
Saturday Evening Post, Independence Square, Philadelphia, Pa.
Scholastic, Chamber of Commerce Bldg., Pittsburgh, Pa.
Scribner's Magazine, 597 Fifth Avenue, New York City.
Short Stories, Doubleday, Doran & Co., Garden City, L.I., N.Y
Southern Review, Louisiana State University, Baton Rouge, La.
Southwest Review, Dallas, Texas.
Story, 432 Fourth Avenue, New York City.
Tanager, P.O. Box 66, Grinnell, Iowa.
This Week, 230 West 41st Street, New York City.
Toronto Star Weekly, Toronto, Ont., Canada.
Vanity Fair, Graybar Building, New York City.
Vernier, 64 Stanley Street, Dumont, N.J.
Virginia Quarterly Review, 8 West Lawn, University, Va.
West, 220 West 42nd Street, New York City.
Woman's Home Companion, 250 Park Avenue, New York City.
Woman's World, 461 Eighth Avenue, New York City.
Yale Review, 125 High Street, New Haven, Conn.

II. BRITISH, IRISH, AND COLONIAL MAGAZINES

Adelphi, 90 Rochester Row, London, S.W. 1.
Argosy, Tallis House, Tallis Street, London, E.C. 4.
Blackwood's Magazine, 45 George Street, Edinburgh, Scotland.
Blue Peter, 12 St. Mary Axe, London, E.C. 3.
Britannia and Eve, Inveresk House, 346 Strand, London, W.C. 2.
Bulletin, 214 George Street North, Sydney, N.S.W., Australia.
Bystander, 346 Strand, London, W.C. 2.
Chamber's Journal, 11 Thistle Street, Edinburgh, Scotland.
Corner Magazine, Fleetway House, Farringdon Street, London, E.C. 4.
Cornhill Magazine, 50 Albemarle Street, London, W. 1.
Criterion, 24 Russell Square, London, W.C. 1.
Daily Express, Fleet Street, London, E.C. 4.
Daily Herald, 12 Wilson Street, Long Acre, London, W.C. 2.
Daily Mail, Northcliffe House, London, E.C. 4.
Dublin Magazine, 2 Crow Street, Dublin, Irish Free State.

Empire Review, Messrs. Macmillan & Co., Ltd., St. Martin's Street, London, W.C. 2.
English Review, 6 Great New Street, London, E.C. 4.
Evening Standard, 46 Shoe Lane, London, E.C. 4.
Fortnightly Review, 13 Buckingham Street, London, W.C. 2.
G. K.'s Weekly, 2 Little Essex Street, Strand, London, W.C. 2.
Good Housekeeping, 153 Queen Victoria Street, London, E.C. 4.
Grand Magazine, 8–11 Southampton Street, Strand, London, W.C. 2.
Happy Magazine, 8–11 Southampton Street, Strand, London, W.C. 2.
Harper's Bazaar, 9 Stratton Street, Piccadilly, London, W. 1.
Illustrated London News, 346 Strand, London, W.C. 2.
John o'London's Weekly, 8–11 Southampton Street, Strand, London, W.C. 2.
Lady, 39 Bedford Street, Strand, London, W.C. 2.
Life and Letters To-day, 26 Maiden Lane, London, W.C. 2.
Listener, Broadcasting House, Portland Place, London, W. 1.
London Mercury, 14 Burleigh Street, Strand, London, W.C. 2.
Manchester Guardian, 3 Cross Street, Manchester.
Modern Scot, 3 South Street, St. Andrews, Scotland.
Nash's-Pall Mall Magazine, 153 Queen Victoria Street, London, E.C. 4.
New English Weekly, 38 Cursitor Street, London, E.C. 4.
New Statesman and Nation, 10 Great Turnstile, London, W.C. 1.
New Stories, Care of Edward J. O'Brien, 118 Banbury Road, Oxford.
News-Chronicle, 19–22 Bouverie Street, London, E.C. 4.
Novel Magazine, 18 Henrietta Street, Covent Garden, London, W.C. 2.
Outspan, P.O. Box 245, Bloemfontein, Orange Free State, S. Africa.
Pearson's Magazine, 18 Henrietta Street, Covent Garden, London, W.C. 2.
Queen, Hatfield House, Stanford Street, London, S.E. 1.
Quiver, Fleetway House, Farringdon Street, London, E.C. 4.
Red Magazine, Tallis House, Tallis Street, London, E.C. 4.
Review of Reviews, 38 Bedford Street, London, W.C. 2.
Saturday Review, 18–20 York Buildings, Adelphi, London, W.C. 2.
Scottish Bookman, 17 South St. Andrew Street, Edinburgh 2.
Sketch, 346 Strand, London, W.C. 2.
Spectator, 90 Gower Street, London, W.C. 1.
Sphere, 346 Strand, London, W.C. 2.
Story-Teller, Tallis House, Tallis Street, London, E.C. 4.
Strand Magazine, 8–11 Southampton Street, Strand, London, W.C. 2.
Sydney Mail, 38 Hunter Street, Sydney, N.S.W., Australia.
Tatler, 346 Strand, London, W.C. 2.
Time and Tide, 32 Bloomsbury Street, London, W.C. 1.[1]
Truth, 10 Carteret Street, Queen Anne's Gate, London, S.W. 1.
20-Story Magazine, 96 Long Acre, London, W.C. 2.
Violet Magazine, Fleetway House, Farringdon Street, London, E.C. 4.
Windsor Magazine, Warwick House, Salisbury Square, London, E.C. 4.
Woman's Journal, Fleetway House, Farringdon Street, London, E.C. 4.

ROLL OF HONOR
1935

NOTE. This list excludes reprints

I. AMERICAN AND CANADIAN AUTHORS

ABEL, HILDE.
Silent upon a Peak in Darien.
ADAMS, HELEN.
Late Afternoon.
AIKEN, CONRAD.
Round by Round.
ALEXANDER, HERBERT. ('JOHN MORTI-
MER.')
Case History.
AMIRIAN, LEMYEL.
Amusement Park Interlude.
ANDERSON, EDWARD.
Bare Legs.
APPEL, BENJAMIN.
Brothers in Hell's Kitchen.
ARGUILLA, MANUEL E.
Midsummer.
BARSÉGHIAN, B.
Link from My Chain.
BASSO, HAMILTON.
Fabulous Man.
BEEMS, GRIFFITH.
Hour among Years.
BENÉT, STEPHEN VINCENT.
Curfew Tolls.
Story by Angela Poe.
BENSON, SALLY.
Christmas Story.
Wife of the Hero.
BIALK, ELISA.
Sainted Sisters of Sandy Creek.
BIRD, VIRGINIA.
Wedding Night.
BISHOP, JOHN PEALE.
Man Who Thought.
BOYLE, KAY.
Astronomer's Wife.
Count Lothar's Heart.
Maiden, Maiden.
Major Alshuster.
White Horses of Vienna.
Winter in Italy.
BRAGDON, CLIFFORD.
Rainy Saturday Afternoon.
BRODY, CATHARINE.
No Lady Like That.
BROOME, JOHN.
Need of Life.
BROWN, DON PARDEE.
Hard Rock Mucker.

BRYAN, JACK YEAMAN.
Dead-Eye.
BUCK, PEARL S.
Heat Wave.
BURLINGAME, ROGER.
In the Cage.
New Interne.
CALDWELL, ERSKINE.
Daughter.
Day's Wooing.
Girl Ellen.
Growing Season.
Honeymoon.
Kneel to the Rising Sun.
Shooting.
Walnut Hunt.
CALLAGHAN, MORLEY.
All the Years of Her Life.
Blue Kimono.
Possession.
Rigmarole.
Shining Red Apple.
With Her Own People.
CANFIELD, DOROTHY.
Murder on Jefferson Street.
CARR, A. H. Z.
Hunch.
CHEEVER, JOHN.
Autobiography of a Drummer.
Of Love: A Testimony.
CHILDERS, BEULAH ROBERTS.
Sairy and the Young 'Uns.
CHILTON, ELEANOR CARROLL.
Very Picture of Grief.
CLEMENTS, ALBERT EDWARD.
He Was Whistling Yankee Doodle.
COATES, GRACE STONE.
Far Back, Far Forward.
COLBY, NATHALIE.
Glass Houses.
COLE, MADELENE.
Mrs. Welsbach's Night of Sin.
CONNOLLY, JOHN.
Memento.
COOKE, CHARLES.
Catafalque.
Introduction and Tarantelle.
Ivory Pavane.
COOMBES, EVAN.
Evening Meal.

North Wind Doth Blow.
COREY, PAUL.
Tombstone of Straw.
DERLETH, AUGUST W.
Stuff of Dream.
DETTE, ESTHER.
Flesh of a Martyr.
DODD, MARTHA.
Poet's Wife.
EATON, EVELYN.
Blind Man's Buff.
EISELEY, LOREN C.
Mop to K. C.
EVANS, NANCY.
I Shall Decline My Head.
FALES, DEAN.
Solo on the Cornet.
FARRELL, JAMES T.
Open Road.
FAULKNER, WILLIAM.
Golden Land.
Lion.
Skirmish at Sartoris.
That Will Be Fine.
Uncle Willy.
FESSIER, MICHAEL.
Over the Hill.
That's What Happened to Me.
FIELD, S. S.
Torrent of Darkness.
FISHER, ARISTA.
Talk of the Town.
FISHER, VARDIS.
Legend of Red Hair.
FITZGERALD, F. SCOTT.
Night Before Chancellorsville.
FLANNAGAN, ROY.
Doorstop.
FLIEGE, LENORE.
Boy Goes to Town.
FOLEY, MARTHA.
Her Own Sweet Simplicity.
FRANCIS, OWEN.
Steel Mill Lullaby.
GIBSON, WILL.
Growing.
GILKYSON, WALTER.
Enemy Country.
GODIN, ALEXANDER.
Descent to the Living.
GORDON, CAROLINE.
Funeral in Town.
Morning's Favor.
GORYAN, SIRAK.
Yea and Amen.
HAHN, EMILY.
Strange Thing.
HAINES, WILLIAM WISTER.
'Hot Behind Me.'
HALE, NANCY.
Great-Grandmother.

HALL, ELIZABETH.
Two Words Are a Story.
HARDY, EVELYN.
Innkeeper's Wife.
HAYES, HOWARD.
How My Wife Got That Way.
HILTON, CHARLES.
Youth Like a Warm Wind.
JAMESON, RALPH.
Something You Belong To.
JOHNSON, JOSEPHINE W.
Epitaph.
KANTOR, MACKINLAY.
Voice of Bugle Ann.
KELLY, FRANK K.
With Some Gaiety and Laughter.
KELM, KARLTON.
Tinkle and Family Take a Ride.
KERMIT, HARRY.
Funny No More.
KNIGHT, ERIC.
Meet Me in the Shadows.
KOMROFF, MANUEL.
Gold Standard Candidate.
Red Course.
That Blowzy Goddess Fame.
Unpardonable.
KRANTZ, DAVID E.
Fragment.
KRAUS, FLORENCE LEE.
Rough Edges.
LARDNER, RING.
Widow.
LARSEN, ERLING.
Kind of a Sunset.
Lover's Return.
LE SUEUR, MERIDEL.
Hungry Intellectual.
Psyche.
Sequel to Love.
LINCOLN, VICTORIA.
All Losses Are Restored.
Waiting for Laurence.
LINNEHAN, SEAN.
Known as a Diversion.
McCLEARY, DOROTHY.
Mail Order Bride.
Shroud.
McWILLIAMS, RICHEBOURG.
They Were Seven.
MALTZ, ALBERT.
Man on a Road.
MARSHALL, ALAN.
I, the Lord, Love Judgment.
MILBURN, GEORGE.
Wish Book.
MILLER, RICHARD.
Man's House.
MORANG, ALFRED.
Auction.
Good Marriage for Bee.

MORRIS, EDITA.
Frail Sister.
MULHOLLAND, D. C.
Memory of Fourteen.
OTIS, RAYMOND.
Girl on the Piano-Stool.
PARSONS, ALICE BEAL.
Midsummer Evening.
POLK, WILLIAM.
Fallen Angel and the Hunter's Moon.
POOLER, JAMES.
Four Fishermen Talk of Wilkie.
PORTER, KATHERINE ANNE.
Circus.
Grave.
PROKOSCH, FREDERIC.
Bandit.
RAMSDELL, CHARLES, JR.
Family Man.
RATLIFF, K.
Something I Don't Know What.
RICHMOND, ROALDUS.
Thanks for Nothing.
ROCHMAN, ROSE.
Report on a Movie.
ROSENBLATT, BENJAMIN.
Sacrifice.
ROURKE, THOMAS.
Fog on the Sound.
Guayana Gold.
RUDOLPH, JOHN.
Walking from the Crowd.
RYAN, STELLA.
I've Got a Son.
SAROYAN, WILLIAM.
At Sundown.
Five Ripe Pears.
Going Home.
Laura Immortal.
Little Miss Universe.
With a Hey Nonny Nonny.
SCRIBNER, FREDERICK.
Pyrrhic Victory.
SEAGER, ALLAN.
Fugue for Harmonica.
SELLER, THOMAS.
Flaw.
SHELBY, K. C.
April Rain.
SHERMAN, RICHARD.
Don't Give It a Thought.
Slow Train through Carolina.
SIMPSON, HARRIETTE K.
Mess of Pork.
SLESINGER, TESS.
Jobs in the Sky.
Life in the Day of a Writer.
On Being Told that Her Second Husband Has Taken His First Lover.
'Times So Unsettled Are.'

You Gi-i-ve Yourself — or Drop the Handkerchief.
SMITH, ROBERT.
Mrs. Kent.
STUART, JESSE.
Battle Keaton Dies.
Three Hundred Acres of Elbow Room.
Woman in the House.
SUCKOW, RUTH.
Auntie Bissel.
SUGRUE, THOMAS.
'Unidentified Man.'
SYLVESTER, HARRY.
All the Brave Young Gentlemen.
Man Going Home.
THILENIUS, HELEN.
Birthday Party.
THOMAS, DOROTHY.
Home Place.
THOMAS, ELISABETH WILKINS.
Traveling Salesman.
THURBER, JAMES.
Man on the Train.
VINES, HOWELL.
Mustydines Was Ripe.
WARE, HARLAN.
Love is a Word.
WEBB, JON EDGAR.
Night after Night.
WEIDMAN, JEROME.
Let Me Explain You Something.
WHARTON, EDITH.
Looking Glass.
WHICKER, H. W.
All-American.
Voyageur.
WHITEHAND, ROBERT.
American Nocturne.
Rotaries Are Constant.
WILLIAMS, ALBERTA.
Roller Vision.
WILLIAMS, CALVIN.
On the Sidewalk.
WILLIAMS, HENRY MEADE.
Marriage Was Made.
WILSON, WILLIAM E.
Lone Pioneer.
WINN, EMERY.
These Little Things.
WINSLOW, THYRA SAMTER.
Dear Sister Sadie.
WOLFE, THOMAS.
In the Park.
Only the Dead Know Brooklyn.
WOODWARD, HELEN.
Day Coach Pilgrimage.
ZINBERG, LEN.
Big Hands.
ZUGSMITH, LEANE.
Betrayal.
Nothing Wrong.

II. British and Irish Authors

BATES, H. E.
  Duet.
  Plough.
CALDER-MARSHALL, ARTHUR.
  Straw Hat.
CHESTERTON, G. K.
  Ring of Lovers.
  Tall Story.
  Three Horsemen.
  When Doctors Agree.
DUNSANY, LORD.
  Jorkens Handles a Big Property.
  Jorkens Retires from Business.
  Return.
FLEMING, PETER.
  Ace High.
GOSSMAN, OLIVER.
  Wayside Spring.
HUXLEY, ALDOUS.
  Visiting Stranger.

JACOBS, W. W.
  Visitor.
JOHNSON, PAMELA HANSFORD.
  Procession.
O'CONNOR, FRANK.
  English Soldier.
  Michael's Wife.
O'FAOLÁIN, SEÁN.
  Meeting.
  Sullivan's Trousers.
O'FLAHERTY, LIAM.
  All Things Come of Age.
  Irish Pride.
PAVEY, L. A.
  Travelers.
STRONG, L. A. G.
  Escape.
  Lobsters.

III. Translations

DUUN, OLAV. (*Norwegian.*)
  Avenger.
GONZALEZ, FRANCISCO ROJAS. (*Mexican.*)
  Cry of Warning.
LU SHUN. (*Chinese.*)
  Medicine.
MANN, THOMAS. (*German.*)
  Disillusion.
  Hungry.
PIRANDELLO, LUIGI. (*Italian.*)
  Captive.

ROMANOV, PANTELEIMON. (*Russian.*)
  May-Flies Before Night.
SALTEN, FELIX. (*German.*)
  Shot in the Forest.
SANDEL, CORA. (*Norwegian.*)
  Embezzlement.
SILONE, IGNAZIO. (*Italian.*)
  Journey to Paris.
TIMMERMANS, FELIX. (*Flemish.*)
  Triptych of the Three Kings.

BIOGRAPHICAL NOTICES

NOTE. These notices refer only to American authors whose work appears in the Roll of Honor in this series for the first time. Biographical notices of other authors included in this year's Roll of Honor may be found, with one or two exceptions, in earlier volumes of the series.

ADAMS, HELEN. Born and grew up in Norton, Kansas, went to school at Washburn College, Topeka, Kansas, is married, and lives in New York City.

ALEXANDER, HERBERT ('JOHN MORTIMER'). Born September 1, 1910, New York City. Graduated from New York University. Has traveled widely in Europe and America since 1931. Has been on the staff of *The Literary World*. Is now doing relief work for New York City.

AMIRIAN, LEMYEL. Born in the Caucasus of Armenian parentage twenty-eight years ago. During the War the fate of his people became his own fate, with all its physical tortures and material privations. Came to America in 1922. Studied architecture at the Massachusetts Institute of Technology. Engaged in theatre work. Lives in New York City.

ANDERSON, EDWARD. Born at Weatherford, Texas, 1905, of Irish and Indian descent. Printer's apprentice, reporter on country newspaper, and news editor at twenty. Trombone player with brass band of a circus, harvest hand in Kansas, and seaman on cotton freighters to Europe. Started writing fiction when twenty-three. From 1930 to 1934 he hunted jobs on newspapers, wrote unsaleable fiction, handled publicity for political candidates, hoboed all over the United States and published 'Hungry Men,' which won one of the two first novel prizes in the contest sponsored by *Story*.

BARSÉGHIAN, B. Born in Adrianople of Armenian parentage. A few days afterwards, her parents were obliged to leave the country to take refuge in Bulgaria where she passed her childhood and part of her youth. Studied literature and pedagogy in the University of Geneva. She married one of the greatest Armenian patriots. Her husband was assassinated by the Turks in the second year of her marriage. She went to Armenia after the declaration of its independence in 1918 and was elected a member of the Armenian Parliament. When the Bolshevik régime was established in Armenia in 1922, she left her country for Constantinople, took refuge later in Bulgaria, and has lived in France since 1924. She has published a book of short stories in Armenian called 'After the Tempest.' Lives in Paris.

BASSO, HAMILTON. Born in New Orleans, 1905. Has lived in various parts of the United States and has worked on newspapers in both the North and South. Has published a life of General Beauregard, and two novels: 'Cinnamon Seed' and 'In Their Own Image.' He is a contributing editor of *The New Republic* and lives in the mountains of North Carolina.

BIALK, ELISA. Lives in Chicago where she was born. Author of the novel 'On What Strange Stuff.' Married.

BIRD, VIRGINIA. Born in New York City twenty-two years ago and still lives there. Educated at New York University, studied law and journalism, and is now employed as a secretary.

BRYAN, JACK YEAMAN. Born in Peoria, Illinois, September, 1907. Left home at the age of sixteen, and has worked at a great variety of jobs ranging from farm hand and dishwasher to social worker and assistant in the teaching of philosophy. Educated at the University of Chicago, the University of Arizona, and Duke University. Has taught at Duke University. Has traveled fourteen thousand miles by highway and freight and conducted research into mental ability of five hundred transients.

Is now employed in the transient research division of the F.E.R.A., Washington, D.C.

BURLINGAME, ROGER. Born in New York City, 1889. Educated at Morristown School and Harvard On the editorial staff of *The Independent*, 1913–14. Associated with Charles Scribner's Sons, 1914–26. First Lieutenant, 308 Machine Gun Battalion, A.E.F. Free-lance writer since 1926. Author of 'You Too,' 'High Thursday,' 'Susan Shane,' 'The Heir,' and 'Cartwheels.' Married Ann Watkins in 1933. Lives in West Redding, Conn.

CARR, A. H. Z. Born in Chicago thirty years ago. Educated at the University of Chicago and Columbia University For seven years analyzed the methods used by fifty industries to get business and wrote about a million words to help them do it. Has written numerous articles, plays, and short stories. Has devoted himself to literature since 1934.

CHEEVER, JOHN. Born near Boston, 1912. Left prep school in his fourth year and has spent the time since then in traveling. Now lives in New York City.

CHILDERS, BEULAH ROBERTS. Born in Berea, Kentucky, October, 1906. His ancestors were pre-revolutionary settlers of Welsh and Flemish stock. His father was a teacher and minister. Educated at Berea College and the University of Kentucky. Married 1928. Lives in Berea, Kentucky.

CHILTON, ELEANOR CARROLL. Born in Charlestown, West Virginia. Educated at the Masters School, Dobbs Ferry, Dana Hall, Smith College, Oxford, and London. Has lived much of recent years in England. Author of 'Shadows Waiting,' 'The Burning Fountain,' and 'Follow the Furies.' Has collaborated with her husband Herbert Agar on a book of literary criticism, a collection of verses, and several plays. Lives in Louisville, Kentucky.

CONNOLLY, JOHN. Born in 1912. Began writing under the encouragement of Howard Baker. Graduate of the University of California, from which he holds a scholarship in creative writing. Lives in California.

COREY, PAUL. Born on a farm in Shelby County, Iowa, the youngest in a family of seven children. His father died before he was two years old, but his mother, with the help of his older brothers, continued the operation of the hundred-and-sixty-acre farm. When he was fourteen, his mother, next older brother, and he moved into the county seat town of the adjoining county, where he studied in high school while working in a jewelry store and later in a music store. During the summers he worked as a farmhand in the community where he was born. He graduated from the University of Iowa where he repaired phonographs, worked as geology librarian, and 'slung hash' at a boarding-house to meet expenses. During the summers he worked as farmhand in the Northwest and as a millman in the redwood mills of California. He did reporting for a trade paper in Chicago for eight months and then moved to New York, where he had various office jobs. He spent a year in Europe, and retired to a farm up the Hudson in 1931. At present he is working on a group of novels tracing the economic and psychological cycle of a section of the Middle West during the past twenty-five years.

DETTE, ESTHER. Born near New York City. Educated at private schools in New York and New England and at Radcliffe College. Is married and has three sons. Lives in Walpole, New Hampshire.

EATON, EVELYN. Born in Switzerland. Spent her childhood between England and Canada. Has published novels and volumes of poetry. Has worked in the scenario department of Paramount Studios in France, and has had other editorial cinema positions.

EISELEY, LOREN C. Born in Lincoln, Nebraska, 1907. Educated at the University of Nebraska and the University of Pennsylvania. Is a trained anthropologist and is now engaged in archaeological work. Has hoboed frequently. Is a contributing editor of *The Prairie Schooner*.

EVANS, NANCY. Born near Macon, Ohio, April 16, 1903. Educated in the public schools at Dayton, Ohio, and at Antioch College. Has worked as a cashier in a department store, as a factory hand, as a playground director and as a bookseller. Married. Has lived in New York City since 1924.

FALES, DEAN. Born at Emerson, Nebraska, 1897. Served a year in the Coast Artillery during the war. Has followed several trades and professions. Author of 'Bill Myron,' 'Village Virgin,' and 'Bachelor of Arts.' Lives in Ponca, Nebraska.

FESSIER, MICHAEL. Born in Angeles Camp, California, thirty years ago. Has worked on newspapers in various parts of California. Is now writing scripts for the cinema. Author of 'Fully Dressed and in His Right Mind.' Married. Lives in Beverly Hills, California.

FIELD, S. S. Born in 1906. Is a newspaper man. Studied architecture at the University of Pennsylvania. Lives in New Orleans.

FLIEGE, LENORE. Has lived on farms all her life, moving here and there, always near a queer old Indian town in Illinois on the Mississippi. Has studied at Cornell College, Iowa and won second prize in a short story contest sponsored by the Forum. Is seventeen. Lives in Gladstone, Illinois.

GIBSON, WILL, is twenty-one and lives in New York City.

HALL, ELIZABETH. Born in Brooklyn, New York, twenty-two years ago. Educated at Swarthmore and Barnard Colleges. Lives in New York City.

HARDY, EVELYN. Born in Philadelphia, 1902. Educated at Smith College and at the University of London. Employed in the British Colonial Office and the American Consulate-General for a number of years. Married. Granddaughter of Arthur Sherburne Hardy. Lives in Cornwall, England.

KELLY, FRANK K. Born in Kansas City, Missouri, June 12, 1914. Educated at Butler University and at the University of Kansas City. Lives in Kansas City, Missouri.

KERMIT, HARRY. Is twenty-seven years old and a reporter on a New York newspaper. Has been a bill collector, helper on a bakery delivery truck, post-office clerk, harvest hand, and factory worker. Has traveled through most of the United States on box cars. Lives in Brooklyn, New York.

KNIGHT, ERIC M. Born at Menston, Yorkshire, England, April 10, 1897. Went to work early as a cap-spinner, fly-spinner, and in engine works and a sawmill. Went to Philadelphia as a boy. Educated in Boston and New York, where he studied art. Served in France during the war with a famous Canadian regiment. Has had varied newspaper experience since then and married three years ago. Has traveled considerably in Central America. Now devotes himself to writing and lives in California.

KRANTZ, DAVID E. Born in New York, 1910. Self-educated. Has been stock-clerk in a sweatshop, assistant to a dental mechanic, messenger boy, dishwasher and waiter, ice-cream vendor, paying-teller, switchboard operator, social service worker, athletic director of a park, bookkeeper in a real-estate office, subscription canvasser, dramatics counselor, and salesman in a department store. He is now in the supply-room of a hospital. Lives in New York City.

KRAUS, FLORENCE LEE. Born in Savannah, Georgia. Has been a stenographer, real-estate broker, and newspaper writer. Lives in Mobile, Alabama.

LARSEN, ERLING. Born in Cresco, Iowa. Spent his boyhood there, in Brooklyn, New York, in the mountains of upper New York, and in Minnesota. Educated in Minnesota and at the University of Iowa. Has studied theology in a Lutheran seminary, traveled in Europe and Asia Minor, and worked on farms and in cinemas. Married. Lives in Northfield, Minnesota.

LINCOLN, VICTORIA. Born in Fall River, Massachusetts, 1904. Educated at Radcliffe College. Has lived for periods of two years and less in the Middle West, Germany, and England, but is essentially a New Englander. Married. Author of 'February Hill.' Lives at Little Compton, Rhode Island.

LINNEHAN, SEAN. Born in Cambridge, Massachusetts, November 21, 1908. Educated in the public schools of Somerville, Massachusetts. Has been an actor, has worked in a glazier's shop and has been a radio announcer. Has been married. Lives in Cambridge, Massachusetts.

McWILLIAMS, RICHEBOURG GAILLARD. Born in Oakhill, Alabama, 1901. Educated at the University of Alabama and at Harvard. Associate Professor of English in Birmingham-Southern College. Lives at Oakhill, Alabama.

MALTZ, ALBERT. Born in Brooklyn, New York, 1908. Educated at Columbia University and Yale School of the Drama. Member of the Executive Board of the Theatre Union. Author of 'Black Pit,' and of two plays in collaboration with George Sklar: 'Merry-Go-Round' and 'Peace on Earth.' Lives in New York City.

MILLER, RICHARD. Born in Illinois, 1903, and grew up in Tennessee. Educated at Columbia University. Married. Has held various jobs in journalism, bookselling, publishing, advertising, and teaching. Divides his time between New York City and Lexington, Virginia, preferring the latter.

MULHOLLAND, DONALD COLPITTS. Born in Minneapolis, 1909. His childhood was spent chiefly in Florida and Arizona. Has lived in Toronto since then. Educated at the University of Toronto. Married.

POOLER JAMES S. Born in Sheboygan, Wisconsin, the son of a Great Lakes fisherman. 'There was a boyhood of growing up in harbors all over the lakes where the promise of better fishing took my father. There was one port on Beaver Island, reached at an impressionable age, which with its people seems to be more vivid in memory than any other. St. James, Beaver Island, is providing the material for my first writings outside of a newspaper's columns. It was from Alpena, Michigan, and fishing with my father — grammar and high school acquired in the transient years — I came to the University of Detroit twelve years ago. Worked at anything until I landed on the Detroit *Free Press* to end schooling with a B.S. and to keep right on with newspaper work.' Shared in a Pulitzer prize in 1931. Married. 'Fortunately I have moved through an America that was before my time, but still was living in the little ports we visited, and now find myself in a time that hasn't jelled yet.' Is thirty years of age. Lives in Detroit, Michigan.

PROKOSCH, FREDERIC. Born at Madison, Wisconsin, of South German parentage, May 17, 1908. Educated in schools in Madison, Munich, Austria, Texas, and Pennsylvania, and at Haverford College and Yale University. Phi Beta Kappa at seventeen. Taught at Yale, 1931–33. Research Fellow in English literature, 1933–35. His father is a well-known scholar who is a professor at Yale. Author of 'The Asiatice.'

RAMSDELL, CHARLES. Born at Austin, Texas, April 5, 1909. Studied anthropology at the University of Texas, and later among the inhabitants of Uruapan, Mexico, and Austin, Texas, where he now lives.

RATLIFF, K. 'Since I was born twenty-eight years ago in a small, loose-tongued little town in Indiana, the world has been a worse place to live in for many people. For seventeen years the citizens suffered my going and coming to and from grade school and high school. I did everything from blistering my throat drinking straight Jamaica ginger to banging cigarette butts on the steps of the library, and my school teachers cussed and cried because they could not effect any discipline in me — poor girls! I visited my little town last week after having been away for ten years. It was Sunday evening, and I walked with an old friend of mine along the quiet main street, trying to talk with him, half-choking in my breast because we had lost the language and were telling lies to each other. "We understand each other, don't we?" he asked. "Yes," I said. "It is still the same, Clarence. We don't have to talk to know, do we?" The spring air smelled nice, and everything was cool and quiet. Old women were coming from church. They had gone in whispering, and had talked about God, and had come out whispering. Their shoes squeaked, and they walked slow whispering. I have spent the past two years at the University of Michigan trying to learn something about writing, hitch-hiked more than a hundred thousand miles across the tangled catwalks of the United States, have worked niggardly in the automobile factories, newspapers, fruit belts, coal fields, and Western grain regions, feeling more and more every year alone, unhappy, brutally driven by an enormous appetite, a hunger for something — I don't know what — a hunger for something that one day, I fear, might have to eat itself.' Lives in Ann Arbor, Michigan.

RICHMOND, ROALDUS. Born in Barton, Vermont, 1910. Educated in Vermont and Massachusetts, and at the University of Michigan. Has had various jobs and now devotes his time to writing. Lives in Westmore, Vermont.

ROCHMAN, ROSE. Born in Poland. Emigrated to New York at the age of eleven in 1913. College graduate. Has taught in a New York City high school. Lives in New York City.

RUDOLPH, JOHN (JOHN RUDOLPH SAROYAN). Born of Armenian parentage in Fresno, California, June 3, 1912. Educated at the University of California. Cousin of William Saroyan. Lives in Fresno, California.

SCRIBNER, FREDERICK. Born in Ellsworth, Maine, 1907. Educated at the University of Maine. Has taught English since then. Now teaches at Greenwich High School, Greenwich, Connecticut. Married.

STUART, JESSE. 'I was born in 1907 in W–Hollow, near Riverton, Kentucky, and I have lived here all my life. My people have lived here since 1896. The Hollow is just a rugged piece of Kentucky earth and there are about ten families living on it. I have hunted over every foot of it. I have gone to church just over the hill to Plum Grove. I went to the one-room school at Plum Grove too. The teacher taught all eight grades. I left school at intervals after I was nine years old. I hired out at twenty-five cents a day. Later, as I grew older, I got fifty cents a day and finally seventy-five cents a day. Then I got a job working with a concrete outfit and I made three dollars a day. I saw children going to high school when we were paving the streets of Greenup in 1922 and I gave up concrete work and entered the high school. In the meantime I had gone a month to a subscription school, taught by my cousin Everett Hilton. About all he taught was grammar and I gave my grammar a brush. In high school I tied for the best grades in my class after four years of football, fun, and some study and a little fighting at first until we all got used to each other. After high school I went back to the farm. Then I ran away and followed a street carnival until they fired me for letting the girls ride free on the Ferris Wheel. Then I went to an army camp and from there to the mills. I worked ten hours each night in a black-smith shop for the steel mills. I would have made a good blacksmith, my boss told me, for I was big and husky for a blacksmith. I had one view in mind: that was to become a writer, and I thought I had to have a college education. I wrote themes in high school and poetry all the time. I wrote them back at Plum Grove too before I was nine years old. I can hardly remember the time when I wasn't trying to write. I went to college and finished in three years at Lincoln Memorial at Harrogate, Tennessee. I worked there at ditch-digging on water-lines, sewer lines, worked in the rock quarry crushing limestone rocks for the campus walks and for the Tennessee state highway. I worked in the hayfields and cornfields, and finally edited the college paper for a couple of years. I made a fairly good college record, to work one half-day and go to school the other half. I came home and taught a school in the Kentucky hills and got into a little mess-up finally with trustees and saw handwriting on the wall. I went back south to Vanderbilt and spent a year in school. I still wrote poetry and tried articles on this and that. I never sent the poetry out except to a few small magazines. It usually was rejected, or three or four lines accepted. Then I was asked to take the magazine. Donald Davidson, professor at Vanderbilt University, advised me to send a sheaf of poetry to bigger magazines. He said my stuff was slated for big magazines. My first poem was accepted by H. L. Mencken for *The American Mercury* for January, 1933, publication. *Virginia Quarterly Review* accepted a sheaf of autumn sonnets that received a good deal of comments. My poetry has been going ever since. I almost starved to death at Vanderbilt. I got two meals a day, then eleven meals a week, and after the fire, that burned our dormitory and cafeteria where we made our meals, on March 19, 1932, until June 2 of that spring I lived on one meal a day, and finished my year in Vanderbilt. I came home, hitch-hiked back to northeast Kentucky (four hundred and fifty miles) on two dollars that I had borrowed from Elizabeth Hale. I decided, then, my going to school was over. I started to farming in Kentucky. We had no rain that summer to amount to anything. Corn wilted to the ground. I started my first book of verse, 'Man With the Bull-Tongue Plow.' I farmed during the summer and wrote poetry. In the autumn I got a broken-down school system on my hands. I was selected superintendent of Greenup County schools. That was a job for a young man when the county school system owed practically everybody in it and the treasury was empty and the bank went blooey like a pin-pricked balloon. I started sending out poetry because I had to send it out and buy my clothes. I worked whole nights on county school problems and went through thirty-some law-suits to get the county back on its feet and to keep it from being devoured by its creditors. I prayed, cussed, and fought for the county. In the meantime I wrote 'Bull-Tongue Plow' in eleven months, lacking one day. The corn burnt to the ground. Some of the poetry I wrote then is still being cussed and discussed. While I was county school superintendent, I plunged into it so hard that I got extremely nervous and after a year I went to Tennessee to rest. In the two months that I was in the mountains of East Tennessee I wrote a 642-page document indicting those who had fought me in the county school system. If that were to be published, I'd spend the remainder of my life on a rock-pile in the state penitentiary at Frankfort, Kentucky. I came back to Greenup County schools as principal of the county high school. I have held that position for the last two years and farmed during the summer. I was always told that I'd never be able to write a short story. It was told to me so much by so many teachers that I was under the impression that I never could, and perhaps this is true. But one day, one winter day, about eighteen months ago, the school buses were water-bound and we didn't have any school. I wrote my first short story and sent it to *Scribner's*. Marion Ives wrote back and told me there was genius in the story, but it was too morbid for magazine use and too long. The next story I wrote was "Battle Keaton Dies." It was accepted by *Story Magazine*. This summer I have written more stories and less poetry. I have placed five stories in big American publications. Only two have appeared up to this time. I weigh two hundred pounds, am six feet tall, twenty-seven years old. You would not take me for a writer of verse. Life has been damned interesting and I have lived it and loved it. If I die tomorrow at twenty-seven, my friends can tell you that I have lived, hated, loved, fought, worked much as any man. I have never been too much of a gentleman to dirty my hands in a fist-fight when it was necessary. My mother's people are English with a strain of Cherokee Indian blood; my father's people are Scotch. We have lived in the mountains all of our days, for generations and generations. We are a sturdy, strong family. The Stuarts helped pioneer the Big Sandy River Valley. They have made good soldiers, have been feudists, Republicans, hard-drinkers, and a few preachers among them. Back in the family but few could read and write. I am the first among them to finish high school and the only one to finish college. The Hiltons have a love for books. There are many teachers among them, many preachers, but only one from that family has finished college. They are Democrats, even more than the Stuarts are Republicans. There is a little dissension in our family around election times.' Lives at Riverton, Kentucky.

SUGRUE, THOMAS. Born at Naugatuck, Connecticut, May 7, 1907. Educated at Washington and Lee University. Has been a reporter on a local newspaper and on the New York *Herald Tribune*. Is now a staff writer on *The American Magazine*. Married. Author with John Lardner of 'The Crowning of Technocracy.' Lives in New York City.

THILENIUS, HELEN. Born in St. Louis, Missouri, October 3, 1911. Has studied a little modeling and pottery and is now a college student.

VINES, HOWELL. Born near Warrior River, Alabama, November 22, 1899. The Vines clan or clans make up the largest Warrior River family, in fact the largest family of people he knows of. 'Oldest child and only son. Two sisters. Born natural heir to my material — grandson to it, to be more specific. Maternal grandfather was the mightiest of the Vineses and is the bobbin of my material. The original earth I grew up in is reflected in my novels. Once hoped and expected to be a major league baseball star. Outside of that never wanted to be anything but a novelist.' Educated at University of Alabama and at Harvard. Married. Taught English in schools and universities for seven years. Now lives at home in the country at Bessemer, Alabama. Author of 'A River Goes with Heaven' and 'This Green Thicket World.'

WARE, HARLAN. Born at Lakota, North Dakota, July 14, 1902. 'Grew up in Winnetka, Illinois. Went on the stage when I was sixteen, but grew no better as I grew older. Then newspapers — police reporting, columning, and finally directed publicity for the Hotel Sherman in Chicago for nine years. During those years wrote at night a novel, a play, a lot of short stories, and a daily radio program. It was the daily radio program that unsettled my reason. Quit, came to California to write. Have a bride, a son and two cocker spaniels named Suspense and Climax.' Lives at Arcadia, California.

WEBB, JON EDGAR. He is thirty, married and has three children. Has been a ghost writer, newspaper man, publicity agent, ad-writer, and editor. Born in Cleveland. At fourteen he had been in every state in the country and every province in Canada. He traveled without a penny and never touched a freight train. He caught rides on the highways in a Boy-Scout suit, and always had the story ready that today was his birthday and that he had just lost his pocketbook. He arrived home with some two hundred dollars in cash. Editor of Sanctuary. Lives in Cleveland, Ohio.

WHICKER, H. W. Born in Indiana, 1895. Most of his life has been spent in the West on the ranges, in the lumber camps and mines in Montana, Idaho, and Washington, or in the newspaper racket, or along the north Pacific islands in a canoe. From college he went into the prize-ring. From the prize-ring he went back into college as an English instructor. He also served twenty-one months in the navy during the world war. Lives at Missoula, Montana, and is associated editorially with *The Frontier and Midland*.

WHITEHAND, ROBERT. Born in San Francisco, March 12, 1910. Has resided in Texas, Minnesota, Kansas, Oklahoma, and Tennessee. He lived from the age of four to twelve in the oil fields of Oklahoma and Texas in tents and temporary shacks. He worked for part of his college education by returning to the Oklahoma oil fields during the summer vacations. He did feature stories and book reviews for *The Tulsa World* for a year. He is now working for his Master's degree in Dramatic Art at the State University of Iowa. Is a graduate of the University of Oklahoma. Intends to write novels and plays. Lives in Iowa City, Iowa.

WILLIAMS, ALBERTA. Born in Southern Illinois and spent her early years there. Educated at Goucher College. Has lived for the past two years in New York City.

WILLIAMS, CALVIN. Born in New Castle, Pennsylvania, September 27, 1914. Has lived back and forth between San Antonio and Mexico City. Educated in San Antonio public schools and at Schreiner Institute near San Antonio. Lives in San Antonio, Texas.

WINN, EMERY. Born in Eufaula, Indian Territory, on Friday the thirteenth, 1905. Has worked on newspapers for the last eight years in Louisiana, Texas and Oklahoma. Now literary editor and daily columnist of *The Tulsa World*, Tulsa, Oklahoma.

ZINBERG, LEN. Born in Ithaca, New York, twenty-four years ago. Educated at the College of the City of New York. Has traveled in Europe. Is a member of the Writer's Union. Lives in New York City.

THE BEST BOOKS OF SHORT STORIES
1935

I. AMERICAN AUTHORS

1. CALDWELL. Kneel to the Rising Sun. Viking Press.
2. DOBIE. San Francisco Tales. Appleton-Century.
3. FITZGERALD. Taps at Reveille. Scribner.
4. JOHNSON. Winter Orchard. Simon and Schuster.
5. KOBER. Thunder over the Bronx. Simon and Schuster.
6. MARCH. The Little Wife. Smith and Haas.
7. NEAGOE. Winning a Wife. Coward-McCann.
8. PORTER. Flowering Judas. Harcourt, Brace.
9. SLESINGER. Time: The Present. Simon and Schuster.

II. BRITISH AND IRISH AUTHORS

10. BEACHCROFT. Young Man in a Hurry. Harper.
11. CHAMBERLAIN. What the Sweet Hell? Holt.
12. DANE. Fate Cries Out. Doubleday, Doran.
13. WEST. The Harsh Voice. Doubleday, Doran.

III. TRANSLATIONS

14. PIRANDELLO. Better Think Twice About It. Dutton.
15. SCHWARZ, *editor*. The Jewish Caravan. Farrar and Rinehart.
16. SILONE. Mr. Aristotle. McBride.
17. SÖDERBERG. Selected Short Stories. American-Scandinavian Foundation.
18. ZOSTCHENKO. Russia Laughs. Lothrop, Lee, and Shepard.
19. ZWEIG. Playthings of Time. Viking Press.

VOLUMES OF SHORT STORIES

Published in the United States and Canada

1935

NOTE. An asterisk before a title indicates distinction.

I. American and Canadian Authors

ADDINGTON, SARAH. *Hound of Heaven. Appleton-Century.
ASCH, NATHAN. *Valley. Macmillan.
BECKER, MAY LAMBERTON, editor. *Golden Tales of the Far West. Dodd, Mead.
BJARNASON, BOGI. Sans the Grande Passion. The Times: Treherne, Manitoba.
BUCKINGHAM, NASH. Shootinest Gentman. Derrydale Press.
BYRNE, DONN. Daughter of the Medici. Appleton-Century. Hound of Ireland. Appleton-Century.
CALDWELL, ERSKINE. *Kneel to the Rising Sun. Viking Press.
CANBY, HENRY SEIDEL, and DASHIELL, ALFRED, editors. *Study of the Short Story. Holt.
CHAMPION, MAY KELSEY. Clad in Doublet and Hose. New London: Bingham Press.
COHEN, OCTAVUS ROY. Black to Nature. Appleton-Century.
DANIELE, F. MICHELE. Yankee Faith. Greenberg.
DAVIS, ELMER. Love Among the Ruins. Bobbs-Merrill.
DERLETH, AUGUST W. *Place of Hawks. Loring and Mussey.
DOBIE, CHARLES CALDWELL. *San Francisco Tales. Appleton-Century.
DRUS, PETER PAUL. Hexenboo. Los Angeles: Privately Printed.
FARRELL, JAMES T. *Guillotine Party. Vanguard Press.
FITZGERALD, F. SCOTT. *Taps at Reveille. Scribner.
FOX, FANNIE FERBER. Chocolate or Vanilla. Knopf.
FREUND, PHILIP. Snow. Pilgrim House.
GRAND, GORDON. Old Man. Derrydale Press. Silver Horn. Windward House.
GRAY, CHARLES WRIGHT, editor. Horses, Dogs, and Men. Holt.
HANSEN, HARRY, editor. *O. Henry Memorial Award Prize Stories of 1935. Doubleday, Doran.
HARRINGTON, GEORGE WHEATON. Silver Lining, and Hannah Stearns. Humphries.
HART, WILLIAM S. Law on Horseback. Los Angeles: Times-Mirror Press.
HENRY, O. Voice of the City. Limited Editions Club.
HICKS, GRANVILLE, and others, editors. *Proletarian Literature in the United States. International Publishers.
HILL, DULCIE M. OAKLEY. Saints in Secret. Milwaukee: Morehouse.
HITCHCOCK, ALFRED MARSHALL. Lucy, Perhaps. Holt.
HOLLISTER, MARY BREWSTER. South China Folk. Revell.
HORNER, DURBIN LEE, editor. Murder by the Dozen. Dingwall-Rock.
JACKSON, BIRDSALL. Pipe Dreams and Twilight Tales. Rockville Centre, N.Y.: Paumanok Press.
JOHNSON, JOSEPHINE. *Winter Orchard. Simon and Schuster.
KANTOR, MACKINLAY. *Voice of Bugle Ann. Coward-McCann.
KIRKLAND, WINIFRED. Return of the Wise Man. Revell.
KOBER, ARTHUR. *Thunder over the Bronx. Simon and Schuster.
KYNE, PETER B. Cappy Ricks Special. Kinsey.
LA FARGE, OLIVER. *All the Young Men. Houghton Mifflin.
LANE, ROSE WILDER. *Home Town. Longmans, Green.
LE SUEUR, MERIDEL. *Annunciation. Los Angeles: Platen Press.
LEWIS, SINCLAIR. Selected Short Stories. Doubleday, Doran.

LINDSTROM, E. GEORGE. Oil Creek Tales. Cleveland: Lindstrom.
McKENZIE, VERNON, *editor*. These Stories Went to Market. McBride.
MacMANUS, SEUMAS. *Bold Blades of Donegal. Stokes.
MacMULLAN, HUGH. Little Bird. Salisbury, Conn.: Housatonic Bookshop.
MARCH, WILLIAM. *Little Wife. Smith and Haas.
MARGULIES, LEO, *editor*. Western Thrillers. Speller.
MARION, FRANCES. Valley People. Reynal and Hitchcock.
MEEK, S. P. Monkeys Have No Tails in Zamboanga. **Morrow.**
MERCEIN, ELEANOR. Sounding Harbors. Harper.
MILLER, MAX. Man on the Barge. Dutton.
MILLINGTON, JOHN A. Five from Life. Paterson, N.J.: Chilusk.
MOODY, CHARLES. Plain English. Meador.
NEAGOE, PETER. *Winning a Wife. Coward-McCann.
O'BRIEN, EDWARD J., *editor*. Best Short Stories: 1935. Houghton Mifflin. **Short Story** Case Book. Farrar and Rinehart.
O'HARA, JOHN. *Doctor's Son. Harcourt, Brace.
PARROTT, URSULA. Dream without Ending. Longmans, Green.
PEEL, DORIS. *Aunt Margot. Houghton Mifflin.
PORTER, KATHERINE ANNE. *Flowering Judas. Harcourt, Brace.
RUNYON, DAMON. Money from Home. Stokes.
SALT, SYDNEY. Contemporary Legends. Majorca, Spain: Caravel Press.
SANGSTER, MARGARET E. Littlest Orphan. Round Table Press.
Saplings. Tenth Series, 1935. Scholastic Press.
SARRIS, THEODORE. Autumn Dream. Chicago: Center Clark Pub. Co.
SCARBOROUGH, DOROTHY, *editor*. Selected Short Stories of Today. Farrar and Rinehart.
SHIPMAN, EVAN. Free-for-All. Scribner.
SIGMUND, JAY G. *Least of These. Muscatine, Iowa: Prairie Press.
SLESINGER, TESS. *Time: The Present. Simon and Schuster.
STARRETT, VINCENT. Snow for Christmas. Glencoe, Ill.: Eileen Baskerville.
TARKINGTON, BOOTH. Mr White, The Red Barn, Hell, and Bridewater. Doubleday, Doran.
WALSH, EDMUND A. *Woodcarver of Tyrol. Harper.
WEGNER, M. C., *editor*. *Albatross Book of American Short Stories. Hamburg, Germany: Albatross.
WINSLOW, THYRA SAMTER. *My Own, My Native Land. Doubleday, Doran.
WOLFE, THOMAS. *From Death to Morning. Scribner.
WOOD, EUGENE. *Back Home, and Folks Back Home. Doubleday, Doran.
YOUNG, STARK. *Feliciana. Scribner.

II. BRITISH AND IRISH AUTHORS

BAILEY, H. C. Mr. Fortune Objects. Doubleday, Doran.
BEACHCROFT, T. O. *Young Man in a Hurry. Harper.
CHAMBERLAIN, PETER. *What the Sweet Hell? Holt.
CHESTERTON, G. K. *Scandal of Father Brown. Dodd, Mead.
CHESTERTON, G. K., *editor*. G.K.'s. Coward-McCann.
DANE, CLEMENCE. *Fate Cries Out. Doubleday, Doran.
DINGLE, A. E. Pipe All Hands. Lippincott. Spin a Yarn, Sailor. Lippincott.
DINNIS, ENID. In Merlac's Mirror. Herder.
DOUGLAS, RONALD MACDONALD. *Strangers Come Home. Macmillan.
GALSWORTHY, JOHN. *Forsytes, Pendyces and Others. Scribner.
GOLDING, LOUIS. *This Wanderer. Farrar and Rinehart.
HARDY, THOMAS. *Indiscretion in the Life of an Heiress. Baltimore: Johns Hopkins Press.
HEARN, LAFCADIO. *Sketches and Tales from the French. Stechert.
MASON, A. E. W. Dilemmas. Doubleday, Doran.
MAYOR, F. M. Room Opposite. Longmans.
O'BRIEN, EDWARD J., *editor*. Best British Short Stories: 1935. Houghton Mifflin.
OPPENHEIM, E. PHILLIPS. General Besserley's Puzzle Box. Little, Brown.
SAYERS, DOROTHY, *editor*. Third Omnibus of Crime. Coward-McCann.

VAUGHAN, HILDA. *Thing of Naught. Scribner.
WALSH, MAURICE. Green Rushes. Stokes.
WEST, REBECCA. *Harsh Voice. Doubleday, Doran.
WODEHOUSE, P. G. Blandings Castle. Doubleday, Doran.
WRIGHT, CONSTANCE. *Silver Collar Boy. Dutton.

III. TRANSLATIONS

BUNIN, IVAN. (*Russian.*) *Elaghin Affair. Knopf.
FEUCHTWANGER, LION. (*German.*) *Marianne in India. Viking Press.
LAGERLÖF, SELMA. (*Swedish.*) *Harvest. Doubleday, Doran.
MAUPASSANT, GUY DE. (*French.*) Short Stories. Dutton. Stories. Peter Smith.
PIRANDELLO, LUIGI. (*Italian.*) *Better Think Twice About It. Dutton.
SCHWARZ, LEO W., *editor*. *Jewish Caravan. Farrar and Rinehart.
SILONE, IGNAZIO. (*Italian.*) *Mr. Aristotle. McBride.
SÖDERBERG, HJSLMAR. (*Swedish.*) *Selected Short Stories. American-Scandinavian
    Foundation.
ZOSTCHENKO, MIKHAIL. (*Russian.*) *Russia Laughs. Lothrop, Lee and Shepard.
ZWEIG, ARNOLD. (*German.*) *Playthings of Time. Viking Press.

ARTICLES ON THE SHORT STORY IN AMERICAN PERIODICALS

1935

A

Addington, Sarah.
    Anonymous. N.Y. Times. Sept. 8. **(22.)**
Allen, James Lane.
    By Charles Angoff. Nat. (N.Y.) Aug. 21. (141:220.)
    By John Cournos. N.Y. Times. Jul. 28. (2.)
    By Stark Young. N. Rep. Aug. 28. (84:78.)
American Short Story
    Anonymous. N.Y. Times. May 19. (16.)
    By E. D. B. Frontier. Spring. (15:252.)
    By William Rose Benét. Sat. R. (N.Y.) Feb. 23. (11:501.)
    By Alan Calmer. N. Mass. Jul. 2. (17.) Aug. 27. (21.)
    By Cora Carter. Books. Nov. 10. (16.)
    By Mary M. Colum. Sat. R. (N.Y.) Nov. 2. (3.) For. Dec. (94:354.)
    By William and Kathryn Cordell. N.A. Rev. Dec. (240:554.)
    By Malcolm Cowley. N. Rep. Jan. 16. (81:281.)
    By Alfred Dashiell. Sat. R. (N.Y.) Nov. 23. (12.)
    By Bernard De Voto. Sat. R. (N.Y.) Oct. 5. (26.)
    By Robert England. Trend. Mar.-Apr. (3:7.)
    By Horace Gregory. Books. Oct. 13. (16.)
    By Alfred Hayes. N. Mass. Jan. 22. (24.)
    By Gerald W. Johnson. Va. Apr. (11:201.)
    By Henry Goddard Leach. For. Dec. (94:321.)
    By Jonathan Norton Leonard. Sat. R. (N.Y.) Jun. 8. (3.)
    By Robert Morss Lovett. N. Mass. Oct. 15. (23.)
    By T. S. Matthews. N. Rep. Oct. 23. (84:309.) Dec. 25. **(85:205.)**
    By Edith R. Mirrielees. Frontier. Winter. (16:156.)
    By Carl Niemeyer. Tan. Oct. (11:29.)
    By Edward J. O'Brien. Sto. Dec. (2.) N. Rep. Nov. 27. **(85:76.)**
    By John Crowe Ransom. Va. Apr. (11:184.)
    By Joseph M. Smith. Books. Sept. 8. (14.)
    By E.H.W. N.Y. Times. Sept. (17.) Nov. 17. (24.)
Anderson, Sherwood.
    By John Hyde Preston. Atl. Aug. (156:187.)
Asch, Nathan.
    By Slater Brown. N. Rep. Oct. 16. (84:278.)
    By James T. Farrell. N. Mass. Sept. 10. (28.)
    By Rose C. Feld. N.Y. Times. Sept. 8. (7.)
    By Horace Gregory. Books. Sept. 8. (6.)
Austin, Mary.
    By Arthur E. Du Bois. S.W. Apr. (20:231.)

B

Balzac, Honoré de.
    By E. Preston Dargan. Va. Jan. (11:146.)
    By André Maurois. N.Y. Times. Feb. 10. **(8.)**
Beachcroft, T. O.
    Anonymous. Books. Mar. 24. (15.)

By William Rose Benét. Sat. R. (N.Y.) Feb. 9. (11:473.)
By Eda Lou Walton. N.Y. Times. Feb. 24. (18.)
Bennett, Arnold.
    By Percy Hutchison. N.Y. Times. Dec. 15. (2.)
    By Isabel Paterson. Books. Dec. 15. (17.)
Blackwood, Algernon.
    By Stuart Gilbert. Transit. Jul. (89.)
Bourget, Paul.
    By Sister M. Jerome Keeler. Cath. W. Feb. (140:554.)
Bradford, Roark.
    By Sterling A. Brown. Opp. Sept. (13:279.)
Brinig, Myron.
    By David Tilden. Books. Sept. 22. (4.)
British Short Story.
    By H. E. Bates. Sto. Nov. (2.)
    By Mary M. Colum. For. Dec. (94:354.)
    By Elizabeth Hart. Books. Oct. 27. (20.)
    By E.H.W. N.Y. Times. Oct. 20. (23.)
Buckingham, Nash.
    By C. McD. Puckette. N.Y. Times. Apr. 21. (13.)
Bunin, Ivan.
    By Obed Brooks. N. Mass. Feb. 26. (24.)
    By Horace Gregory. Books. Feb. 10. (4.)
    By Alexander Nazaroff. N.Y. Times. Feb. 3. (2.)
    By Harry Salpeter. Lit. A. Apr. (2:260.)
    By Mary Stack. Com. Apr. 5. (21:659.)
Byrne, Donn.
    Anonymous. Books. Jul. 21. (10.)
    Anonymous. N.Y. Times. Jul. 21. (18.)
    By Geoffrey Terwilliger. Books. Feb. 3. (8.)
    By M.W. N.Y. Times. Feb. 10. (16.)

C

Caldwell, Erskine.
    By Louis Adamic. Sat. R. (N.Y.) Nov. 9. (10.)
    By Gerta Aison. Lit. A. Jul. (2:482.)
    Anonymous. Nat. Jun. 19. (140:720.)
    By Sterling A. Brown. Opp. Oct. (13:311.)
    By Kenneth Burke. N. Rep. Apr. 10. (82:232.)
    By Whit Burnett. Books. Jun. 16. (6.)
    By Robert M. Coates. N. Rep. Jul. 24. (83:312.)
    By Louise Maunsell Field. N.A. Rev. Sept. (240:379.)
    By Lewis Gannett. N.Y. Her. Jun. 7.
    By Albert Halper. N. Mass. Dec. 10. (22.)
    By Randall Jarrell. So. R. Autumn. (1:397.)
    By Ferner Nuhn. Nat. (N.Y.) Oct. 30. (141:518.)
    By Edwin Rolfe. Part. R. Jul.-Aug. (61.)
    By Arthur Ruhl. Sat. R. (N.Y.) Jun. 8. (5.)
    By Harold Strauss. N.Y. Times. Jun. 9. (6.)
    By Robert Van Gelder. N.Y. Times. Dec. 15. (9.)
Callaghan, Morley.
    By H. J. Davis. C. For. Dec. (15:398.)
Chamberlain, Peter.
    By Ferner Nuhn. Books. Oct. 20. (18.)
    By Edith H. Walton. N.Y. Times. Nov. 3. (7.)
Chekhov, Anton.
    By Alexander Bakshy. A. Merc. Sept. (36:1.)
Chesterton, G. K.
    By Kay Irvin. N.Y. Times. Oct. 13. (20.)

Cohen, Octavus Roy.
 Anonymous. N.Y. Times. May 12. (15.)
Conrad, Joseph.
 Anonymous. Sat. R. (N.Y.) Oct. 12. (12.)
 By Ford Madox Ford. A. Merc. Jun. (35:169.)
 By Percy Hutchison. N.Y. Times. Sept. 29. (4.)
 By R. G. Lillard. P.M.L.A. Mar. (50:316.)
 By H. L. Mencken. Nat. Oct. 16. (141:444.)
 By Clara Gruening Stillman. Books. Sept. 22. (8.)
 By Morton Dauwen Zabel. N. Rep. Dec. 18. (85:180.)
Craddock, Charles Egbert.
 By Edd W. Parks. E.T.H.S.P. 1934. (6:67.)
Crane, Stephen.
 By Ford Madox Ford. So. R. Jul. (1:20.)
 By Claude Jones. A. L. Mar. (7:82.)

D

Dane, Clemence.
 By Garreta Busey. Books. Nov. 24. (16.)
 By Edith H. Walton. N.Y. Times. Oct. 20. (18.)
Daniele, F. Michele.
 By Edith H. Walton. N.Y. Times. Dec. 15. (23.)
Davis, Elmer.
 By F.T.M. N.Y. Times. Mar. 31. (7.)
 By David Tilden. Books. Mar. 31. (14.)
Derleth, August W.
 By James Crissey. Frontier. Winter. (16:154.)
 By Elizabeth Hart. Books. Jun. 9. (8.)
 By Edith H. Walton. N.Y. Times. Jun. 16. (7.)
Dingle, A. E.
 By Lincoln Colcord. Books. Mar. 10. (12.)
 By P.H. N.Y. Times. Mar. 17. (6.)
 By William H. Taylor. Books. Oct. 27. (22.)
Dobie, Charles Caldwell.
 Anonymous. N.Y. Times. Oct. 20. (27.)
 By Wilson O. Clough. Frontier. Winter. (16:155.)
 By Will Irwin. Books. Sept. 22. (7.)
Dostoevsky, Fyodor.
 By Edwin Berry Burgum. N. Mass. Aug. 6. (26.)
 By Kenneth Burke. New Republic. Mar. 27. (82:192.)
 By John Cournos. Yale. Spring. (24:632.) N.Y. Times. Jun. 9. (9.)
 By Joseph McSorley. Cath. W. Jan. (140:492.)
Douglas, Ronald Macdonald.
 By Elizabeth Hart. Books. Jul. 14. (8.)
 By Edith H. Walton. N.Y. Times. Jun. 30. (7.)

E

Engström, Albert.
 By Gurli Hertzman-Ericson. Scan. Jun. (23:161.)

F

Farrell, James T.
 By Frederick B. Maxham. Wind. Winter. (2:277.)
 By Ferner Nuhn. Books. Oct. 6. (5.)
 By Lionel Trilling. Nat. Oct. 23. (141:484.)
 By Edith H. Walton. N. Y. Times. Oct. 13. (7.)
Faulkner, William.

By W. J. V. Hofmann. Lit A. Mar. (2:193.)
By Camille McCole. Cath. W. Aug. (141:576.)
Feuchtwanger, Lion.
By Basil Davenport. Sat. R. (N.Y.) May 11. (19.)
By Margaret Cheney Dawson. Books. Mar. 3. (4.)
By Harold Strauss. N.Y. Times. Mar. 3. (6.)
Fitzgerald, F. Scott.
By Elizabeth Hart. Books. Mar. 31. (4.)
By William Troy. Nat. (N.Y.) Apr. 17. (140:454.)
By Edith H. Walton. N.Y. Times. Mar. 31. (7.)
Fox, Fannie Ferber.
Anonymous. Books. Sept. 8. (8.)
By Edith H. Walton. N.Y. Times. Sept. 15. (18.)
Freund, Philip.
Anonymous. N.Y. Times. Jul. 7. (15.)

G

Galsworthy, John.
By Percy Hutchison. N.Y. Times. Oct. 27. (2.)
By George Libaire. Books. Feb. 24. (19.)
By Isabel Paterson. Books. Nov. 3. (12.)
Glasgow, Ellen.
By Douglas Southall Freeman. Sat. R. (N.Y.) Aug. 31. (11.)
Gogol, Nikolai.
By John Cournos. Yale. Spring. (24:632.) N.Y. Times. Jun. 9. (9.)
Golding, Louis.
By Elizabeth Hart. Books. Jan. 27. (8.)
By Edith H. Walton. N.Y. Times. Jan. 27. (6.)
Gordon, Caroline.
By Robert Penn Warren. S.W. Winter. (Supplement, 5.)]
Grand, Gordon.
Anonymous. N.Y. Times. Jan. 20. (12.)
By Ben Ray Redman. Books. Jul. 14. (12.)
Graves, Merle Dixon.
Anonymous. N.Y. Times. Jan. 27. (18.)

H

Hardy, Thomas.
By Samuel C. Chew. Books. Jun. 16. (9.)
By Percy Hutchison. N.Y. Times. Apr. 28. (9.)
By R. G. Lillard. P.M.L.A. Mar. (50:316.)
By Christopher Morley. Sat. R. (N.Y.) Mar. 16. (11:551.)
By Carl J. Weber. Books. Jul. 14. (15.)
Hawthorne, Nathaniel.
Anonymous. Essex. Apr. (71:150.)
By Fannye N. Cherry. A.L. Jan. (6:437.)
By R. H. C.S.M. Jul. 1.
By Randall Stewart, N.E.Q. Mar. (8:3.)
By Arlin Turner. Tex. Jul. (15:38.)
Hearn, Lafcadio.
By Bertha S. Coolidge. Sat. R. (N.Y.) Apr. 27. (11:654.)
By M. G. N. Rep. Aug. 28. (84:83.)
By Frank Jewett Mather. Sat. R. (N.Y.) Jun. 29. (7.)
By Clara Gruening Stillman. Books. Jun. 9. (4.)
By Edward Larocque Tinker. A.L. May. (7:224.) N.Y. Times. Jun. 9. (5.)
Hemingway, Ernest.
By Bernard De Voto. Sat. R. (N.Y.) Oct. 26. (5.)
By Clifton Fadiman. N.Y. Nov. 2. (96.)

By Paul Harris. A. Crit. Dec. (13.)
By Granville Hicks. N. Mass. Nov. 19. (23.)
By W. J. V. Hofmann. Lit. A. Feb. (2:111.)
By T. S. Matthews. N. Rep. Nov. 27. (85:79.)
By C. G. Poore. N.Y. Times. Oct. 27. (3.)
By John Hyde Preston. Atl. Aug. (156:187.)
By Carl Van Doren. Books. Oct. 27. (3.)
By Edmund Wilson. N. Rep. Dec. 11. (85:135.)
Henry, O.
 Anonymous. State. Jan. 26. Feb. 9.
 By Paul S. Clarkson. A.L. May. (7:195.)
 By Ida B. Henderson. State. Feb. 2.
Hergesheimer, Joseph.
 By Henry Alden. Tan. Feb. (10:29.)
Hilton, James.
 By Eric F. Gaskell. C. For. Apr. (15:281.)
Hughes, Langston.
 By Alain Locke. Opp. Jan. (13:8.)
Huxley, Aldous.
 By Henry Alexander. Q.Q. Spring. (42:96.)

I

Irving, Washington.
 By Susan S. Bennett. S.C.H.G.M. Oct., '34. (35:130.)
 By E. H. Hespelt and S. T. Williams. P.M.L.A. Dec., '34. (49:1129.)
 By William R. Langfeld. N.Y. Times. Dec. 15. (1.)
 By Henry A. Pochmann. A.L. Mar. (7:106.)
 By Coleman Oscar Parsons. A.L. Jan. (6:439.)
 By Robert E. Spiller. Sat. R. (N.Y.) Dec. 21. (17.)
 By Aubrey Starke. A.L. Jan. (6:444.)
 By Ralph Thompson. A.L. Jan. (6:443.)
 By George F. Whicher. Books. Dec. 22. (3.)
Ivanov, Vsevolod.
 By John Cournos. N.Y. Times. Dec. 29. (9.)

J

James, Henry.
 By Ford Madox Ford. A. Merc. Nov. (36:315.) So. R. Jul. (1:20.)
 By Eleanor Lowden. Tan. Mar. (28.)
 By Austin Warren. A.L. Jan. (6:455.)
Jewett, Sarah Orne.
 By Gladys Hasty Carroll. Sat. R. (N.Y.) Nov. 9. (3.)
Jewish Short Story.
 By John Cournos. N.Y. Times. Dec. 1. (38.)
Johnson, Josephine.
 By Eleanor Clark. N. Rep. Sept. 25. (84:194.)
 By George Dangerfield. Sat. R. (N.Y.) Aug. 31. (16.)
 By Elizabeth Hart. Books. Aug. 18. (6.)
 By Mary McCarthy. Nat. Aug. 21. (141:220.)
 By Edith H. Walton. N.Y. Times. Aug. 18. (7.)
Joyce, James.
 By Leon-Paul Fargue. Transit. Jul. (130.)
 By Armand M. Petitjean. Transit. Jul. (133.)
 By L. A. G. Strong. A. Merc. Aug. (35:433.)

K

Kantor, MacKinlay.
 By William Rose Benét. Sat. R. (N.Y.) Aug. 31. (4.)
 By H. I. Brock. N.Y. Times. Aug. 25. (7.)

By Thomas Caldecot Chubb. N.A. Rev. Dec. (240:550.)
By Caroline Gordon. N. Rep. Oct. 23. (84:312.)
By Edward Larocque Tinker. Books. Aug. 18. (5.)
King, Grace.
    By Bess Vaughan. L.H.Q. Oct., '34. (17:752.)
Kipling, Rudyard.
    By William Rose Benét. Sat. R. (N.Y.) Nov. 30. (7.)
    By Edith Mirrielees. Va. Jan. (11:37.)
Kober, Arthur.
    By Newman Levy. Books. Oct. 13. (4.)
    By Beatrice Sherman. N.Y. Times. Oct. 6. (2.)
    By George Stevens. Sat. R. (N.Y.) Oct. 12. (6.)
Kyne, Peter B.
    Anonymous. N.Y. Times. Aug. 18. (15.)

L

La Farge, Oliver.
    By William Rose Benét. Sat. R. (N.Y.) Aug. 17. (10.)
    By Wilson O. Clough. Frontier. Winter. (16:155.)
    By Grace Haxton. Books. Aug. 18. (3.)
    By Haniel Long. N. Rep. Aug. 28. (84:80.)
    By Edith H. Walton. N.Y. Times. Aug. 25. (7.)
Lagerkvist, Pär.
    By Gurli Hertzman-Ericson. Scan. Jun. (23:161.)
Lagerlöf, Selma.
    By Percy Hutchison. N.Y. Times. May 5. (2.)
    By Hanna Astrup Larsen. Scan. Spring. (23:7.) Summer. (23:113.) Autumn.
        (23:207.) Winter. (23:309.)
    By Mary Ross. Books. Apr. 21. (3.)
Lane, Rose Wilder.
    By Garreta Busey. Books. Oct. 13. (10.)
    By Margaret Wallace. N.Y. Times. Oct. 13. (21.)
Lawrence, D. H.
    By Henry Alexander. Q.Q. Spring. (42:96.)
    By H. J. Davis. C. For. Jan. (15:158.)
    By Vera Fulton. Mod. M. Jan. (8:701.)
Le Sueur, Meridel.
    By Nelson Algren. N. Mass. Aug. 20. (25.)
    By Wilson O. Clough. Frontier. Winter. (16:155.)
    By Richard Leekley. Wind. Fall. (3:78.)
Lesnik.
    By Alexander Nazaroff. N.Y. Times. Aug. 18. (8.)
Lewis, Sinclair.
    By Clifton Fadiman. N.Y. Jul. 13. (64.)
    By Eleanor Godfrey. C. For. Aug. (15:333.)
    By Peter Monro Jack. N.Y. Times. Jun. 30. (3.)
    By Howard Mumford Jones. Sat. R. (N.Y.) Jul. 6. (7.)
    By Mary Ross. Books. Jul. 7. (4.)
London, Jack.
    By Edmundo Peluso. I.L. Feb. (75.)

M

MacManus, Seumas.
    By Paul Allen. Books. Sept. 1. (9.)
    By Jane Spence Southron. N.Y. Times. Sept. 8. (21.)
March, William.
    By William Rose Benét. Sat. R. (N.Y.) Feb. 9. (11:473.)
    By Elizabeth Hart. Books. Feb. 10. (3.)

By Fred T. Marsh. N.Y. Times. Feb. 17. (2.)
By Harry Salpeter. Lit. A. Apr. (2:260.)
Marguerite of Navarre.
By Florence Finch Kelly. N.Y. Times. Dec. 15. (9.)
Mayor, F. M.
Anonymous. N.Y. Times. May 12. (6.)
Meek, S. P.
By Paul Allen. Books. Mar. 17. (13.)
Anonymous. N.Y. Times. Mar. 17. (19.)
Melville, Herman.
By N. Bryllion Fagin. A.L. Jan. (6:433.)
By R. S. Forsythe. N.E.Q. Mar. (8:99.)
By Percy Hutchison. N.Y. Times. Jul. 7. (2.)
By H. A. Larrabee. N.Y.H. Apr., '34. (15:144.)
Miller, Max.
By Burton Rascoe. Books. Feb. 17. (4.)
By Edith H. Walton. N.Y. Times. Feb. 10. (6.)
Moore, George.
By Charles Morgan. A. Merc. Oct. (36:176.)
By Horace Reynolds. N.Y. Times. Dec. 8. (5.)

N

Neagoe, Peter.
By Lionel Abel. Nat. May 29. (140:636.)
Anonymous. Sat. R. (N.Y.) April. 27. (11:649.)
By Whit Burnett. Books. Apr. 21. (2.)
By Harold Strauss. N.Y. Times. Apr. 14. (18.)
By K. W. N. Rep. Oct. 9. (84:251.)
Norris, Frank.
By Willard E. Martin, Jr. A.L. May. (7:203.)

O

O'Hara, John.
By William Rose Benét. Sat. R. (N.Y.) Mar. 2. (11:517.)
By Fred T. Marsh. Books. Mar. 3. (17.)
By Edith H. Walton. N.Y. Times. Feb. 24. (7.)
Oppenheim, E. Phillips.
Anonymous. N.Y. Times. May 19. (16.)

P

Page, Thomas Nelson.
By W. D. Orcutt. C.S.M. Mar. 22.
Parrott, Ursula.
By Jane Spence Southron. N.Y. Times. Nov. 3. (24.)
Peel, Doris.
Anonymous. N.Y. Times. Feb. 17. (17.)
By William Rose Benét. Sat. R. (N.Y.) Feb. 9. (11:473.)
By Whit Burnett. Books. Feb. 17. (8.)
Pilniak, Boris.
By Alexander Nazaroff. N.Y. Times. Aug. 18. (8.)
Pirandello, Luigi.
Anonymous. Wind. Fall. (3:77.)
By Clifton Fadiman. N.Y. Jan. 12. (72.)
By Elizabeth Hart. Books. Jan. 6. (3.)
By Percy Hutchison. N.Y. Times. Jan. 6. (2.)
By Sada F. Kiteley. C. For. Jul. (15:289.)
By Arthur Livingston. Nat. Jan. 30. (140:134.)
By Jerre Mangione. N. Rep. Aug. 28. (84:82.)
By Frank Scully. Esq. May. (37.)

Poe, Edgar Allan.
    By Mozelle Scaff Allen. Tex. Jul. (15:63.)
    Anonymous. R.N.L. Apr. 15. Oct. 5.
    By Edward J. Breen. Com. Dec. 27. (23:250.)
    By Killis Campbell. A.L. May. (7:220.)
    By D. K. Jackson. M.L.N. Apr. (50:251.)
    By Una Pope-Hennessy. A.L. Nov. (7:334.)
    By Rolls G. Silver. A.L. Jan. (6:435.)
    By J. G. Varner. A.B.C. Feb. (6:56.) Four Arts. Jan.–Feb. (2:4.)
    By Ross Wells, R.T.D. Oct. 6.
    By George F. Whicher. Books. Feb. 3. (13.)
    By M. B. Whiteside. Pers. Autumn, '34. (15:315.)
    By J. H. Whitty. R.T.D. Jul. 21.
Porter, Katherine Anne.
    By Charles Angoff. A. Sp. Nov. (11.)
    Anonymous. Nat. Mar. 27. (140:369.)
    Anonymous. Sat. R. (N.Y.) Dec. 14. (16.)
    By Howard Baker. So. R. Jul. (1:178.)
    By Eleanor Clark. N. Rep. Dec. 25. (85:207.)
    By Malcolm Cowley. N. Rep. May 29. (83:79.)
    By William Troy. Nat. Oct. 30. (141:517.)
    By Eda Lou Walton. Books. Nov. 3. (7.)
    By Edith H. Walton. N.Y. Times. Oct. 20. (6.)
Pushkin, Alexander.
    By John Cournos. Yale. Spring. (24:632.) N.Y. Times. Jun. 9. (9.)
    By Alexander Nazaroff. N.Y. Times. Nov. 3. (8.)

R

Rich, Barnabe.
    By D. W. Thompson. M.L.N. Feb. (50:99.)

S

Salt, Sydney.
    By Norman MacLeod. N.M.Q. May. (5:122.)
Saroyan, William.
    By Ernest Hemingway. Esq. Jan. (21.)
    By W. J. V. Hofmann. Lit. A. Jan. (2:25.)
    By Joel Lloyd. Ar. Feb. (26.)
Shipman, Evan.
    By Frank de Mercado. N.Y. Times. Nov. 3. (7.)
    By Stuart Rose. Books. Dec. 22. (5.)
Short Story
    By Harry Hansen. World. Jul. 6. (15.)
    By William Saroyan. Sat. R. (N.Y.) Jan. 5. (11:409.)
    By Tess Slesinger. Sat. R. (N.Y.) Jul. 6. (12.)
    By Edith H. Walton. N.Y. Times. Jul. 21. (7.)
Sigmund, Jay G.
    By Charles J. Finger. A.W. Sept.–Oct. (4.)
    By E. H. W. N.Y. Times. Sept. 8. (21.)
Silone, Ignazio.
    By Whit Burnett. Books. Oct. 13. (10.)
    By James Burnham. Nat. Oct. 9. (141:416.)
    By Jay Gerlando. N. Mass. Nov. 12. (23.)
    By Richard Leekley. N. Rep. Nov. 20. (85:55.)
    By Fred T. Marsh. N.Y. Times. Sept. 29. (8.)
Slesinger, Tess.
    By Gerta Aison. Lit. A. Jul. (2:482.)
    By Charles Angoff. Nat. Jun. 19. (140:716.)
    By William Rose Benét. Sat. R. (N.Y.) May 25. (5.)

By Whit Burnett. Books. May 26. (7.)
By Robert M. Coates. N. Rep. Jul. 24. (83:312.)
By Randall Jarrell. So. R. Autumn. (1:397.)
By A. K. Mod. M. Sept. (9:319.)
By Edith H. Walton. N.Y. Times. May 26. (7.)
Söderberg, Hjalmar.
Anonymous. Books. Jul. 21. (10.)
By Harold Strauss. N.Y. Times. Feb. 17. (7.)
Spofford, Harriet Prescott.
By Ima Honaker Herron. A.L. Nov. (7:355.)
Stevenson, Robert Louis.
By Edward D. Snyder. Sat. R. (N.Y.) Aug. 3. (11.)
Strindberg, August.
By Gurli Hertzman-Ericson. Scan. Jun. (23:161.)
By Alma Luise Olson. N.Y. Times. Jul. 28. (8.)

T

Tarkington, Booth.
By Murray Godwin. N. Mass. Jul. 2. (36.)
By L. Cabot Hearn. Sat. R. (N.Y.) Nov. 9. (5.)
By Mary Ross. Books. Dec. 8. (5.)
By Beatrice Sherman. N.Y. Times. Nov. 24. (6.)
Twain, Mark.
Two Letters. Sat. R. (N.Y.) Nov. 16. (9.)
Unpublished Diaries. Cos. Aug. (24.) Sept. (48.)
Twain, Mark.
Anonymous. N.Y. Times. Aug. 4. (5.)
By Newton Arvin. N. Rep. Jun. 12. (83:125.)
By E. Douglas Branch. Frontier. Winter. (16:160.)
By Henry Seidel Canby. Sat. R. (N.Y.) Oct. 12. (3.)
By Cyril Clemens. Opp. Mar. (13:79.) Com. Oct. 11. (22:591.)
By Mary M. Colum. For. Nov. (94:276.)
By Bernard de Voto. N.Y. Times. Oct. 27. (1.)
By Theodore Dreiser. Eng. J. Oct. (24:615.) Esq. Oct. (22.)
By Frances G. Emberson. U. Mo. S. Jul. (10:1.)
By Gordon S. Haight. Yale. Autumn. (25:212.)
By Stephen Leacock. Q.Q. Spring. (42:68.)
By Fred W. Lorch. A.L. Jan. (6:460.) Nov. (7:350, 351.)
By Robert Morss Lovett. N. Rep. Nov. 20. (85:50.)
By Edgar Lee Masters. A. Merc. Sept. (36:67.)
By Christopher Morley. Sat. R. (N.Y.) Nov. 2. (15.)
By Charles O. Paullin. W.M.Q. Jul. (15:294.)
By Dorothy Quick. N.A. Rev. Sept. (240:342.)
By Ben Ray Redman. Books. May 5. (12.)
By Carl Van Doren. Books. Sept. 29. (8.) Oct. 13. (1.)
By Mark Van Doren. Nat. Oct. 23. (141:472.)
By A. L. O. W. Q.Q. Summer. (42:272.)
By James J. Walsh. Com. Aug. 23. (22:408.)
By Owen Wister. Harp. M. Oct. (171.547.)

V

Vaughan, Hilda.
By Edith H. Walton. N.Y. Times. Dec. 22. (7.)

W

Walsh, Edmund A.
By Jane Spence Southron. N.Y. Times. Dec. 22. (7.)
Walsh, Maurice.
By Louise Maunsell Field. N.Y. Times. Sept. 22. (6.)
By William C. Weber. Books. Sept. 15. (3.)

West, Rebecca.
    By Obed Brooks. N. Mass. Feb. 26. (24.)
    By L. Cabot Hearn. Sat. R. (N.Y.) Feb. 2. (11:457.)
    By Mary Ross. Books. Feb. 3. (5.)
    By Edith H. Walton. N.Y. Times. Feb. 3. (7.)
Wharton, Edith.
    By Marcel Tirol. Q.Q. Winter. (42:559.)
Wilde, Oscar.
    By Lloyd Lewis and Henry Justin Smith. Harp. M. Nov. (171:686.) A. Merc.
        Dec. (36:434.)
Willis, Nathaniel P.
    By William Purviance Fenn. A.L. Jan. (6:421.)
Wilson, Harry Leon.
    By Thomas Beer. Books. Jun. 16. (1.)
Winslow, Thyra Samter.
    By William Rose Benét. Sat. R. (N.Y.) Aug. 10. (12.)
    By Mary Ross. Books. Aug. 18. (4.)
    By Edith H. Walton. N.Y. Times. Aug. 11. (6.)
Wodehouse, P. G.
    By Paul Allen. Books. Sept. 29. (14.)
    By Beatrice Sherman. N.Y. Times. Sept. 22. (7.)
Wolfe, Thomas.
    By Clifton Fadiman. Books. Nov. 16. (107.)
    By Peter Monro Jack. N.Y. Times. Nov. 24. (6.)
    By Howard Mumford Jones. Sat. R. (N.Y.) Nov. 30. (13.)
    By Ferner Nuhn. Books. Nov. 17. (7.)
Wood, Eugene.
    By Anita Moffett. N.Y. Times. Sept. 1. '35. (7.)
Wright, Constance.
    Anonymous. N.Y. Times. Feb. 17. (19.)
    By May Lamberton Becker. Books. Feb. 10. (6.)

Y

Young, Stark.
    By Emily Clark. Va. Oct. (11:026.)
    By Henry S. Commager. Books. Jul. 28. (3.)
    By Elmer Davis. Sat. R. (N.Y.) Jul. 27. (5.)
    By Clifton Fadiman. N.Y. Jul. 27. (54.)
    By Randall Jarrell. So. R. Autumn. (1:397.)
    By Richard Dana Skinner. Com. Oct. 25. (22:645.) N.A. Rev. Dec. (240:553.)
    By Rebecca W. Smith. N.M.Q. Nov. (5:282.)
    By Margaret Wallace. N.Y. Times. Jul. 28. (6.)

Z

Zostchenko, Mikhail.
    Anonymous. Nat. Oct. 23. (141:489.)
    By Mary M. Colum. For. Dec. (94:354.)
    By John Cournos. N.Y. Times. Oct. 13. (8.)
    By William Cunningham. N. Mass. Oct. 1. (40.)
    By O. F. N. Rep. Oct. 23. (84:306.)
    By Elizabeth Hart. Books. Sept. 8. (14.)
Zweig, Arnold.
    By Obed Brooks. N. Mass. Oct. 22. (27.)
    By Samuel Nock. Sat. R. (N.Y.) Jul. 13. (6.)
    By Mary Ross. Books. Jul. 14. (4.)
    By Harold Strauss. N.Y. Times. Jul. 14. (6.)

INDEX OF SHORT STORIES IN BOOKS

1935

I. AMERICAN AND CANADIAN AUTHORS

II. BRITISH AND IRISH AUTHORS

III. TRANSLATIONS

MAGAZINE AVERAGES

JANUARY 1 TO DECEMBER 31, 1935

The following table includes the averages of distinctive stories in nineteen American periodicals. One, two, and three asterisks are employed to indicate relative distinction. 'Three-asterisk stories' are considered worth reprinting in book form. The list excludes reprints. Figures in columns three and six represent stories with one or more asterisks: figures in columns four and seven stories with two or more asterisks.

PERIODICALS	Number of Stories Published	Number of Distinctive Stories Published			Percentage of Distinctive Stories Published		
		*	**	***	*	**	***
American Mercury	32	31	25	17	97	78	53
Anvil	31	19	9	2	61	29	7
Atlantic Monthly	22	19	14	6	86	64	27
Collier's Weekly	269	18	3	3	7	1	1
Cosmopolitan	120	23	6	2	19	5	2
Esquire	157	86	37	15	55	24	10
Frontier and Midland	32	24	15	6	75	47	19
Harper's Bazaar (New York)	55	27	15	6	75	47	19
Harper's Magazine	23	18	13	8	78	57	35
Manuscript	68	29	10	1	43	15	1
Pictorial Review	56	15	9	7	27	16	13
Prairie Schooner	24	18	9	4	75	38	17
Red Book Magazine	92	21	7	5	23	8	5
Saturday Evening Post	231	39	5	2	17	2	1
Scribner's Magazine	33	31	24	12	94	73	36
Story	102	96	66	41	96	66	41
Vanity Fair	54	36	18	8	67	33	15
Windsor Quarterly	17	9	6	5	53	35	29
Woman's Home Companion	54	7	2	0	13	4	0

The following tables indicate the rank, by number and percentage of distinctive short stories published, of eleven periodicals coming within the scope of my examination which have published an average of 50 per cent or more of distinctive stories. The list excludes reprints, but not translations.

BY PERCENTAGE

1. American Mercury . . . 97%
2. Story 96%
3. Scribner's Magazine . . 94%
4. Atlantic Monthly . . . 86%
5. Harper's Magazine . . 78%
6. Frontier and Midland . . 75%
7. Prairie Schooner 75%
8. Vanity Fair 67%
9. Anvil 61%
10. Esquire 55%
11. Windsor Quarterly . . . 53%

BY NUMBER

1. Story 96
2. Esquire 86
3. Vanity Fair 36
4. American Mercury . . 31
5. Scribner's Magazine . . 31
6. Frontier and Midland . . 24
7. Atlantic Monthly 19
8. Anvil 19
9. Harper's Magazine . . . 18
10. Prairie Schooner 18
11. Windsor Quarterly . . . 9

The following periodicals have published during the same period seven or more 'two-asterisk stories.' The list excludes reprints, but not translations.

1. Story	 66	10. Harper's Bazaar (New York) . . 13
2. Esquire	 37	11. Manuscript 10
3. American Mercury	. . . 25	12. Prairie Schooner. 9
4. Scribner's Magazine	. . . 24	13. Anvil 9
5. New Yorker	 20	14. Pictorial Review 9
6. Vanity Fair	 18	15. New Masses 9
7. Frontier and Midland	. . 15	16. Red Book Magazine 7
8. Atlantic Monthly	. . . 14	17. Forum 7
9. Harper's Magazine	. . . 13	18. Southern Review 7

The following periodicals have published during the same period four or more 'three-asterisk stories.' The list excludes reprints, but not translations.

1. Story	 41	10. Atlantic Monthly 6
2. American Mercury	. . . 17	11. Frontier and Midland . . . 6
3. Esquire	 15	12. Southern Review 6
4. Scribner's Magazine	. . . 12	13. Windsor Quarterly 5
5. Harper's Magazine	 8	14. Red Book Magazine 5
6. Vanity Fair	 8	15. Direction 5
7. New Yorker	 8	16. Prairie Schooner 4
8. Harper's Bazaar (New York)	. 7	17. Yale Review 4
9. Pictorial Review .	. . . 7	18. Hairenik 4

Ties in the above lists have been decided by taking relative rank in other lists into account.

DISTINCTIVE SHORT STORIES IN AMERICAN MAGAZINES

1935

NOTE. Only distinctive stories are listed. The list includes a few American stories published in British periodicals. One, two, or three asterisks are used to indicate relative distinction. Titles of stories with three asterisks qualify for the 'Roll of Honor.' The figures in parentheses refer to the volume and page number of the magazine. Where successive issues of a magazine are not paged consecutively, only the page number is given. While every effort has been made to indicate correctly the nationality of authors, I assume no personal responsibility for the accuracy of my classification in this or in other lists.

I. AMERICAN AUTHORS

A

ABEL, HILDE.
***Silent upon a Peak in Darien. Man. Oct. (3.)

ADAMIC, LOUIS.
**My Friend in Herzegovina. W.H.C. Jun. (14.)

ADAMS, BILL.
*Decent Sailorman. Adven. Apr. 15. (43.)
*Golden Emblem. Adven. Jun. 15. (58.)
*Jukes. Adven. Nov. (132.)
**Muffler. T.W. Jun. 9 (3.)
*Never Get Excited. Adven. Jul. 15. (70.)
*One Thing at a Time. Adven. Aug. 15. (100.)
*Sea Chest. Esq. Jul. (50.)
*Silk and Sixpenny. C.G. Jul. (14.)

ADAMS, HELEN.
***Late Afternoon. Pr. S. Spring. (9:79.)

AIKEN, CONRAD.
***Necktie. (R.) Gol. Jul. (22:54.)
***Round by Round. A. Merc. Apr. (34:461.)

ALDEN, HENRY.
*Charm from the Sky. Tan. May. (3.)

ALDRICH, THOMAS BAILEY.
*Untold Story. (R.) Gol. Aug. (22:192.)

ALEXANDER, HERBERT. ('John Mortimer.')
***Case History. N. Mass. Jul. 2. (23.)

ALGREN, NELSON.
*Lumpen. N. Mass. Jul. 2. (25.)

AMIRIAN, LEMYEL.
***Amusement Park Interlude. Hai. Jul. 26.

ANDERSON, EDWARD.
***Bare Legs. Sto. Jun. (67.)

ANNIXTER, PAUL.
*King Crumb and the Uka Mauler. Esq. Aug. (30.)

APPEL, BENJAMIN.
***Brothers in Hell's Kitchen. Lit. A. Jun. (2:422.)
*City Soul. Lan. Sept.–Oct., '34. (41.)
*Crazy Kid. Man. Feb. (22.)
*Dog's Family. Frontier. Spring. (15:191.)
*Friday We Crack the Bank! Red. Bk. Mar. (30.)
**Movie of a Big Shot. An. May–Jun. (12.)
*9th Avenue Pipe Dream. Red Bk. Feb. (40.)
**Red Mike, Mabel and Me. Lit. A. Sept. (2:626.)
*Shrimpereno. Red Bk. Jan. (30.)

ARGUILLA, MANUEL E.
***Midsummer. Pr. S. Fall. (9:225.)

ARMFIELD, EUGENE.
**Little Acorns. Sto. Oct. (35.)
**Old Block. A. Merc. Feb. (34:209.)

ASCH, NATHAN.
*Be Careful, Mrs. Hopkins! L.L. Dec. (13:154.)
**Greatest Story. N. Mass. Feb. 5. (17.)

ASHERY, R. E.
*No Fire on Mount Carmel. Sto. Feb. (5.)

AYDELOTTE, DORA.
**White Bread. For. Feb. (93:119.)

B

BABB, SANORA.
*Farm in Alaska. N. Mass. Jul. 9. (19.)

GOODLOE, ABBIE CARTER.
*Claustrophobia. (*R.*) Gol. Jul. (22: 67.)
GOODMAN, STEVE.
*Handout. Man. Apr. (73.)
GORDON, CAROLINE.
***Funeral in Town. Westm. Winter. (23:278.)
**Last Day in the Field. Scr. Mar. (97:162.)
***Morning's Favor. So. R. Autumn. (1:271.)
**One More Time. Scr. Dec. (98: 338.)
GORYAN, SIRAK.
***Yea and Amen. Hai. Mar. 22–29, '34.
GOWEN, EMMETT.
*Mr. Pink. Sto. Jan. (74.)
*Southern Mother. N. Mass. Aug. 27. (18.)
**Witch's Blood. Esq. Mar. (55.)
GRAFTON, SAMUEL.
**Matilda Receives Her Callers. A. Sp. Aug. (7.)
GRANBERRY, EDWIN.
***Trip to Czardis. (*R.*) Gol. Aug. (22: 209.)
GRAY, MARGARET.
*Woman Known Only as Jen. Tan. Mar. (12.)
GRAYSON, CHARLES.
*Lord's Day. Esq. Jul. (28.)
GREEN, PAUL.
**Love and a Fiddle. Jale. Jun. (24: 782.)
GREENE, WARD.
*Hymns before Murder. Lit. A. Mar. (2:196.)
GRIFFIN, MYRON.
**Tell Me Always. Am. P. Nov. (1:28.)
GRIMWOOD, ALFRED.
*Fall of Lucifer. Sto. Mar. (75.)
GROGAN, ELMIRA.
*Bound Boy. W.H.C. Dec. (23.)
GURGANUS, RANSOM.
*Die You Sinner! Manu. (35.)
*Dust in the Light. Manu. (28.)

H

HAARDT, SARA.
*Baby Chile. Harp. B. (N.Y.) Jul. (70.)
HAHN, EMILY.
*Ghost of Susie. N.Y. Jul. 6 (24.)
***Strange Thing. Sto. Jul. (47.)
HAINES, WILLIAM WISTER.
***'Hot Behind Me.' Atl. Jun. (155: 683.)
HALE, NANCY.
***Great-Grandmother. N.Y. Dec. 7. (33.)

*Spring on the Pincian Hill. V.F. Jan. (37.)
HALL, EDWARD FITCH.
*Soft Spot. Sto. Jan. (21.)
HALL, ELIZABETH.
***Two Words Are a Story. Sto. Nov. (24.)
HALPER, ALBERT.
**Doctor Winton. Atl. Dec. (156:703.)
*Milly. Red Bk. May. (42.)
HANLON, BROOKE.
*Ranny. S.E.P. Nov. 9. (14.)
HANSEN, JOE.
**Dave Comes to Dinner. Frontier. Summer. (15:275.)
*Donovan and Gary. Frontier. Autumn. (16:17.)
**Man Swinging a Hammer. Frontier. Winter. (16:101.)
HANSON, BIP.
**Horseflesh. Pr. S. Summer. (9:196.)
*Love. Man. Feb. (61.)
*Purgative. Man. Oct. (15.)
HARDY, EVELYN.
***Innkeeper's Daughter. N.S. Jun.–Jul. (2:198.)
HARPER, LAWRENCE A.
Memory of Joseph. Man. Oct. (54.)
HARRISON, CHARLES YALE.
*Story for Mr. Hemingway. Mod. M. Feb. (8:731.)
HARRISS, R. P.
*Red Coat Day. Sto. May. (26.)
HART, ELIZABETH.
*'April is the Cruellest Month —.' Sto. Apr. (80.)
HARTE, BRET.
***Man from Solano. (*R.*) Gol. Jan. (21:69.)
HAYES, HOWARD.
***How My Wife Got that Way. A. Sp. Nov. (2.)
HEALY, J. V.
*Professor. Sto. Feb. (83.)
HENRY, O.
*Ferry of Unfulfilment. (*R.*) Gol. May. (21:499.)
HILTON, CHARLES.
***Youth Like a Warm Wind. Frontier. Summer. (15:257.)
HOLDEN, RAYMOND.
*Trust. Scr. Oct. (98:232.)
HOLT, ACHILLES.
**Desire. Mag. Jan.–Feb. (2:195.)
HORGAN, PAUL.
*Slow Curtain. Harp. M. Feb. (170: 323.)
**Tribute. Scr. Oct. (98:216.)
*Trunk. Mad. Nov. (11.)
HOW, ROGER F.
*September Night. Sto. Sept. (34.)

II. CANADIAN AUTHORS

III. British and Irish Authors

A

AUSTIN, F. BRITTEN.
*Heritage. Red Bk. Mar. (15.)
*Smile from Lucrezia Borgia. S.E.P.
May 11. (18.)
*Who Worships Gloriana? S.E.P.
May 25. (31.)

B

BARRIE, J. M.
*Two of Them. (R.) Gol. Apr.
(21:355.)
BASHFORD, H. H.
*Abbot of Herridge. Pict. R. Apr. (20.)
BATES, H. E.
***Duet. V.F. Feb. (21.)
***Plough. Frontier. Spring. (15:203.)
BENNETT, ARNOLD.
*Nocturne at the Majestic. (R.) Gol.
May. (21:502.)
BENTLEY, PHYLLIS.
**Whole of the Story. W.H.C. Sept.
(11.)
BERESFORD, J. D.
*Other Way. Esq. Mar. (26.)
BLAND, MRS. E.
*Mystery of No. 17. (R.) Gol. Aug.
(22:165.)
BOTTOME, PHYLLIS.
*Ear of Caesar's Wife. Red Bk. Mar.
(52.)
**Vocation. (R.) Gol. Jun. (21:573.)
BURKE, THOMAS.
***Beryl and the Croucher. (R.) Gol.
Jul. (22:94.)
*Happy Ghosts. Esq. Jan. (49.)
*Lonely Inn. Esq. Jul. (85.)
*Two Gentlemen of Chinatown. Esq.
Aug. (74.)

C

CALDER-MARSHALL, ARTHUR.
***Straw Hat. V.F. Apr. (51.)
CHESTERTON, G. K.
***Ring of Lovers. Col. Apr. 20. (20.)
***Tall Story. Col. Apr. 27. (16.)
***Three Horsemen. Col. Apr. 13. (7.)
***When Doctors Agree. Harp. M. Aug.
(171:329.)
COLLIER, JOHN.
*Aviary. Harp. B. (N.Y.) Apr. (78.)
*Elephant. Esq. Apr. (33.)
*Sentimental; Story. Harp. B. (N.Y.)
Feb. (83.)

COPPARD, A. E.
***Poste Restante. (R.) Gol. Apr.
(21:293.)
CRONIN, A. J.
**Christmas for Agnes. Cos. Jan. (56.)
*Country Doctor. Cos. May. (37.)

D

DICKENS, CHARLES.
*Great Winglebury Duel. (R.) Gol.
May. (21:468.)
DUNSANY, LORD.
***August in the Red Sea. (R.) Gol.
Jan. (21:63.)
***Jorkens Handles a Big Property.
Harp. M. Jul. (171:138.)
***Jorkens Retires from Business. T.W.
Mar. 10. (4.)
***Return. Atl. Jun. (155:742.)

E

EDGINTON, MAY.
***Purple and Fine Linen. (R.) Gol.
May. (21:409.)

F

FLEMING, PETER.
***Ace High. For. Mar. (93:156.)
FORESTER, C. S.
**To My Darling. Esq. Sept. (70.)

G

GALSWORTHY, JOHN.
***Acme. (R.) Gol. Jan. (21:92.)
GIBBON, PERCEVAL.
*Did They Marry? (R.) Gol. Jun.
(21:609.)
GOLDING, LOUIS.
*Anything to Oblige a Gipsy. Harp. B.
(N.Y.) Dec. (100.)
GOSSMAN, OLIVER.
***Wayside Spring. Sto. Apr. (55.)

H

HEWLETT, MAURICE.
***False Brother. (R.) Gol. Aug.
(22:147.)
HILTON, JAMES.
*Gerald and the Candidate. Cos.
Mar. (38.)
*Mr. Chips and Young Waveney. Cos.
Oct. (34.)

IV. TRANSLATIONS

A

ALEICHEM, SHOLEM. (*Yiddish.*)
***Hotel. (*R.*) Gol. Aug. (22:172.)
ANDERSEN, KNUD. (*Danish.*)
**Phosphorescence. Scan. Mar. (23:64.)
ARZUBIDE, HERMAN LITZ. (*Mexican.*)
*Greetings, Comrade. Part. R. Jul.-
Aug. (26.)

B

BALZAC, HONORÉ DE. (*French.*)
***False Courtesan. (*R.*) Gol. May.
(21:457.)
BARBEY D'AURÉVILLY, JULES. (*French.*)
**Don Juan's Greatest Love. (*R.*) Gol.
Jun. (21:623.)
BARBUSSE, HENRI. (*French.*)
**Child. A. Sp. Jul. (4.)
BARTA, ALEXANDER. (*Hungarian.*)
*Village is Saved. I.L. Dec. (24.)
BIRABEAU, ANDRÉ. (*French.*)
*Barber's Miracle. (*R.*) Gol. Aug.
(22:204.)
BOCCACCIO, GIOVANNI. (*Italian.*)
***Friar and the Lady. (*R.*) Gol. Mar.
(21:202.)

C

CANKAR, IVAN. (*Slovenian.*)
**Her Grave. Sky. Jan. (3.)
CHEKHOV, ANTON. (*Russian.*)
***Zinotchka. (*R.*) Gol. Apr. (21:331.)

D

DAUDET, ALPHONSE. (*French.*)
***Elixir of Father Gaucher. (*R.*) Gol.
Feb. (21:108.)
DUUN, OLAV. (*Norwegian.*)
***Avenger. Scan. Dec. (23:353.)

F

FRANCE, ANATOLE. (*French.*)
***Undress Parade. (*R.*) Gol. Apr.
(21:289.)
FREUCHEN, PETER. (*Danish.*)
*Nauja the Desired. Esq. Dec. (92.)

G

GERASIMOVA, V. (*Russian.*)
*Tadjikan Shadieva's Last Contest.
I.L. Feb. (6.)

GERGELY, SANDOR. (*Hungarian.*)
**Simple Story. I.L. Oct. (34.)
GONZALEZ, FRANCISCO ROJAS. (*Mexican.*)
***Cry of Warning. Part. R. Jul.-Aug.
(24.)
GORKY, MAXIM. (*Russian.*)
**Pogrom. Esq. Jul. (24.)

H

HSI-CHEN, SUN. (*Chinese.*)
*Ah Ao. Asia. Nov. (35:693.)

I

INBER, VERA. (*Russian.*)
**Nor-Bibi's Crime. I.L. Jan. (20.)

K

KLEIST, HUGO VON. (*German.*)
***Day of Judgment. (*R.*) Gol. Apr.
(21:347.)

L

LAN-CHI. (*Chinese.*)
*End of Wang Po-pi. I.L. Nov. (48.)
LEON, MARIA TERESA. (*Spanish.*)
*Acorns. N. Mass. Apr. 9. (16.)
LING, TING. (*Chinese.*)
*Flood. Asia. Oct. (35:631.)
LOUYS, PIERRE. (*French.*)
*Extraordinary Adventure. (*R.*) Gol.
Apr. (21:380.)
LU SHUN. (*Chinese.*)
***Medicine. Asia. Feb. (35:118.)

M

MANCISIDOR, JOSÉ. (*Mexican.*)
*Home. Part. R. Jul.-Aug. (20.)
MANN, THOMAS. (*German.*)
***Disillusion. Yale. Autumn. (25:77.)
***Hungry. Esq. Mar. (22.)
***Little Louise. (*R.*) Gol. Jan. (21:78.)
MARGUERITE OF NAVARRE. (*French.*)
***Cure for Folly. (*R.*) Gol. Jul. (22:102.)
MAUPASSANT, GUY DE. (*French.*)
***Mademoiselle Fifi. (*R.*) Gol. Mar.
(21:230.)
MAUROIS, ANDRÉ. (*French.*)
**Young Girl in the Snow. Esq. Dec.
(53.)

THE END